THE FORKED PATH

BOOK 2 *of the* WRAITH CYCLE

THE FORKED PATH

T·R· THOMPSON

ODYSSEY
BOOKS

www.odysseybooks.com.au

First published in 2018 by Odyssey Books

A Cataloguing-in-Publication entry is available from the National Library of Australia
ISBN: 978-1-925652-39-0 (pbk)
ISBN: 978-1-925652-40-6 (ebook)

Cover design by Michelle Lovi

The roots that sink the deepest

The forked path of the mind

The soul that splits is weakest

Future and past entwined

Part 1

He is fifty feet above ground when the first rock hits. It cracks into his left thigh, sending pain burning up his leg and freezing him in place, his hands clinging to the surrounding branches. The next stone rips through the wet leaves beside his ear, and he surges onward, upward, away from the threat below.

He climbs faster than he ever has before, forcing the pain out of his mind, no longer looking at the ground disappearing beneath him, eyes always searching for the next hand and foothold, scuttling up the enormous trunk of the tree.

Another rock strikes him, in the back this time, and his right hand flies from the tree, out of control, almost twisting him free of the trunk. His arm spins in the air wildly, windmilling himself back against the trunk, his cheek pressed against the rough bark as he gasps in and out.

Not fair. Not now, now he was so close.

A cackle of laughter below, and another stone thuds against the trunk beside his head. Six inches to the left and he would have been done for.

He feels the first tickle of fear bloom in his chest; the doors swinging open inside his mind.

Forget that. Forget everything. Just climb.

When the final rock hits, he doesn't feel it. Suddenly the tree is no longer beneath him, he is falling, the world silent and shrinking down into a dark tunnel. He closes his eyes as the branches tear past, surrendering, waiting for the ground to take him.

The vision fades and I am alone again, wandering these endless paths. Time has narrowed my senses, wrapping itself around me, pulsing into my nostrils and swamping me, churning me inside out until I no longer recall which way is up, which direction is forward, what is past, and what is yet to be. This is what death is, perhaps. A falling out of linear time. A narrowing of possibilities down to a single, final point.

I remember how time once stretched before me, its passing painfully slow, each year an eternity, unable to be fully glimpsed. Now the weeks and months flicker by, their advance unmarked.

The trees toy with me, aware of my age, my weakness. They trap me in place, wrapping themselves around me and forcing me to bear witness as their strange children run wild. I do not remember ever being one of them, and yet I must have been. They play their cruel games on each other, but the trees do not recognise how flawed their creatures have become. How darkened.

The wind shifts and I find myself free again, my thoughts travelling back in time and pulling me with them, down into the damp soil at my feet, recognising the pull of the earth, the yearning to return. And I feel again the tremor of his presence, shocking me into action.

He is coming. The spark flickering into flame, seeking out the shadows to chase them away. I can feel the warmth and sway of the trees he passes through, ever deeper, pushing down toward the end of my days. He is a harbinger of change. I should not fear him, but I cannot do otherwise.

The trees do not yet recognise what he might become. His threat. His promise.

Only a final few steps remain for me. I force myself forward and block my ears to the warnings whispered on the wind.

Chapter 1

The cat stalked through the broken shadows of the forest, belly low to the ground, eyes wide and staring out through the dimness at its prey. A heavy, constant rain drummed on the leaves and trees, a rolling applause that drowned out all other sound. The cat crept along slowly, circling around behind the large wild pig that snuffled industriously at the foot of the tree. The pig seemed focused on its task, oblivious to all else, but the cat knew better. He had been tracking this one for most of the morning and had already spooked it twice, a careless step cracking a twig the first time, a sudden change in wind direction betraying his presence the second. The wind had brought with it the rains, and now the cat shivered as he readied himself to spring.

Don't mess this one up. I'm hungry.

The cat's features twisted into a scowl as the strange thought brushed across his consciousness.

Leave him be, Higgs. Besides, you can't be hungry, there's nothing of you to feed.

I don't care what you say, Biore. I'm still hungry. And cold. What we need is a nice dry cave, a roaring fire, and this pig roasting over a spit. Then I might be in the mood for your lectures.

The cat licked his lips, the strange thoughts forgotten as he concentrated on the task at hand.

The pig had scratched out whatever had interested it at the base of the tree and now held its head high, sniffing the air. The rains were waking the forest, a wet, earthy smell rising from its floor. The cat waited, satisfied that his scent was covered. There would be no mistakes this time.

The wild pig stood at least two feet high, its haunches roped with muscle, its dark brown skin glistening in the rain. Its hooves were large and well used, pointed at each end as though sharpened purposefully, and two long tusks curved out from its lower jaw, reaching almost to the level of its eyes, prodigious weapons when wielded by the thickly corded neck of the beast.

Don't give it a chance to use them.

The cat allowed himself to enjoy the tickle of his silver claws sliding out from the ends of his paws, then sprang.

He landed on the pig's back, claws digging into flesh and clinging on as the pig bucked and screamed, kicking its back legs high into the air. The cat tried to reach a paw around to get at the pig's throat, but it bucked again, almost throwing the cat clear if not for its claws locked deep into muscle.

The beast ducked its head and launched forward, trying to pin the cat between itself and the trunk of a large tree, but the cat swung to the side at the last moment, releasing his hold to land safely on the ground as the pig crashed full bodied into the thick trunk. The cat didn't hesitate, swatting out with both paws to almost sever the pig's head from its body, hot blood pouring out in a sudden rush as the creature's veins were sliced open. The pig collapsed, a long last sigh of life breathing out as it sank into death.

The cat stared at it, watching the light fade from its eyes.

Constant rain still filled the air, washing the blood of the fresh kill deep into the soil and the waiting roots.

The next moment the cat was gone; in his place was a young man, squatting on his haunches, a long silver knife hanging from his hip. Wilt tossed his hair back from his face and stood up, tugging his worn black cloak around his shoulders.

Now what?

Now we find somewhere warm and safe to cook our meal.

Wilt bent down and pulled the pig's legs together, steadying his feet in the mud. With a grunt he heaved the carcass up onto his shoulders, almost slipping with the sudden weight. There was enough meat here to last them for days.

Him. To last him for days.

By the time he'd stumbled back to the cave with his prize and had it stripped and dressed and roasting slowly over a low fire, Wilt was exhausted. He lay on the smooth dry rock of the cave floor and stared at the fire, letting the dance of the flames wash his mind clear.

The heat from the fire was fighting a losing battle against the unnatural cold that filled the enclosed space, but Wilt felt none of it. He was floating in a still, grey emptiness.

You're wearing yourself out like this. You're no ranger.

Wilt allowed himself a small smile in reply. *What am I then?*

You're a Black Robe. One of the skilled. And one of the most powerful of our kind I've ever encountered.

Biore. Wilt let the words dredge up a memory: him standing on a stage, facing down the combined might of the Nine Sisters, becoming one with the weld within him, turning their power against them.

You're a thief. One of the Grey Guild.

Higgs's voice brought forth a second memory: he watched himself run along the night highway in Greystone, leaping over gaps between buildings, a shadow against the night sky.

The shadow darkened, and the world dropped away, and he was a cold, still emptiness standing alone in the centre of a room, reaching out again and again to the onrushing guards, his hand a thousand writhing black snakes, his touch death.

I'm a killer.

You're my friend.

Delco. Wilt let the dark memory sink back into the depths.

Where have you been hiding? I've been trying to run things practically single-handed.

Sorry, Higgs. When I'm with Rawick … it's hard to keep track of time.

At least you two know some forestry skills. More help than Biore's been.

Wilt sat up and drew himself away from the chatter inside his mind, the impossible separate consciousnesses that dwelled somewhere within the welds themselves, inside the depths. Depths that were now a part of him.

He pulled out his long silver knife and sliced a thin strip of meat from the roasting carcass. The flesh was still slightly pink, but looked cooked enough.

Wilt bit into it and hot juice filled his mouth, the texture and pull of the meat against his teeth bringing him back to the physical world, the grey shadows of the cave brightening into colour, the cold air warming for a moment as life re-entered the room.

He swallowed and immediately cut another slice, wolfing this one down as well, leaving the cold and silence of that other world far below as he gave into his hunger. He hadn't eaten properly in days, and now attacked the carcass with an animal rush, ignoring the hot fat that seared his throat. Its warmth filled his belly, silencing every other thought. Only this was real. The heat of the fire, the taste of the meat.

Some time later he lay back on the warm rock, watching as the bright colours of the cave walls faded back into uniform grey. The cold settled over him like a blanket, separating him from the living world.

Feel better?

Wilt lay his cheek against the stone and closed his eyes.

Higgs?

Yes, Wilt?

Go to sleep.

The wind shifted again in the night, bringing with it a drop in temperature, whistling through the high stone ceiling of the cave and sparking the low coals of the fire into a dull red glow. With it came the murmur of the Tangle, the deep mutterings of an ancient consciousness. Wilt's dreams morphed as it washed over him, and his unconscious mind could almost make out the words the wind whispered into his ear.

Words of longing, words of pain and patience and an inhuman yearning for eternity. Words of warning. Words of fear.

The words brought with them visions that slid across his mind, not leaving any trace in his memory as he slept on, the Tangle murmuring its dark lullaby into his ears.

Stop! Thief!

He ducked under the guard's swinging arm and swerved into the alley, dropping half his haul as he went, not thinking for a moment about stopping to recover any of it. A loud crash behind him told him the guard hadn't been quick enough to change direction and had crashed into the fruit stall that lined one wall.

He grinned, tucking the two loaves he still held into his shirt as he ran, turning again as the next opening reared up, not slowing until he could no longer hear the heavy boots of the guards stomping after him. Even then he took two more twists deeper into the nest of alleys behind the market square before he slowed and risked a look back.

Safe. He was safe.

He leaned back panting against the nearest wall, tying his shirt tighter around the bread he'd swiped and glancing around the narrow alley to be sure no other street rats were thinking of trying to relieve him of his hard-won prize. After a moment to catch his breath, he turned to the wall and began to climb.

In seconds he was up on the roof, scurrying along the night highway, angling his path to the north of the market square, to his sorry excuse for a home. The grey skies opened as he ran, a heavy rain soaking him to his skin, threatening to turn the fresh loaves he carried into sodden mush. He slid and skidded across the greasy roof tiles, finally recognising the twisting lanes below him and dropping to the street, out of the worst of the weather.

All around him poor folk were fussing with their hovels, pulling thin wooden coverings into place to shelter from the persistent rain. He scurried past, holding his arms against his chest to protect the bread from the weather and hide it from any curious onlookers.

He turned into the small narrow opening between buildings that he called home. He pulled the thin canvas sheeting closed behind him as he entered and sat down on his pallet, eager to eat. Eager to ease the angry ache in his stomach.

'What do you have there, Meat?'

He curled into a ball, but it was too late. His father reached for his arm and tore it away, almost wrenching his shoulder out of its socket and sending the two loaves spilling into a scummy puddle on the ground.

'Look what you've done now!'

He tried to shrink himself tighter as the blows fell, his red hair streaming into his face as the rain and tears blinded him.

When he awoke, dawn was breaking grey and still across the sky. Wilt busied himself blowing life back into the coals of the fire, though his body felt no need for its heat.

What we need now is coffee.

Wilt smiled at Higgs's words and sat back as the flames caught. Coffee. Fresh bread. Bacon and eggs. He'd almost forgotten what such luxury tasted like. How long had he been gone? How long had he been out here, alone?

Too long. Too long with only our voices for company. Too long in your other form, your mind lost to human thought.

Had it really been so long? The dawn seemed earlier each morning, and frost no longer marked the grass of the forest floor, but were the seasons changing or were these merely signs of his steady progress south, toward the warmer weather, away from the high cold stone of Redmondis?

He caught himself. Human thought?

You've been spending more time away, Wilt. Ignoring us.

It was true the voices in his mind were more distant in his animal form. The world itself was different, brighter, sharp-edged, more immediate. The smells and textures a thousand times more vibrant. Was that why he spent so much time there, or was it this place, the Tangle itself, that made his other form seem more fitting? Perhaps it just took less food to fill his belly.

There are other hungers.

Biore's words brought his mind back to the present. He was right; the call of the depths and his other, darker form had been getting stronger each day, and it was becoming a burden to resist them. Why fight it, especially here, where he could do no harm?

Why else was he here at all? The Tangle was where he had thought to find answers to his some of his many questions—the true nature of the shadow form Wilt and Biore had both shared, the source of the still darkness beneath the chaos of the depths, the power that lay there, waiting for him.

He rubbed the strange lenses Higgs had formed that covered his black eyes. They itched.

Delco?

Yes, Wilt?

Any luck getting Rawick to open up about where in this place we should start looking?

It's … not that simple. The trees are troubled, that much I can say. But what causes it is … concealed. I am trying, Wilt. But their way of thought is so alien. South. There is a pull in that direction.

Biore?

Just another reason to give ourselves free rein, at least for a while. Let us see what the shadow realm can show.

Higgs?

I prefer our animal form, but if you must. Just be sure not to spend too long. You know the dangers.

Wilt rocked to his feet, his mind made up. He kicked at the

fire, scattering the coals and banishing the flames back into nothingness. A moment later and all that remained was a black scorch on the rock floor. He looked around the cave for any other signs of his presence. It was empty and still, already waiting for its next occupant.

Very well. We should pick up the pace anyway.

Where are we going, Wilt? What is our destination?

South. Delco is right; it's calling, drawing me toward it. Something that knows the depths as I do. Something that waits for me.

With a whisper Wilt's human form was gone and a dark shadow blew out of the cave, cutting down through the forest. It snaked through grey shadows, ignoring the curved animal track that marked the forest floor, slicing straight through any tree or barrier that blocked its path.

There was nothing to mark its presence, just a thick bubble of cold silence that moved through the forest, stifling all animal noises as it passed. The trees themselves seemed to bend out of its path, and no life stirred in the cold earth left in its wake.

Chapter 2

Shade ran through the forest, flickering in and out of the sunlight that filtered through the trees high above, dancing between and around the roots and branches that reached playfully into his path. He was fast, faster than any of the Others. He was just as Nurtle said he was: fast as a shadow, just as fast as his name.

Shade felt a smile stretch across his face as he moved, forgetting everything but the rush of air past his cheeks, the smell of the packed dirt forest floor, the whisper of the wind in the leaves. Suddenly the sound changed, and a muffled laugh from the Others cut across his thoughts.

He reached out his senses to identify the threat. He flew around the next tree, and there it was: a thin wire line stretched at neck height across the path. Shade didn't slow, he merely dropped his body to the ground and dived into a skid, leaning back as he moved under the glistening thread. He kept his eyes locked on the wire as he slid beneath it, feeling the forest floor against his back, seeing the ground through his own body as the physical world disappeared into grey shadow.

No fair!

A voice protested from off the side of the path, then was silenced by other whispers. Shade lay still on the path, the world dark around him, the light and heat of life in the bushes to his side showing him where the Others hid, watching. He reached for them, something inside him yearning to stretch out and grasp them, then he shook his head and the shadows retreated as the light of the forest returned.

A hurried scuffle of footsteps in the bushes and the whispers and laughter returned, fading from hearing as the Others moved farther away. Shade listened to them, trying and failing to picture their smiles. Then a leaf from high above drifted across his vision as it spiralled through the air, and he forgot about everything else.

The leaf swayed back and forth as it sank, until it cut across the waiting wire line, the sharpened thread slicing through it easily, and the leaf became two, each half falling faster now, in a race to the bottom.

One becomes two,
Sliced right through.

Shade stared up at the wire, running the simple rhyme back and forth in his mind, watching the sunlight glint along the stretched, thin metal. Just staring at it like this brought forth many different thoughts. Many different possibilities.

Finally he sighed and pulled himself to his feet, reaching into his pocket for the small folded blade he always carried, the one Nurtle had given him. He cut the wire at both ends, enjoying the humming twang as it snapped loose, then wound the metal thread into a tight loop and slid it into one of his many pockets.

For the Guardian, a gift,
To help heal the rift.

Then he was moving again, racing through the shadows, gliding on the breath of the trees.

Hours or perhaps days later Shade followed a well-beaten trail through the trees, a wide path made for more than one man to pass along, as close to a main thoroughfare as the trees ever allowed to form. Usually these trails curved around the few villages spotted along the edge of the forest, and Shade kept off them, not liking the heat and scent of human life that swamped them, knowing that

Nurtle had warned him to be careful not to be seen. Humans didn't understand. And what they didn't understand, they feared. And what they feared, they hated.

Shadow and silence both were made,
Safe for little wandering Shade.

This path, though, this one was different. It was cold, with no recent life marking its surface. Even the trees on either side had bent in toward each other, beginning the process of closing it off, erasing it from existence.

He felt lightheaded and satisfied, his belly still warm from the treeblood he'd taken from one of the Elders that morning. It wasn't stealing, not from the old ones. Not when it was just a little taste. It filled his belly and helped to silence the Others for a time, letting him enjoy the morning air in peace. He wouldn't tell Nurtle though; she was always warning him not to take too much.

She was always warning him about everything. Stay hidden. Watch out for the Others and their tricks. She warned him about the trees themselves sometimes, when she could tell he was really listening. He liked to please her, even though he knew she couldn't understand it. She was only human after all. He was something more.

He looked down at his hand as he walked, trying to will the change on, to sink down into that silent grey world that opened around him all too rarely, all too fleetingly. He could never hold on to it, like a pool of water pouring out of his palm. The tighter he gripped it, the quicker it faded away.

For a moment he thought he saw his hand fade, but then the wind shifted and the leaves above him swayed with it, and a bright glitter of sunlight brought him back to the surface.

The morning light shone down on his matted black hair, his grime-coated face. His clothes were a muddy mix of greens and browns that smeared into each other and merged with the surrounding forest, almost completely concealing him. He was short, four-foot tall on tiptoes, and as his cloak swayed and folded around him in the breeze it revealed there was nothing to his body. He looked like he was in danger of the wind lifting him away were it to get any stronger.

All that marked him as anything more than a mischievous young boy were his eyes. They were dark, too dark on closer inspection, as though the whites themselves had become stained a dull grey. They darted around as he walked, like those of a wild animal, flitting from point to point, always on the lookout for the next danger, the next threat.

Shade froze as he realised he had reached the end of the trail and was standing at the edge of a large clearing, at the border of a village. He slid off the trail into the trees, melting into the shadows. He almost turned and fled, but something in the air held him in place. A silence. A burnt silence. And something else. Death.

He slunk further back into the forest, keeping his eyes locked on the village, but there was no movement. No threat. All was still.

His boot crunched on something and he looked down to see a small pack lying in the undergrowth. He crouched and flipped it open, eager to discover new treasures.

Something sharp sliced into his finger and he jerked it back out with a hiss, thrusting the bleeding finger into his mouth and sucking the metallic warmth back into himself. With his other hand he pulled the bag upside down and poured its contents onto the ground in front of him.

A small glass statue—that was what had cut him. It looked like it had once been shaped into a tree, or something like it perhaps. It was beyond repair, not even a shard large enough to form into a blade, or perhaps a necklace. Shade sighed at the waste of it, the possibilities all shut off with one careless crunch of his boot.

Beside the scattered glass was a small hard biscuit. Trail food, the sort that humans often took with them when travelling. Shade had tasted its like before. It filled the belly but made the mind slow, stopped the ears, and dulled the senses. He left it where it lay. Some other forest creature would find it and enjoy a feast.

He pulled his finger out of his mouth and studied it. A single thin line cut across the tip of his finger; it darkened and filled, then pooled into a round droplet of black blood. He shoved the finger back into his mouth.

Why was the pack left here, in this bundle of bushes?

Shade looked around and noticed it immediately. The tree here, just next to where the pack had lay. It was different. Silent.

He stood up and studied the wide trunk, walking slowly around its base. There. Just above his head on the far side. Something horrible.

Shade held his breath as he watched it, and the wounded finger dropped out of his mouth. He'd never heard of such a thing, not even from the foolish villagers that Nurtle suffered to live with. Someone had wounded this tree.

He reached out and traced the outline of a rectangular gash in the trunk of the tree, not even just in the bark but cut into the timber itself, inches deep, a handhold or foothold. And above it another one, then another. Shade leaned back and followed the path of steps that had been cut into the trunk, all the way to the first thick branch that thrust out ten metres above the ground.

Why would someone do this? To climb it? Why couldn't they use their hands and feet?

He placed his whole hand inside the horrible thing, feeling for any sense of life underneath the silence. Nothing. Then his wounded finger scratched along the rough inner surface of the foothold, a single drop of blood streaking across its ridged surface, and the world dropped away.

Ache. A sick ache. Deep within the roots. Pulling on it, pulling on all its brothers and sisters, calling for it to sink back down into the soil, pull into the past, into safety.

Night. Still and calm, the forest silent. One of the humans who had hurt it perched up in its limbs, cradling a bow. Arms wrapped around legs in the chill air, eyes staring out into darkness.

Then the scratching ache again. The spreading stain as the dark things came. Leaking out of the night itself. Passing through the weakened barriers no longer strong enough to hold them back. Pouring into the village and snuffing out every life they met in an instant.

The human stands and looses its first arrow with a terrified scream, but all it does is advertise its presence. In moments one of the dark things is upon it, silencing it forever, leaving it to drop to the forest floor and drain its life into the waiting soil.

Familiar, these dark things. From a time long past. A sickness that should not be suffered inside these borders.

Brothers and sisters. So weak. So distant. Retreating down into the roots, away from the light and dark of the world.

Shade pulled his hand back with a gasp and fell onto his back, his mind still reeling from the vision that had swamped it. His heart was racing. Dark things. Evil things. Spider-shaped and impossibly fast. Here, inside the Tangle.

He rolled to his feet and stuttered up into a run, gaining pace with every step, leaving the dead village behind. He ran faster than he ever had before, faster than thought, his mind dropping into the grey world of shadow, fleeing the dark wake of the past.

Chapter 3

The shadowed world drifted by; now and then a bright flash of life illuminated the grey fog, the sign of an animal too foolish to heed the unnatural silence of the forest. Some were ignored, spared and left shivering in the sudden cold that seemed to drop over them from the sky. Others were not so fortunate. They flashed briefly as he touched them, their final memories filling his vision as their life burned out in the cold depths.

The voice of the Tangle spoke to him as he went, the whisper clearer in this form, though his conscious mind was too distant to understand its words. Its heavy, ancient voice rumbled through his core, the burning flashes of life and deep silent pools of shadow adding to the strange language he swam through.

He forgot all else, letting the voice of the Tangle carry him onward, deep into its heart and out the other side, the air warmer now, thick with a jungle scent. The flashes of life became more frequent. He found his pace slowing as he allowed the endless hunger that swirled within him try to sate itself, but no matter how many times he let himself turn from the path, no matter how many bright flashes of terror and sudden silence he encountered, the hunger stayed the same. Always turning, an endless whirlpool roaring within him, too deep to ever be filled, to ever be contained. There could be nothing else.

Wilt.

The grey trees shot past, each shape the same as the last. Even the voice of the Tangle seemed muffled and distant now, lost in the depths.

Wilt. Stop this.

He could spend eternity haunting these shadows, snuffing out any life he found. He could become death itself, and still nothing would change. Nothing would alter the flow of the great vortex surging within him.

At the edge of his vision a small glowing spark drifted, catching his eye, leading his mind back from its contemplation of the dizzying brink.

Wilt. Come back.

That voice. He knew that voice. It wasn't the Tangle; it was a part of him. Within him. He was human.

Wilt.

Higgs.

The grey world bled away and Wilt found himself standing in a small forest clearing, the flickering sunlight glowing down through small breaks in the tree cover, reflecting off tiny mites of dust that floated back and forth in the fresh breeze. He took a deep breath, his first in days.

Well, it's about time. We were beginning to worry.

Biore? How … how long have I been gone?

Too long, boy. Days at least. Far too long for any to spend in the shadow realm. Any who still wish to return. It was only through Rawick that we could lead you back at all.

Rawick. Wilt saw again the spark floating past his vision, dancing before his eyes, leading him away from the sucking depths.

I … I asked him to help find you. I think he understood me.

Delco. I saw him, I think. At least, some manifestation of him. He helped me—

Helped you back from the edge, from the lure of that which turns in the depths of the welds, that which calls all of those who draw on its powers. You lost control of your hunger, and it led you away. It is much stronger in that form. I should know.

Yes, Biore.

Perhaps we should take things a little slower now. It was foolish to go as far as we did, especially here. This forest shares an ancient connection with that which lurks beneath—you can feel it in the air itself. The stillness and silence. We will need to be more careful.

Besides, we've travelled a long way. Look around, even the trees are different here. We're near the southern edge of the forest, I believe.

Biore was right. As Wilt looked around, he realised he was in a whole new world from the one he had last seen. Great pines no longer towered above him; now thick vines twisted around themselves to form a jungle of vegetation, a solid green wall that funnelled him down a thin forest trail out of the small clearing. The air smelled different, heavy with moisture and heat, sticking his shirt to his back. He slung off his worn old cloak and dropped it to the ground.

Won't be needing that anymore.

Above him the trees still closed off the sky, reaching out to wrap their branches around each other in a protective shell, only allowing the smallest slivers of sunlight to leak through. The forest floor was thick with rotting leaves, the cloying scent of death undercutting the fresh breeze that forced its way through the walls of vegetation around him. Even the sounds of the forest here were different, louder. More filled with life.

A human voice called out, followed by the sound of something heavy moving through the undergrowth, and suddenly the cat was high above the clearing, perched on a thick branch, peering down into the space where Wilt had stood a moment before.

'You could at least try to move more quietly,' a gruff voice called from further down the path. A soldier appeared under the cat's tree and stopped when he saw Wilt's cloak lying on the ground. 'Emaus! Look at this!' The man crouched down and examined the ground around the cloak as his companion huffed into the clearing.

'What is it, Gul?'

'What's it look like? Someone's been through here.' Gul picked up the cloak and weighed it in his hands. 'Still feels warm.'

Emaus stood panting, resting his hand on his sword hilt, peering around the clearing. 'Well, you're the tracker, Gul. What does the trail tell you?'

Gul was still examining the ground around the discarded cloak. 'I don't know, it's strange.' He walked further into the clearing then turned around again. 'There are footprints, but they appear out of nowhere, then disappear again just as suddenly. Into thin air.'

Gul stood back up and both men drew their swords.

'Do you think—?' Emaus's voice was no longer gruff. It was almost a whisper.

'I don't know. There have been no sightings this far south before.'

'But the others—'

'The others haven't seen anything either. It's all been vague reports of strange sounds, sudden cold. Soldiers with loose tongues making each other nervous.'

'This cloak though.'

'It's just a cloak.' Gul bundled it up and wrapped it under his arm. 'C'mon, we'll have to report this. Keep your eyes open.'

He turned on his heel and marched out of the clearing, back down the path from which they'd appeared. Emaus followed, his eyes still scanning the surrounding trees, as if he expected an attack at any moment. Neither man sheathed their sword.

The cat watched the humans disappear back into the forest, the sounds of their movement fading into the general jungle hum.

Careless.

I know, Biore.

Wilt landed lightly back on the ground and stared down the path the two men had taken.

They were guards.

Soldiers. From the capital, to judge by their uniforms.

From Sontair? But we're still miles from there, aren't we?

Yes. Something big must have happened to bring them this far into the Tangle.

Wilt still stared down the path. He felt a sudden rush of

loneliness and for a mad moment considered calling after them. Just to have another human voice to talk to. There was something else there too. A deeper craving, waiting to be acknowledged.

Don't be foolish.

They were nervous. As though they were expecting something. Something bad.

Maybe we haven't been careful enough, in our other form. Too rushed. Too eager.

No. They weren't thinking about us. It might be wise to follow them, find out more before we stumble further into trouble. Soldiers from Sontair patrolling this far into the Tangle must be looking for something.

Or someone.

Come. Let us see what we can learn. Wilt, perhaps your cat form would be most appropriate.

With that the conversation ended, and the cat trotted out of the clearing, down the forest path, following the scent of the two soldiers. The wind brushed through the trees, whispering its secrets as it went.

Chapter 4

Shade sat alone high in the trees, squatting on a round, thick branch, watching the clumsy humans pass below him. They rattled and stomped and cursed, shoving branches out of their way as they moved, eyes forever shifting left and right, searching for some threat or victim to take out their nervous energy on. They stunk of sweat and fear.

But the treasures! So many glittering, colourful things, stark against the dull greens and browns of the forest, calling out to Shade to reach down for them, free them from their current resting places. He rubbed his fingertips together as he watched, rocking up on his toes, the thrill of anticipation tickling down the back of his spine.

It wouldn't be long now until they stopped to rest at a clearing the Tangle opened up for such a purpose and surrendered to their fatigue. They would pitch their heavy tents and stoke their fires, cook their strangely scented meals and sleep deeply, far too deeply to notice little Shade passing among them, lightening them of what treasures called to him.

All he had to do was wait. Wait and watch and, when the time came, slip past the weary guards who patrolled the edge of their camp, eyes blind in the darkness, ears filled with the thousand strange shiftings and callings of the forest. Never hearing Shade's furtive steps.

The last of the column moved past and Shade placed his palm

against the trunk of the tree, closing his eyes and listening for the deep murmur just below hearing. It was like the treasures the soldiers carried, out of reach yet still calling to him, urging him onward.

He could almost grasp it, almost hold it in his mind, yet it slipped away again. All he caught was a glimpse of a clearing, a clear night sky, and a scattering of campfires burning low in the cool air.

Very well. He would follow them, let their clamour and noise lead him on his way.

From darkness to light.

Silent as night.

He dropped out of the tree and slipped effortlessly into the shadows, stepping around fallen roots and leaves, his feet almost floating above the forest floor so silently did he move. He kept his eyes up, trusting his instincts to stop him from stepping anywhere he shouldn't. Now and then a glint of colour flashed out through the shifting leaves as he trailed along behind the soldiers.

'How much farther, Ged?' A panting, heavy voice. Husky with fatigue.

'Can't be long. Last glimpse of sky I seen looked grey, have to be almost twilight by now, not that you'd know it in this place. Sarge's probably just waiting to find the right spot.'

'Hope so. I'm done. Too much marching. Give me a real fight any day, not this wandering about.'

'Don't be so sure, Thron. You saw that village yesterday same as the rest of us. And you've seen the others. Don't know anything that can do that. Don't think I want to meet it anyways.'

'My own damn fault for signing up in the first place, I suppose. Thought I'd get two hots and a cot and all the fighting my sword arm could want. Never thought it'd mean trudging around the Tangle. No good can come—'

'Hold! You feel that? It's ice cold.'

Shade immediately stopped, and only now realised he could see the two figures clearly in front of him, shining lights of life against a dull grey background. Past them stretched the whole column of men, at least twenty of them all turned toward the rear, toward him, weapons drawn and ready.

For a silent moment he felt himself pulled toward them, called onward by the glittering lights.

Then he fled, the forest a blur as he shot through it, away from the soldiers and their treasures, away from the shining figures of light. Away from the call that came from somewhere both without and within, urging him ever deeper.

Shade recognised the trap, a scattering of leaves somehow too randomly strewn across a bare stretch of path. The colour of the dirt was wrong as well, too dark compared to the rest of the packed earth, too loose and recently disturbed. The Others were getting bolder with their tricks, but not clever enough. Not for his eyes.

He stepped along the edge of the suspicious patch and passed around it, grabbed the nearest heavy rock his hand came to, and tossed it lightly over his shoulder to land smack in the centre of the path. As soon as it landed the ground itself seemed to open, a stretched and tanned hide folding in on itself as it collapsed into the pit below.

Shade edged up to the hole and peered in. Sure enough, multiple sharpened stakes lined the floor of the trap, shining strangely in the dim sunlight. Coated with something, some sort of poison. There were a thousand possibilities, and the Others knew all of them. As did Shade. Nurtle had taught him most of them, and the few really nasty ones she'd kept silent about he'd discovered in the heavy journals of knowledge she kept so carefully hidden in her cabin. Not carefully enough. Not from fingers as quick as his.

He lay on his stomach and leaned over into the pit, careful not to touch any of the spikes, eventually wresting out the thick hide that had fulfilled its part in the trap. It was heavy, coated in mud to help it blend with the ground, but not too worn and seemingly only a few weeks old, judging by its smell. He gave it one solid shake, scattering leaves everywhere, then balled it up as best he could and continued on his way.

Warmth from the cold,

For bones shrivelled and old.

He broke into a giggle at his little joke but immediately caught it. It wouldn't do to add further insult to what the Others already put the Guardian through. That trap was another sign of their growing confidence in their little mischiefs. He didn't want to be like them.

The hide would make a fine addition to the offerings. And who knew? Perhaps there would be a gift for him waiting in the secret knothole. Some sign. The forest was on edge these days, troubled as it had never been in Shade's memory. Perhaps there would be something to show him the way.

Less than an hour later he drifted off the path he had been following, careful not to appear too sure of his surroundings, stepping through the shadows of the closely grouped trees, ears alert for any sign of danger. There was nothing. He was alone. Suddenly he ducked around the corner of the tree he was passing and seemed to completely disappear.

In reality, he dodged under an exposed root and slid down a short incline into his secret place: a small circular grove only a few feet wide, surrounded by an almost solid wall of thick trees. The sunlight seemed unwilling to intrude into the space, and Shade waited a full minute for his eyes to adjust before crouching at the base of one particularly large tree.

He lay the hide he had just discovered out on the ground and rummaged through the multiple secret pockets of his cloak. Moments later arranged neatly on the hide were a bright red sweat-stained kerchief, a goblet formed from dull silver, and the thin, sharp wire one of the Others had tried to hurt him with days before. Shade sat back on his haunches as he stared at the loot and nodded. A good haul.

With a sigh he wrapped the hide closed and stuffed the whole package deep into the knothole at the base of the tree, determined not to look at the treasures any longer. As he reached in, he tensed, as he always did, his fingertips electric for the touch of anything the Guardian may have left for him in return. Sometimes it was something simple, like a sweet fruit from the distant reaches of the Tangle. Other times it was more elaborate, like the strangely carved wooden mask he had found over a year ago that now adorned a wall in Nurtle's hut. Most times there was nothing at all.

But today there was. Shade caught his breath as his fingers brushed across a thin cloth bundle. He let his hands tickle its surface, prolonging the tension, trying to form a picture of what it could be. Finally he gave in and grabbed it, pulling it free.

It was a dull, dirty green cloth, rolled tightly, held in place by a simple loop of twisted wood. For a moment Shade felt a pang of disappointment, then shook his head and held the prize up to the light. There was something carved into the coiled wood. Words of some sort. As his fingers moved across the clasp, it seemed to come to life and sprung open, toppling the cloth to the floor.

He turned the opened clasp back and forth in the dim light, trying to make out the words scratched into it. As he recognised the characters, his lips moved automatically, the power in the words forcing themselves to be heard.

Future and past entwined.

The surrounding forest dropped into instant silence, and he stood perfectly still in the hush, waiting until the first scratchings and shufflings of the trees filled the air again. It was as though the forest had caught its breath at his words and was only now slowly exhaling.

He looked back at the clasp. As though the words themselves had unwound it, it was now three separate long threads, sticks really, nothing special about them. He dropped the twigs to the floor, and they seemed to disappear into the scattered refuse of the forest.

Shade nodded to himself. That treasure's job was done, whatever that job had been. The real gift must be the green cloth.

As soon as he grabbed it he knew he was right. A spark of familiarity lit his fingertips as he touched it, and raising it up from the ground he could see it was a cloak, just his size of course, lighter and richer by far than the worn cloak he currently wore. He hurried out of his old garment and slipped the prize over his shoulders, feeling it wrap itself around his shoulders.

Immediately he heard them. The Others, whispering to each other, giggling and scheming. Impossibly close. He dropped to the ground and scuttled as far into the shadows of the trees as he could, desperately hoping for the voices to pass by and leave him undisturbed. How had they snuck up on him?

Well, it's about time, I say.

Time has nothing to do with it. Action is what matters.

He's old and weak. That's what matters.

But only one of us can replace him. You know the rules. You know what the forest asks.

You heard it just as clear as me. He's done it. Must be desperate to use a kid like that.

We're all kids. And if you're right, he can probably hear us right now. That's how it was when he chose me.

And you failed just like the rest of us. Just like he will. Isn't that right, Shade?

Shade froze in place, all senses on edge as the voices called to him. Without thinking he dove into himself, dropping into the shadow realm where all life stood starkly against the shifting grey background. He scanned the area, turning a full circle to seek any lights of life. There was nothing. He was alone.

Ah, leave him be. Let the challenge do its work.

And just like that, the voices ceased.

Chapter 5

'Report.'

'We found this, Sergeant.' Emaus proffered the bundled cloak, but the sergeant simply stared at it, keeping his hands locked behind his back.

'And what is this?'

'A cloak, sir. A … It was left in the middle of the trail, still warm from its owner.'

'Or some other creature that stumbled across it.' The sergeant sniffed.

'There were no trails to or from the area.' Gul interjected, then immediately regretted it. The sergeant stared down at him as though Gul were something unpleasant he had stepped in. Gul swallowed and ploughed on, determined to make his point. 'We found human footprints around the cloak, but they went nowhere. As if whoever had made them just disappeared.'

'Yes, well, let's not make too many assumptions.' The sergeant hiked his belt up higher around his ample waist as he considered the news. 'Sounds like the Tangle is continuing to play its games.'

He swung around to scan the line of dark trees bordering their camp as if expecting an answer. When none came, he turned back to the two soldiers.

'Good work, I suppose. Go and get some hot food into you. We've had reports of another village attack. We move out at first light.'

The sergeant turned to the chart spread out in front of him, and Gul and Emaus saluted quickly and moved off toward the nearest campfire to see what food they could scrounge up.

The camp was large, with five separate main tents billowing in the light breeze, each with their own fire blazing. Shadowed forms moved in and out of their light. A double guard patrolled the border of the clearing, the men alert and nervous, making Wilt's job of sneaking past them more difficult than he'd expected. Eventually he found himself curled on a high tree branch looking down at the patrolling guards. As the men passed beneath him they shivered in the cooling night air.

Can they feel us?

I don't think so, Wilt, it's just the cold. The whole camp looks built for warmer weather. Look at the tents, the thin canvas walls. And the soldiers, all with cloaks over their armour. No, these men are used to a warmer climate. Southerners.

And their banner?

The cat peered out over the camp, studying the pennants of each tent fluttering in the evening breeze.

Sontair. The jewel of the South. These soldiers are from the capital.

We need to find out what they're doing here.

Another soldier had just passed beneath the tree, and the cat waited for him to move on before scampering down the trunk and creeping further into the camp. He angled toward the nearest campfire and crouched low in the flickering shadows. The fire was burning in front of a large tent, its front flap flung back and pegged into the ground. The cat slipped behind this and settled down in the shadows to see what he could learn.

Almost immediately, soldiers began moving back and forth from the fire, spooning out stew from the large pot that bubbled over the flames. The smells of cooking meat and rich gravy wafted over the cat, filling the air with a rich, warm scent.

Gods. Smell that. We haven't had a real meal in ages.

Higgs was right. Wilt hadn't eaten in the traditional sense since the wild pig he'd killed days ago, yet he didn't feel hungry. The thought skated across his animal mind, unable to find the purchase it should.

Listen now.

Two soldiers strode up to the fire and helped themselves from the pot, not interrupting their conversation.

'And the third patrol reported it too. I tell you, Jenks, there's more to it than the usual soldier's nerves.'

'Well, we've both been on patrol long enough to know that men's minds have a way of filling the time with phantoms, and our sergeant isn't helping any with his obvious nerves. I haven't seen anything, neither have you. Until we do, there's no point worrying at it.'

'But we've both felt it. I have, and I know you have—I saw you last night. You felt the ice touch just as clear as any of us.'

Jenks turned his attention to his food and didn't reply for a few moments. Eventually he lifted his head and wiped his mouth on his sleeve. 'There was something strange in the woods last night, I'll give you that. Sudden cold, like all the air had left the forest. But I don't know what it was, and neither do you, and it's no good filling up our heads with dark images based on what we think it might be. We patrol, we report what we see. We pray to all the gods that the sergeant or the captain or someone else even higher up sees sense and brings us home in one piece. No more.'

'Well, something is responsible for what we saw in that village. Those poor folk didn't do that to themselves. You've heard the stories about those demons in the north, the wielders from Redmondis. Maybe they're—'

'Whatever took that village will bleed just like you and me. It's no good wondering—when we find them, we'll punish them. And those folk will have their revenge, just like any of the king's villages.'

'But what if it's … You've heard the stories too, Jenks. A dark spirit haunts these woods. The trees themselves talk to it, guide it on—'

'Enough of that, man. Child's stories. Tales told by worried mothers to keep their young ones from wandering too far into the Tangle. No more talk. Eat your food.'

The two men walked away, leaving the cat alone in the shadows, watching the low flames and considering their words.

A dark spirit? Can they mean—

No, Wilt. We haven't been this far south. And we haven't—

We haven't killed anyone.

I'm more interested in hearing about this village. Sounds like raiders, but they've never dared come this far inland before. We need to find out more. We need to see what that man saw.

The cat sat up, his eyes bright in the firelight.

I don't know if I can control it.

We need to know. We'll help you, Wilt. We'll help you maintain focus.

Suddenly the cat was gone and a black mist haunted the space he had left, a thousand black welds squabbling for position. A deep, bone-chilling cold filled the air, fighting for dominance with the low campfire.

Wilt dropped his senses deeper, the world around him becoming a grey sea of shadow. Bright forms burned around the edges, calling to him, but he ignored their pull and focused on his target. A single black weld swam out through the night air toward the guard who had stood by the fire just moments before.

Jenks, still deep in conversation with his partner as they walked across the campsite, stopped mid-sentence as the weld slid straight into his mind and Wilt began rifling through his memories. It only took a moment to find what he wanted.

He stands at the edge of the forest clearing, staring out across what used to be a village. Fires still smoulder in the wrecked huts and a thick, acrid black smoke fills the air. At the village border are fallen guards, armour only half on, as though they had been caught by surprise, cut down as they struggled to gather themselves into something resembling a formation. The killing wounds were clean and quick. Professional.

His experienced eye takes in the scene and stores it for later evaluation and report. He reaches out and punches one of his men on the shoulder, gesturing them onward, into the village. Maybe there will be survivors, someone they can help. He knows even as he has the thought that it won't be true. They are hours too late.

Deeper into the village, the smell of the smoke is choking now. The bodies scattered around them are no longer just those of armed men. The raiders have left no witnesses. He spits on the ground and lets his eyes drift across the scene, taking it in but refusing to allow his eyes to dwell on any one horror.

At least they died quickly.

A call from one of the men, and he hurries over, eager to have a task, something to occupy his mind. A woman's body is stretched out on the ground, impaled on a thick, curved black sword, the first of any foreign weapons they have seen. The blade itself radiates evil, the edge strangely serrated and dimpled, as though it were grown rather than forged from steel, its inky surface a dark scar on the world. The guard who called him over reaches out to touch it, then pulls his hand back sharply with a cry.

'Agh! It's cold, colder than ice. It burns!'

At the man's touch the blade collapses in on itself, crumbling into black dust, the wind carving it away to join with the smoke that fills the air.

He hawks and spits again at the thought of that black air filling his lungs, then turns and marches away.

The image faded as the weld snapped back to Wilt, leaving Jenks to shake his head at the sudden dizziness that washed over him. A moment later the spell passed, and he continued on his way.

Wilt opened his eyes to the world of the present. The campfire was almost out, the coals smoking and smouldering, fighting to create some sort of heat in the sudden, unnatural cold.

That sword. It looked—

It wasn't a sword. It looked more like a limb.

We should worry about that later. It's time to leave.

More soldiers were approaching the fire, rubbing their hands in anticipation of a hot meal. Wilt heard a crack as he shifted his feet and looked down to see the grass around his feet was frozen white.

The next moment a black cat streaked through the campsite and into the shadows of the forest, unnoticed by any of the guards. A cry of dismay chased it deeper into the Tangle as the soldiers discovered their stew had somehow turned ice cold.

Chapter 6

Daemi weighed the dummy training sword in her hand, trying to adjust her mind to its foreignness. The wooden blade was the correct weight, but the balance was all wrong. Whoever formed it had paid too much attention its appearance, ensuring the hilt, handle, and blade looked as close to the real thing as a wooden version could, rather than the more important overall balance of the sword. It felt top heavy, and the tip of the blade kept wanting to dive forward into the dirt.

Daemi tossed it to her other hand and reached for a second one. She'd just have to work with what they had. Maybe after this afternoon's session she'd find time to speak with Petron and get some crafters to work on more realistic weapons for them.

She stood up and stepped into the circle, flexing her arms, swinging the two blades back and forth. As soon as she did so, two more guards joined her in the duelling ring, and she put all other thoughts out of her mind.

The two guards wore full faced helms, and each carried their favourite training weapons. The man on the right—Daemi could tell they were both young men by the set of their shoulders and their wide stance—carried a staff, weighted on one end to resemble a halberd. The other wielded a long sword and shield. Daemi dropped her arms to her sides and bowed briefly to each opponent.

'Begin.'

The gravelly voice of the master called out from the edge of the circle of guards lining the duelling ring marked out in the packed dirt. The audience of guards roared out in answer, and her two opponents started in, wasting no time closing the space between themselves and her. As soon as they were in range they split, circling in opposite directions, eyes wide and wary behind their helms.

The sounds of the world faded as Daemi watched them, waiting for the first attack.

The halberd wielding guard swung suddenly, a fast cutting blow that sailed easily over her head as Daemi ducked and rolled to her left, straight toward her attacker, bringing her much shorter blades into range. The guard swung, dancing his feet in a circle to avoid her approach, bringing the tip of his weapon back around to point at her as he backed away to the far side of the circle.

Daemi continued her roll back up to her feet and grinned at him. It was a feint, nothing more. The other would be striking …

Now.

A shuffled step was all the warning she needed as the second guard closed in. He swung a vicious diagonal cut at her, a blow that would have sundered any armour had it been made by a real sword. Had she still been standing there. As it was, Daemi was already behind him, a double spin to his sword arm side bringing her into range. Her duel blades shot out together, punching cruelly into the guard's side, right where the front and back plates of his armour buckled together, the shock of the blow blasting all the air from his lungs and dropping him to his knees.

He recovered well, turning his collapse into a roll to bring himself back to his feet, reversing his blade into a horizontal slash that was far too slow to trouble Daemi, but gave him time to step away, his blade pointed at her chest.

Daemi smiled again, watching the point of his blade droop as the bruising blow she had struck had its effect.

'Raise your blade, Talis.' The master was quick to notice too, and called out his correction.

The first guard moved in, hoping to take advantage of the distraction. Daemi was too quick again, throwing herself forward this time to roll into range, both blades chopping out in a lightning-quick cadence, smacking into the handle of the staff where the guard's gloved fists held it. The first blow shocked the weapon itself and the second landed squarely across the guard's gauntlet. His hand dropped, and the halberd almost fell before he gathered himself and trotted away from her again.

It was too easy, only two against one. The master had to see that. He would have something else planned.

Daemi let the two guards gather themselves, allowing the shock and pain of her blows to sink in. Let their next attacks be more measured, more precise. Let them learn to fear the consequences.

'What are you waiting for, men? Attack!'

Another cheer rang out in answer to the master, urging the guards on. Both stepped toward her now, eager to strike her down. Too eager.

The first guard swung his halberd again; it was obviously too heavy for him now and his attack lacked control. As Daemi ducked, she clapped her two blades into it, adding force to its momentum, sending it straight into the second guard, who had moved too close to his companion. The second guard raised his shield just in time, deflecting the blow but sending himself sprawling to the side, out of range. Daemi ignored him for the moment, eager to finish things off quickly.

Her strike on the halberd turned into a quick spin as she shot out her trailing leg, sweeping the feet of the first guard out from under him. Instantly she was on him, her dual blades rapping out a quick staccato of strikes across his chest and helm.

The guard shot his hands into the air in surrender, and Daemi spun back to her one remaining foe.

'Move in, Talis. You do no good hanging back.'

The master's tone was one of exasperation now, and the sound brought a grim smile to Daemi's face. He'd been trying to best her with these arranged duels for weeks now, yet every time she'd won out. Done it easily, too. It was beginning to look a little embarrassing for the rest of the troop.

As Daemi watched the guard close in, the skin across her back tightened, as though an icy breeze had blown down the back of her neck. She continued to circle, studying the way the guard stepped toward her, the way the tip of his blade pointed up straight at her heart.

It was the merest flicker of a glance that gave it away. Daemi made out the guard's eyes behind his helm, the way they moved suddenly up and over her shoulder, and Daemi rolled to the side just in time to avoid the sudden thrusting attack of a third opponent stepping out from the ring of guards.

So, the master had had enough of playing fair. Now he simply wanted to win.

Daemi completed her roll and spun back to her feet, keeping low to the ground, watching as the two guards moved in toward her. The new opponent held twin daggers, shorter than Daemi's swords but probably faster. He must have been picked especially in response to her choice of weapons, the master hoping to nullify any speed advantage she had.

The scarred skin on her back was aching now, tight and hot and stretched. Daemi forced the thought out of her mind to focus on the duel.

Both guards stepped to the side and closed in, aiming to attack simultaneously from separate angles. It was no good waiting for them. Take the initiative.

Daemi decided and attacked. She cut straight at the sword and shield wielding guard, her blades a blur of movement, cracking hard into the man's shield. She wasn't concerned about him blocking the blows, merely wanting to distract him for a key moment.

As the shield moved to block, Daemi stepped further to the side and threw three heavy blows into it, spinning it, and the man holding it, around—right into the second guard, who had been about to launch an attack of his own. Suddenly the first guard found himself blocking the blows of his own companion, Daemi having stepped behind him. The next moment he was on the ground; four hard shots into his back and legs and he dropped like a stone.

Daemi didn't stop to admire her work, leaping over the prone man to bring both blades slicing down at the remaining guard's head. The guard raised his daggers and just blocked the blow, but the force drove him onto his knees. Daemi's high attack flowed effortlessly into a low swinging kick that caught the guard right in his exposed stomach. His arms dropped, and two more quick strikes on his helm ended the battle.

'Enough.' The master's disappointed tone left no doubt as to his opinion of the fight. 'You are victorious again, Captain.'

Daemi stood to attention and saluted in reply.

'Some day one of these dogs will best you, I'll make sure of it.'

'May that day be soon, Master. I'm in danger of becoming bored.'

The master's eyes widened at Daemi's disrespectful words, before his mask cracked and a wide grin broke out across his face.

'Ho now! I will have to come up with more surprises next time then, little cat.' He turned back to the other guards, his face freezing in an expression of cold command. 'You lot, back to the training grounds. We have a long afternoon ahead.'

He nodded in salute to Daemi and led the guards away. Daemi watched them go, standing perfectly still at attention until the last of the guards had moved out of sight. As soon as they were gone she slumped down, pulling her tiger-faced helm free and shrugging the tight training leathers off her shoulders.

Sure enough, the inside of her armour was streaked with red. Her scars had opened again.

Daemi grabbed her cloak from the pile of belongings to the side of the duelling ring and threw it over her shoulders to hide the stains that marked her undershirt. She hadn't felt the rip this time, just the tightness that had come to be so familiar since she'd woken weeks ago with the scars marking her back. The scars from the touch of the nightmare creature that had almost ended her. The scars Wilt had given her.

Daemi shook her head to dismiss the thought and trotted out of the training yard, her regular armour in hand. There was only one healer in Redmondis with the skill to close these wounds. She had to see Petron.

By the time Daemi had climbed the worn stairs to Petron's chamber, high in the twisted structure that used to be known as the Black Robes' tower, the blood from her scars had dried, cracking and falling away as she raised her arm to knock on his door.

Before her fist touched the heavy timber, his voice called out. 'Come in. You made too much noise trooping up those stairs to bother knocking.'

Daemi pushed the door open to reveal a large, brightly lit chamber, sunlight streaming into the room through a massive opening knocked out of the stone wall that faced the open sky and the green sea of the Tangle far below.

She stood there dumbfounded for a second, lost in the yawning space and freedom of the heavens. The world spun with sudden vertigo and she edged toward the door until Petron's voice snapped her back into the moment.

'Like it? I got some younger crafters to help redecorate. Remove the stuffiness.'

Daemi found her mouth was hanging open, and she shut it with an audible click.

'Yes, that was my first impression too. They went beyond themselves. Probably trying to impress me.'

Daemi finally regained control of her senses and turn toward his voice. Petron was sitting at his desk, a tired smile on his face. 'I ... uh ... imagine they succeeded.'

'Yes, they did at that.' Petron chuckled.

The smile dropped as he studied her, noting the arch of her shoulders, the way she held herself to stop the raw skin on her back from rubbing on her shirt. 'Again?'

Daemi nodded glumly and moved across the room to the bed, pulling her garments free as she went. Petron had been treating her wounds ever since they had been inflicted, so many weeks ago now, and she had long since lost any sense of modesty around him.

Petron stood and joined her at the bed as she lay down on her stomach. He pulled her undershirt up as gently as he could; the dried blood had stuck it to her skin and ripped cruelly as he pulled it free. Daemi made no sound, but the tensing of her back was all the sign needed of the fresh pain he was causing.

'Ah.'

Petron sat back as he studied the reopened scars, running his fingers around the edge of the wounds. He tried to keep his tone light though was grateful Daemi had her head turned away from him and couldn't see the concern in his eyes.

'Is it very bad?'

'No worse than the last time.' Petron patted her on the shoulder and moved to retrieve the unguent he'd made for just this purpose. It seemed to heal the wounds well enough, though they kept reopening after a few days, as though the wounds themselves were resisting any attempts to remove their mark from Daemi's skin.

Daemi's shoulders shuddered as he spread the medicine.

'And your dreams? Still troubled?'

Daemi waited for the shudder to pass before turning back to face him. 'Yes. You know how it is.'

Their eyes locked in mutual understanding. Each of them suffered from the nightly terrors that seeped into their dreams. Every time the vision was the same. A writhing figure of darkness, reaching for them, then the cold touch of death. The same silent emptiness waiting for them until their eyes opened to find the world still there and breath still in their lungs.

'I had hoped that in time, seeing as how busy we both are—'

'You hoped they would fade like these scars of mine. And I suppose they have, in that neither these scars nor our dreams have healed yet.'

Petron noted the resigned edge to her words and turned his eyes back to his work. Finally the last of the long scars closed under the healing power of the medicine, and the skin on her back looked almost normal again. 'I've been thinking about that.'

He sat back and tossed the unguent across the room to its place among the strange figurines, powders, and bottles accumulated in one corner of his room. 'I believe it's time we tried something new.'

Daemi sat up and pulled her clothes back on. 'And?'

'And I think perhaps this new Redmondis of ours needs to stop licking its wounds and re-emerge onto the world's stage.'

Daemi stood up and finished buckling her armour around her chest. She gave it a thump with her fist to settle it into place. 'Well, it's about time.'

Chapter 7

The cat trotted quickly along the forest floor, his mind clear and still, senses alert, following the pulsed, insistent command to track back to where the soldiers had been, back to where the man Jenks had seen the ruined village.

It was easy to find; the trail of memory left by the shared weld helped, but it wasn't long before the scent of death and smoke was clear enough for his own nose to follow without difficulty.

Wilt stood at the edge of the trees, staring out at what had once been a village. It was changed from the vision the weld had shown him. Low, broken huts, a thin black smoke fuming out from them, the fires that had consumed them almost entirely burned out now. All their fuel had been used up.

He stepped carefully through the remains of the buildings, trying to make sense out of what he saw.

It couldn't have housed more than twenty or thirty people, a tiny village such as this, judging by the number of huts and the modest size of the ploughed fields lining its outskirts. Farmers and their families scratching a living out of the ground. Raiders would find nothing of value here. What could the villagers have done to deserve such a fate?

The soldiers must have buried the dead.

Higgs's voice pulled Wilt out from his dark thoughts. There was no sign of any bodies.

No. The barn closest to the fields, to the north, it's still burning.

The patrol must have started that fire themselves. A sort of mass cremation.

Wilt turned to face the barn Biore had pointed out. He was right; the smoke was thicker there, the fire still doing its work.

Wilt felt dazed and numb, and not just because of the ruin that surrounded him. It was as though a secret voice that spoke only to him, a constant whisper at the very edge of his hearing, had suddenly been silenced. It had happened just as he had stepped out of the shadow of the trees. He wondered whether the others had noticed it, how much of his mind they really shared.

He ambled toward the smoking barn. There were no flames visible, and no heat radiating out from it, but Wilt was cautious of getting too close. The smoke was thicker here, and he didn't want to breathe any of it in. There was something else as well, something familiar.

A gust of wind blew a black cloud across his vision, and as it passed, he saw another figure at the far edge of the village. A soldier. A guard, standing alone. Hands on hips. Her hips. He recognised her immediately, just from her stance. Daemi.

The smoke passed, and the vision was gone, and Wilt shook his head to clear it.

What are we waiting for? Higgs's familiar tone was impatient.

Did you see that?

See what?

Wilt hesitated, no longer sure of himself.

Nothing. I thought I saw something, but it was just the smoke.

The sudden vision had brought with it a warm rush of longing that took his breath away, and the feeling grew stronger as he approached the barn. The walls of the structure had collapsed inwards as the roof had caved in, and a low heap of timber smouldered into ash. There was nothing recognisable left, no sudden terrors of familiar human forms, yet to Wilt what remained was almost as bad. That so much life had become nothing more than dust.

There's nothing here.

Biore's voice almost sounded disappointed, though Wilt understood what he meant. He had been half hoping for some other sign of what the guards had discovered, like that strange-looking sword, or limb, or whatever it had been. Something not of this world.

Wilt turned away from the barn and stared at the Tangle, the tall trees forming a solid wall delineating the edge of the village from the wilderness beyond. The tops of the trees swayed mockingly in the breeze.

Why build a village here, in the Tangle? Growing up in Greystone all knew well enough to stay clear of its borders, though no one was ever really clear why. What was different for these poor folk?

Maybe they thought it a good source of food. Maybe they were hunters as well as farmers.

Surely even simple farmers knew better than that.

The Tangle had been a place of fear for generations, a cautionary tale told by mothers to their children at night. Maybe the villagers thought it was nothing more.

Wilt turned away, not wanting to hold the trees' gaze any longer. What horrors had they witnessed?

You heard the soldier last night. There must be other villages nearby. This one was too small to survive out here in total isolation.

Delco, ever the practical one. He was right; there was no way a village of this size could provide everything for itself, no matter how determinedly the farmers worked the land. There had to be others.

He walked out of the village, away from the smoke and ash and the silence of death.

Wilt lay within a still black pool of sleep; images floated to the surface and a low whisper slithered through his mind. As each vision blurred into form, the words became clearer, as though they themselves helped snap the pictures into focus, capturing scenes viewed through other eyes. A line of trees shifted in the wind, watching him. Waiting for him.

Flows with you and without you.

A red-robed figure pulling back her hood to reveal a cold, terrifying beauty. Eyes staring through him, past his desire, past his fear. Lips curved into a knowing smile.

The blood within the stone.

A twisting nest of serpents coiling over each other, waiting in the depths, waiting for any mind to drift within reach.

Writ for you and about you.

A circle of stone figures falling in order, the spiral shield, the wave continuing around its endless path, bringing with it a throb of warmth and life, pulsing like a heart.

Together and yet alone.

A tall soldier standing alone, facing a mirror. Pulling her helm free to reveal dark curled hair and green eyes that seemed to stare through the shimmering vision, straight into him.

Wilt awoke with a start and almost dropped the small pot of water he was somehow clutching over the fire.

Careful now, Wilt, I've been working on this for hours.

Higgs? What is happening? I was—

I was being careful. Just thought that while you rested I could take over for a little while, get some work done.

Wilt shook his head, the shreds of the dream sliding from his mind as he took control again, like his fingers were slipping back into a familiar pair of gloves.

Wait a second. You were controlling my body?

Don't get upset. I wasn't doing anything to get worked up about. Just taking it for a spin.

I warned him it might come as a shock.

Biore? You knew about this?

It was his idea. Well, maybe not in so many words, but he mentioned the possibility.

I simple noted that it might theoretically be—

Theoretically?

And it is! Look! Look what I crafted while you were sleeping.

Wilt looked down at his hand, only now aware of the weight resting in his palm. It was a ring, formed from stone, glowing red in the firelight, as though the stone captured the flickering light of the flames, caught and held it within its form.

Put it on.

Higgs couldn't disguise the childish eagerness in his tone.

What is it?

It's a ring, of course. A heat ring—no, that won't do for a name. We'll need to think something up. But I got the idea from our trip into the guard camp. You drew the heat from their campfire, sucked its energy up into you and used it. I thought that if we had our own source of heat, and made it powerful enough, you could draw from it. Maybe that way you could …

I could what?

Rejoin the human world again, Wilt. You've spent too long on your own, too long in the dark.

Biore's words brought snatches of Wilt's dream back up to the surface. Daemi standing in front of a mirror, staring back at him.

Wilt shook his head and focused back on the ring sitting in his palm.

So you're saying that while I was asleep Higgs took control of my body and decided to try some crafting?

I wasn't sure it would work, and it took a bit longer than it should have, but the stone still responded to my touch, and I could feel the life inside it. It was great, Wilt, it was like I was really there.

Wilt's anger subsided as he recognised the plea in Higgs's tone.

You are really here. All of you. You're with me.

I know. It's not the same though.

Rest assured we were keeping an eye on him, Wilt. We wouldn't let anything happen to you.

Wilt bounced the heavy stone ring in his palm as he considered the possibilities.

So you're saying that by wearing this I can just walk up to people and not ... Not have them ... Not drain the world around them. Not have them feel the cold, the icy pull of the depths. Not be such a danger to them.

It's worth a try, isn't it?

Wilt saw Daemi again, standing alone, her green eyes shining.

Yes. Perhaps it is.

Chapter 8

The shadow cut through the forest, ignoring the trails that wound in and around the heavy trunks of the trees. Any obstacle in its path was simply passed through, the light of the world fading momentarily as it merged with and pushed through the foreign forms. Any trees it moved through produced a deep sigh of pleasure in its heart, a cooling plunge into a fathomless pool of consciousness that recognised and welcomed its presence, sending it on with a calming caress that stilled the rush and panic of the world around it. Eventually the murmur of the trees found a foothold in its mind—his mind—and the shadow slowed to a top.

A bright beam of sunlight flashed into the clearing and seemed to burn the shadow away, leaving a small boy to stand in its place, leaning back against the nearest tree, shaking with exhaustion.

Shade stared at his feet as he panted for breath; the pointed toe of his boot dug into the moist earth, stamped down the thick moss that covered the forest floor. He waited, aware of the worms that moved beneath his feet, the simple life forms that consumed what the forest let fall. He cleared his mind, letting no thought enter until the stillness returned and he had control again.

Shade pushed away from the tree and looked around, trying to get his bearings. He had been near the southern edge, watching the soldiers prepare for their patrol, his eyes soaking in the various treasures they carried with them. So many shiny things to collect.

He'd kept the soldiers in sight as they started off, heading into the Tangle, stumbling in their heavy armour. It was easy to stay out of sight. They were oblivious to the small dark shape that followed them, watching them pass before him one moment, then flitting ahead to wait high in the branches of the trees as they moved underneath.

The soldiers wouldn't have been able to hear anything over the racket they made, their blades and armour clanking, snagging in branches that seemed to reach across the trail and wind themselves purposefully around them. The column stretched, and the faces of the men tightened with tension as they wound deeper into the forest.

Perhaps they could hear the trees after all, beneath the noise they made. Perhaps that was what caused their fear.

Shade drifted closer; at times he was close enough to reach out and touch them, tug at them with his outstretched finger as they passed, just as the trees did, feeling the cold, dead touch of their armour.

That was when he heard the voice.

It was as if the forest song changed, dropped a register, ignoring the men now, focusing all of its energy on speaking to him.

Come, little Shade. Little wraithling.

Shade forgot everything except the voice. He moved through a grey, shadowed world, lit only by the bright flashes of life that passed him in single file.

The forest whispered its will, and the next moment he was cutting through the trees, angling right for the front of the column. His mind was clear, filled with hunger. He followed it without thought.

Then something else was there. Something foreign. A black, twisted shape. It recognised him, saw through him, turned its attention away from the men it had been lying in wait for to face him. The voice changed again and his mind was flooded with panic, sending him fleeing out through the forest, following the voice that called him on, led him away from the danger he had stumbled upon.

The black thing leaped after him in pursuit. He felt the burning cold of its breath at his heels, urging him onwards, pushing him past the limit of what he thought possible. Then it had dropped away as he powered on, too fast for it to follow. Eventually the whispers of the trees returned, and he found his steps slowing. Found himself here, far from where the guard column had been, back in his own mind and body. Feeling strangely used.

Secrets and lies,

Shadows and eyes.

Shade shook his head at the memory and pushed himself up from the tree. He was safe here, the forest still and quiet around him. The threat left somewhere far behind in his blind flight.

Was that what the forest had wanted? To lead the threat away from the men who stumbled through it? Or had it wanted him to drive them away, out of its borders. Perhaps its patience had worn thin.

Shade gave up trying to get his bearings from the forest floor and pulled himself up into the tree. He felt the pulse of life underneath his fingers, the troubled dreams of the ancient ones. In moments he was near the top, balancing on thin branches barely strong enough to hold his weight, scanning the surrounding area. There, to the south-east, a thin column of smoke curled into the clear sky, as though from a large campfire. It had to be the guard column; no one else would be foolish enough to risk a fire within the borders of the Tangle.

He watched the smoke twist and fade into nothingness in the wind, feeling the tree beneath him sway in the same breeze. It was a very black smoke.

No campfire made that.

As he moved closer to the site of the smoke, he began to recognise the forest around him. He was right near the village of Weverly, one of the neighbouring villages scattered along the southern edge of the Tangle, crouching within its borders for protection.

The thought reminded him that Nurtle had given him a task, a mission to fulfil. She had told him it was direct from Jared himself, their village chief, though Shade had no way of knowing if she spoke the truth. Perhaps she was lying to him, making fun of him, like the Others.

No. Not Nurtle. The Others, yes, but not her.

Jared wanted a report. The trees had been whispering about another village taken, just like the others. Taken by the dark.

Nurtle had tried to find out more, had spoken with the trees themselves, but they wouldn't make their meaning any clearer to her. Besides, one couldn't ever trust the trees to tell the whole truth. Too often they whispered to those with the power to hear them, to lead them astray or cause mischief for their own amusement. Nurtle was always telling him that. Only ever listen to the trees with one ear, she said. You never know what their goal might be.

Nurtle had been angry when he'd first returned to her in his new cloak. He'd tried to tell her it was a gift from the Guardian, had used his best rhymes to win her over, but she had just shaken her head and turned away. Shade could tell something worried her, but he kept that thought to himself.

Don't touch anything. She had been specific about that.

Shade flittered through the trees, a smile on his face as he remembered her words. An abandoned village would hold all sorts of treasures for his collection. What Nurtle didn't know wouldn't hurt her.

By the time he approached the edge of the clearing that marked the outer boundaries of the village of Weverly, Shade's smile had dropped away. It was the trees' fault. They were disturbed, their troubled mutterings urging him onwards, filling his thoughts with strange black shapes that danced away again as soon as he tried to focus his attention on them. Dark things. Dark things had come. Silence had eaten its way across the village and left nothing behind.

Eventually Shade decided he would ignore them, block out their voices. They were much louder now, seemingly determined to scare him away from his task.

When he reached the edge of the clearing that marked the

borders of Weverly, he stood silently and waited. It was immediately clear that something was wrong. There was no sound of life from the village before him, no noise at all other than the constant nervous chatter of the trees.

A single fat column of smoke rose from the far side of the village, black and greasy, smudging across the sky as the wind took hold. Its source was obscured by broken, empty-looking huts. Shade watched the smoke warily. He wanted none of it near him.

He cut around the edge of the village, staying upwind, then moved in toward the abandoned buildings.

The villagers had been given little warning. Each hut he passed had been sacked, valuables scattered across the floors, doors hanging on their hinges where they had been thrown open in panic. Shade glanced inside each one he passed, his curiosity drawing him. He never let himself cross a threshold though, not wanting to pry too deeply into such recently ended lives. Whatever these people thought they could salvage would now be curling up into the sky with the rest of them.

He saw the source of the smoke now, a large central building where the villagers would have once gathered together for celebrations and events. He kept it downwind and circled around it, not wanting to see any of the dark, twisted shapes he knew would be there.

Shade had enough information for Nurtle; he didn't need to see anything else. But he had glimpsed other huts on the far side of the village, other buildings that didn't look as lived in. Ones where he might find something for him. Perhaps even another gift for the Guardian.

Sure enough, a row of half-finished huts squatted in the dirt close to the line of trees that edged the clearing. Empty door frames and partial roofs let the forest breeze blow through, removing any lingering scent of the black smoke that smouldered in the centre of the village. Shade smiled to himself, forgetting everything else in the sudden hunger for treasure.

An hour later he was halfway through the third hut, his pockets bulging with interesting knickknacks he'd claimed as his own. Smooth river pebbles, bright strips of dyed cloth, even a couple of rolls of glittering ribbon. He'd hit the jackpot in this latest hut though: a massive ball of twine, metres and metres of it, all handwoven. All his, if he could get it out of here. He tried lifting the large ball—it was bigger than his head. He could probably carry it if he had to, but he knew he would have to be prepared to run if any of the Others found him on his way back through the Tangle. Maybe he should just take as much as he could fit into a pocket, cut the twine there, and hide the rest in the forest to come back for later.

He was busy weighing his options when he heard it; a deep sigh from the trees just metres away, followed almost immediately by an intense cold. It seemed to reach for him through the wall of the hut. Shade lost all thought but that of flight; he shot out through the open doorway and darted around the next hut, bending his run to angle for the trees while keeping the sense of cold behind him.

It was one of them, one of the dark things. Still here, waiting for any who had escaped to return.

Shade reached the edge of the Tangle and ducked under the low branches, focusing all his energy on flight. He'd escaped them once already, he could do it again. He danced around trees impossibly fast; the world around him drained of colour as he sped on and on, losing himself in the shadows.

But he wasn't fast enough this time. He could feel the cold reach for him, kissing the heels of his feet. Somehow it was keeping up with him, gaining on him, coming closer with each step. He almost looked back, if only to get one final look at whatever it was that would end him.

It was the trees who saved him. They parted suddenly, a wide open space appearing where none had been before. Shade knew immediately what had happened. The trees had seen his desperate flight and done the only thing within their power to help. They had called the Guardian.

Shade skidded to a halt as soon as he burst into the clearing and fell face down onto the ground, clasping his eyes shut and driving his nose into the dirt so as not to catch a glimpse.

There was a single whisper, right at the edge of hearing, then darkness.

Chapter 9

Wilt slid the weld blade quickly along the rabbit's limp body, angling the blade up at the last moment to leave a flap of pelt hanging from its legs. He put the knife down and grabbed the flap in both hands, flipping the rabbit in the air, snapping his wrists at the high point of the loop and ripping the skin from its body in one jerk. He caught the body and hung it from the hook Higgs had formed in the stone wall of the cave.

See? Told you having crafter skills on hand would prove useful.

Not bad at all, Higgs. Rawick himself would have been proud.

Delco? I wondered if we'd ever hear from you again. It's been days.

Has it? I'm sorry, Wilt. It's hard to keep track of time when I'm—

When you're trying to communicate with Rawick. I understand. Wilt bent down to wipe his knife clean on the rabbit's discarded fur. *Besides, without the knowledge you passed on to me, I would have starved in the first week out here.*

A sudden warmth bloomed on Wilt's back, then floated away again, a spark dancing in the breeze. *Was that …?*

Yes, I think so. It's hard to tell sometimes.

Wilt slid the long knife back into the sheath on his hip and sat down to poke at the fire. The coals were a deep red now, the flames low. Just about perfect for cooking.

Have you ever wondered how you came to learn about wilderness survival, Delco? I mean, he must have taught you some things, but did you gain the knowledge when he—

When he used the white weld on me? When he almost killed me? It's okay to talk about it.

Well?

I'm not sure. We used to go out into the woods a lot, camping, hunting. But the muscle memory, the way your hands know where to be, how to move—, you can't learn that from being taught. I think it comes from somewhere deeper.

Wilt looked up at the cleaned and dressed rabbit hanging from its hook. *Deeper. Like the welds. I think you might be right. I still don't understand half of what I find my hands doing out here.*

He reached out with the stick he'd been using as a poker and hooked it around the loop of the rabbit's back legs, then arranged the whole on a small spit he'd built over the fire. A rich smell filled the small cave immediately.

It's part of what I wanted to talk to you about, Wilt. It's hard to know what he means sometimes, hard to get any words out of him at all, but in the last few days he's become more insistent. More urgent, like he's trying to tell me something.

And?

It's the trees. He says the trees are speaking to him, directly to him I mean. They say they've been waiting for him. For us.

Us?

For you, Wilt. They've been watching you.

A flame flared in the fire as hot fat dripped from the rabbit's body, and Wilt stared into it, his eyes losing focus. Inside it, dancing in orange and white, he saw himself standing on the edge of the river, just outside the walls of Greystone. Across the river were the trees of the Tangle, waving slowly in the wind. Staring back at him. *Why?*

That's where it becomes less clear. Something about the dark. A darkness. Something from the depths. Something they've seen before, long ago.

The words brought another vision, foaming waters filled with serpents, twisting angrily about themselves in their hunger, desperately searching for a way back to the surface world. Beneath them, below the wash and the fury, was the darkness.

But what does it mean, Delco?

I don't know. I've tried, tried everything I could think of to make sense of it. I can't. I don't think Rawick himself understands what they mean. They're so old, Wilt, so alien to us. But there is one. He says there's one who can help us. He says …

Wilt could feel the hesitation on his tongue as though Delco's thoughts really were his own.

He says it's waiting for us.

We will have to do something about your clothes.

Wilt looked down at himself, suddenly aware of his appearance. The physical realm had become less important in the past few weeks. He was still wearing the remains of his black robe from Redmondis, hardly recognisable now. Below his waist the robe had been ripped and shredded, scraps of cloth bound around his legs into something that passed for trousers. Above it the material was in better shape, though it hung loosely from his frame, billowing about his chest and arms.

You've lost a lot of weight. Biore's tone was scolding.

Any suggestions?

The village we saw. There must still be something there we can use.

The idea of returning to the ruined village disturbed Wilt. The silence and finality of it.

You can't see other people looking like this, Wilt. Besides, it should be better now. It's been days. The fires—

Must have run out of fuel by now.

Wilt crept through the village, his left fist clenching and unclenching around the thin stone ring he wore on his middle finger. It felt heavy and cold on his skin, colder than he had expected.

Did you expect it to feel hot? Give me some credit, I'm more of a crafter than that. You shouldn't feel it at all. Just know that when the need arises, it can provide the heat required, especially when you … do your thing.

Wilt smiled and stopped fussing with it. He scanned the broken buildings with fresh eyes now, looking for a likely source of clothing. Most of the huts had completely collapsed, the fires and elements having had their way with the timber frames. Further out from the centre, though, there were still one or two stone huts that seemed in better shape.

There. They look almost untouched.

As he strode closer, Wilt saw why. These huts were only half built, the timber roofs not yet spanning the stone walls completely, the newly sawn timber still moist and green. Wilt circled the closest hut, trailing his fingers along the thick roof beam. Immediately he thought of the Tangle, of the wall of trees staring at him, and snatched his fingers away.

Did the villagers really fell trees from the Tangle? Can you imagine anyone in Greystone even considering such a thing?

No, Higgs. But then Greystone has been surviving at the edge of the Tangle for decades, and this village is only a few years old. Maybe they didn't know any better.

Maybe the Tangle got its own revenge.

Wilt shook his head and ducked under the beam, into the shadows of the hut. Sure enough there were a few scattered sacks and crates stacked in the shelter of the half-roof. They looked untouched.

See if there's anything we can use. Hurry, this place still makes me nervous.

Wilt sorted through the containers. He was lucky; in one crate was a pile of old clothing that looked like it would fit him. At any rate, it was in better shape than the scraps he wore now.

Minutes later he stepped out of the hut feeling like a new man. He had cut the bottom half of his black robe free and replaced it with trousers made of a thick, hardy looking material that felt like suede. Over the remains of his robe he buttoned a thin leather vest.

You look like a woodsman.

Wilt smiled and stretched in the sunlight. *You mean we. We look like a woodsman.*

A sudden snap of noise brought his arms down, all his senses instantly alert.

The other hut. Behind us. There's something there.

Wilt dropped into a crouch and scurried around the side of the hut, hand on the hilt of his blade. He reached the corner of the stone wall and waited, peering around its edge.

There was nothing, only silence. The Tangle itself seemed to be holding its breath.

Your other form. These walls mean nothing to it. Biore couldn't hide the hunger in his voice, but Wilt had to admit he was right. It was the surest way.

The next moment a black mist cut directly through the stone wall, surging straight toward the second hut, toward the bright glow of life that huddled there, so obvious in the grey shadowed world he floated in.

Wait, Wilt. Don't hurt it.

The welds urged him to ignore Higgs's words, the hunger in the pit of his stomach roaring for satisfaction. His mind was almost overrun by it, the roar morphing into a strange music that washed over him, blanking out everything else but the pulse of life that called it onward.

He stopped outside the hut, his hand reaching toward the spark of life crouching on the other side of the wall, his blood calling for him to take it, to snuff it out. To feed.

The blood. The blood within the stone.

The next moment his human hand was in front of his eyes, resting against the solid wall. He had almost …

A clatter of movement snapped him from his thoughts as whoever had been hiding made a break for safety. He glimpsed a short, thin body leap out of the hut, heading straight for the Tangle. Wilt hurried after it, around the hut and into the trees.

Catch him.

It was him. A young boy, moving incredibly quickly.

Wilt ducked into the shadows of the Tangle and felt the world close around him. The boy was already stretching his lead, moving faster than ordinarily possible, dancing between the thick trunks. With each step Wilt dropped further back, losing sight of the figure as it flittered in and out of the broken sunlight.

We can go faster than this.

No sooner had Higgs made the thought known than a large black cat took Wilt's form, streaking ahead, matching and then gaining on the boy. The trees surrounding them seemed to lean in, reaching out to try to hinder and slow the cat, but it pushed on.

He almost had him. Just one more leap.

The trees gave way to a large bright opening, a clearing in the forest, and the cat was suddenly bathed in sunlight.

The cat stopped, the boy it had been pursuing forgotten as it stared at the strange figure standing in the middle of the clearing.

It was a man—at least, it may have been once. The skin showing through his long green robe was cracked and broken, almost like bark, and from his brow two long antlers grew out, twisting together like twin sharpened branches. One hand clutched a tall wooden staff, and the other was held palm outwards, as if in greeting.

For a long moment the cat stared at the impossible figure.

Then the man broke the silence, his voice that of the trees themselves, an aged creak of timber with the whistle of the wind through leaves.

'So. At last we meet, young spark.'

Chapter 10

The water was perfectly calm, a still, silver mirror reflecting the face that stared into it. The skin of the water bent slightly with the force of the breath pushing down on it, but did not break as the words poured out and spilled over its membrane. The words suggested a shape to the liquid, and it flowed as ordered, arranging itself into the requested form. A final word of command, and the silver surface darkened, and other images appeared.

A dark shape, scuttling and rushing through a forest, leaped at its target, another shape, a human. A man. Armoured. A guard perhaps? Or a soldier, though the markings were unfamiliar. More chaos as shapes broke into movement all around, and all that could be made out of the confusion of images were flashes of green leaves high above, sunlight struggling to break through and illuminate the scene. A sudden splash of red and the waters darkened again.

The lips leaning over the bowl whispered again, more urgently this time, and the images shifted in time and place, finding another scene. A strangely lit forest clearing, rows and rows of fallen trees re-purposed as pews. A single figure sitting at one end of the clearing, on something like a throne. A twisted timber structure that seemed almost to grow out of the figure. The figure sat perfectly still, perfectly patient, then raised its head to stare straight ahead.

Heather jerked her head away with a gasp, snapping the connection instantly. Her heart was pounding, and her breath surged in and out of her lungs. The figure in the vision. It was almost as if it had seen her …

She pushed her chair back from the table and looked up at the ceiling, trying to calm the panic that rushed through her. She focused on her breathing, slowing it, bringing her heart rate down. In and out. Stay calm. Stay focused. Stay as still as the water itself.

Finally her body relaxed, and she noticed she was clasping her necklace with one hand. She smiled to herself and relaxed her fingers from around it.

She dropped her eyes back to the bowl in front of her. The surface was still and clear again, a perfect mirror reflecting only what stared into it. A young girl, almost a teen, face wrinkled in concentration and concern. Long, slightly curled hair tucked behind her ears, eyes calm and cold and somehow sad. Eyes that had seen much.

'Heather!'

The door to the room burst open and Heather turned to see the young Black Robe stumble in, almost tripping over himself in his haste. The sight took the last of her concentration, and a surge of anger almost made its way to her lips before she recognised who it was. She smiled.

'Frankle. What brings you to the crafter's halls this early in the morning?'

'Early? It's—' Frankle stood flummoxed for a moment, glancing out the window at the low sun peeking up above the horizon. 'Well. I suppose it is a little early. But we have much to do! I wanted—'

Heather's smile widened as he hurried out his explanation. It was almost comical the way he stood in the doorway, arms waving along with his words, almost drowning in the oversized black robe that hung from his thin frame.

'You wanted to be sure we were ready for our presentation. It's okay, Frankle. I understand.'

Frankle hurried into the room and sat down on the bed. 'It's just that I haven't had to … perform like this before. In front of other people, I mean. I know we're—'

'I was nervous my first time too. Everyone gets nervous.'

Frankle finally gave up trying to explain himself and smiled shyly back at her.

Heather pushed the vision bowl away from her with a whispered command, and it joined the general clutter of trinkets and knickknacks scattered across her desk.

'Is that …?'

'Yes, Frankle. You know what it is.'

He watched as she stood up and rummaged through the items on her desk. He wanted to ask another question, even though he'd been told it was considered rude to pry like he did. To ask so many questions all the time. But Heather always had such interesting answers he couldn't help himself.

'Did you … did you see anything?'

Heather looked at Frankle as if weighing him up. 'Yes.'

Frankle knew that look, had suffered under it ever since he could remember. The look that said he was too young, too small, not yet ready.

'You don't have to tell me if you don't want to.'

Heather smiled at the sulky tone of his words, instantly melting their frostiness. 'Don't be silly, Frankle. I'll tell you when there's something to tell. Remember what Petron says, we can't always trust the visions the waters show us. They don't always obey the rules of time and place like we want them to. They might show you something that happened generations ago, or something from a possible future. Better to be sure about what you know before telling anyone what you see.'

Frankle sat for a moment pondering her words, then grinned, and any insult was forgotten. 'You're right, I guess. You know, sometimes you sound just like Delco.'

Heather returned the smile, happy that Frankle could now talk about his lost friend without getting upset. He was making progress.

She turned back to her rummaging. 'So. You think you're ready to show the Masters what we can do?'

Finally she found what she was looking for. Frankle didn't reply straight away, his attention fully captured by the long thin blade in Heather's hand. It was a short sword, one of the long knives the guards all carried. Nothing special about it. But with what they now knew, what they could turn it into …

He gave a quick nod and stood up. 'Yes. I'm ready.'

The Great Hall of Viewing seemed even larger than normal this morning, its high ceiling streaked with clouds that drifted across it, mirroring the sky outside through some long forgotten crafter skill. Heather stared up at it wistfully, transfixed as always by its magic. She was determined to one day figure out how it had been done.

Frankle sat beside her at the front of the hall, jiggling his legs nervously under his robe. He didn't understand how Heather did it, how she calmed her nerves so easily. She seemed oblivious to the large crowd forming in front of them. The eyes staring up at them. The doubt and judgment in their gaze.

Ugh. He felt like he would throw up.

'And how are the two stars of the show?'

Frankle looked up to see Petron smiling down at him, his eyes kind. Immediately the wave of nausea passed. 'Um … okay I guess. When do we start?'

Petron studied his face without replying, then turned to Heather. 'Still trying to figure out how they did it?'

Heather snapped out of her musing and smiled warmly at Petron. 'I'll work it out one day, you'll see.'

'I've no doubt of it.' Petron chuckled.

'Do you think they'd let me up there, to study the surface first hand? After this, I mean?'

Petron studied the crowd: the various crafters, Black Robes, and guards chatting together, mingling and sharing knowledge in a way that would have been impossible only a few months previously. Before the Sisters fell, before Cortis. Before Wilt.

He turned back to Heather and Frankle, his face serious. 'If you can prove what you said you could do, if you can show others how it is done, then I don't think anyone here will have the power to stop you getting as close as you want.'

Petron patted them both on their shoulders and moved to the front of the audience. The ceiling above was a deep cobalt blue as he raised his hands toward it and all chatter in the hall instantly ceased.

'Good people of Redmondis. Masters. Crafters. Wielders. Guards. Those who have yet to find their true path. Welcome.'

Over a hundred pairs of eyes locked on Petron. There had been rumours circulating through the stone corridors about this morning's presentation. Wild rumours. If even half the gossip was true, the event was one not to be missed.

Petron himself had started this new tradition, this forum to encourage the schools to share knowledge between them, to break down the walls of habit and prejudice that had formed around them under the rule of the Nine Sisters. Everyone had already found value in it in some way, and each attendee looked forward to the weekly assembly. It was just one of many small alterations to the conditions within Redmondis that Petron had implemented with a far reaching effect.

'I won't waste your time with introductions. You should all know our two subjects.'

Petron waved Heather and Frankle to their feet and they both shuffled forward.

'Heather is a young crafter who has shown just some of her value to all of us in the recent weeks. Frankle is an even younger wielder, perhaps not so well-known as yet. But I suspect that will soon change.'

Frankle's shy smile deepened and red flushed his cheeks.

'They are here to show us something extraordinary.'

With that Petron moved to the side and joined the audience, his eyes keen.

Heather and Frankle stood silently in front of the crowd for a few moments, dumbstruck. Then Heather spoke.

'We all here know of the recent troubles. We were all touched in some way.'

The understatement in Heather's words sent a murmur of agreement rippling through the crowd, but it soon quietened.

'One of the rumours you have all no doubt heard is that of the moonsteel blade the Cantor Cortis wielded. The weld blade.'

The murmurs grew in volume again. Everyone had heard that particular tale, though not all believed it. Moonsteel was such a rare and little studied element that its very existence was often questioned.

'I can only assure each of you here that such a blade does exist. I held it myself.'

Heather drew a long guard's knife out from behind her and held it up for the crowd to see. 'This, of course, is not a moonsteel blade. Simply a guard's sword, like so many of you carry.'

Heather waved the blade back and forth as if to further demonstrate its ordinariness. 'I have made some modifications to it, though I doubt even other crafters would easily recognise that fact.'

She spun the blade in her hand and offered it hilt first to the nearest guard. 'Here. Please. Does this blade strike you as in any way altered?'

The guard—a young man not long out of the training grounds by the look of him—took the blade and gave it a few swings before shaking his head and smiling shyly.

'Pass it around if you will,' Heather continued. 'See if any of our learned friends here have anything to add.'

The guard passed the blade to his neighbour, an elderly crafter who held the steel close to her face before sniffing and shaking her head. She then passed it on to a master standing beside her, his black robe stained with age and dust. He too seemed to find nothing amiss.

So it went as the blade was passed along the first row of the audience. Finally it made its way to Petron's hands. He was about to pass it back to Heather without comment when he stopped and tilted his head as if listening to a faraway sound. 'There is something. Faint … an openness.'

Heather accepted the blade from his hands. She turned to the crowd.

'As always, Petron is correct. Opened is a very apt term, as it happens. We all know that strong steel is forged by folding metal, layer upon layer, hammering each together to become a single, stronger form. So too was this blade. What I have done is not so much reverse that process as … loosen it. The result is a blade much weaker than it looks. If I were to raise this weapon against any of the others in this room, it would shatter in the first few strikes. However, if my wielder friend would help me …'

Frankle almost missed his cue, finally stumbling forward, his face still flushed with embarrassment.

Heather smiled and whispered to him. 'Forget them. Just do as we practised. You know you can do this.'

The words calmed the rush in Frankle's mind, and he forgot his embarrassment, forgot the crowd and the surrounding hall, focused all of his attention down on the blade. He calmed his breathing and felt himself dropping into a weld.

All sound died away, and he floated in stillness. Far below a rushing river of power surged and flowed, aware of his presence yet unable to reach him. Always waiting, calling to the secret part of his mind. In front of him, a hundred possibilities stretched out, welds waiting to be formed and wielded, sent out to strike down onto his enemies. Frankle's mind remained calm and separate.

That's right. Like this.

The voice came from all around, from the weld itself. A familiar voice, one he had known for too short a time. One he knew could not be here, but listened to nonetheless. Instructive and calming, a guiding light in the darkness.

Delco's voice.

A memory stretched out before him, a shimmering weld wall, a blade entering it and merging with its form. A reimagining of what was possible.

Some part of Frankle reached out and took the blade from Heather's hands.

The memory changed. No longer did Frankle watch from the background as Delco merged the moonsteel blade with the weld wall; instead he now stood beside him, the shimmering surface right in front of his face, another blade in his hand. He reached toward it and the weld wrapped around him, sucking him down into its vortex, pouring out and up his arm, into the hungry steel.

The weld folded itself into the waiting blade, its essence captured and held in this new form. Frankle could feel the blade bend and flex in his hand as it welcomed the power into itself, stretching and testing its new boundaries. He watched it run silver as the weld entwined itself into it, fascinated by the sight, yet always aware of the figure standing beside him.

Frankle knew Delco no longer existed except here, in the timeless land beneath the surface world. He wanted to turn, to grab his moment and whisper a few words, make a connection, but his neck was locked in place. At last, by force of will, he moved his head.

'Frankle. Open your eyes.'

Too late. Always too late. The memory dropped away, and he rushed back toward the surface world, the real world. Back to the limitations of time and space.

'Frankle?'

Heather's voice brought him all the way back, and he opened his eyes to see her studying him. He smiled, and the concern in her eyes melted away.

'I'm okay.' He whispered the words, yet they seemed to echo in the silence of the hall. He looked down and saw both his and Heather's hands wrapped around the hilt of a shimmering silver blade. A weld blade. Moonsteel.

They turned to face the audience and held the blade aloft, and a gasp of astonishment burst out from the crowd. A moment later chaos broke out, a hundred voices all demanding an explanation of the impossibility they had just witnessed.

It took Petron some moments to calm the bedlam and make himself heard. 'Please, good people, be silent. You have questions. We all do. What I will say is, what you have seen here is not a trick. And perhaps most importantly, it is repeatable.'

The consequences of Petron's words slowly made their way into the mind of each audience member, and all sound died away in a hush of awe.

A weld blade. They had found a way to forge moonsteel! A force armed with such weapons could shake the world.

Petron turned back to Heather and Frankle, who still clasped the blade between them. He smiled, though his eyes spoke of a deeper concern. 'You have done a great thing today. A great and dangerous thing. Redmondis will never be the same. Let us hope it is not the first step down a dark path.'

Chapter 11

When Shade opened his eyes, he found himself crouched in the dirt, the clearing he had stumbled into no longer there, wiped from existence. The trees huddled close around him now and the sky above was darkening to grey.

Night was coming. He was already late.

At fall of night

Wise spirits take flight.

A weak glow to one corner of the sky where the sun was setting pointed him in the right direction, and he hurried off, consciously keeping his eyes down, not wanting to risk glimpsing anything more.

The surrounding trees were silent, each knowing what he had almost seen. The Guardian. Forbidden for any to lay eyes upon— even the Others respected that much. He would likely face trouble when he got back to Nurtle. The trees had sent word ahead, of course. They couldn't help themselves.

The silence and lengthening shadows played on his mind as he travelled, twisting his thoughts, swamping him in guilt. He had spent too long in Weverly. Angered something. He should have just seen what he could and headed straight back to make his report. Instead he had scavenged.

Like a common rat, Nurtle's voice in his head scolded. *Like a common rat.*

When the last bank of trees finally gave way to open sky, the stars twinkling into being in the fading light, he had wound himself so tight with worry that he half expected an escort to be waiting for him at the edge of the small village he called home. Waiting to take him and march him straight to Jared. Instead, the few villagers he saw seemed not to notice his passing.

As he moved further into the township, away from the over-bearing trees, he found his thoughts lightening. A smile found its way onto his face and he waved a greeting at a couple of folk still toiling in their fields, determined to make as much use of the dwindling light as they could. He recognised one of them. Stord. He'd delivered some of Nurtle's medicines to his family the past winter. The man stood up and stretched his back, returning Shade's greeting with a distracted wave, and the last of Shade's fear seemed to melt away. He was home.

Maybe he had gotten away with it.

'Shade!'

Nurtle's angry cry rung out across the village, impossibly loud, immediately wiping all positive thought from Shade's mind.

'Shade! I know you can hear me. Come home, now!'

He shrunk into himself as he heard the words. She sounded furious. Shade sighed and sped up into a trot, headed for the far side of the village and Nurtle's lone hut.

How much had the trees told her?

Rounding another hut he could see Nurtle silhouetted in her doorway, hands on hips, tapping her foot impatiently. Her eyes narrowed as she spied his figure in the darkening air, and she swallowed whatever her next cry was to have been, concentrating on staring him down as he hurried up to her.

As soon as he was within reach, though, her pose changed and a wide smile lit up her face. 'You're late.'

She reached out and pulled him into a hug, almost suffocating him as his face disappeared into her waist. Finally she released him and Shade stepped back, panting for breath.

He wanted desperately to explain, but didn't know where to begin.

'Never mind what you were up to.' As always she could read his thoughts completely. 'Come inside.'

Nurtle rested her hand on his tousled hair and shepherded him into the hut.

A wave of heat blasted his face as soon as he stepped past her. The fire in the hearth was blazing, baking the entire inside of the hut. He turned to ask her what it was for when he saw the other occupant of the room, lying on a single bed up against the far wall. A stranger.

Shade turned to Nurtle, his question clear on his face, but she simply nodded toward the figure on the bed. He stepped closer and suddenly knew the reason for the fire.

On this side of the room, only a few steps in, the heat of the fire was losing its battle against a deep cold. A bone cold, as if death itself were reaching out for him. Immediately his mind went back to Weverly, to the hut, to the thing that had chased him.

'He's sleeping. Leave him be, child.'

Nurtle approached the prone figure on the bed and replaced the cloth resting on his forehead. Her breath steamed out as she leaned over him, but she showed no sign of discomfort.

Shade looked down at the man, studying him. He was younger than he had first seemed. His face was drawn and gaunt, and his skin was pale and clammy in the firelight. He didn't look at all healthy. His clothes, too, were a mess, none of them seeming to fit, a worn-out black shirt the only item that seemed like it actually belonged to him. He looked like he had been living rough for quite some time.

Nurtle finished tending to her charge and sat back, her voice tired. 'He is someone who walks a dark path, one few have walked before and even fewer returned from.' She turned to Shade then and smiled. 'But you've met him before, haven't you?'

Shade shook his head.

'You don't remember. Perhaps you didn't encounter him in this form. But you recognise the pull, don't you? The cold?'

Shade nodded, feeling suddenly guilty.

'You thought it was one of them, one of the dark things that overran the village. You're almost right.' Nurtle stood up and moved back to the fire, rubbing the blood back into her hands. 'He has gone deep, this one. Deeper than any wielder I have known. No wonder he caused so much trouble with the Sisters.'

Shade's ears pricked at her words.

'Redmondis. Yes. But he has left that life far behind now.'

Shade studied the man with renewed interest. From Redmondis. That meant he knew of the Black Robes.

He looked again at the black shirt the man wore, only now seeing the rough edges of the material where it had been torn short.

A Black Robe.

His pulse quickened at the possibilities. Maybe he could teach him about welds and wielders and crafters and all the legends he only ever heard people whisper about. He'd never actually laid eyes on—

He caught a glint on the far wall of the room, right beside the bed at the man's head. A long silver knife was propped against the wall, glistening strangely in the firelight. Glowing almost. It called to him.

He reached toward it.

Nurtle followed his outstretched hand and grunted, throwing a blanket over the blade, hiding it from view.

Immediately Shade felt something let go, as though a grip around his mind had melted away.

'That is something best kept hidden, and certainly not for one such as you.' She turned back to Shade and studied his face. 'Now, young Shade, tell me about your day.'

Shade tore his eyes from the spot where the cloak covered the silver treasure and looked into Nurtle's eyes. As ever, he lost himself in their depths and she saw through him completely, knew everything about him, inside and out. He let himself be guided to a seat in the centre of the room where the heat from the fire and the strange cold from the bed mixed into something approaching a comfortable temperature.

He gave her everything—the ruined village, the treasures he had found, the black smoke, the strangely silent trees, the cold that reached out for him through the stone, the rushed flight through the forest, the appearance of the Guardian himself just before darkness fell.

When he finished, he found his mind was clearer, as though he had freed himself of some burden he hadn't been aware he carried.

Nurtle pushed a steaming bowl of soup into his hands. 'You did well. Now drink. You need your strength.'

The thick, steaming soup calmed his thoughts even further as it warmed his belly, and he found his eyelids becoming heavy instantly.

'That's good. Now sleep. There is work still to do this night.'

Nurtle caught the half full bowl as it slipped from his hands and guided him down onto the rug on the floor as his eyes closed and his breathing dropped into a heavy rhythm.

As he slept, Nurtle covered him with a thin blanket, then stood with her hands on her hips, looking back and forth between the two sleeping forms.

Both so young. Too young. Or is that just what us old ones always think?

'Sleep well, boys. There is no darkness here.'

With that she turned back to the fire and continued with her work. She was determined to be ready for what was coming.

'What do you have there, Meat?'

He curled into a ball but it was too late. His father reached for his arm and tore it away, almost wrenching his shoulder out of its socket and sending the two loaves spinning into the air.

He dropped and twisted simultaneously, squirming free of the hand gripping him, one leg shooting out behind to swipe the legs out from under the bigger man. As his leg connected he reached out and caught one of the loaves before it hit the ground. He heard and felt the impact of his father's body falling, but didn't bother turning around to confirm it with his own eyes. He shot away, back into the relative safety of the alleys, the one dry loaf clutched safely to his chest.

His mind was singing, unable to grasp what it was he had just done. He'd fought back. Finally. Convincingly. And saved his prize.

He smiled as he bit into the crust of the bread and savoured the warm scent filling his nose.

A silver tingle tickled the back of Shade's eyelids as he slept, and some secret part of his mind readied itself for what it knew was about to occur. The tickle became a shudder as a wave of silver broke across his vision.

He was staring down at a large, detailed map spread out on the table in front of him. One corner was held down by a polished stone, the other held in place by his own hand. He stared, momentarily confused by the sight of his hand. It was enormous—weathered and roughened by years of use, thin grey hairs curling around the knuckles. He flexed it slowly in front of his face, and the map rolled back up into a spiral.

'Jared?'

Another hand reached out and brushed the map back into position. He looked up into the eyes of the guard captain staring at him.

'Captain Mont,' he answered without thought.

'Is there something the matter?'

Jared shook his head and the strange feeling that had overcome him faded away. He cleared his throat with a grunt.

'As you can see, Captain, here is Copring. Following along the southern edge of the Tangle, to the west lies Weverly and Reggon, both recently attacked. Further along, Verson, also taken. And Jarlyle—we have no news from there.'

'I can confirm Jarlyle was hit not three weeks ago. It is no more.'

Jared paused and looked up at the stern faced captain. 'Then there is no question. Copring must be the next target.'

'I can have my patrol stationed outside the village by nightfall.'

'Do so. The western border has the most room. There are even a few abandoned huts still standing your troops may wish to take advantage of.'

'The western edge? Isn't that where the—' Mont caught himself before spluttering the insult. 'Where she abides?'

Jared pulled back from the desk and stood up to his full impressive height, placing his hands on his hips and staring coldly down at the captain, letting his gaze say all that needed to be said. He knew the sort of prejudices these soldiers held.

'Nurtle will keep well away from your men. They have nothing to fear from her.'

Captain Mont dropped his eyes from Jared's glare. 'Very well. We'll begin preparations. With your leave?'

Jared nodded, his face still cold, and Mont backed out of the hut. As the door swung closed behind him, Jared sighed and let his arms drop to his sides.

Can you blame them? Were you so very different, all those years ago, when you first encountered wild magic?

He turned away from the desk and stared into the tall polished glass mirror propped against one wall of the hut. The reflection mercilessly reminded him how long ago those days were.

He was a middle-aged man, dressed in the forest colours all the villagers wore. His hair was clipped short and greying at the temples, his vest stretched out over his growing belly, but despite these signs he still radiated an air of competence and authority. His long arms were thickly muscled, and his set jaw spoke of a man who expected and generally received respect and obedience from all around him.

He looks just like Lodan.

The strange thought popped in and out of his mind, and he shook his head at his reflection.

Suddenly the vision vanished and Shade sat bolt upright.

He was still in Nurtle's hut. He looked to the side to see the stranger still stretched out on the cot, showing no sign of returning from his deep slumber.

The fire in the hearth had burned low, and the temperature in the hut was dropping. Shade's breath steamed out in front of him. How long had he been asleep? It had seemed only moments.

He shook himself to clear the last remaining cobwebs of the dream from his mind and stood up, clapping his arms around himself to get the blood flowing again.

Apart from the stranger in the bed, the hut was empty. Nurtle must be in the Tangle.

Jared. He had dreamed of Jared. More than that, he'd actually been Jared in the dream. How was that possible?

And that strange voice. Lodan. Who was Lodan?

Shade stared at the sleeping stranger. He looked too old for the voice Shade had heard in his dream. But if it hadn't been him, then—

He pushed the thought away. There would be no answers here.

He turned toward the door then stopped, unable to resist the single flash of mischief that lit up his mind. He skipped across the room to the blanket Nurtle had thrown over the strange silver blade. He wanted one more look, perhaps the chance to touch it, weigh it in his hands.

He moved as quietly as he could, half expecting the stranger to wake up or Nurtle to come storming into the hut just in time to catch him. He reached out and lifted the edge of the covering.

There was nothing there.

The blade was gone.

Chapter 12

Petron had finally extricated Heather and Frankle from the crowd of probing questions that followed their display, insisting they be given a chance to rest and regain their strength. More than a few angry glances flashed his way as a result but they soon faded as it became clear how much the presentation had taken out of the two young ones, and they were allowed to retreat to the comfort of their beds. They were both probably deeply asleep by now, their dreams blank and empty, sleeping the sleep of the innocent.

Petron grimaced at the jealous rush that followed that thought. He hadn't slept properly in months, not since Cortis's uprising. Not since Wrex.

He grunted and pushed the painful flash of memory back down. Not here. Take my nights if you must but not here.

'Petron.'

Daemi stepped forward from the stream of people still milling about the Great Hall, and the sight of her instantly raised his spirits.

'I was wondering if you would catch our little display.' He smiled.

Daemi clapped him firmly on the shoulder in the guard style of greeting. The two of them had grown close in the last few weeks, each drawing comfort from the other's presence. 'You weren't kidding when you said it might prove interesting.'

Petron chuckled, and they both turned to watch the audience

slowly file out of the hall. Voices were still raised in excitement, eyes shining with eagerness at the possibilities ahead. 'You will need to keep a close eye on them. Protect them, now that the secret is out.'

Daemi nodded, and Petron was once again filled with a wave of gratitude at how much this young woman, barely out of her teens, was willing to shoulder. She had proven herself indispensable in his efforts to reimpose order on Redmondis since the uprising.

Petron's smile faded as he considered all he still had to ask of her.

Heather and Frankle had done a great thing, proven that moonsteel could be formed through the teamwork of crafter and wielder, yet until they could teach others how it was done they remained the only ones who could perform such a valuable task. That made them targets.

'In fact, I was hoping to speak to you about that.'

Daemi turned back to him, suddenly more alert. 'You want me to take them with me when I go.'

Petron shook his head and smiled. 'I should have known you'd be one step ahead of me.' He moved to help the group of younger crafters who had begun stacking away the chairs that had been arranged for the presentation. 'Here. Give me a hand with these, will you?'

Daemi nipped in front and ushered him away from the workers, angling him toward the nearest chair. 'Sit, old man. Sit and tell me what you have been cooking up in that tower of yours.'

Petron allowed himself to be led and sank into the chair with a sigh. Daemi quickly stacked the rest of the furniture away, her young, strong body moving the heavy old wooden benches with ease. Petron watched her silently, feeling the years pile over him.

'As I was telling you, we need to try to re-establish contact with the capital—with Sontair. We have heard nothing from them in weeks, not since before ...' He waved his hand vaguely around the room in a gesture that seemed to encompass all of Redmondis. 'Before all of this. Wrexley himself was the last official contact we had, and from what little he told me even that didn't go well. Whatever gulfs have opened between us must be addressed.

'In light of their persistent silence our best option is to keep things formal. We should send a representative from each of the main classes—each must have their figurehead. Politics, you know. I was thinking that you, Heather, and Frankle would be ideal. Getting those two out of here and away from the constant questions sure to come their way is a bonus.'

'And once we reach Sontair, you intend for them to repeat their trick?' Daemi tossed the last of the benches onto the stack and turned back to Petron.

He noticed enviously that she wasn't even breathing heavily. 'What do you think, young captain? Would it be wise to show our hand so quickly?'

Daemi pondered his words, then shook her head. 'No. We don't want to be seen as a potential threat. But then politics was never my speciality. That was more—' She stopped, but it was too late.

'That was Wrex's department,' Petron completed.

Daemi blanched. 'I'm sorry, I didn't—'

'Don't be foolish, child.' He waved the words away. 'I do not intend for them to repeat their performance, still I want you to take them with you. For all your sakes. The road to the south has not become any easier in recent times, if the few scattered reports we've received are to be believed. The darkness is spreading, Daemi. You see them in your dreams just as I do. The dark things, getting more distinct every night, floating ever closer to the surface.'

Daemi nodded.

'I do not know what awaits in the capital itself,' Petron continued. 'I have heard rumours, troubling rumours. For now it would be best to keep this particular skill a secret as long as possible. Moonsteel is valued throughout the kingdom. Word may well reach Sontair before you do regardless of our efforts.'

Daemi marched up and raised her arm to her chest in a salute. 'I will protect them with my life. They will not come to any harm.'

Petron smiled as he stood up. 'I know you will do your best. Now come, we have much to prepare.'

By the time Petron finally trudged up the last few steps to his chamber at the top of the wielder's tower, the sun had long since set and the clear sky was scattered with twinkling stars. In his room Petron stood at the edge of the large opening along one wall, letting the cool night breeze ruffle his hair. When he closed his eyes, it was almost like he was out there, flying again.

He opened his eyes and scanned the stars, picking out the patterns of constellations automatically. The bear. The eagle. The great river. But there, at the last turn of the river, a star was missing. He stared at the spot where he knew a light should be, wondering if a bank of weather was moving in from the south, then the star next to it also disappeared.

For a mad moment he felt a rush of terror, a flash of memory from within the welds, holding Wilt's hand, floating impossibly above the chaos of darkness that spiralled in the depths, calling to him.

Another star blinked out, and he took a step back from the edge of the window.

A moment later he heard beating wings, and he hurried to give his visitor some space.

With a gust of air that scattered the papers on his desk across the room, a large eagle soared out of the black sky and landed, its long claws scratching fresh marks on the heavy rock of the chamber floor. It perched there for a moment, its cold eyes studying Petron as though he were a potential meal.

Petron gathered himself and stared back. He nodded his head once in greeting.

The next moment the eagle was gone and in its place stood a lone woman, stooped with age, leaning on a tall carved wooden staff and scanning the room with a critical eye.

'Not one for keeping things in order I see.' She clucked and stepped away from the edge of the window. Without asking permission she headed straight for a chair sitting by the fire and settled herself into it with a sigh.

Petron moved to join her. 'Nurtle? To what do I owe the—'

'Don't say pleasure, for the gods' sake,' she interrupted, continuing to stare around the room. 'Never thought I'd be inside these walls again. Cold stone. Gives me the shivers.'

'I wasn't sure you'd accept my invitation. I know Redmondis has not been kind to your kin.'

'My kin? Yours too, unless you forget. Us wildlers need to stick together, more so these days.'

'Ah, so you've claimed that particular insult as your own?'

'"Wildler" you mean? It's accurate enough. Besides, we've had more to concern ourselves with than the names others call us.'

'That's why I asked you to come. I was hoping to rebuild some of the—'

'Ha!' Nurtle coughed out a laugh that silenced him again. She chuckled as she noticed Petron's discomfort and reached out to pat his knee. 'You have already done more than has been done in decades. Even *they* talk about it.' She nodded her head toward the open window and the blank slate of the Tangle breathing far below.

'They talk a lot, don't they?'

'Oh yes. Of late they have been telling some particularly interesting tales. Strange creatures haunting the shadows. Hunting. Things that do not belong in this world.'

Petron saw a flash of vision from his dreams, a black spider-like creature diving at him. He shook his head to clear it, to banish the nightmare from these waking hours.

Nurtle's hand on his knee tightened then moved away as she pulled herself to her feet. 'Here. Let me brew you something that will help.'

'It's nothing, just—'

'You see the visions too. They haunt the dreams of all who have the sense to see. Some more than others, of course. And they're getting more vivid.'

Petron nodded, aware suddenly that he wanted to talk openly about this to someone. 'Each night they stay a little longer, become clearer. It's … exhausting.'

'That is their purpose, I expect. One of them, at least. They are trying to weaken any who stand in their way.'

A richly spiced scent filled the room as Nurtle pulled something from deep within her cloak and dropped it into the kettle. Petron's spirits lifted immediately, as though the smell itself had pushed his tiredness away.

'Now, not too much of this, just a cup each night before bed.'

Nurtle pushed a steaming cup of tea into his hands and sat down again. 'I'll leave you enough for the next week or so. I expect I'll be back by then.'

Petron sipped the brew and grimaced at the strong, piney taste. A moment later the heat spread throughout his body, melting the tension from his muscles.

Nurtle watched the tea do its work, Petron sighing and leaning back in his chair. He looked so much older these days, so weighed down by the world.

'The trees have been telling other tales as well. Tales of strange visitors with even stranger powers. Young men wearing tattered robes that perhaps once haunted these halls.'

Petron raised one eyebrow and frowned at Nurtle. 'That was just one reason I contacted you. Wilt is … important to me.'

'Important to all of us, I suspect. Look what I stumbled across.' Nurtle grinned and pulled out a shining silver blade from within her cloak.

Petron almost dropped his cup as he sat up straight again, all fatigue gone in an instant. 'Wilt's weld blade! How did you—'

'Relax, old man.' Nurtle smiled and gestured him back into his seat. 'Your young friend is safe.'

Petron frowned again, calculating to himself. 'So he travelled all that way already? To the very southern edge? That's imposs—'

'Oh come now, Petron. You know better than to use that word. Besides, he has abilities even I don't understand. And I've seen many more summers than you.' Nurtle's voice dropped into a whisper. 'You are wrong to fear that power. It may be the only thing that saves us.'

Petron shook his head. 'You didn't see what … What it did to Wilt. What he became.'

'A wraith, you mean? I told you, your young friend is safe. He has more control than you realise. Besides, such forms are not unfamiliar to us, you know.'

'There are others?'

'There are some who draw from that same source, at least some part of it. The Tangle itself could be said—'

'That's not what you mean though, is it?'

'No.'

It was Nurtle's turn to sigh now. 'Shade, our … son. He shares it.' She let the words soak in as she stared around the room, her eyes focused on a point far distant. 'I, too, feared it when I first saw glimpses of what he was capable of. What they wanted from him. But Petron, if it could be harnessed—'

'We cannot harness the dark. Not without consequences.'

'Do not speak to me about consequences.' Nurtle's tone was hard, her words edged with pain. 'Not until you spend three decades apart from the only mind that truly shares yours. Not until your child is taken from you, and returned, changed forever. Not until you are asked to sacrifice him all over again.'

Petron let the angry words wash over him and sipped his tea. 'I know about sacrifice, Nurtle. We all do.'

Petron's simple words seemed to break the spell that had come over her, and Nurtle shook her head. 'I … apologise. We all know what Wrex—'

Petron waved the words away and put his empty cup back on the table. 'The problem remains.'

'You see it as a problem. Perhaps it should be viewed as an opportunity. You are sending a representative to Sontair, are you not?'

Petron grimaced. 'I see Redmondis' ability to keep a secret hasn't improved.'

'You underestimate us wildlers once again. We have ears everywhere. Some closer than you'd expect.'

'It is true. The guard captain I've told you of, Daemi, will lead a small group. She is perhaps our best officer, and a break from these stone walls will do her good.'

'Ah yes, the one who shares the connection with Wilt. He will also be sent south once he finishes his task with us. I've no doubt they will find each other.'

'Is that really—'

'It is unavoidable. From what you've told me their minds are deeply linked. I can recognise the signs in others.'

'Daemi is not a wielder. They could not become what you are. What I and Wrex—'

'But Wilt is more powerful than either of us. Who can tell what they are capable of sharing?' Nurtle nodded to herself, her eyes shining in the firelight. 'Are you so certain of the limits of this power, Petron? Haven't we all learned by now not to underestimate the depths?'

Chapter 13

Why can't I wake him up?

Higgs's voice had an edge of panic. For too long now he'd been floating in still darkness, waiting for the familiar light of Wilt's consciousness to illuminate the world, but there was nothing.

Wilt will wake in time. He is safe, can't you feel it? He needs to rest. His mind and body both need time to repair. He hasn't been taking care of himself.

You mean we, Biore. We haven't been taking care.

I don't think there's any significant damage. Nothing rest won't cure.

What if he never wakes again?

You don't believe that. Besides, that … thing … was not our enemy. You must have felt it, the familiarity. It spoke like it knew who we are.

It was a wildler. A very strong one.

You know what it was, Delco?

Rawick does. He recognised it immediately. He's become much more talkative all of a sudden. Much more present. Like something woke him up.

And he knows about this …

Wildler. Like him, in a way. Like all the others who slipped out of Redmondis' grasp. Some escaped, some were forced out, some were lucky enough never to have been siphoned up in the first place.

Like Petron.

No, Higgs, Petron had some training. This one was much more free. Much more dangerous. Some wielders let the welds themselves consume them.

More like Rawick then.

Yes, but Rawick didn't mean for what happened to him to occur.

Like Wilt will become if we continue to let him spend so much time in the shadows.

It said something about a spark. You think—

I think it was talking to Rawick.

Ah. Now that is interesting.

But it doesn't help us. How do we wake up Wilt, Delco? What does Rawick say?

He's not … it's hard to get him to focus on a subject. It's not a conversation. He says … he says we should go back there, to the forest. We need to speak to the Guardian again.

The Guardian?

'That's quite enough of that. Time to quieten down in there. Let your friend return to the surface world for a time. He is safe in my care.'

There was a long silent pause as the world seemed to freeze in place.

'Open your eyes, young wielder. Open your eyes and return to the waking world.'

Wilt followed the command automatically, and stared up into the lined grey face of an old woman, her eyes burning into him with a strange blue glow. As he focused on them the glow faded, and the edges of her mouth curved into a knowing smile.

'Those lenses you wear are clever. Real crafter work. I suppose we all need our little disguises. Here now, drink.'

A cup of something warm and strangely spiced was held to his lips, and again he followed the command, swallowing without thinking, the thick syrup coating his throat as it slid down, lighting a fire in his belly as soon as it hit. It was the most delicious thing he'd ever tasted. He tried to sit up and reach for the cup to pour more of the golden liquid into his mouth, but the woman was too quick for him, pulling the cup away and hiding it behind her, her smile growing wider.

'Ah! You are thirsty, you still have your appetite. That is good. But this particular brew is not something you should take too much of. Not at your age.'

Wilt sat up and looked around. He was in a small hut, much like the ones in the deserted village he had found. Before he chased the boy. Before he saw—

'Where am I?'

His voice sounded strange in his ears. Weak and thin. He wondered when was the last time he'd used it.

'You are in Copring, at the southern edge of the great forest you know as the Tangle. My name is Nurtle. You are under my care. You are safe here.'

Wilt pulled his eyes back to the woman standing over him. His mind was flooded with questions, he needed to slow the rush with simple facts. The woman blocked most of his view of the room. She seemed enormous, her features oversized, her head impossibly large. Long strands of grey hair curled down from her scalp and disappeared behind her back, tied in a long ponytail. She looked friendly enough, the cracked skin of her face pulled into a thin smile. Cracked skin, almost bark-like. Almost like—

'How did I get here? I was in-'

'You were somewhere few have seen and even fewer have returned from.'

Her smile was fading as she stared at him, the strange glow returning to her eyes. He could feel himself slipping into them.

'There was a ... thing. Waiting for me.'

He tried to resist the pull, but the edges of his vision were already turning dark. Her eyes were the whole world now, her firm palm pushing down on his forehead, guiding him back into unconsciousness.

'You have walked a dark path, young wielder. Or should I call you wraith? You have spent too long in that long forgotten form, too long under its spell. Too long in the forest. Those trees can play tricks on even the strongest minds. Sleep now.'

Wilt couldn't help but fall back into darkness.

'Sleep. That goes for all of you in there.'

Wilt opened his eyes and stared out the single square window, the only light in the dim room. He swayed, his memory reaching back to another time, a cut hole in a canvas canopy, an old wagon rolling and bouncing along a rutted mountain track, cutting through the Tangle on its way to Redmondis. A high cloud slid slowly across the dawn sky, a giant hand reaching out and spinning the world back up to speed.

Suddenly another shape loomed into view, a shadowed head that popped up from the edge of the sill and froze as their eyes met. A boy. Wilt recognised him instantly. The boy he had chased through the forest. The one who had led him—

Wilt sat up in a rush and the world lurched sickeningly to the side.

'Easy there. Not so fast.'

A firm hand gripped his shoulder and held him upright as he began to fall. He closed his eyes and shook his head, trying to will away the fog that swamped his vision.

'What—'

'Be quiet. Be still. You have slept deeply. Wait for the dreams and memories to clear.'

Wilt focused on the hand gripping his shoulder and the voice that seemed to anchor him to the physical world. He sniffed and smelled the open fire and the recently cooked breakfast, and other, stranger spices in the air.

Finally the universe tired of twisting his mind, and he focused on the blanket that covered his legs. It was thick and warm and not at all rough on his skin. His skin. He was naked.

The thought brought with it a strange panic and he stared up at the woman holding his shoulder, his mouth moving again but no sound coming out.

'Be still, wielder. You have come a long way. You are safe here.'

The woman—Nurtle, that was her name—smiled down at him. Her eyes looked normal, no longer glowing with that strange light that had held him before. He shook his head and the troubling memory faded back into the depths. She was just an old woman.

'I'm Nurtle. You remember. I have been taking care of you.'

'Copring. I'm in Copring.'

'That's right.' Her hand patted his shoulder a final time, and she turned back to the fire. 'I haven't completely lost my touch then.'

Pots and pans crashed together as she rummaged about the hearth. 'Copring. A village on the southern edge of the great forest—the Tangle as you call it. You were found wandering, lost. Quite the worse for wear. Haven't been eating properly, haven't been looking after yourself. Neglecting your physical needs.'

She turned to flash a raised eyebrow at him, as though they were both in on some secret he was only dimly aware of.

'You called me 'wraith'?'

'An old name for the shadow form you dwelled in. Long forgotten now. For the best perhaps. You have spent too long in its thrall.'

There had been something else—he had seen something.

He spun around to face the window again, and sure enough the small head was there, dropping out of view with a muffled yelp.

'Don't let the child bother you. Shade is his name, and one well suited to his nature. Curiosity is the gift and the curse of youth. One thing age has taught me is that we simply have to suffer it.'

Wilt turned back from the window as Nurtle placed a plate of food in his lap, and he suddenly forgot everything except his hunger.

'Eat. Your body needs it.'

He needed no further encouragement. He dove into the food— eggs, bacon, sausage, potatoes, and some sort of spinach he hadn't tasted before. It was all delicious. Better than anything he'd eaten in …

'That's a start at least. You need to put some meat back on those bones of yours.'

Wilt swallowed what was in his mouth and blushed at his nakedness. He pulled the blanket up over his chest.

Nurtle chuckled and turned back to the fire. 'Ah. You flatter an old woman. Here.' She tossed Wilt's clothes over her shoulder to land on his lap. 'If your modesty insists, dress yourself.'

She resumed pottering over the fire as he pulled his clothes on. With a sudden rush of panic he remembered the heat ring, but it was still on his finger. Where was the moonsteel blade?

As if in reply, Nurtle pointed to the far corner of the room. 'And I don't want to know how you stumbled upon that particular treasure. I've already had to hide it from prying eyes. Keep it hidden if you must carry it about.'

Wilt buckled the long knife back onto his hip and stood, self-consciously adjusting his clothes.

'All part of the same problem, of course,' Nurtle continued to mutter to herself. 'Humans with no understanding of what they're dealing with, digging themselves ever deeper.'

She turned back to face him and smiled. 'There now. You look very smart. Feel better?'

'Er … yes. Thanks.'

Wilt stood awkwardly in front of her as her eyes moved up and down his body, as if studying him for leaks. Her gaze skipped over the blade on his hip, as if she found the sight troubling, then froze on the ring on his finger.

'And as for that.' Her hand shot out impossibly fast and pulled his fingers up close to her face. 'This I have never seen before. A rare thing, in this world. Clever. Very clever.' She dropped Wilt's hand and stared at him, the strange blue glow lighting her eyes again, hypnotising him. 'Your young friend is smarter than he looks.'

The next moment the glow was gone and Wilt was left gazing into an amused old woman's eyes. She patted him gently on the shoulder and turned away. 'You still have much to learn, and no time in which to learn it. Here.'

She flung a deep green cloak over his shoulders, fixing it in place around his neck before he knew what was happening.

'You lost your cloak in the forest, didn't you? That's all right, it wasn't made for this climate anyway. This …' She smoothed the material and Wilt felt an immediate comforting warmth spread over him. 'This is much more suitable. Think of it as a gift. From the trees.'

Wilt stood dumbly in front of her, not knowing what to say. Finally his mind caught up to her words. 'How did you know about my cloak?'

'The trees see many things.' Her voice was low and serious, then her face broke into a wide smile. 'And they gossip worse than a gaggle of old women. Trust me, I should know.'

Nurtle turned him around and guided him toward the door of the hut. 'The village leader, a man by the name of Jared, is waiting to speak with you. Your arrival here is timely in more ways than one. He is in the large hut in the centre of the village, you can't miss it. I'm sure you'll recognise him quickly enough.'

Wilt glanced back at Nurtle. She grinned knowingly and opened the door. 'Now it is time for you to rejoin the human world, young wielder. Try not to get into too much trouble.'

Chapter 14

Wilt stood outside Nurtle's hut and surveyed the scene laid out before him. Copring. It was small, smaller even than the ruined village he'd discovered in the Tangle. That thought brought another rushing to the forefront of his mind and he whirled around three hundred and sixty degrees. No wall of tall, silent trees stood guard around this village.

He was finally outside the Tangle. For the first time in days, perhaps weeks. The first time since leaving Redmondis.

He waited for an answering voice from inside his mind, from Higgs or Biore or even Delco, but there was nothing, only a strangely warm silence. As though the voices hadn't left but were simply muted somehow.

He licked his lips, the strange taste of the drink Nurtle had fed him still lingering on his tongue. Had she drugged him, altered him in some way?

Had he lost them?

No. He felt sure Nurtle hadn't done him any harm. His mind felt fuzzy, yet content, as though he were floating on a warm cloud.

Wilt stretched and breathed in the clean open air and felt more himself than he had in … he wasn't sure how long.

A large bonfire smouldered in what seemed to be the centre of the village, its grey smoke coiling high into the clear blue sky above. The bare ground around its edges was packed down, and a well-worn trail snaked out from there to the entrance of the large central hut that had to be the one Nurtle had mentioned.

He followed the path, nodding now and then to the villagers who passed him, all seemingly informed of his presence and told to ignore the young stranger in their midst. They smiled blankly but averted their eyes as soon as they met and it was clear none of them wanted him to speak with him. There was something else too, something not quite right about the whole picture. He couldn't put his finger on it, but once again the strange surge of contentment wafting over him blurred that thought away before it could trouble him any further.

Before he knew it he was standing at the door of the central hut, his hand already pushing it open. At the last moment he realised he should probably announce himself and coughed out a greeting. 'Uh, hello?'

The door to the hut swung open at his touch to reveal a large, well-lit room. At the far end, an enormous table was pushed against one wall, its surface covered with scattered papers and maps. Over this bent a tall, muscular man, his attention focused on some detail in the papers. The man stood and turned around, and Wilt felt an immediate rush of vertigo as he stared into eyes he had once looked out from in a dream.

Jared. This was Jared.

'Ah, Wilt. I'm glad you've come.'

The voice seemed to wrap out across the room and wind around him, pulling Wilt further in. He found his feet moving, until he stopped, catching himself and resisting the strange pull trying to take control. It was almost like a weld, yet different. Less focused. It was as though a wide net of smaller welds had been cast over his mind, covering it rather than striking into its centre. He studied it for a moment before slamming down the walls of his mind and severing it.

Jared flinched as the connection broke, but his smile only widened. 'Aha! So Nurtle wasn't exaggerating. Sorry about that, but I had to be sure.'

'You're … a wielder?'

Jared shook his head, his smile twisting into a rueful grin. 'The Nine Sisters would not have agreed with that assessment. Think of us as your weaker cousins. We had some talent, a lot less focused than yours, a lot less human, you could say. A lot less useful for the powers that claimed Redmondis.'

'Wildlers.' Wilt wasn't sure where he'd heard the term, but it popped into his mind automatically.

'That is one of the names they tarred us with in the north. Aimless. Unfocused. Dangerous. Wildler is good enough. Our talents share a great deal with the wild forest. It is where our powers come from. It is where we will eventually return.'

Suddenly the vision of the strange creature Wilt had stumbled upon in the forest washed over him. 'I met someone, in the Tangle. Something. It knew me.'

'The forest Guardian. The tree shepherd. The spirit of the shadows. He, too, has many names. And much in common with you, if Nurtle is to be believed. Apparently he's very interested in you. Has been for some time.'

Jared's smile grew wider as he saw the effect of his words on Wilt. 'Try not to let an old man's mysticism worry you too much. You're still feeling the effects of the treeblood Nurtle fed you. You have questions, and not all of them can be answered right now. Here.'

He patted Wilt on the shoulder and pointed at the desk with his other hand.

Wilt looked down at the large map spread out on the table in front of Jared. It was the Tangle, all of it, a massive green belt of trees that spread across the entire table, a full two metres each side. There at the far north edge were the mountains where Redmondis sat, and here, miles and miles south was the village of Copring, right against its southern edge. Through the centre of the forest ran a wide river, one Wilt had never even knew existed.

Wilt felt a wave of dizziness as he tried to make sense of the sheer size of it all. The scale of the forest seemed to mark out the entire world. Had he really travelled all that way on his own? He had spent weeks alone wandering its shadows and still only seen a fraction of it.

'Hard to comprehend, laid out in front of you like this, isn't it?'

Wilt could only nod dumbly, his eyes pulled along the myriad of forest trails marked out across the enormous map.

'You are one of the rare ones who can fully appreciate the size of the Tangle, having travelled across its length yourself. Long ago I too made that journey. As did Nurtle, as did many of the others you may meet in the villages scattered along the Tangle's southern edge. Which is part of the reason we find ourselves here, of course. Never quite able to leave it behind once it's touched us.'

Finally Wilt found his voice. 'You were in Redmondis.'

'That was long ago. A lifetime ago.' Jared smiled and pointed at the southern end of the map. 'Here is where we are. Copring. A small village of no account. Easily missed, easily ignored, just how we like it. Here'—his finger slid a few centimetres to the left—'is Weverly. I understand you know already what happened there.'

Jared's finger moved further along the southern edge of the map, picking out small towns as he went. 'Reggon. Verson. Jarlyle. All small, quiet villages made up of those Redmondis saw fit to discard so many years ago. All now gone.'

'How?'

Jared's hand curled into a fist and thumped the table. 'Now, that is the question.'

He suddenly rolled up the enormous map and replaced it with another, far less detailed one. This was little more than a rough, hand-drawn sketch, marking out a string of townships curling from the southern edge of the Tangle southwards.

'This is what the soldiers from Sontair have shown us. Village after village razed. It's not just wildlers that are being attacked. This trail leads all the way south to the capital itself. Somewhere there is the source.'

'The source of what?'

'Of whatever is trying to wipe us out.'

Jared stood up and looked at Wilt, sizing him up. 'Now, Nurtle would have us believe that you, young wielder, have been sent here to help find out exactly what it is we're dealing with.'

Chapter 15

Daemi woke with a groan of pain, rolling onto her side, away from the depths of sleep, away from the familiar dream that had taken hold of her once again. She had been fighting the wolves, focusing every ounce of muscle, every instinct her training had honed, every breath of effort into holding them back. But they didn't stop. As soon as one great fanged beast fell another took its place, snapping at her, always pressing her back, always pushing her that little step further toward the brink of her endurance.

Then the dream changed, away from her twisted memories of the day Cortis had taken Redmondis, into something altogether blacker. Her adversaries had morphed into something less recognisable, darker, not of this world. Black, clawed indefinable shapes, seemingly formed from long sharpened limbs that shot out without warning. She fought them too, holding them back as she pushed herself beyond her limits, beyond her human body and into the essence of battle itself.

Then dawn broke, somewhere on the far horizon, and she was left standing alone, surrounded by her victims.

Daemi sat up, wincing as her nightshirt caught on the wounds on her back and tore at the dried blood around their edges. The cuts had reopened during the night, responding to strains her body made in her nightmares, the blood mingling with her sweat to soak through her clothes and into the mattress. She grimaced and pulled her nightshirt free, ignoring the new fire of pain the movement cost her, forcing the cloth up over her head and tossing it into the corner of the room. She ignored the mirror on the wall as she walked over to the stone sink with its pool of icy clean water waiting for her. Her reflection would tell her nothing her body didn't already know.

Minutes later she marched out of her room, shoulders pushed back, furiously ignoring the weight of the armour putting pressure on the open wounds on her back. She could feel the warm blood still leaking through the cracks in the skin, soaking into her underclothes. Either the dreams were getting worse or Petron's remedies were losing their potency. She pushed the thought from her mind. There was no point feeling sorry for herself. No point worrying over things she could not control.

Twin guards at the entrance to the tower snapped into a salute as she passed, and she acknowledged them with the briefest nod of her head. She'd been promoted to captain months ago, in the weeks before Cortis's gambit, but still found herself momentarily confounded whenever her fellow guards responded in the way her rank demanded. She doubted she'd ever get used to it.

Daemi strode away from the guard tower, noting the thin covering of snow on the ground as she marched. Winter was deepening, the cold nights stretching longer. Soon enough the hours of true daylight could be counted on one hand. One guard's hand at that.

She grimaced at her own joke and flexed her fist, the tight skin where her little finger used to be still reminding her of the sacrifice she had made at the start of her journey. When the world was a different, much simpler place. When her path had seemed clear and straight.

Two more guards saluted as she passed through the doorway of the wielder's tower, and this time she remembered to return the gesture, her fist thumping into her chest plate. The movement sent another shot of pain across her back, and she quickened her step into the tower and up the stairs as she felt fresh warm blood flow from the wounds. Soon enough the blood would begin dripping out, marking her trail, and she didn't want to have to explain that away. None of these men would understand.

Only one man truly understood. Well, perhaps more than one, but Wilt wasn't here anymore.

Daemi forced the thought away as soon as it appeared, angry with herself for letting it pop into existence at all.

Moments later she pushed open the door to Petron's chamber and her mind soared as she stared out through the open walls into the clear blue sky. The sight took her breath away, and she had to resist the urge to step back from the yawning edge.

'Good morning, Captain.'

Petron's voice was tinged with amusement, and Daemi gathered herself, aware she was gawping. As she pulled her eyes away from the scene, she immediately noticed he wasn't alone.

She snapped to attention. 'Your pardon, Petron. I didn't—'

Daemi spun on her heel to leave the room. Petron was just raising his hand to stop her when they were both interrupted by the visitor, an old woman with bright, sparkling eyes, whose voice was edged with command.

'Don't be silly, girl. Come. Sit. Petron, you really are losing your touch. Can't you see she's wounded?'

Petron stepped quickly to Daemi's side, concern wrinkling his face as he noticed the unnatural hunch of her shoulders. 'Again?' he whispered.

Daemi nodded, allowing herself to be led across the room as weakness washed over her. Petron guided her to the bed next to where the old woman was sitting, and she collapsed onto it, all strength abandoning her legs as he pulled her armour up and over her head.

The next moment she was lying on her stomach, eyes closed, listening to Petron's whispered mutterings as he surveyed the damage. There was the sound of movement, then the woman's voice joined in.

'Oh dear. This is much worse than you told me on my last visit, Petron.'

'It is much worse than it was. The wounds seem to not want to heal.'

'These wounds were not caused by natural means. It will take more than natural means to heal them.'

Daemi tried to lift herself from the bed, but a firm hand patted her lightly on the head and her strength faded.

'Hush there, child,' the woman's voice ordered. 'Let Nurtle do her work.'

Daemi could feel the darkness calling to her and knew she couldn't avoid falling into it.

'Come Petron, this will require both of us.'

Daemi listened as the voices moved above her, now and then a light touch pressing against the sides of her wounds, sending a bright spark of pain to illuminate her growing drowsiness. The old woman chanted under her breath as she worked, and moments later Petron's voice joined with it, a perfect harmony instantly forming and twisting around itself, knitting together as she felt the skin across her back tighten and the pain begin to fade.

She tried to muster one last push to the surface of consciousness, but her eyelids wouldn't obey her commands, and she finally let herself fall into the depths as the two skilled healers did their work. The last words she heard were from the old woman.

'There. Let her rest now. Let the weave do its work.'

Daemi slept for almost two days in Petron's chambers, her dreams non-existent or too deep to read from the outside, her face untroubled the entire time, her breathing slow and regular.

Over the hours Petron watched her wounds heal, the skin bonding itself together across her back. Nurtle's healing touch had performed its magic, leaving her skin looking almost unscarred by the time the work was done.

When Daemi finally woke, Petron warned her to take things slowly, that the healing was not yet complete, that such wounds could never completely close, but she only nodded in reply and hurried on her way. Petron watched her leave, shaking his head at her stubborn eagerness to get on with planning for the upcoming expedition. He knew his warnings would be ignored.

'She is young. There is nothing any of us can do in the face of youth.' Nurtle was sitting on a chair by the fire, smiling at him with shining eyes.

'You enjoy watching these children torment me, don't you?' Petron growled.

'I enjoy watching a leader take form. A father figure. You cannot deny it.'

Petron sunk into the chair next to hers. 'They do not understand the dangers they face. I'm not sure if that's a blessing or a curse.'

'And you, Petron, do you understand?'

'I know the consequences of fighting back.'

He looked away then, out to the massive opening cut into the stone wall of his chamber, out to the wide open sky. Far in the distance a bird circled high above the deep green of the Tangle, eyeing some unsuspecting prey far below.

His fingers curled into the arms of his chair, his nails clawing at the dark wood.

'Petron,' said Nurtle, disrupting his reverie.

He pulled his eyes away from the outside world and looked at her, gathering himself when he noticed her tone.

'What has become of Cortis?'

'Dead.' Petron coughed, his face twisting into a grimace. 'Or gone, at least. No longer of this world.'

'He is still down there?'

'In the catacombs, you mean? Of course. I allowed no one to touch him. His body has failed, yet there is still some spark there, some part of his mind twisting in the depths. It was too dangerous to move him.'

'Dangerous for whom?'

'For all of us, I suspect. Whatever dark power he thought he served lost patience with him, consumed him. Whatever hell he abides in now is of his own making. Leave him to pay his own price. He deserves everything he gets and more.'

'You have heard the reports, from my lips and others.'

'The attacks on the villages? There have been scattered reports for months—since before Cortis.'

'But now they are more frequent.'

Petron sat up straighter in his chair. 'You think they are related?'

'I think that whatever door Cortis opened may still remain ajar. And more than one nightmare may force its way through it.'

Petron sat back and stroked his chin, considering her words.

'And the prophecy? You still do not believe?' Nurtle continued.

Petron clucked his tongue angrily at the thought, but measured his words. 'I've found many things can be explained by many prophecies. I saw what happened to the Nine Sisters. I saw how much their prophecy helped them.'

'It was never their prophecy. And you have not spent the time I have speaking with those whose roots sink the deepest. You cannot appreciate how ... convincing they can be.'

'They cannot be trusted. You know that.'

'We do not need to trust them. We just ... they are not our enemies.'

'Nor are they our friends.'

Petron stood and paced back and forth across the room. Nurtle watched him silently, allowing his thoughts to reach their conclusion.

Finally he raised his head. 'You think we should see what we can learn from Cortis? That there is something to gain? Something that could help Daemi and ... the others?'

Nurtle nodded and turned back to the fire. 'We should try everything we can.'

Chapter 16

Well, that was interesting.

Higgs! Wilt stopped in his tracks in the middle of the village street. *Where have you been?*

Here. I think. It was the strangest thing. I was asleep, yet more than that. Unable to wake, but there was no panic or danger in it. There was something almost … reassuring about it.

And the others?

We're here, Wilt. Delco and Rawick as well. There was no danger. It was Nurtle's doing. I think she wanted time for you to regain some of your humanity. We'd spent too long in the forest, too long in your other form.

Biore. I haven't been able to hear any of you since we ran into that … thing in the forest.

It was a spirit of some kind. Deeply linked to the trees themselves. There have always been rumours of a Guardian haunting the Tangle. I never really believed them until now.

And Nurtle? What is she?

A wildler, as Jared said. One of the many wielders banished from Redmondis by the Nine Sisters when they took power. Judging by how easily she silenced your mind she's quite a powerful one at that. We should be grateful she doesn't seem to hold any grudges against us.

So, Biore, you heard everything Jared told me?

Yes, I think so. It's confusing … almost as though it was a dream.

Just as you dreamed the meeting between Jared and the captain of the guard patrol, perhaps.

That was more than just a dream. I recognised him.

Yes, but we must be cautious. What you saw may only be a reflection of a reflection of the truth. Long ago there were wielders who specialised in using the depths to draw out prognostications of the future. Bending the welds across time and space. Rarely were they ever one hundred percent accurate. Our human minds bend the welds to our shape, even when we don't intend them to.

The boy. The one I … we chased from the village. The one we saw through the window of Nurtle's hut. Shade. He shared the vision with us. He guided us along.

Yes. I'd be very interested to meet with that boy again. Look around this village. Notice anything in particular?

Wilt scanned the surrounding village, searching for something out of the ordinary. Biore was right; there was something off about the place, but he couldn't put his finger on it.

There aren't any kids around.

That's right, Higgs. In Redmondis, one of the early rumours to spread about wildlers was their inability to procreate. That something in the way they joined their minds together interfered with their biology. It was never proven, of course.

But, Shade. I thought … I guess I assumed he was Nurtle's son. Or grandson, I suppose.

Perhaps he was. Nurtle and Jared have only told us as much as they think we need to know. Perhaps in time we will find out more.

Uh, Wilt? What are we doing? asked Higgs.

Wilt smiled and resumed his march, resting his right hand on the hilt of the long knife hanging from his hip. *We're following orders. Going to see the captain of the guard patrol camped on the edge of this village. Jared suggested we offer our services.*

At that moment Wilt rounded a wall, and a guard stepped out into his path. He immediately lowered the long pike he was carrying to point directly at Wilt's chest.

'State your business.'

Wilt stopped and raised his hands before catching himself and dropping them to his side. 'Uh … hello there. My name is Wilt. I'm here to see your captain. Captain Mont.'

The guard took a moment to look Wilt up and down, unimpressed with what he saw. 'Another villager, are you? What business do you have with the captain?'

Wilt drew himself up and tried his best to sound haughty. 'No business of yours. Tell him Jared sent me. I have a message for him.'

You're wasting time. Use your skill, boy. Convince him.

For a moment Wilt considered doing just as Biore suggested, sending a black weld into the man's mind and taking control, but something held him back. Some memory from his time in the forest, the lost days and weeks spent alone. He knew where that particular path led.

Wilt stared silently at the guard, daring him to doubt his word. Eventually the man shrugged, and the pike was lifted up and away from Wilt's chest. 'Very well.' He sniffed. 'Proceed.'

Wilt felt the guard's cold glare as he passed, but he shrugged it off and held his head high, as though he really did have an important message from the village leader.

So, Wilt … what's the message?

Oh, I don't know, Higgs. We're just going to volunteer our services, like Jared suggested.

Services?

Now you haven't been paying attention. Look around.

Wilt was walking through the centre of the guard camp now, picking his way past low campfires and hastily raised tents. He felt the guards watching him, each studying him coldly, their hands never far from their weapons, as though they weren't convinced he wasn't about to transform into some sort of monster and attack.

There are no Black Robes with these soldiers, no wielders at all. I think Jared's right, the captain has a need for one. And no, Biore, I'm not going to just use a weld on him.

These guards sure are nervous.

They've been on patrol too long, Higgs. Seen too many strange things. The Tangle has well and truly got to them.

Wilt continued on, ignoring the looks and grunts his passing caused, until he came to the centre of the camp, a large, double-roomed tent with two guards posted at its entryway.

It looks just like Wrexley's tent. Remember?

Wilt smiled at Higgs's words and the memory of their first trip to Redmondis. So long ago now.

He was shaken from this thoughts by movement at the entrance to the tent as the two guards snapped to attention. Captain Mont stepped out, acknowledging their salute with a distracted wave as he marched away.

'Captain Mont!' Wilt hurried to catch up.

At the sound of his name, the captain stopped and turned, staring at Wilt as he trotted toward him. 'And you are?' His tone was tired.

'Wilt, Captain. My name is Wilt. Jared sent me.'

'Oh. Another scout are you? Go back to Jared and tell him we've more than enough already, especially considering how the last few village "scouts" had a remarkable tendency to disappear as soon as we entered the forest.'

'Not a scout, Captain. Something far more useful.'

Wilt reached up and slid the lenses covering his black eyes free, at the same time sending a single weld slithering into the captain's mind. Immediately the captain's right hand waved in the air as though he were greeting a friend. Then he pulled the weld free and released his hold on the captain.

He bowed his head to give the captain time to regain his composure and slid the lenses back into place.

'So. Another witch, are you?' The captain's strained voice was the only sign something had shaken his nerve.

'A wielder, sir. Trained in Redmondis. I believe you may find my particular skills quite useful.'

The captain grunted and looked Wilt up and down again. 'You don't look like a Black Robe.'

'No, sir. I'm not. Not anymore. There have been some recent changes.'

'Yes.' The captain snorted. 'I've heard rumours of the recent happenings in the north.'

What does he know about Redmondis? Ask him about Petron, and Daemi, and—

Wilt smiled and pushed Higgs's thoughts down. 'Suffice to say things have improved for the better. I can assure you I am just as skilled a wielder as any who wear the black robes, and just as useful to a patrol who intends to enter the Tangle.'

The captain continued to study Wilt, then gave a quick nod. 'Very well. The next patrol leaves in an hour. Report to the scouting party—Sergeant Gould. I'll send word ahead so you're expected. They'll be waiting for you at the northern edge of the camp. We travel light and fast and if you can't keep up you'll be left behind.'

'Sir!' Wilt saluted.

The captain turned and marched away, calling out over his shoulder, 'Perhaps you can help us avoid the tricks the Tangle likes to play.'

Chapter 17

Shade had to admit it. He was lost.

He hadn't thought it possible. He'd spent all his life in the Tangle, wandering its paths, listening to its low murmur and avoiding the random cruel tricks the Others liked to play. Now though, none of the surrounding trails seemed familiar. As soon as he found one worthy of pursuing, it seemed to curve around on itself until he was somehow back where he started.

He'd even tried climbing some of the trees, though they too resisted his efforts, bending themselves out of his way and shifting branches and boughs suddenly out of reach. Finally he'd glimpsed the late afternoon sky and got a sense of direction, but as soon as he was back on the forest floor, the trees seemed determined to shepherd him away from his chosen path. After only a few steps he'd be faced with an impossible solid wall of trees that even his thin figure was unable to squeeze through. And so he'd be forced to turn around and try to flank them, but the forest always seemed one step ahead.

And the Others, their voices much clearer now, as though they too were all converging on this one spot. Their conspiratorial whispers seemed to leak out of the shadows to fill his ears.

A challenge!

So soon?

Long overdue. Look how weakened we are.

But none have succeeded. Even the strongest of us.

And little Shade hopes to succeed?

He squeezed his eyes closed and tried to ignore them. Nurtle had warned him about this as soon as she'd seen the cloak the Guardian had gifted him. How it would open certain doors, certain paths that normally remained closed.

Future and past entwined.

The words on the clasp that had held it. The words forced out of him. Had he brought this on himself? Or was it the Guardian, drawing him ever deeper. Was this what Nurtle had feared?

Time to climb, little Shade.

Climb for your life.

Or your death.

It's all the same to us, you know.

Shade let their words wash over him, not paying attention to their meaning. His mind was buzzing, as though the forest's song itself had grown in strength. Their words were just another breeze in the leaves. He kept his eyes closed and let the voice of the forest hum his heart into stillness.

When he opened his eyes again, he was deep in the forest, the light dim, the high sun blocked out by ranks of close-growing trees. The air was thick and muggy, heavy with moisture and the warmth of rotting things, making it hard to breathe.

He was standing in front of an enormous trunk, easily twenty feet across. It was the biggest tree he'd ever seen.

The Challenge Tree!

How high can little Shade climb?

How fast?

Not high or fast enough.

Not a runt like you.

Hurry up and start, boy.

We'll be right behind you.

Shade ignored them, staring up at the mighty tree in front of him. He craned his head back until his neck ached, and still he couldn't see the top. The tree seemed to disappear into the high shadows, growing up into the clouds itself. There was no telling how tall it was.

As the Others continued their chatter, Shade stepped forward and placed one palm on the mighty trunk, closing his eyes to better hear the whispered voice deep within. This had to be the oldest tree he'd ever encountered. Its voice would lie deep.

Scared?

Shade opened his eyes and looked back at the source of the voice, the set of wild black eyes that stared out at him from the forest shadows.

He shook his head and smiled, and suddenly the air was filled with wild animal cries, screeches and hisses, squawks and barks.

Still the Others remained in the shadows, only their black eyes visible. Waiting for him.

Shade faced the trunk and focused his mind on it, reaching out again with both hands now to feel the throb of life under his hands. He could sense the power running under his palms, the thrum of life surging through the bark, the silent song of the tree calling to him. He turned his head and placed his ear against the tree, tuning himself to it, letting it take him where it would.

Finally he stepped back and shrugged his cloak free from his shoulders. The Others stopped their cries and silence descended on the clearing as though the forest itself was holding its breath.

Shade broke into movement, sprinting right at the tree, taking three quick steps directly up its trunk and leaping out and up to grasp the first low branch. His momentum sent his body swinging around the branch; he tucked his legs in and let go of his grip, flying through the air to land feet first on the next branch over.

Some Others let out a small cheer at the sight.

Shade looked down and smiled, waving briefly before turning back to the tree and scampering upwards, disappearing into the shadows.

He's fast.

Faster than we've seen in an age.

But is he strong enough?
Brave enough?
Open enough?
Quickly now.
We'll have to catch him at the Twist.
We're coming to get you, little Shade.

Shade had left all thought of his pursuers far behind, concentrating instead on the continuing deep hum of the tree under his fingertips as he climbed. He could feel it urging him ever higher, lending his limbs strength with each step. The leaves on the surrounding branches joined the song, the wind that stirred them pushing at his back and shoulders, until he forgot about his hands and feet entirely and let the forest song overwhelm him and lift him up the tree.

This was what Nurtle meant by the spirit of the forest, surely; this other intelligence, teasing him, dancing at the edge of his mind, almost making itself known and understood.

The surrounding branches melted away suddenly, and he faced a long gap in the trunk of the great tree, still ten feet wide even at this height. The trunk seemed to bow and twist around itself here, as though the tree long ago had to bend around some obstacle now lost to the past, warping itself as it pursued the sunlight.

Shade studied the twining shape, trying to understand what had caused this anomaly. There was something there, some note deep in the song thrumming under his palms, a dark edge of threat.

He closed his eyes. It was right there, a scurrying shadow flitting just out of reach.

Something cracked into the trunk beside his head and his eyes snapped open, the vision wrenched away. He looked around, but there was no sign of any threat.

Be careful not to fall, little Shade.

The call came from metres below, and Shade knew suddenly

what danger he faced. A spark of fear bloomed in his chest, bringing with it other thoughts, other possibilities.

He swallowed and pushed the panicked thought away, concentrating on each hand and foothold, trying to keep his mind focused on the task. The hum of the tree under his palms rose in volume in response, rising against the sudden fear, pulsing in time with his heartbeat, then taking it in hand and leading it back down to a steady rhythm.

A second rock smacked against the trunk, this time just to the side of his right hand, showering it in tiny pieces of wooden shrapnel. He looked down, following the path of the missile, and saw a single set of black eyes staring back at him from the edge of the shadows below.

Shade closed his eyes and turned back to the trunk, letting the tree guide his hands and feet now, forgetting the world around him. Forgetting all but the tree and the life that flowed under his fingers.

As he moved he felt other presences, other beings moving with him, below him, on the edge of his skin. Closed minds that scurried carelessly upwards.

Finally he felt leaves and shoots under his hand again, and Shade opened his eyes back to the surface world. He'd reached the end of the bizarrely twisted, bare section of trunk and could pull himself up into the relative safety of thick foliage again.

A third rock flew past his head, ripping through the leaves around him as it went. It thudded into the trunk above him so hard it caused the tree to shudder in response, the hum inside it rising in volume again.

As if it were angry.

Shade climbed, faster than he had before, his mind filled with the song of the Tangle, the deepening drone wiping all other thought away.

He could feel the Others dropping further behind, losing interest in the chase as he disappeared from view.

No. One still came. He could feel the heat of a life force moving across the twisted section of trunk now metres below. One wasn't going to give up.

The tree hummed under his fingers again and Shade slowed his ascent. Why was he running? Why not stop and wait in the shadows? Wait for him to come.

Shade shook the dark thoughts from his mind and continued to climb. He was impossibly high now, yet still the sunlight only flickered in and out of view from still higher. How long had this great tree stood here, watching the forest grow up around it? How many other trees were its children?

What kind of mind inhabits such an ancient thing?

The tree hummed again in answer, louder now, until the sound filled his mind. He felt sure the noise had to be heard all across the forest, the song washing all thought clear.

This way, little Shade. Climb, and forget all else.

The voice creaked through him. His awareness narrowed and stretched, bending away, leaving his body behind.

He looked up from studying where to place his hands and feet to catch a glimpse of the boy, but he was much higher now, still moving fast. Where had the runt learned to climb like that? Even the Twist had only slowed him momentarily.

His forearms ached with the strain of climbing, the tension of clutching each branch tighter than the last as the ground sunk further away. He grunted, scanning the shadows for some sign of his prey. He only had two more rocks. He had to make sure.

The tree seemed to bend and twist under his hands as though trying to shake him loose. He could feel the ground far below calling to him, sucking him toward it. He looked down again and felt the world turn around the tree, spinning him into dizziness.

Shade shook himself and was back in his own mind, staring at his hand on the trunk of the tree. Those hadn't been his thoughts. That was the Other. The one following him.

A single bead of sweat ran out of his tousled hair and tricked down the side of his face.

That's right, little Shade. That's just how it is done.

Shade closed his eyes and reached out again for what he knew was there.

The tree twisted under him again and he almost lost his grip, catching himself in a last scrambling moment to cling on. The tree was actively fighting him now.

He reached into his pocket and withdrew the small sharp knife he carried there. He dug it slowly into the bark in front of his face, twisting it cruelly as it went to carve out a round hole in the timber.

That's what you get. That's why you don't cross me.

Somewhere deep below his consciousness a howl of fury and pain cried out in answer.

He dropped the knife, and it disappeared into the shadows below. He stared at the hand that had let it fall. It looked foreign to him, not his hand at all. It was smaller, much smaller than his own.

He watched as the hand reached out to the trunk and pushed itself away, letting gravity take hold. He was nothing more than a great weight, plummeting through broken sunlight, through the dimness to the darkness and oblivion waiting below.

Shade opened his eyes and examined his hand, the same hand he had just seen through other eyes. He stared at the trunk until the final image, the moment when the body met the ground, faded slowly from his mind.

Come. Climb. See what power awaits, little Shade. Little wraithling.

He climbed ever higher, up into the light.

Chapter 18

Wilt trudged along the path slowly, struggling to peer through the dim light that filtered to ground level through the rows upon rows of branches and leaves high above. The soldier was only three metres ahead, but was barely visible. The man's cloak was little more than a shadow that swung in and out of focus as they made their way along the thin forest trail, deeper into the Tangle.

No wonder these guards have been seeing things.

Wilt grunted at Higgs's words and ducked as a low branch suddenly loomed into view through the fog. The man in front hadn't called out a warning; there was hardly any noise at all, just the dull thump of heavy boots on the damp forest floor. Even the birds had fallen silent.

Unnatural. A forest shouldn't be this quiet.

It was never like this for us, was it, Biore? I don't remember much, Wilt replied.

Perhaps we'd be better off in another form, Wilt. One that is more comfortable moving through the shadows.

What did Nurtle call us? A wraith? Are you sure we're strong enough to risk that here?

Wilt ignored the thoughts and kept moving, concentrating on keeping the shadow in front of him in sight so he didn't lose his way. The trail they were following was little more than an animal track, all too easy to wander from if you weren't paying attention.

Or if the trees feel like playing games.

Delco's words were forgotten as the guard in front suddenly became clearer, and Wilt almost stumbled into his back before realising the column had stopped.

The man turned his head and muttered over his shoulder. 'You. The sergeant wants you up front.'

His duty done, the man leaned against the nearest trunk and rummaged in his cloak pockets for pipe and tobacco, eager to take advantage of any halt in the long march. Wilt pushed past him and moved toward the front, past a thin line of guards he had heard no sound from in the eerie silence of the forest.

At the front of the column Sergeant Gould waited, muttering to his second in command, his face stern and still. 'Wielder.'

Wilt nodded and stood at attention as the sergeant looked him up and down.

'From Redmondis, the captain says.' He punctuated these words by spitting to the side of the trail, as though the name left a sour taste in his mouth.

The second in command's face twisted at the sergeant's words, but he held his tongue.

'I've met some of your kind before,' the sergeant continued. 'Can't say I found them too useful. But the captain feels otherwise and what the captain wants, the captain gets.'

'What can I help with?'

The sergeant nodded down the path that snaked away from them into the shadows. 'This point marks the deepest we've moved into the Tangle so far. Ahead is virgin territory. I'd appreciate anything you can do to ensure we don't stumble into a surprise.'

Wilt tried to peer through the dim light, but could see nothing.

We're not going to see anything that way, boy.

Of course. 'Wait here.' Wilt didn't wait for a reply; he strode ahead down the trail, leaving the soldiers to stare at his back as it faded into the fog. In only a few steps he was alone.

Now perhaps we can stop wasting time?

Biore's right. Don't worry, Wilt. We'll be here with you.

Wilt felt a chill shudder over his shoulders as a black mist of welds took his place. A moment later the wraith cut down the forest trail, a silent, cold shadow on the world.

Wilt studied the surrounding forest, but could find no sign of life. No bright glow of heat and blood burning against the grey world he now inhabited. The forest wasn't just silent, it was empty.

Something has caused this stillness. Something has chased all life away.

You know, Delco, your forest knowledge is appreciated and all, but could you try not sounding so ominous all the time?

Wilt smiled to himself at the voices in his mind, so much clearer and more present in this form. He could easily take a step into the tunnel, into the waiting dark, and he'd be there with them.

He shook the thought away and moved into the trees, pushing past branches that almost seemed to reach out to touch him, to brush past his shoulder as he passed, to draw sustenance from his being. As he moved he noticed another sound, the murmur of the forest itself, a sigh or groan that was the foundation for all other sound in the deep woods. The whisper of the Tangle was also much clearer in this form, much more vivid once he sank beneath the surface world.

Be cautious, Wilt. Don't let the Tangle lead you.

Biore's voice brought him back. He was right; that was exactly what the Tangle was doing. It had done it before. He'd spent weeks in thrall to its song as he moved south, telling himself it was easier this way, ignoring the hunger of his body, letting himself drift ever further from life. It was too dangerous, taking this form here in the Tangle. Too easy to forget.

We're with you, Wilt. We won't let you lose yourself.

Higgs keeps saying your name. And it helps, it really does.

A sudden shudder tingled up his spine and all other thought dropped away. There was something here. Someone else.

He scanned the surrounding forest, but there was no sign of life.

Behind you. Something looped around.

Wilt spun and raced back toward the guards, his wraith form cutting a direct path through the trees, ignoring any physical barrier. He felt each trunk and branch he passed through as a deeply cold kiss, beckoning him back down.

Soon enough he could make out the guard column, a single line of glowing life curving through the forest. Men standing and shifting, trying not to make too much noise. Nervous men.

There was nothing.

No—there, just to the north of the column, a black spot, another shadow on the world.

Wilt cut toward it, bending around the guards, leaving them shivering in the sudden cold of his wake.

The shadow in front of him altered its path immediately. It had been arrowing straight for the front of the column, but turned away sharply as Wilt approached, fleeing the scene.

It's … another wraith, isn't it?

Higgs was right. The dark form shot away back into the depths of the Tangle, moving faster than Wilt thought possible. In a moment it was gone, completely out of sight.

Whoa. Maybe not so much like us after all.

Or maybe just further along the path. I think we just saw a glimpse of what one day we might become.

Wilt shook his head at the naked hunger in Biore's tone. There was so much he did not see—good things, light things. Things not worth leaving behind.

He thought of Daemi then, standing alone in her room, staring into the mirror.

A cry rang out through the forest, from the rear of the guard column, and the sounds of battle broke out.

Wilt forgot all thought of pursuit and raced back toward the guards.

In moments the source of the commotion was clear. At the rear of the column two guards were already down, their bodies prone and cold on the forest floor, the heat of life already draining into the waiting soil. Three more men stood with their blades drawn, their heads moving back and forth, desperately trying to identify their attackers before they too fell.

There was no sign of the threat that had already claimed two victims. Three heads moved as one to the left and suddenly two more men were down. Their bodies grappled with some invisible presence for a second, then went limp, and the glow of life that burned so clearly in Wilt's vision faded into the background.

What is it? We can't see—

Use the welds, Wilt, Biore instructed.

But there's nothing to wield against, nothing to—

The guards. Send a weld into one of the guards.

Immediately Wilt understood what Biore was trying to explain to him. He sent out a thick black weld, directly toward the third guard, the one still standing among his fallen comrades. The weld slipped in easily; the man's mind was a sea of panic, all mental barriers ripped away. One thought echoed through the chaos.

This is it. This is the moment you die.

The guard, Per was his name, scanned the dense forest on either side of the path, unable to make out anything. Behind him he could hear the rest of the patrol trying to form into a defensive position on the narrow, twisting path.

Too late. Too late for any of us. The best you can do is die well. Hope you can sink your blade into one of them before they take you.

At his feet he was aware of his fellow soldiers, already dead. The dark things, the nightmare shapes that had appeared from the shadows, had ended them in a moment, then disappeared.

Wilt, try to direct him. Try to take control.

The cold, it bites. Don't think about it, just keep your blade up and steady. Remember your training, forget everything else.

Suddenly it was upon him, a spindly, spider-like shape, all sharp limbs and frenzied speed, leaping out of the shadows to land on his chest, pushing him to the forest floor. Then a swipe of a long, barbed claw, a mind-clearing pain, and the cold and the panic left him, and he melted into the waiting darkness.

Now, Wilt. Go back up into the creature itself, just like—

Just like I did in Redmondis, with Cortis. Right, Biore? Use the pain itself as the key.

Wilt felt the pull of the depths call to him as the guard, his vessel, sank down into death, the cool still breath of the long tunnel calling to him. He wrenched his eyes from it and pushed the weld up and out of the guard's mind, back along the limb that had ended him, back into the creature itself.

For a single, endless moment he stared into it, into the still, dark emptiness, no life in it at all, a simple nightmare in living form. No thought other than to kill, no will other than to do that which the depths ordered it to do, no mind in which to dwell. The darkness itself wrapped around him, holding him in place.

So. We meet again. A single, world-encompassing voice whispered into his ear, blasting all thought away. He felt himself sink into the floor of the ocean, swallowed by the dark. Then it flung him away, out of the depths, back into the living world.

Wilt lay to the side of the forest trail, guards moving all around him, their blades drawn, hunting out whatever threat had just attacked and taken down five of their fellow men. He heard himself whimper, then tried to sit up, but his vision clouded with stars and he sank back down.

The forest floor was warm under his ear, and he could almost feel the life within it pulsing into his flesh, revitalising him, bringing him back from the edge.

The stars in his eyes burned themselves out and drifted away, sparks floating on the breeze.

That voice, Wilt. What was that?

It knew us, Biore. It recognised us, or at least, recognised him.

Wilt has seen it before, Higgs. Or it has seen him before.

The creature, the thing that attacked us, is it gone? Where is it?

Wilt sat up more slowly this time, feeling still in the commotion that surrounded him as the guards tried to organise their ranks. On the ground nearby lay five bodies, their eyes blank and empty, staring at sights none on this side of life could see. Deep, wide gashes were cut into their bodies, across the throat and chest. One man's torso had almost been split in two. There was no sign of the thing that had performed the grisly work.

It had been quick. At least they had that mercy.

'Form up, men!'

Sergeant Gould's voice rung out across the forest, instantly taking control. Guards snapped to attention, their training overcoming their blind panic.

'Did anyone see it?'

'Aye, Sergeant,' more than one voice called out in answer, their voices too loud, trying to mask their fear.

'Which way did it go?'

'It … vanished, Sergeant. As soon as Per fell.'

Wilt looked at the guard who had spoken. He was standing closest to the fallen men, his sword gripped tight in his fist. His face was a tight mask of concentration, fighting to keep control.

He's right, boy. That thing disappeared as soon as it took its last victim.

The sergeant pushed through from the front of the column and paused as he took in the scene. He scanned each of the victims, capturing the memory, then shifted sideways to look at Wilt. For a moment Wilt saw hatred in the man's eyes, hatred born of fear of all wielders, their mysterious powers, and the damage they could do to honest men.

Wilt stood up quickly, feeling suddenly ashamed.

'You. What happened?'

'We were attacked. The guards were attacked.' Wilt corrected himself instantly, seeing the anger flash in the sergeant's eyes. 'A black thing, like an enormous spider. Impossibly fast.' He held his hands out, struggling to explain what his brain still refused to process.

Something not of this plane.

'What was it? And why—'

'It was something … I think it was something from the place beyond. The place where welds come from. The depths themselves.'

The sergeant studied Wilt's face as he spoke, as though he could learn more there than from Wilt's stuttering explanation. 'And where is it now, wielder?'

There was no mistaking the accusation in his voice.

This is a man who knows something of the ways of the weld. It wouldn't surprise me if he served in Redmondis, many years ago, though I don't recognise him. Tread carefully, Wilt.

Tell him we saved the others, Wilt. Made the thing disappear.

'It's gone. Back to where it came from, I think. I … used a weld on it, tried to take control, to stop it. But its mind … there was nothing there, nothing but emptiness. It wasn't real.'

The sergeant snorted and nodded to where his men lay in the dirt. 'Real enough for them.'

'No—I mean it wasn't … natural. It wasn't anything more than a tool, an extension of the depths.' Wilt dropped his hands to his side and shook his head, aware he wasn't making any sense.

The sergeant stared at him silently, then spun away, back to his men. 'Form up. We return to camp. Get a stretcher built. We're not leaving these men here.'

Instantly the guards moved into action, thankful for something to do, some real problem to tackle and solve.

Wilt watched them work around him. Now and then one of them glanced up at him, their eyes shadowed.

They fear you. They think you brought that thing to them.

Wilt thought about Biore's words, and about the cold stillness of the creature's mind, the familiar call of the depths, the voice that had whispered his name.

Perhaps they are right.

The bodies began to turn almost as soon as they were hauled onto the stretcher.

Wilt wasn't the first to notice. One guard marching behind the makeshift pallet called out, his voice over-loud and edged with panic. Sergeant Gould spun around instantly to reprimand him, not wanting his fear to infect the other men, assuming it was still a hold-over from the earlier grisly encounter. The next moment he too cried out, more in dismay than fear, and within moments Wilt found himself beside them, his gaze following the guard's shaking finger to the bodies laid out on the rough timber frame.

It was as though each body had been dipped in ink, the skin on their faces and hands blackening gradually. Then their features collapsed in on themselves as the ink seemed to eat away at them, their chests caving in next and their bodies sinking down into hollow husks. In moments only their armour remained, and the black dust that had been their bodies was whipped up and away in a sudden gust of wind.

Wilt turned his head instinctively as the dust rose around them, not wanting any of it to touch him.

Don't breathe any of it in.

The other men must have had the same thought; they each covered their faces and turned away until the strange dust had cleared, the wind sucking it out and away, as though the trees themselves had stirred it up to purge the stain from within their midst.

'Gods. What happened to them?'

It was the first guard, his voice even younger than his face, and Wilt almost stuttered out a reply before a second guard spoke, his voice much harsher. 'Wielder work.'

Wilt turned to see the man staring straight at him, his features twisted with disgust.

The sergeant stepped in and clapped the man on the shoulder. 'Leave it, Dale.' The clap became a push, propelling him toward the front of the column. 'Give them a hand up front. We head south, out of the forest. Leave the stretcher where it is. There's no point now.'

Without another word the guards resumed their march, following the trail out of the depths of the Tangle.

As they marched, Wilt could feel the dread and fear lift from his shoulders as though it were a physical thing. The Tangle's power to influence his thoughts and mood faded the further south they moved, the closer they came to its borders.

It is a strangely troubled mind. Delco's voice was much quieter now, more distant, as though he were leaving the physical realm further behind.

The trees you mean? Can you understand them?

It isn't—it's not like there is one mind to comprehend. The trees are so ancient, so deeply rooted.

Are they a threat?

Not to us. Not directly. But I wouldn't let your guard down.

Within hours the column was back on the edge of Copring, and Wilt found himself a stranger again, the soldiers obviously displeased to have him share their company. He couldn't blame them, not after what they had just seen.

Don't let their fear trouble you, Wilt. That's all it is. Fear born of ignorance.

I know.

'The witch comes.'

The soldiers, who had been relaxing and settling into camp, snapped to attention at the call, readying their weapons. Wilt followed the voice as the men parted to reveal a hooded figure standing at the edge of the camp, one hand resting on a tall, knobbed wooden staff.

Nurtle. She's looking for you.

Wilt waved his hand vaguely at the guards as he walked toward her, trying to get them to relax their state of alert. They ignored him completely. Whatever displeasure they felt in his company was nothing compared to the open fear the sight of Nurtle elicited in them.

Nurtle didn't move from her spot at the edge of the camp and didn't seem to notice the commotion her presence caused. Finally Wilt closed within hailing distance and she raised her head to an almost audible sucking in of breath from the guards.

'Come, wielder. I need to make use of your skills.'

With that she turned and strode away from the camp, never giving it a second look. She obviously expected Wilt to follow.

There's something wrong. She seems different. Worried.

Wilt nodded. Higgs was right, there had been a definite edge to her tone.

Nurtle didn't speak again until they were back at her hut, and she disappeared into the shadows of its doorway. Almost immediately she reappeared, holding a small green cloak in her hands. 'Here. Take this. What can you read from it?' She seemed distant, as though some important part of her had shut down and she was simply stepping through automatic motions.

'Nurtle? Has something happened?'

She shook the cloak, urging him to take it. 'Just try. There's no time.'

Wilt reached out and took the cloak. It felt strangely light for its size.

It's the boy's. Shade's.

Something has happened to him, Wilt.

But what can I—

Do you not feel it, the energy within the fibre? It feels almost like—

The weld blade. Biore's right, Wilt.

Yes, I think we can use this.

Wilt shook the cloak out and held it in front of him. It didn't look remarkable at all, just the same smudged greeny-brown colour all the villagers wore. The same as his own new cloak. Only the weight was unusual.

Put it on.

Wilt pulled his cloak free and swung his arms up and around his head, throwing the new garment over his shoulders. It settled over him with a sigh, and he felt a spark of recognition in his mind.

He looked up at Nurtle, who was studying him intently.

'Where did you find this?'

'Such questions will have to wait, wielder. I promise I will give you answers in time, only help me now. We need to find him. Quickly. The Guardian is weakened and due to pass on. Shade must be there, and so must you. You have to ease the way. Help me, please.'

Wilt held her gaze and nodded, knowing implicitly he could trust her. He closed his eyes and fell into himself, into the dark river that flowed beneath the surface world.

Chapter 19

Shade opened his eyes to find himself sitting on a felled trunk in an open forest clearing, facing forward, his hands clamped onto the seat on either side of him, holding himself in place.

He had no memory of travelling here. No idea what time of day it was. His last memory was clouded; he had images of climbing, of heading toward the top of an impossibly tall tree. Feeling it rock and sway beneath him as a thick black smoke stained the sky.

'You have done well, child. More than you realise.'

Sitting at the front of the clearing, on a high, intricately carved wooden throne, was the Guardian. Shade wanted to close his eyes, to blind himself to the sight, yet he couldn't. His eyes were drawn to the figure, pulled along the strangely curved carvings of its throne.

The Guardian didn't move, yet its voice seemed to come from everywhere at once, filling Shade's mind. He couldn't focus properly on the face in front of him. All he could see was a blur of features where the face should be, as though a hundred separate visages were shifting across it, no single set staying in place long enough for his mind to grasp.

'And your talents have brought our guest to us.'

Shade couldn't help but close his eyes at the words, as though they carried a secret command. As soon as his heavy lids closed, he found himself awash in a rushing stream of thought.

What is happening? Where are we?

We're in the Tangle, Higgs. It called us here.

Delco! Where is Wilt?

Wilt is here, just as we are here. We are one.

Biore, can you make any sense of this?

I think—I think whatever it is can hear us.

'You are correct, Master Biore, and you are welcome. As are your companions. Rawick, who himself came so close to becoming what you see before you. Delco, who through the strength of his love for his brother called him back from oblivion. And Higgs, who is himself the key.'

How is this possible? We were in Nurtle's hut, she gave us Shade's cloak, and then—

'And now you have found what you seek. Come, Wilt. Join us.'

Shade opened his eyes again and slowly turned his head. Somewhere within his mind he felt a tearing, a slow peeling away of something that didn't rightly belong inside him. The next moment he was staring at another figure sitting beside him. The wielder, the Black Robe from Nurtle's hut.

'Welcome, Wilt.'

Wilt stared at Shade, who looked just as lost and surprised as him. He turned back to the figure at the front of the clearing.

To Wilt's eyes the Guardian was a tall, thin man in a mottled green cloak, his entire face covered by a wooden helm carved into the likeness of a stag, complete with two long twisting horns curving out of the top.

'We have been watching you for some time now, little spark. Watching and waiting for you.'

The Guardian's voice seemed to come at Wilt from all directions. The trees lining the clearing shifted and swayed in response, splashing long shadows across the Guardian's helm. It moved and shifted as Wilt stared at it, until another creature entirely stared back at him, a badger or beaver-like animal, the twin horns now sprouting leaves and branches of their own, until the shadows shifted again and the vision faded.

Wilt shook his head, trying to pull his eyes away from the dizzying sight.

Ask what it wants.

'What *I* want?' The Guardian chuckled—a creaking, cracking sort of sound. 'Youth always searches for reason, I should remember that. It has been many, many years since I was young.'

The face on the helm twisted again in the shifting light, and now an ancient, knotted trunk stared out at them, a stretched, worn face carved into its grey wood.

'I want you to look at those fallen trees upon which you sit. Those ancient, long silent ones. They have lain in that position for longer than I have wandered these woods, longer than the five Guardians before me served, and each of those attended to their tasks for ten lifetimes of normal men. Still, their spirit remains. Their voices survive. When you listen for them, what do they tell you?'

Wilt looked at his hands clutching the brittle wood on either side of him. He closed his eyes to listen, dropping into himself, holding himself just above the raging river that flowed beneath the surface. He heard nothing.

They hunger.

Wilt's eyes snapped open at the words; they seemed to echo inside his mind just as Higgs and the others did, but they came from the boy. From Shade.

'Very good. They hunger. What do they hunger for?'

For life. For us.

The Guardian shook his head.

'They hunger for *a* life. One that has long been held out of their reach. They hunger for me.

'These trees have protected us for centuries, waging a silent battle on the dark that would seep to the surface world should they allow it. They protect us and yet they fear us. Fear us and loath the necessity of our existence.

'Your parents, Shade. Nurtle and Jared. They are wildlers, they too came close to the seat I find myself in. They know the hunger of which we speak. They know too of your affinity with this place, with the depths. With your ability to ride the shadows. They know why you are here.

'And you, Rawick.' The Guardian turned to face Wilt. 'You came close to this point. You felt their power.'

What is he talking about, Wilt? Are the trees a threat to us?

'Not to you, little thief. You have nothing to fear from them.'

I … I think I know why we're here.

Delco? What is it?

It's Rawick. This is … this is what he has been searching for.

'You have always been able to read your brother's thoughts better than any human, young wielder. That is why you, too, are required.'

The Guardian looked between the two young men sitting across from him, his mask shifting again in the light to form a new face, a sad face, its bark worn down by the winds of time. His head dropped, and his voice became much quieter. 'I have waited for this moment for many years. Waited for it and dreaded its arrival.'

He raised his head again, his voice much stronger now. 'It is long past time for another to take on the mantle, to replace me as Guardian. I am old and weak—my inability to prevent the recent attacks within our boundaries prove that. At one time these servants of the dark would never have dared show themselves so openly. But my strength has faded, and with it the protection of the Tangle itself.'

The Guardian stood slowly, his body creaking like old wood, and raised his hands to his helm. 'So, Shade. So, Rawick. So, Delco. I pass this task on to you.'

Wilt and Shade stood in unison, their bodies again following a silent command. The Guardian raised the helm from his head and a searingly bright shaft of sunlight flooded the clearing. There was only white—white, and a whisper in Wilt's mind.

Farewell, Wilt. I … We … Rawick and I … have to stay here. To help Shade. To serve the forest. Thank you for holding us in the world for so long. Now it is time to let go.

Through the white fog Wilt saw two sparks drift and dance across his vision, twirling around each other. At the same time he felt a separation in his mind, a sudden emptiness.

This is where we are meant to be. This is what we were meant to do.

As his vision cleared, Wilt discovered he was sitting alone on the fallen tree. Shade was no longer next to him. On the throne in front of him sat the Guardian, the rich red wood of his carved helm shining in the sunlight as it raised its face to the sky.

'Shade?'

The Guardian seemed only then to notice his presence. 'You. I know you.'

The voice was changed, stronger and louder now, filled with the shift and sway of young saplings, the creak of aged timber, the naked threat of the living trees that loomed around them. It was not Shade's voice, or Delco's. It may have been Rawick's, but Wilt had only heard that in whispers at the edge of his mind.

'You have served your purpose here, wielder. You will be permitted to leave.' The Guardian raised his head, as though sensing the wind. 'The others that are here. The dark ones. They will not be so fortunate.'

The carved helm moved back to face him, and Wilt flinched as the visage twisted into a terrifying rendering of a human face at the height of pain. 'Travel quickly, young spark. The trees are hungry, and not so easy to control. They will not wait long.'

A great wind suddenly gusted through the clearing, throwing whirlwinds of dust and leaves into the air, blinding Wilt completely. He found himself on his feet, arms covering his face as the wind pushed him out of the clearing and branches whipped across him. He stumbled on unthinking, his feet hardly seeming to touch the ground as he was impelled out and away.

The sound in the forest grew as he went, the trees seeming to urge themselves on to greater thresholds of anger and noise.

Every few steps Wilt tried to glimpse his path, but could only see movement and chaos before the dirt blinded him again and he was pushed onward, always out, always away from the heart of the storm.

Finally, with one last great shove he was spat free, stumbling out into clear sunlight, out from the wall of trees lining the edge of the Tangle, into the silence and stillness of open grassland. He collapsed on the ground, his mind a whirl, the rushing tide of the depths calling to him, begging for him to sink down into them, bringing with it a wall of darkness that wrapped around him and wiped his consciousness away.

Part 2

The spark has fulfilled his promise and I am reborn. The world sharpens around me, as though a veil has been lifted from my eyes. The dark abyss of the past has been lit however briefly by his light, the forking branches of possibility revealed. I recognise what has occurred, more voices joining the chorus within me. I feel no loss for the one I used to be. I walk these endless paths, somehow wandering each one simultaneously, parts of my mind racing through the hidden depths of the forest, ejecting what dark creatures remain, cleansing the way.

The trees watch me cautiously as I move through them. Their senses strain to reach me. They do not yet know what to expect from this new Guardian. What form my revenge might take. They fear me once again.

I keep my silence. I remember their tricks, their cruel games, but I look on them as a father does a wayward child. They will be corrected but not punished. Their strange children have disappeared into the past, where they belong, where they will linger until enough time has passed for them to once again be remembered and return to this world.

The elder ones creak and shift in place, their dreams troubled. They know the work is not yet done. The dark stain has been removed from their presence, yet still it remains, the barriers holding it back weakened, leaks springing forth and creatures that should not walk the surface world rushing to escape.

The spark moves on, out of my reach, yet I still feel his connection. Part of his mind now lies within mine. He too feels the pull.

Others are coming, other visitors who share a connection with him. Perhaps they will help me further shape his fate. All of our fates. All tangled around him like the snaggled roots of an elder, delving too deep, too far into the past. Altering what once was.

We have not seen the last of each other. Of that I am certain.

Chapter 20

Wilt woke in the sunlight, face down in the dirt. For a moment he lay perfectly still, soaking in the warmth and heat, until the memory of where he had just been rushed in and he sprang to his feet, ready to face any threat.

There was nothing. He was safe.

He stood at the edge of the Tangle, a single uninterrupted wall of trees facing him. They seemed to shift and sway with the breeze, pulsing back at him a warning as clear as if it were shouted to the heavens.

He turned away from them and headed south, not wanting to provoke any further reaction.

His head felt light and clear, as though a great weight had been lifted. He hadn't been aware how much room inside his mind Delco and Rawick had taken up, or at least how much of his mind was always concentrating on maintaining the connection to them. He felt the sun and the air more fully, as though he had taken two great strides back from the brink of the depths, toward the light and noise of the surface world. Toward humanity.

We're still here, you know.

I know, Higgs. It's just that … I guess I didn't realise how tiring it was becoming, holding you all in there.

It is a danger I have been thinking long about, Wilt. The human mind is not designed to hold such connections for so long. We could be putting you in danger. That is why Nurtle drugged you when she found you, to shut us out, at least for some time. To let you return from the edge.

I'm fine, Biore. There's nothing for you to worry about.

What about Shade?

What about him?

Well, he's gone now too, isn't he? Won't Nurtle want to know what happened to him? How are we supposed to explain that?

Higgs's thought snapped Wilt out of his reverie. He wasn't sure what had happened inside the Tangle himself, so how was he going to explain it to anyone else?

All too soon Wilt found the path under his feet becoming cleared and better maintained as he approached the edge of the village. He stepped off it, knowing it led to the centre of the village, heading instead for the small hut on the outskirts where Nurtle lived. There was nothing else for it, he'd just have to explain what had happened. How he had failed.

'So, wielder. You have news, I expect.' Nurtle stood in the open doorway of her hut, hands planted firmly on her hips. Her mouth was twisted into a frown, and immediately Wilt tried to stutter out an explanation.

'I … Sorry. It's a little …'

Nurtle continued to glower at him for some moments before her face broke into a wide smile and she held her arms out toward him. 'Come here, boy. Today is a momentous day for our family.'

Before he knew what was happening, Wilt was wrapped in a hug, his head pressed deep into Nurtle's chest.

'Let the boy go, woman. He'll pass out from lack of oxygen in there.'

Nurtle's hug relaxed and Wilt pulled his head back to see Jared standing behind them, a wide smile on his face.

As soon as her arms relaxed, Nurtle stepped toward Jared and they linked hands. 'Come, sit down, child.' She waved him inside the hut and pushed a steaming mug of something spicy into his hands.

'It's okay.' She smiled at Wilt's questioning look. 'This is a simple herbal tea. Drink, it will be good for you. We owe you an explanation. Let me begin at the beginning.'

Nurtle and Jared sat next to each other on the bed, facing Wilt, their hands still intertwined as though neither could stand being too far removed from the other.

'You are from Redmondis,' Nurtle began. 'You must know something of what happened to those who refused to submit to the rule of the Nine Sisters.'

'Wildlers.'

Nurtle grinned at the words. 'Yes, that is what they called us, hoping to insult us, I expect. I quite like the term.'

She and Jared locked eyes then, as if some secret message was passing between them. Then Nurtle turned back to Wilt.

'Many years ago, before the rise of the Nine Sisters, Jared and I found ourselves recruited into Redmondis. We each had talent, some of the skill the Black Robes are so proud of. But we differed from them. It didn't take the masters long to recognise that fact.'

Jared took over the telling, his words bleeding into Nurtle's. 'Understand that times were very different then. Many more variations of the skill were accepted, even encouraged. Nurtle and I discovered in each other a kindred spirit of sorts. We shared many things. Many appetites.'

Nurtle slapped Jared's thigh with her free hand. 'That's more than enough of that.'

'What I mean to say, Wilt,' Jared continued, 'is that we found each other's skill complimentary. The way we accessed and shaped the welds worked better together than apart. So much so that the next step seemed the only one that made sense. Some wielders take on other forms, as you know. Others have wards who share part of their minds and some of their powers. We went one step further.'

Oh. I've heard about this.

'We took on each other's form completely. Became one.'

They turned to each other again, smiling shyly at some shared memory before Nurtle took up the story again. 'The Tangle showed us the way. The trees—they share a consciousness while still maintaining separate bodies. But it was not such a simple task, joining in this way. It required work and sacrifice.'

Wilt had a sudden flash of understanding. 'Shade.'

'Yes.' Nurtle's smile twisted into sadness. 'Our child, Shade. He was the product of two wild ones who shared the same mind. Something that shouldn't have been possible. Yet, with the help of the Tangle, it was done.'

Wilt remembered the strange, otherworldly knowledge that lurked within the small boy's eyes. The sense that he was more than human.

'Shade was our gift, and our price. The trees, they are strong, wild, but they require a voice, a Guardian to help guide their appetites. The current Guardian was ageing, had been old for generations already. The Tangle was weakening. Threats haunted its shadows, threats that only a decade ago would never have been possible within its borders. A new shepherd was required, one with a special affinity for the voice of the trees. So Shade was given to us to guide and help to grow. And it became obvious very early on that he was not what you would call a normal child. He was forest touched, forest born. In time he would be called.'

Nurtle's eyes misted over as she spoke. 'And you helped guide him through the transition, Wilt. Somehow, it was eased because of your presence. You helped him to answer the Guardian's call.'

Delco. Rawick. This is why they were needed. This is why we were brought here. Led here, by the forest. By the Guardian itself, I would guess.

'It wasn't me,' Wilt whispered. 'It was Rawick.'

Jared sat up straighter at the name. 'Ah. Rawick. I've heard that name before. The trees have spoken of him. He was another wildler, though he went even further … joined with the welds themselves, it was said. I thought—'

'We thought that meant he had surrendered his life completely. It is good to know that is not the case.'

Jared wrapped his other hand around Nurtle's. 'Now our task here is completed. The trees have told us of the new Guardian, the new strength they feel. It is time for the next phase.'

Wilt looked between them, aware he was missing something. 'What do you mean?'

'This village can no longer survive on the edge of the Tangle,' Jared answered. 'The days of humans entering its depths whenever they wish are over, at least for now. To cleanse itself the Tangle has closed its borders. It will no longer be a source of trade or food for our people.'

Wilt remembered the closed ranks of trees, the loathing he'd felt emanating from them. The naked threat.

Nurtle continued. 'It is time the villagers moved south, away from the dangers lurking in the shadows. The soldiers from the capital will return to Sontair soon. The villagers will travel with them.'

Something in her tone told Wilt what they really meant. 'You're not coming, are you?'

Nurtle smiled and nodded. 'You are a quick one. No, Jared and I have played our parts here. We have a few duties remaining, then perhaps we too will be rewarded with a place within the Tangle's borders.'

Wilt watched them gaze at each other again, saw the way information seemed to flow between their eyes, not requiring words at all.

Just like the trees. They share a consciousness, but it is no longer human.

Wilt had a sudden vision of the tens of thousands of trees that formed the Tangle, and wondered how many of them were once human, like these two. Wild and unsatisfied in their current form. Always seeking something more, some place into which they could sink their roots.

They seemed suddenly aware of Wilt's thoughts and broke off their silent conversation. 'So, Wilt. We wanted to thank you for what you have done. For us. For Shade. Here.'

Nurtle stood and pulled a deep green cloak out from somewhere behind where they had been sitting. 'I always seem to be handing you clothing, don't I? Take off the poor imitation I gave you earlier. Here is a true forest cloak.'

She handed the cloak to Wilt, who took it without thinking. As soon as his fingers touched the soft fabric, a spark flashed through his mind.

'You recognise it, no? It led you to Shade, led Shade himself to where the Guardian needed him to be. Now perhaps it can help lead you to where you need to go. Put it on.'

Wilt found his hands obeying the order before his mind could make sense of the strange rushing sensation still pouring through him. As the cloak settled on his shoulders, it seemed to fit itself around him, nestle into his shape as though wrapping him in a hug.

'It will keep you warm and dry. And should the need ever arise, it will allow you entry into the Tangle. Even the oldest of the trees still recognise its authority.'

A strange whisper ghosted across Wilt's mind at Nurtle's words. A spark floating in the darkness.

'Now go, young wielder. Travel south with the villagers, toward Sontair. Help to keep them safe. The dark stain still spreads and the capital itself seems its most likely source. Seek your answers there, and be always on your guard.'

Jared and Nurtle stood as one, and Wilt let them led him out of the hut, his mind still rushing with the strange floating sensation and a thousand questions he still had.

Tell them to look after Delco.

'Take care of them. Of Shade, and Rawick, and Delco.'

Jared smiled and patted him on the shoulder. 'Have no fear of that, younger wielder. They are more than capable of looking after themselves. And when the time comes, if it does come, look to the north, to the borders of the Tangle. We will be there for you.'

Chapter 21

The wolf slunk slowly forward, eyes fixed on hers, its steps measured and confident. Daemi tried to raise her blade again, but her arm wouldn't respond to her brain's command, and a low simper of pain bubbled over her lips as she tried to force her body to move. It was no use. The muscles across her back and shoulders had been carved open by claws and teeth, and the flow of blood down her spine was now a constant stream as her life leaked out of her. The wolf wavered and blurred as she stared at it, her vision darkening at the edges and stretching into a long narrow tunnel.

The wolf stopped just outside the range of her blade and watched her, licking its lips. All colour drained from the scene as a chill wind blew through, bringing with it a deep, bone-numbing cold.

This is not the way. Not what was or what will be.

Daemi heard the voice, recognised its familiarity but couldn't bring her mind to make any further connection. She fell to her knees.

Come. Let this go, Daemi. Leave this apparition.

The tunnel narrowed again, until all that was left was darkness, and the grinning mouth of the wolf waiting for her.

Wake up.

The mouth opened, and death closed its jaws on her.

'Wake up!'

Daemi sat up quickly, sliding the dagger out from her pillow in one smooth move.

'Whoa! I surrender!'

She blinked in the bright sunlight streaming through the open window of her chamber and let the world arrange itself. Frankle stood at the foot of her bed, his hands held high in the air. 'Sorry, didn't mean to startle you, it's just that Heather said we need to move.'

Daemi stared at him, wondering why he was standing the way he was, until she realised she was still holding her dagger, its tip pointed straight at his chest. She slid it back under her pillow and swung her legs out of bed. 'What time is it?'

'An hour past dawn. Heather said—'

'You should have woken me earlier. We were due to leave at dawn.'

'Heather said we should let you rest, that it would be good for … you know.'

Daemi glared at Frankle, the look on her face sending him backing out of the room, his hands still held high above his head as though he'd forgotten their existence.

'Still, never mind that. I'll meet you downstairs, shall I? Give you time to—'

'Tell Heather I'll be two minutes. Be sure everything is ready.'

'Yes, ma'am.'

Frankle ducked out of the room, away from Daemi's withering glare.

She watched him go, his black robe rippling out behind him as he ran, and shook her head. A boy, just a boy, pretending to be a man, hoping nobody would notice.

And you? Sleeping past your watch? What is your excuse, little girl?

Daemi stood up and stamped across the room to her dresser. A large bowl of icy cold water stood in front of the mirror. She plunged her hands into it and threw water over her face and shoulders, letting the shock of it bring her fully into the waking world.

She stared at her reflection as the water dripped down her face.

It was just a dream. Just another dream.

She turned her shoulder to examine her back in the mirror. The wounds were still closed. All that could be seen was a dull pink scar reaching down from her shoulder and disappearing under her nightshirt.

Good. One less thing to worry about. Now move.

Daemi dressed and gathered her belongings quickly. She was travelling light; they all were, hoping to make the trip to Sontair in a week or so, at least so Petron had promised them. He'd been particularly vague about how they were supposed to cover such a distance in so short a time, but she had learned in the last few weeks not to question him. Petron would find a way, he always did.

You trust him. Almost as much as you trusted Wrex. And look where that got us.

She splashed more water on her face on her way out of the room, washing such thoughts from her mind.

The rest of the travelling party had gathered by the gates of Redmondis and were busying themselves with last-minute adjustments. Heather was helping Frankle into his oversized pack, clapping him on the shoulder as he sagged under its sudden weight, all the blood draining from his face as he struggled to stay on his feet.

Heather watched him stumble and stepped forward to hold him up. 'You see? You don't need to carry so much, Frankle. You're not used to it. Petron said we'll only be gone for around two weeks. Here.'

She pulled the pack off his shoulders and let it drop to the ground with a thud. 'Now lighten it. If it's not at least half the size by the time we get going, I will have to do some reorganisation of my own.'

Frankle looked ready to protest, then stopped as pain flared in his shoulders where the pack's straps had been. He sighed and sat down, opening his bag to see what treasures he could do without. 'You know, we wouldn't have this problem if Petron let us have some horses.'

His grumble faded as he worked, and Heather turned away to see Daemi marching toward them. 'Be quick about it. I don't think Daemi wants any more delays.'

Heather's words gave Frankle's hands speed. He'd already seen the mood Daemi was in. Best not add any fuel to that fire.

'Ready?' Daemi glared down at Frankle and the mess surrounding him, but addressed her words to Heather.

'Just about.' Heather smiled, determined to melt the ice in Daemi's tone.

Daemi dropped her own pack to the ground with a grunt. It was twice the size of Frankle's, yet she seemed to carried it with ease. 'And where're your things?'

Heather gestured proudly to the small shoulder bag she had slung over one arm. It was no larger than a day pack and looked almost empty.

Daemi looked unimpressed. 'You know we're likely to be gone for at least a couple of weeks. Probably more.'

'I know.' Heather patted the bag fondly. 'It's a little trick a crafter friend showed me once.'

To demonstrate, she swung the bag off her shoulder and flipped it open. She reached in and pulled out a large blanket, far too large to have fit inside the bag.

There was a clang as Frankle dropped a round metal bowl in surprise. 'Where did you get that? Why can't I have—'

'Higgs made it, a long time ago.'

Heather's quiet words stopped Frankle's protests immediately.

'I've never been able to get it quite right,' she continued. 'Perhaps it's something you can help me work on, while we're on the road.'

Frankle nodded quickly and turned back to his things, his cheeks flushed.

Daemi stared at the Black Robes' tower, ignoring them both.

'And where's Petron? Don't tell me he slept in too. It's bad enough he's not letting me take any guards with us.'

'Didn't he explain?' Heather replied. 'I mean, he did tell you how we were travelling, didn't he?'

Daemi peered back at Heather, her suspicions raised. 'No, he didn't.' Her eyes narrowed. 'What do you mean?'

Heather just smiled and turned away, looking up at the sky as if studying the weather. 'Shouldn't be long now.'

Daemi's question was answered by a high cry in the distance, and she looked up to see two large eagles circling slowly in the wind far above their heads. The birds spiralled down, their silhouettes growing in size as they sank closer, becoming impossibly large as they came into clear view.

Daemi raised her hand to shield her eyes from the morning sun. There was something odd about one of the shapes in the sky, other than its size. Its outline looked wrong, as though ... There was something attached to its back.

'Oh no.' Daemi dropped her hand and gulped.

The two giant eagles, far too large to be anything other than magical, gave one last lazy circle before banking into a turn and skidding to a stop just metres from them. They were each the size of a large horse, wings stretching fifteen feet across at least, and sitting on the larger one's back in a weirdly shaped saddle was Petron, his eyes wide and tears streaming down his cheeks.

'Good morning!' He waved as he slid off his mount and stumbled toward them, wiping his cheeks clear.

Heather trotted out to greet him, sliding her arm around his back to steady him.

He grinned down at her. 'I'd almost forgotten how disconcerting flying can be.'

'What is that?' Daemi pointed at the enormous bird, her eyes locked on Petron, her tone stern.

'Ah.' Petron patted Heather on the shoulder and gently pushed her away. 'I had a feeling you might have reservations.'

Daemi was about to spit back a reply when she was interrupted by a shimmer in the air and suddenly the smaller of the two great eagles had disappeared. In its place stood two figures, holding hands.

'Sometimes it's best to show rather than tell, dear,' Nurtle said.

Daemi stared back and forth between the two. Nurtle, the healer who had helped close the scars on her back, and another man she hadn't seen before. Her mouth opened and moved, but no sound came out.

'Wildlers.'

Frankle's quiet awe broke the silence and Nurtle and Jared turned to him, their expressions calm, but wary.

'Many things once forbidden have returned, young wielder,' Nurtle replied. 'It would be best to keep your mind open.'

'Oh, I know.' Frankle smiled at her, removing all tension in an instant. 'Believe me, I've already seen ... well. You know.'

He nodded to the long silver blade hanging from Jared's hip. A weld blade, the one he and Heather had formed only days before if he wasn't mistaken. Jared lifted the blade to glint in the sunlight. 'Impressive work, this. Something even Nurtle hadn't thought possible. Of course she'd never admit that out loud.' He winked at Frankle and slid the blade back into place.

'Yes, well.' Nurtle coughed. 'It's good to see evidence of the changes Petron keeps promising me have been made around here. You'll be interested to know the blade also seems to help with our joining. Jared and I hadn't been able to merge fully like that since ...' Nurtle broke off and gestured vaguely around the high rock cliffs that walled them in. 'Since before all of this.'

Frankle was about to quiz them both on this new aspect of the weld blades before Petron interrupted.

'Questions will have to wait. We've spent enough of the day already.' He turned to Daemi, who was still frozen in place, her face grey. 'Daemi? Is this going to be a problem?'

'Um.' Daemi seemed to be trying to force words out, but her throat wasn't giving up the fight just yet.

'Without the aid of this mount it will be weeks before you even reach the southern edge of the Tangle, let alone Sontair. That's if you make it there at all.'

'And if you can even enter the forest.' Nurtle's quiet tone brought all eyes back to her. 'The Guardian has sealed its borders. Even we can no longer pass through. So you must go over.'

Jared patted her lightly on the shoulder, as if comforting some secret pain.

'So we'd best get started then. How do we ...' Heather's eager tone lightened the mood instantly.

'Just climb aboard and hold on. Stax here is an old friend of ours, he knows what he's doing. The saddle is more for your comfort than anything else.' Jared grinned. 'He won't let you fall.'

'And perhaps keep your eyes closed, Daemi,' Petron whispered to her. 'Those without a head for heights may find the experience ... uncomfortable.'

Daemi nodded silently, not wanting any more of her terror to show.

'He'll take it easy on you, I promise. We will travel beside you, at least until the edge of the Tangle. No harm will come to you.' Nurtle turned back to Jared, grasping both his hands in hers and closing her eyes. A moment later the air shimmered with a silver mist and the figures morphed into a single form. The air cleared and an enormous eagle squatted before them, its piercing golden eyes staring through them as its great claws gouged deep groves in the dirt at their feet.

'All aboard,' Petron called. Heather eagerly ran up to the saddled eagle and pulled herself up and onto its back, sinking her fists deep into its feathers. 'Oh! Its lovely and soft. And warm, too. Come on, Frankle.'

Frankle hurried up, hauling his pack off his shoulder to sling it up ahead of him. Heather caught it easily and watched him clamber somewhat less gracefully into position behind her.

'On you go, Daemi. Try not to worry, it's perfectly safe.' Petron kept his voice low, not wanting to add any fresh bruises to her ego.

'I know … it's just—'

'Something you have to learn, young lady, is the ability to let go. Trust in your friends, they are all we truly have in this life.' Petron patted her gently on the shoulder and pushed her forward.

Daemi stumbled into a walk, then a trot, as though her legs had forgotten how to move forward and she didn't want to allow them to freeze into place again. She pulled herself up onto the great bird with a grunt and wrapped her arms around Frankle's narrow hips.

'That tickles.'

'Be quiet. I don't want to hear another word from either of you until we're back on solid ground.'

With that she closed her eyes, sinking into herself to try to maintain control in the face of her fear.

Petron ran a hand over the great head of the eagle, staring into its golden eyes. 'Take care of them.'

He turned to the other eagle, seemingly still focused on its task of ploughing the dirt. 'And return quickly. We still have much to do.'

With that both eagles dropped their heads and sprang into the air, Heather letting out a wild whoop of joy as they rose high into the sky and left the cold stone of Redmondis behind.

Chapter 22

The great eagle banked slowly in the cold rushing wind, sinking ever lower in the sky, angling toward the treetops tens of metres below.

Heather clung to its neck, her fists wrapped in its feathers, her heart leaping with each soaring turn. It was magical, beyond anything she had ever experienced before. The freedom, the power. She closed her eyes and tried to capture the feeling in her memory, box it in, keep it safe, aware even as she did so that she would never be able to truly replicate the exhilaration of flight. Still, she was determined to try.

Seated behind her, Frankle stared down at the Tangle stretched out like a green carpet below them. He could feel its power, its threat, just as he could recognise some part of the wielder's art in the eagle's form he rode upon. Recognise it, but never replicate it. This skill was too wild, too close to the edge. Too dangerous. The same menace radiated out from the Tangle below. So this is what it meant to be a wielder outside the security of Redmondis. Always on guard, always in danger of losing yourself.

Clinging to his waist, Daemi sat with her eyes clenched shut, a low murmur tumbling over her lips the only sign that she was conscious. She was chanting to herself, controlling her terror by limiting her awareness to the cadence of the words and nothing else. The wind rushed past her face, but she pushed all thought of it and what it meant away, drowning it in the rhythm of her chant. She would survive this. Survive it and never speak of it again.

The eagle let out another wild cry and banked again, sinking ever closer to the treetops.

'What is it doing?' Frankle screamed into Heather's ear, trying to be heard against the roaring wind.

'We're going to land,' Heather shouted in reply.

'What?'

Heather smiled at Frankle's cry and turned back to the front, determined to soak up as much of this experience as possible.

Sure enough the eagle seemed to spot what it was looking for and banked into a spin, sinking lower with each revolution.

Daemi's arms tightened around Frankle's waist until he squirmed in discomfort.

In moments they had sunk below the tops of the trees, spiralling down toward a small clearing that only now became clear to their human eyes. The ground rushed up at them, and Heather felt a moment of panic as it seemed they were about to plough directly into the earth, before the eagle reared back at the last second, skidding to a halt on its outstretched legs.

Suddenly they were still, the eagle bending its head low and turning one eye toward its passengers, waiting for them to take the hint.

'I guess we're here,' Heather said, sliding easily off the eagle's back.

'Where exactly is here?' Frankle replied, pulling at Daemi's arms, which were still firmly locked around his waist. 'Daemi, you can let go now.'

Daemi peeked one eye open to make sure they were on the ground, then released Frankle from her vice-like grip and tumbled quickly off the great eagle. 'The Tangle,' she murmured, staring around her at the thick ring of trees that bordered the small clearing. 'Why did we land here?'

Frankle was having trouble getting his legs untangled from his robe and over to one side of the eagle and he fell face first onto the forest floor. Daemi reached down and pulled him to his feet.

As soon as all three had dismounted and retrieved their packs, the eagle leaped back up into the sky, its enormous wings taking it up and out of their reach within seconds, a thick cloud of dust blinding them as it left.

With three beats of its wings it was away, disappearing out of view. The dust slowly settled around them and they dropped their arms from where they held them to shield their eyes.

'Well, I guess we're on our own,' Heather said, turning back to the others.

'Perhaps not.' Frankle pointed past her shoulder to the far side of the clearing.

Daemi followed his gaze and drew her blade, stepping in front of the other two. Standing just at the edge of the small clearing, in the shadows of the trees was a man wearing a green flowing robe and a complicated, horned helm. The man stood perfectly still, watching them.

'Uh, Daemi, I don't—' Whatever Heather had been about to say was lost as the man raised his right arm in a sort of wave or salute, palm outward.

Then he closed his fist, and the world disappeared.

A song echoed in the darkness, flowing in and out of range, its tune forming the boundaries of the blackness Heather floated in. As she listened to the tune her lips formed into a smile, her body reacting before her mind recognised the heartstone's song. She opened her eyes.

She was lying on a bed of thick moss at the base of an enormous tree, its uppermost branches too high to see, its thick trunk seeming to loom over her as she stared up at it, the sky spinning around its axis until she felt dizzy and had to look away.

It was then that she noticed the small boy sitting next to her on a large, overgrown root. He was holding the heartstone's sounding bowl in his lap, one hand hovering over it, a rapt expression on his face. For the briefest flash she thought it was Higgs, then the last webs of dream fell away from her mind and she could clearly see this was someone else.

Heather raised herself up on one arm, aware somehow that she was perfectly safe, that there was nothing to be concerned about.

The boy looked over at her and a smile lit up his dark features. He moved his hand away from the sounding bowl and its song faded out. He put the bowl back onto the round with a sheepish grin.

'It's all right.' Heather sat up completely and saw all of her belongings set out on the ground.

The boy smiled again, his eyes clouded and shy.

'It seems you've been busy.' Heather reached out to pack her things into her bag, then stopped as a thought occurred to her. She held up the small crafter's bag. 'How did you open this? It's only supposed to respond to my touch.'

The boy sprang to his feet and walked a few steps away, watching her stuff her belongings back into her bag. Finally she finished and jerked the drawstring closed.

She stood up and offered her hand. 'My name is Heather.'

The boy blushed and stepped toward her, snatching her hand before dropping it again and stepping back away. It was almost as though he feared her.

Shade.

Heather watched him, rubbing her fingers together where they had touched his hand. They were tingling strangely, and she suddenly knew that something important was happening.

'This is the Tangle, isn't it? We landed in the Tangle.'

The boy nodded and smiled again.

Heather's brain didn't seem able to gather its thoughts in order, as though her mind was being channelled down a narrow stream, its high banks only allowing for certain questions. 'Shade. I feel like I should know that name.'

The boy giggled then and sprung past her, leaping up the tree to perch on a wide branch directly above her.

Heather studied the strange child, his shock of black hair half covering a grimy face, his grey eyes bright and knowing. He was younger than Higgs, but there was definitely a resemblance.

'You remind me of someone I used to know.'

Shade rewarded that with another grin and leaped higher, up to another branch.

A sudden thought stopped her. The sounding bowl should only have reacted to the heartstone that Higgs and she wore, just as her bottomless pouch was only supposed to open for her touch.

Tears sprang to the corners of her eyes. This was a dream. It had to be.

Shade spun around the trunk to appear on another branch, flitting in and out of her view, drawing her eyes ever higher up the tree as he climbed.

Inside the depths, and inside your heart.

If you're looking for him, that's where you should start.

Tears flowed freely down Heather's cheeks as she stared up into the heights. The sky was spinning again, taking her consciousness with it.

The dark shape of the boy disappeared into the mist of the upper reaches of the tree, and Heather felt herself falling as the world around her spun into oblivion.

When he next knew conscious thought, Frankle found himself walking alone along a narrow forest trail, the trees on either side of the path looming over him, curving to form a high canopy that filtered the sunlight into a strangely blurred glow, as though he was walking through a memory.

He couldn't be sure where he was, or how he had come to be there, but he felt no concern. He wasn't lost, or late for some appointment, or forgetting some task he had been sent to perform. He simply walked, enjoying the fresh air in his lungs, tracing his fingers lightly over the tree trunks he passed.

Suddenly another figure was walking beside him, matching his stride. He didn't look over to see who it was, just accepted their presence. He felt no curiosity or cautiousness. He just let the dream flow over him.

'You've come a long way since we last spoke, Frankle.'

Delco. He smiled but continued staring straight ahead. 'I've been shown many things. A lot has changed.'

'Oh, yes. Tell me, how are the other Black Robes adjusting?'

Frankle's smile widened as he thought of his friends in Redmondis, those who had been with him through the dark days and others he had met since. 'They're well. Most are still there, growing in knowledge. Petron is in charge of things now. He's encouraged the wielders and crafters to work closer together.'

'The "lesser skilled".'

Frankle chuckled. 'Yes. That's a term that's fast fallen out of fashion. The boundaries have blurred between our two schools. It's already producing surprising results.'

'That is good to hear. I'm glad you're enjoying yourself more.'

'Me too.'

Frankle stared down the path, unable or unwilling to turn and study his old friend. A small voice in the back of his mind was whispering to him now, whispering something important, something he didn't want to hear just yet.

'Although, I'm not sure how much longer I can stay in Redmondis. Since—'

'Since it happened.'

'Yes. It's become clear to me the high stone walls protect us, but they also blinker us somehow. We need to spend more time in the real world if our skills are to be of any real use to people.'

'You have grown in wisdom, Frankle. And here you are, outside those walls, on a quest of your own. You are already taking the first steps.'

Frankle looked around, aware that the air had changed, the light brightening, the dream ending.

'Be sure you don't forget what you learned in those days you would rather not remember. Be sure you can still recognise the dark when you next encounter it.'

The secret voice in Frankle's mind was louder now, though he still avoided picking out its words. He wanted to turn toward Delco, just for one moment, but his neck wouldn't move.

'You aren't really here, are you, Delco? I saw your body. Your remains.'

A tingle of fear tickled up Frankle's spine as he spoke. He didn't want to anger whatever it was that walked beside him, but when the voice spoke again it sounded just as warm as before.

'You know better than that by now, Frankle, surely. You've seen beyond the surface world. You know the depths that the welds draw their power from. Do you doubt there are other places you are not yet aware of, eddies within the greater flow that—'

'It doesn't matter,' Frankle cut in, aware suddenly that he was running out of time. 'I'm just glad to speak with you again. I wanted to thank you, for looking after me, for helping me when you did. And I wanted to tell you I remember that, and I'll keep trying to live up to your example. I won't let you down.'

The glow surrounding him brightened again, the air warming in an amused smile.

'Goodbye, Frankle. We will talk again, I promise. Keep on your path.'

The presence next to him halted, but Frankle walked on, the surrounding glow blurring away the trees, his consciousness disappearing into the fog.

Daemi opened her eyes and lay still, watching the leaves far above her shift and sway in the wind. The damp smells of the forest filled her nose, and the thick moss underneath her formed a surprisingly comfortable bed. She let herself wake up slowly, enjoying the tingle of each of her senses coming up to speed, then sighed to herself, aware suddenly that she was keeping somebody waiting.

She sat up, feeling rested for the first time in weeks, months perhaps. There had been no dreams to trouble her, no flashes of the past or glimpses of the future, no visions seen through other eyes. Just blank emptiness.

She was sitting in a small forest clearing, her bed of moss under a high tree at one end. In the centre of the clearing rows of fallen trees seemed to have been twisted and shaped into primitive benches, polished pews all facing away from her, toward the other end of the clearing and a large timber throne. In it sat a strange creature. A long green cloak rising seemingly from the forest floor itself to a carved wooden helm that covered the creature's head, twisting into twin horns, antlers almost, that reached up toward the sky high above.

'Good morning, Daemi.'

The words echoed in her mind rather than her ears, and with them came an instant knowledge. This was the Guardian. The heart of the Tangle.

'I hope you will forgive the … theatre of this.' The Guardian waved his hand dismissively round the clearing. 'A relic of former times. Former lives. Still, it is important to keep the past always in mind, if we wish to avoid making the same mistakes.'

The Guardian's hand waved again and a sudden vision of fire and battle washed over Daemi. Out of the thick smoke a large grey wolf stalked toward her, its eyes locked on hers. Then, just as quickly as it had come, the vision disappeared.

'It must be troubling, this connection you share. With the past, with other eyes. With the depths themselves. Especially for one not trained to deal with such power.'

The hand waved again, and the vision returned, the wolf almost upon her now, drool dripping from its open maw, its golden eyes burning through her soul. Its jaws stretched wide, ready to take her, to consume her and force her to leave life behind.

'But enough of that.'

Instantly the vision was gone, and she was back in the clearing, her panting breath the only sign that anything out of the ordinary had occurred.

'Wilt seems to have opened more than one door. My predecessor believed he held the power to save all of us from what lies below, from what is even now bleeding to the surface. The trees share that faith. I have known them my whole life, I know something of their nature, so I reserve the right to harbour doubts as to their true purpose.

'This connection you share is of course the reason for your troubled dreams. You have become a target. Perhaps I can help to ease this pain.'

Somehow, without seeming to move, the Guardian stood directly before her, his great horns looming over her, twisting up into the branches of the tree. His cloak parted, and a single gloved hand reached out to her, as though to help her to her feet. Without thinking, she grasped it.

Once again reality was washed away, and she found herself in another place, a wide open sky of stars stretched out above her, the coals of a low campfire lighting the scene with a dim orange glow. A hand was still clasped in hers, though this one was not gloved. It was warm, and familiar. It squeezed hers softly.

She looked to the side, and there lay Wilt, staring back at her.

Chapter 23

Wilt knew he was dreaming, but he didn't care. He could feel Daemi's hand in his, hear her breath moving in and out of her lungs, see the steam rise from her lips as the living warmth blew into the cold night air. He lay perfectly still, not wanting to do anything that would cause the dream to end.

A sudden breeze blew through the campsite, turning the low burning coals of the campfire a deep orange, and wiping the dream away. With it came another vision, a wall of trees swaying in the wind, beckoning him, lulling him into other dreams, other minds.

A shadowed figure flitting in and out of the dappled sunlight of the forest, moving impossibly quickly, patrolling its borders, hunting out that which did not belong.

A shimmering weld wall, a lone young Black Robe standing before it, reaching out to it with a shining silver blade.

An icy shock down her spine as the nightmare form reaches out and tears its claws through her armour to burn deep gashes into her back.

A heartstone, sitting in a stone bowl, its song filling the room.

Wilt sat up, instantly awake. The low fire cast its orange glow across the scattered camp, and beyond its reach the night was spotted with other fires, other sleeping figures. To the north the darkness was deeper, no fires stretching in that direction, and a cold wind whistled down from the distant mountains to flow through the camp.

Wilt turned to face the breeze, enjoying its touch on his cheeks.

You miss them, don't you?

Of course.

Do you think what we see … do you think it's what is really happening to them, or has happened? Or do you think—

I don't know, Higgs. You're supposed to be the clever one.

Petron said wielders and wards can share their minds, that it allows them to see what the other is doing, feel what they're feeling. But I've never heard of a wielder having more than one ward.

I don't think it's about wards. It's the welds, the links between us, between our minds. Besides, most of those visions were from other memories.

Delco, standing in front of the weld wall. I saw that.

And I did not, though you told me about it. That vision was from your memory, not mine.

Perhaps we're bleeding into each other, our memories crisscrossing and jumbling together. One more thing we should watch out for.

Wilt's thoughts were interrupted by the heavy boots of a guard marching past the border of his camp, patrolling the edge of the great sprawling exodus of villagers and soldiers that he was at the back end of. Wilt watched him pass, saw his eyes scanning the night, his hand resting on the handle of the axe on his hip.

Nervous. He doesn't believe we've left the danger behind in the Tangle.

I think he's right.

Wilt stared out into the darkness to the north, back toward the Tangle, its closed borders, the now empty villages spotted along its edge. Deserted, dead towns, stripped of all life.

Biore, do you think Del—the Guardian will be able to stop them, the dark things that attacked us?

No. I think the Guardian will keep the Tangle secure, but that won't stop whatever those things were from rising in other areas. You heard what Jared told us. Other villages and towns have been attacked, not just the ones inside the Tangle. From the sounds of things, everyone's retreating to the capital for protection.

The guard continued on his patrol, disappearing into the heavy shadows. Wilt watched him leave, then lay down and rolled over, putting his back to the warmth of the fire, waiting for sleep to take him.

The air was noticeably warmer now, and the few villagers who travelled toward the rear of the long, haphazard column had removed their cloaks in the heat of the day. Wilt hadn't even thought about removing his, he didn't feel hot in the slightest. He recognised the change in the air, but it was as if the temperature couldn't penetrate him. He rubbed his fingers across the stone ring on his left hand, accepting the surge of fire as he touched it with his mind. Perhaps he was beyond feeling any temperature changes. Perhaps he was no longer human enough.

Perhaps it's just the forest cloak Nurtle gave us.

Or that. Wilt chuckled at his dark thoughts and attempted to push them away. The sun was shining, the path they trod was dry and flat, the fields to either side of them shining bright green with the growth of early spring. Even the river that curled past them on one side shone, glinting silver in the sunlight.

The Boroni. It will widen as we continue south, until it wraps around the walls of Sontair itself on its way to the far sea. Its source is high in the mountains, above Redmondis, and it cuts a lone path through the Tangle on its journey south. Its waters are cold and deep. And troubled.

Wilt watched the river flow past them, the current flowing faster than they moved, though its surface seemed calm enough.

If it goes all the way to Sontair, then why don't we let it carry us along, instead of marching like fools beside it in the hot sun?

Many others have had the same thought before, young Higgs. And no one has ever seen them again. You note none of the villagers or soldiers have suggested such a plan. They know better.

Some of the other travellers seemed to be sharing Wilt's

thoughts. More than one of them glanced toward the rushing waters before dropping their heads and marching on. They had just left one menace behind, they weren't eager to wade into another.

There was something strange about the surface of the water, something suggestive about the way it swirled and twisted. On impulse Wilt dropped into himself and sent out a weld.

A rushing tide, a swirling chaos. A deep coldness, an ache, reaching for warmth, for life. Dark depths, watching the lights far above, waiting to rise.

Wilt snapped back up to the surface world with a gasp.

There's something there, in the depths. Something ancient.

Something not to be disturbed. Come, Wilt, leave such dark thoughts. We have a long way to travel.

Wilt nodded and turned his eyes south, away from the river.

Chapter 24

Petron sat alone in his chamber, his chair turned to face the open sky, his eyes closed, feeling the wind against his cheeks and remembering the soar and bank of flight. If he let his mind go, let it float free in the memory, he could almost lose himself in it. Almost remember the doorway in his mind that led to that form, the doorway that was now lost to him. The doorway that perhaps no longer even existed.

A single tear rolled down his cheek, cold against the wind, and he felt himself being pulled back.

He opened his eyes to stare out across the sky, his mind still somewhere in the past. A knock at the door brought him completely back, and he stood to greet his visitor.

'Master Petron.' A young guard strode into the room and saluted, his boot heels clicking together to send an echo bouncing around the thick stone walls of the chamber.

Petron returned the salute with a wave and a smile. They were so serious, these soldiers.

'What do you have for me, Pierce?'

The guard seemed taken aback by the use of his name, but quickly regained his composure.

'Uh, the last allocation of the moonsteel—'

'Weld blade, Pierce, please. Let us all learn to use its proper name,' Petron corrected gently.

'Yes, sir. Weld blades. The quartermaster reports that the last allocation has been dispensed. We're awaiting more from the crafters.'

'Tell the master he shall have them by the end of the week. The wielders and crafters are working as fast as they can to replicate Heather and Frankle's work. It is slow going now without them here to help, but we will get there.'

'Yes sir.' The guard snapped into another salute.

'And tell your master to send me five of his best men by sundown. I have a task for them.'

'Yes sir!' Pierce's salute was even more vigorous this time. Every Redmondis guard was desperate for action. They'd spent weeks on end training and drilling within the high stone walls. There would be a clamour of volunteers for this new duty.

Petron waved him out of the room as a high cry echoed out from the open sky.

In the far distance, only just visible against the grey, a black shape approached, gaining in size even as Petron watched.

Moments later the shadow had coalesced into the form of a giant eagle, its enormous wings beating heavily against the rushing wind. Petron watched it, not allowing his thoughts free rein, refusing to let his mind return to that place of want and loss.

They know how much it costs you, seeing them together. Don't make it any harder for them.

He turned away from the opening and began preparing a large pot of tea over the fire, busying his hands as he contemplated what they had planned. The guards were a precaution; he doubted they would be needed. No, the danger tonight would not be physical.

'Petron.'

He finished pouring the tea and turned toward the voice, holding out two steaming cups.

'Nurtle. Jared. You made great time.'

The road to the Redmondis garrison was still rutted with deep trenches at regular intervals, but the high guard towers that had once spiked up along its length hadn't been rebuilt. Their rubble and lumber had been cleared up and carted away for use in other parts of Redmondis, and the only remaining trace of them were a few indentations in the land where their foundations had once stood.

The trenches too had fallen into disrepair. If Petron had had his way, these too would have been filled in and the twisting network of tunnels that linked them collapsed in on themselves, but even he had to admit finally that the effort required would not be worth it. Instead the tunnel entrances had been sealed to ensure no curious wanderers stumbled into harm, and the rest was left to time to do its work.

The guards had been agreeable, eager even, to help break down the defences that surrounded the garrison. Those who had willingly followed Cantor Cortis in his ill-fated uprising had either fallen in battle or scattered to the winds once his reign had been overthrown, and the remaining guards were keen to wash the stain of that dark time in their history from the land.

Petron had made things clear. No longer would Redmondis require a fortress heart in which to squat and hide. The new Redmondis they were building required nothing more than the skills of its members—wielders, crafters, and guards—working together to become more than their individual parts. The weld blades were just the most recent example of this. Redmondis was flourishing, growing in size and power. It had no reason to fear.

Petron watched the small guard patrol he had requested spread out across the road in front of him, scrutinising each trench they passed, each shadow, on alert for any sign of a threat.

'They're wasting their time. There's nothing here,' Jared mumbled.

'They know that. They're just … keeping in shape,' Petron replied.

'Perhaps they grow impatient as well,' Nurtle added, squeezing Jared's hand in hers. 'They do your leadership proud, these soldiers, Petron. They respect you.'

'They have good teachers, that is all.'

The group moved past another line of trenches, and Petron

shuddered at a cold touch on his shoulders as they passed the small sealed door hidden in the shadows.

Nurtle raised her head as if sniffing the wind. 'Something remains here, soaked into the land. You feel it, Petron.'

'I do.'

'Good. That is what we will use. That will be our key.'

'Our key to where?'

'To the depths themselves, Petron. To the darkness that hides within them. To the threat we have yet to face.'

The guards had reached the end of the road and were standing at attention by the great double door that led inside the garrison. Petron sighed as he stared up at it, unable to push the memory of the last time he had been here from his mind.

He stepped forward and slowly traced his fingers in an intricate design across the centre of the door, then stood back and whispered something in a language none of the guards could understand. A deep glow surged seemingly within the timber itself, then flashed as the magical barrier dropped away. Petron waved to the guards, and they stepped forward to lean their shoulders against its weight. With a grudging sigh the heavy door swung open.

'Come then,' Petron whispered. 'Let's see what still lurks in the dark.'

The guards plunged through, into the shadows.

Moments later Petron stood on the threshold of the garrison, sniffing the stale air that wafted out, waiting for the guards to give the all clear. It smelled of metal and blood, the scent of battle still lingering, clinging to the cold stone walls.

'This place needs a good airing out.' Jared coughed and shifted his feet as they waited.

'The door was sealed for a reason,' Petron said.

'And now we open it for a reason,' Nurtle replied. 'It is never a good idea to lock our troubles away. They can only grow and fester.'

'All clear, Master Petron.' A guard appeared out of the shadows.

'Very good. Two of you take positions outside. Close the door behind us and don't allow anyone in or out unless I give the order personally.'

Petron strode past the guard and Nurtle and Jared followed, hands still locked together. As soon as they entered the garrison, the heavy door swung shut behind them with a low boom.

The shadows seemed to melt into retreat as they moved into the entrance chamber, their eyes adjusting quickly to the dim light that seeped in from some hidden window in the ceiling high above. Three guards remained at attention on the far side of the room, and Petron waved them on as he walked.

'Can you still feel it?' Nurtle asked.

Petron nodded and continued on in silence. The cold dread he had first felt on the approach to the garrison was stronger now, its weight sinking over his shoulders like an old cloak. Wrapping itself around him and settling in.

The guards ahead darted in and out of their path as they proceeded into the building, ducking into side rooms to ensure no threats were missed. Petron guided Nurtle and Jared along a particular path, taking sudden turns left and right seemingly at random, feeling his way along the twisting corridors, guided by the chill that crept ever closer to his heart.

Finally he stopped by the entrance to a side room, his head bowed.

'What is it, Petron? Is it Cortis?' Nurtle whispered.

Petron shook his head, unable to form the words. He waved vaguely into the room, his hand dropping limply to his side and his shoulders shuddering.

Jared and Nurtle stepped past him into the chamber. It was bare except for a long table in the centre. No, not a table. A rack. A device for torture.

Nurtle looked around, noting the heavy shackles that hung from the far wall, and the deep brown stains soaked into the timber of the rack. She squeezed Jared's hand in sudden comprehension. 'Come. Petron doesn't need to see this.'

She bustled Jared out and slipped her free arm into Petron's, pulling him past the doorway to leave the silent chamber behind.

What is it?

Jared's question bloomed in her mind.

It is the place where Wrexley was broken. The place where Petron lost everything. Her response was couched in sensations of empathy and terror. Both Jared and Nurtle knew in their hearts that they could never survive such a separation, and the very idea of it sent a cold shiver of dread aching through them. Petron and Wrexley were wielder and ward, not quite as deeply connected as the wildlers who had been forced out of Redmondis, not quite as without limit in the sharing of souls, but a deep bonding of minds nevertheless. To have it torn away would drive most men mad.

A whimper escaped Petron as they continued away from the room, his head still bowed and face in shadow, but the further they walked the more strength he seemed to gain, until he raised his head and shook himself free of Nurtle's supporting arm. His eyes blazed, a deep anger fuelling the fire inside them.

'Come. Cortis is not far. What is left of him.'

The guards had already scouted ahead and stood at attention by a doorway at the end of the corridor. Petron's step quickened as they approached it, eager now to face the chill that still clutched at him.

Through the door the room opened out into a wide formal chamber, much bigger than most of the rooms they had passed by. It was circular, the stone walls bent and curved strangely to form pockets of shadow for guards to lurk in, and in the middle of the room carved stone steps led up to a small stage of sorts, a platform dominated by a single large throne. Sitting on the throne was a corpse, a shrunken, shrivelled husk. Long dead.

Petron stood at the base of the steps leading up to the throne, fists clenched and shaking. He looked ready to charge up the steps and strike the remains of the man who had taken so much away from him, but he held himself in place.

Nurtle stepped past him, patting him gently on the shoulder as she went, still clinging to Jared with her other hand. Neither of them wanted to let go, not here, not with what they could sense haunting the place. Both were secretly terrified that if they dropped their hands they would somehow never get their connection back.

As they moved closer, it was clear the body on the throne was not simply a desiccated corpse. Its skin was shrunken against the bone, its eyes hollow craters staring at them from the other side of life. It looked wholly unnatural. The normal stages of decay should have broken the body down much further by this stage; all that remained should be just stripped bones and dust. Something had preserved this form, almost as if to leave a reminder for all who witnessed it of what waited for them once the light of life was snuffed out.

'Cantor Cortis,' Nurtle whispered. She wanted to touch the thing, to feel its reality, to be sure of what she was witnessing, but her instincts halted her hand as soon as it reached out.

'What is it?' Jared could sense her unease.

'I don't … I'm not sure. But I don't think anyone should touch it.'

As if in response, a chill wind breathed through the room, its taste stale and cold.

'I thought the door was closed,' Jared said.

'It is,' Petron replied. 'This draft comes from deep within the tunnels that riddle this place.'

The breeze died as quickly as it had appeared.

'Now we are here, what is it exactly you had in mind, Nurtle?' Petron's voice was stronger now, clearer, as if all doubt and fear had been shrugged away.

'I'm not sure,' Nurtle admitted, turning back to face him.

'Hold!' Jared's urgent call brought all three guards sprinting up to the platform, their weapons drawn, eyes scanning the room for any threat.

'Jared?'

Jared pointed past Nurtle's shoulder, his finger shaking, to where Cortis's remains perched on its throne. 'It moved.'

Chapter 25

Wilt sat close to the small fire, though there was no chill in the air. The campsite was quiet, the weary travellers making the most of the opportunity to rest. He stared into the flames of his campfire, enjoying the feeling of them cleansing his mind.

Just like we used to do. In Greystone.

Wilt smiled, then stared out into the dark.

There's a lot more space here than we had in Greystone. A lot more world than we ever imagined.

Speak for yourself. I was always destined for great things.

Wilt turned back to the fire. The only sounds in the night were the crackle of flames and the occasional splash of movement from the river, shrouded in darkness.

We should not have camped so close to the Boroni.

The thought immediately snapped Wilt out of his reverie. He held his breath as he listened, searching for some clue to the sudden tension in the air, but there was nothing to hear.

Are you trying to scare us, Biore?

It's too quiet. Where are the guards?

Wilt sprang to his feet and looked around. Biore was right, there was no sign of the usual guards patrolling the edge of the stretched column of travellers.

Perhaps they've relaxed their patrols, now we've left the Tangle behind.

Whatever attacked us in the Tangle is just as likely to strike here, Higgs.

But the Guardian closed the borders.

Higgs is right, wasn't the goal to seal whatever those creatures were in?

The Boroni flows through the Tangle, Wilt. The trees can't close that.

Another splash from the direction of the river brought Wilt's eyes around and his hand to the weld blade on his hip. He stepped away from the light of the fire to allow his eyes to better penetrate the darkness.

It's no good. There's no moon, the night is too dark to see anything.

Use your other sight, boy. Use the gifts you have been given.

Wilt obeyed the command without thinking, and padded further out into the inky darkness on four feet, his cat's vision cutting through the gloom with ease. To one side of the campsite flowed the Boroni, its troubled surface rippling and swirling with the fast flowing current. The river seemed pure silver to the cat's sight, but no shape broke its surface.

Nothing. There's nothing there.

A sudden flare of light from the edge of the camp gave the lie to that thought. Sparks crackled into the air as a campfire was kicked by a flailing leg, and a very human cry of pain cut through the unnatural silence of the night. Suddenly chaos broke out on all sides.

They are already among us. You have another form, Wilt. Give it full rein.

Wilt felt the hunger in Biore's voice, and knew the danger that indulging such a craving could lead to, but he had no other choice. The cat disappeared and darkness itself seemed to take its place as the wraith sliced through the night, arrowing straight toward the sounds of battle.

To Wilt's eyes the world was a grey, flat plain, lit here and there by firelight and the brighter flash of life, a glow that called to him, urging him onward to reach out and extinguish it. Glimmering shapes lay all around him, prone bodies still wrapped in sleep, unaware of the dangers that threatened not metres away. Further on, at the edge of the camp closest to the river, a struggling figure seemed to be wrestling with the night itself before falling in a heap, its light fading into the soil. There.

He blinked across the campsite, arriving just as the last of the light from the human form seemed to melt into the grey of the landscape. From the direction of the river, what looked like enormous black crabs were scuttling over each other, pouring out of the waters to flow over their waiting victims. They were about the same size as the wild boars Wilt had hunted in the Tangle, though now and then one reared up on its hind legs and became large enough to strike a man in the chest.

The first few travellers taken didn't know what hit them. They were swamped in moments, flailing under the swarm of creatures, their cries of sudden terror smothered by the evil things that ended them so effortlessly.

Wilt reached his hand out to the closest creature, his fingers a twisting nest of thin black welds that shot out toward it. As they struck they seemed to fuse into the thing, not slowing it for a second, and Wilt felt only the briefest glimpse of a connection, a yawning cavern of silence where the creature's mind should have been.

The nightmare form turned and darted straight at him, leaping at the last moment to land squarely on his chest. Were he in human form his life would have ended then, sucked out of him in a flash of pain as claws ripped him apart. But Wilt was no longer simply human, he was something more. The creature fell through the black mist of welds that was Wilt, and the surface world dropped away as they both sunk into the chaos of the depths.

He was riding a horse, the sun hot on his back as he bounced in the saddle. Catherine rode beside him, her long blonde hair flowing in the wind, falling across her shoulders until she reached up to pull it back, and then turned to smile at him. He returned the smile and urged his mount on, faster and faster, each racing the other to the edge of the river bank, to the shaded spot they'd discovered weeks ago. Their secret place. Where they could rest and be sure of no disturbance. Where they could lay together. Where nothing else mattered.

—Wilt.—

The world shifted, and he was standing in a darkened hut, a blacksmith's hut. Standing beside his father, holding tight to his enormous hand as they watched the smith do his work. The blacksmith wielded a hammer bigger than his head, bigger even than the tools in his father's workshop. He doubted even his father could lift the thing, and his father was the strongest man in the village. The smith struck down on the anvil one last time, then doused the blade he was shaping in a large bucket, sending clouds of steam into the air. He coughed and wiped his eyes to clear them, then stared as the smith smiled and held the small sword out to him, hilt first. 'Go on,' his father urged. 'It's yours.'

—Wilt, these are not your memories. Don't lose yourself in the welds. Come back to the surface.—

Seline lay on the pillow, trying to catch her breath, adrenaline coursing through her as she stared up at the beams of the ceiling, willing them to stay in place as the world spun around her. His hand tightened on her shoulder, and she tried to smile in return but her face would not obey. Then the midwife urged her again, and the pain took over, until the world suddenly opened with a baby's cry, calling out to its mother, calling out to her.

—Biore, what can we do? It's too much, too much to hold. Too fast.—

—These must be the memories of people the creature has already taken. Maybe if we try to redirect the flow to …—

Her sword slashed down, cutting directly through the weak point at the shoulder of her attacker. The soldier fell with a choked cry, and she spun around to face the next one, aware there was no time to think, just act, trust her training and her honed instincts. Her blade shot out and up, parrying the death blow that had been slicing down at her head. She wheeled around with the force, allowing her blade to drop as she pirouetted, then reversed its direction and slashed across the soldier's belly.

—Someone closer. That's it. We have to direct them out of the flow, back into Wilt's mind. This one. Hold this one.—

She was bent over double, hands on her knees, hair falling over her face and sweat dripping from her forehead to mingle with the blood pooling on the ground. Breathe. Recover. There are more coming.

She stood up and held her blade directly out, challenging her next victim. It was a wolf, far larger than was natural, its eyes filled with a knowledge that was more than animal, more than human. It padded toward her, its bared teeth grinning in anticipation.

—Daemi. We're seeing through Daemi's eyes. How is that possible?—

—She shares a very strong connection with Wilt. This is a memory, a dream, not to be trusted. But it might just be something we can use.—

The wolf sprang, its front paws on her impossibly quickly, and it was all she could do to fall and roll with its momentum, allowing the wolf's claws to rake her chest piece, trusting in the strength of the steel, then bouncing to her feet. The wolf was quicker still, already in the air, launching at her legs now, knocking her feet from under her to send her cart-wheeling over its back. As she spun she glimpsed bright blue sky and the shadow of an eagle high above, circling the battle.

She landed on her knees and only just brought her blade up in time to bat the wolf's next strike away. It adjusted its leap in mid-air, twisting to the side and out of reach, landing on all four feet and circling her, its grin now a snarl of frustration, its eyes wary of this human's speed and skill. Still, it was confident. It was faster. Too fast for her.

—Here. Let me try. I think I can ...—

A shadow passed over the wolf's vision then, a strange black mist that took its attention away. Something foreign, something that didn't belong, not in this world, not in this time. Its hackles raised and a low growl emanated out of its throat.

—Biore? What are you doing? Where are you … ?—

—It's the only way, the only way to bring him back. To bring you both back. Ah! The rush of it. To be truly inside the welds, bending them, taking control. This is what true power means.—

—But …—

—I know what I'm doing! Trust me, after searching for so many years, to have finally found this. I think it's what I was always meant to do.—

The wolf hadn't attacked. It just stood there, growling at her. No, not at her, at something else. Something only it could see. She didn't question her luck. She surged to her feet and charged, her blade held high, ready to deliver the killing blow.

The wolf saw the human coming and knew it was lost, but couldn't do anything to save itself. It was held in place, its mind locked by something dark and cold, something that wormed into its mind and stayed there, pushing its animal consciousness down.

She sliced the blade down with all her strength and cut deep into the wolf's skull, ending its life in an instant. Its eyes faded out, and for a moment she saw a spark of recognition that burned out into stillness and death. She fell to her knees in exhaustion, her blade dropping from her hand.

The vision faded as they rose out of the depths, up to the surface world and the reality of the present.

Wilt opened his eyes and sat up. He was surrounded by bodies, human bodies, their eyes open and devoid of life. He sprang to his feet and spun around, searching for the creatures that had attacked him.

Wilt? It worked. We're back.

Back from where?

I don't know. That thing sucked us down into the depths, further than we've ever been, into a wash of other people's memories, the flashes of life they saw before they died. We were drowning in them until Biore … I don't think he came back with us.

Wilt didn't have time to figure out what Higgs meant. Only

metres away another of the nightmare shapes was scuttling toward him, its evil claws held high, ready to claim another easy victim.

Without thinking Wilt drew the weld blade and dropped into a fighting stance he had never been trained for. The creature threw itself at him and he spun underneath it, twirling the blade in an arc above his head as it passed over him, slicing into its carapace. The weld blade seemed to melt into the creature, cutting through it without resistance. A moment later only black dust remained, dust that held its form for an instant before collapsing into nothingness.

Wilt stared at the spot where the creature had been, and then down at the weld blade in his hand. It was shining silver-blue in the darkness, calling to him, speaking to something in his mind that recognised it and answered its call. He felt the power and hunger that lurked within him flare into life. His body faded into a black mist and the wraith moved away, glowing sword in hand, searching for its next victim.

Another of the creatures leaped out of the darkness and the wraith moved inhumanly quickly to meet it, the weld blade spinning out of its form in a deadly thrust that pierced the centre of the scuttling body. As it sunk home, its pool of stolen memories flowed into the blade and through Wilt, no longer taking his consciousness with them, sinking through him and down into the spinning depths.

Wilt.

I'm here. I'm okay.

Biore did something, gave us something from the memories. A way to fight back. Something from Daemi too, a part of her. It's like we've taken on her training, her abilities.

I know. Now we need to use them.

The wraith cut across the campsite, toward the sounds of struggle and the glow of still living forms falling under the onrushing tide of darkness that flowed out from the riverbank. All thought was forgotten, the wraith no longer aware of Wilt or Higgs in its mind, not recognising anything but the hunger, the pull of the depths that reached out to each scuttling thing, draining it completely, its sword striking home again and again, pulling each one with it into oblivion.

It seemed to take only moments, but dawn was breaking when Wilt next became aware of himself, of the separation between the surface world and the depths, between the past and the present, between reality and dream. He took a deep, shuddering breath, his lungs burning with the cold morning air.

They're gone. They're all gone.

Wilt looked around at the scattered bodies at his feet, all human. No sign remained of the nightmare creatures that had ended so many lives. He raised his eyes to the river, a dark vein cutting through the landscape, its water black and silent.

The weld blade. It—

Drained them. Fed on them, just like a wraith.

Wilt looked at the blade still clutched in his hand. It no longer glowed with a blue light, its liquid silver surface seeming almost natural in the growing dawn.

Chapter 26

Heather woke to the sound of the wind in the trees, a heavy sigh building to a roar before fading again, like the rhythmic rush of the ocean—at least, that's what she had always been told the ocean sounded like. She'd never been closer than a week's travel from its endless blue horizons. A sudden memory flashed before her of her uncle leaning down to hold a shell to her ear, her thoughts wiped away in an instant as the waves came to life inside her mind.

'You're awake.'

Heather opened her eyes to see Daemi standing above her, all three packs at her feet, an impatient expression on her face.

'We need to move. We're still days away from the capital, if we can even find our way out of this place.'

'Where's Frankle?' Heather asked sleepily as she sat up.

Daemi pointed to her left and Heather saw Frankle lying on the thick moss of the forest floor, a low snore rattling out of him. She grinned at the sight. Who would have thought such a little body could make such a racket in its sleep?

She turned back to Daemi. 'Did you see—'

'Never mind what each of us saw.' Daemi stopped the conversation before it began. It was obvious from her tone there would be no more discussion. Whatever Daemi had experienced here in the Tangle, she wasn't ready to share it. 'Wake him up.'

Heather rolled to her feet and padded over the soft ground to where Frankle lay. She reached out and shook his shoulder gently.

'Huh?'

Frankle stared up at her, not recognising her face, his mind still lost in a dream.

'Frankle. It's me. Time to get up.'

'Heather. I was having the strangest …'

He sat up and looked around the forest clearing, noticing Daemi's impatient stance. 'Though I don't suppose now's the time.'

'Come. You can tell me about what you saw later. I don't think Daemi's in the mood.'

Heather helped him to his feet and walked them over to where Daemi stood, glaring at them. 'We need to get moving. We've already wasted too much time here.'

'It's okay, Daemi.' Frankle smiled into the face of her grumpiness. 'I'm sure our friends are on the way.'

'What do you mean?'

A high cry echoed across the sky, and Heather called out and waved with joy at the sight of the giant eagle spiralling down through the air currents toward them.

'Oh no.' Daemi's shoulder's slumped as she watched the creature approach.

'You didn't think they'd abandon us here, did you?' Frankle's smile just got wider. 'Don't worry, Daemi. I'll look after you.'

With that he sat down on his pack and waited as their transportation glided down from the open sky.

Frankle grinned and Heather let out another exalted cry of joy as the great eagle they were riding leaned into a swooping turn, racing over the fields below, somehow seeming to gain even more speed as it banked.

His grin morphed into a grimace as Daemi's fists squeezed his waist in response. A low groan of nausea and dread reached his ears, and he thought momentarily about turning to check on her, but decided against it. Whatever she was going through, he couldn't help. She'd just have to ride it out until their journey was ended.

That wouldn't be too far away. Already they had left the southern edge of the Tangle behind, the green carpet of trees ending abruptly to be replaced first by barren plains, which then separated into fenced off squares, the browns and greens and yellows arranging themselves into a chequered blanket of farmland.

They'd been flying for over half the day, not stopping for any breaks, as though the eagle knew of a new sense of urgency to their mission. More than once Frankle had considered speaking up, screaming something into Heather's ear about taking a five-minute break, allowing Daemi some mercy from the experience she so clearly dreaded. Yet he never quite did, always being held back by something he couldn't put into words, almost weld-like in its feeling. A knowledge that there were deeper powers at work, and that now was not the time to influence them.

Heather had a similar feeling. She had no problem flying onward, the eagle soaring in and out of the low clouds, banking low to gain speed before curving up into the heavens. Each pitch and turn sent sparks of adrenaline shooting through her, though she remained aware of how Daemi was suffering. There simply wasn't any way to help until they were back on firm ground, and it was clear the eagle was planning on completing their journey in as short a time as possible.

That was something else she'd noticed—the change in the eagle itself. Previously she'd been able to perceive an inkling of humanity inside it, some hint of the man that had shared the creature's mind. Stax, that was the name Nurtle had used. That humanity was buried deep now, deeper than she could sense. On their first flight it had felt as though that consciousness had been hidden under a thick cloak, its shape still there to be made out once they knew what they were looking for. Now even that was gone, and there was only a tingling sense of something *other* about the creature they rode upon. The wildness had grown, had fully taken over.

Her thoughts snapped back to the present as the first sight of towers in the distance appeared, thin tall structures jutting out of the landscape. The farmland below them had become increasingly compressed, and roads crisscrossed through it, but this was their first glimpse of what had to be their destination. She kept her eyes locked on the buildings, watching them grow taller as they raced toward them.

Unlike Redmondis, Sontair was a sprawling city built with no thought other than revelling in its own glory. No planner had designed its layout, no logic plotted its streets. It had twisted itself out of the ground in increments as more and more people flooded in over the decades, towers and walls forming up around them, fencing them inside a great stone city the like of which none of the young travellers had ever seen.

Even Daemi ceased her groaning as they flew closer and the full size of the capital dawned on them. It was enormous, easily ten times the area of Redmondis, which itself had been the largest township any of the three had experienced in their short lives. The outer wall that ringed the city's borders had to be at least twenty feet high, and inside them seemingly every second building was a tower that reached up toward the sky, straining in competition with its neighbours to be the tallest, the most glorious, the envy of its neighbourhood. The whole city seemed to surge out of the ground, the streets twisting up the central hill of the city to the grand silver castle that formed its shining centrepiece. Sontair. The jewel of the south.

The eagle let out another cry and banked again, sharply now, curving away from the sight of the city and heading out toward the deserted farmland. Minutes later it was gliding in to land, in the centre of the closest empty-looking field. As it touched down, Sontair had once again shrunk to a distant bump on the horizon.

All three of them tried to catch their breath as the dust cloud the eagle had created settled around them.

Finally Heather spoke. 'I guess this is as far as it will take us.'

She slid off the eagle's back easily and held up a hand to help Frankle down. He clambered off far less gracefully but landed on both feet, then turned to catch Daemi as she slumped, exhausted, from the great bird's back.

As soon as her feet touched the ground, Daemi hobbled a few steps, waving Heather and Frankle's offered hands away, then collapsed on the ground, her head between her knees, sucking in deep breaths.

Heather watched her for a few moments then turned away. She would be okay, she just needed some time to herself.

The eagle had lost interest in them immediately and was pecking idly at the furrows it had carved into the soil. It was almost funny to watch, as if anything it found there could be enough to satisfy its bulk. Perhaps it was simply another sign of instinct taking over.

That thought brought other, more troubling ones to the surface. Frankle interrupted her thoughts, his mind having followed a similar path. 'It's completely wild now, isn't it? Whatever humanity had remained before, it's gone.'

Heather only nodded in reply, silently examining the magnificent creature that had carried them so far. She wasn't sure how she felt about what she was watching. There was a sadness to it, but overriding that was something more, a sense of triumph perhaps, of victory. As though the shackles that had held a mind separate from its true nature had finally slipped off.

'Do you think that's what becomes of all the wildlers eventually, Heather?' Frankle asked, his voice tiny. 'Do they all reach a point where coming back becomes impossible?'

'Maybe it's a choice in the end. Maybe it's what they always wanted.'

The eagle raised its head then and fixed them both with a piercing gaze. It let out another great cry in response.

Heather gripped Frankle's hand, and he returned the squeeze as they watched the eagle launch itself into the sky. Dust billowed around them as its enormous wings lifted it up into freedom, and in seconds it was far above them, curving into a soaring turn as it circled ever higher. It let out another cry, this time of farewell, and shot off toward the north.

'It's gone then?'

Daemi was standing behind them and they dropped their hands quickly as if caught.

'Uh, yes,' Frankle stammered. 'I guess we walk from here.'

'Seems fair enough. If I was a giant magic eagle, I wouldn't want to get within bowshot of that place either.' Daemi nodded toward the silver castle glinting in the distance.

'Do you feel—'

'I'm fine,' Daemi cut Heather off. 'Let's march.'

Her tone brooked no argument. Heather and Frankle grabbed their packs and fell into step behind the tall guard captain. It was clear, now they were back on solid ground, who was in charge.

'Daemi?' Frankle spoke up again after a few steps. 'What are we planning to do once we get there? I mean, do you have a plan?'

Daemi grunted, then finally replied. 'We walk up to the gate and introduce ourselves. Then we take it from there.'

She quickened her step to shut down any further conversation as her two young companions shared a silent smile and hurried to keep up.

Chapter 27

'So, wielder. Once again you seem to be at the centre of trouble.'

Wilt looked up from where he was sitting by the fire, under the watchful gaze of two heavily armed guards. Walking toward him was Captain Mont, one hand still clutching the hastily written reports his junior officers had given him, each one trying and failing to make any sense of the mess that had been made of the rear end of his column overnight.

Captain Mont stopped at the fire and frowned at the young man, little more than a boy, who seemed to have been the lone survivor of the attack. 'Care to explain why you still stand when by the latest count fifteen of my men and at least thirty others won't wake to see the morning?'

Wilt stood up, dusting himself off and pulling his shoulders back. He knew there was no point trying to explain. He barely understood it himself. The eyes of every guard who had passed him since the attack last night had marked him as guilty. 'I told you before, Captain. I'm not without my talents.'

If Wilt's defiant tone shocked the captain, he hid it well. He turned and waved at a subordinate standing behind him and held out his hand. 'Show me the blade.'

A guard stepped forward and handed the captain Wilt's weld blade. He had surrendered it immediately just hours before, not wanting to get into any further scuffles with an exhausted and traumatised column of well-armed soldiers.

'And this? Moonsteel, isn't it? I've heard of the stuff, but never seen it before.' He waved the sword back and forth in the air. 'Perfectly balanced.' He flipped it quickly and caught the flat of the blade, offering the hilt to Wilt. 'Take it. From what my guards tell me, you know how to wield it well enough.'

Wilt reached out slowly and took the offered blade. A throb of warmth radiated up his arm as his fingers closed around the grip.

'However, I will have to insist you travel in a more secure manner for the remainder of the journey to Sontair. Up front, with me. You'll be quite comfortable, I assure you.'

Wilt nodded, keeping his face blank as he slid the blade back into place on his hip.

'Word has already been sent ahead, and my superiors in Sontair are eager to make your acquaintance. Even more so since your little adventure last night, I'm sure.'

The captain looked him up and down once more, as if giving himself one final chance to change his own mind. 'I can trust you not to try anything foolish, can't I?'

Wilt smiled and nodded his assent. It was clear the captain was well aware he could walk out of any prison they put him in. What he was trying to do was restore order in his men. Wilt understood. Besides, he could do with resting his feet for a while.

'Good.' The captain turned to leave. 'We're still two days' march from Sontair. Let's try our best to make them uneventful.'

Wilt sat alone in the dark wagon, his eyes closed, smiling as the cold wind rushed past his ears. He felt the heat of the enormous feathered body beneath his legs, leaned with it as it banked and swooped in the invisible current of air, and heard a high yelp of joy in reply.

Wilt, that sounds like Heather.

Wilt kept his eyes closed, aware that he was experiencing another place and time, through another set of senses.

Daemi. It must be. Why can't she see anything?

The feel of his hands wrapped around another's hips, the tension in his fingers, the tightness of their grip, gave him the answer. Daemi was terrified.

Maybe that's why the vision is so clear now. Maybe her fear has lent strength to the connection you share. See if you can make her open her eyes. I want to see where they are.

Wilt frowned as he concentrated, trying to force his will back along the strange link that joined his and Daemi's minds. It was like a weld, but different, not as responsive to command. The vision warped and bent in response, and far away the great eagle they were riding banked again, fighting against the air now, twisting and bumping its riders uncomfortably.

'Ugh.'

Frankle let out a groan as they tilted to the side again, and Daemi felt his hands lock over hers. At least she wasn't the only one suffering.

As if in response, Heather let out another whoop and Daemi's eyes snapped open. She snatched a glimpse of Heather's hair streaming in the wind, high clouds rearing up around them and a thick green carpet stretched out far below. The Tangle.

The image shut off as quickly as it appeared, and Wilt was back, alone in the tent.

What happened? That was Heather's hair, I almost—

Wilt tried to drop into the vision, reaching for the connection that had joined them, but it had danced away and his mind was left clutching at nothingness.

It's gone.

Try again! We have to make sure they're not in trouble.

It's okay, Higgs. Daemi was scared, but they were perfectly safe.

Wilt thought again of the rush and height the vision had shown them, the stomach dropping clamour of it all.

At least, not in any direct danger.

How can you be sure?

I … It's like you said, Daemi's fear lent the connection strength, but when there's real danger I see more. It's almost like I become part of her. I think we only saw that glimpse because she was scared. She's scared of heights, I think.

Daemi? I didn't think she was scared of anything.

Well, I wouldn't mention it to her if I were you.

His thoughts were interrupted as the lock on the rear door of the wagon slid open with a heavy clang.

'Good afternoon.'

The flap of the canvas covering whipped back and Captain Mont pulled himself up and in, looking around the spare, dim space with a critical eye. 'Not too dark in here, is it? I could get you a lantern or something.'

He stared at Wilt, hands on his hips, waiting for a reply.

'Uh, no, it's fine.' Wilt coughed, finding his voice.

The captain glanced around the small space impatiently before finally grabbing a crate from the corner and settling down on it. He leaned forward and stared at Wilt as if trying to decide something. 'I've had experience with you wielders in the past, you know. Redmondis. Black Robes.' He waved one hand in the air as if dismissing the terms. 'Not interested in the labels, just in how useful an individual can be. What I'm wondering is, how useful can you be?'

He punctuated his last words with a pointed finger jabbed toward Wilt's chest. When Wilt didn't react he sighed and lowered his tone. 'What do you know of those creatures that attacked us? You must know something.'

Wilt stared warily at the captain, wondering how he could even begin to answer such a question. How to describe the strange dark things that seemed to be formed from the welds themselves, that he had dived into, sunk through, drawing them down into oblivion far below?

'The creatures, they're … not of this plane. They're from the depths, from the place where all wielders draw their power.'

'Like welds, you mean?'

Wilt nodded quickly, glad the captain knew something he could build his description around. 'I think they're formed of the same stuff and that they are drawn to the fears of their victims. Attracted by them.'

'Hmm.' Captain Mont leaned back, considering the words. 'So perhaps we're not entirely powerless.'

After a moment he seemed to remember where he was and snapped out of his reverie. 'I wanted to thank you, for not making a scene earlier. I'm sure you understand.'

'Your men have seen too much strangeness recently. I understand.' Wilt smiled. 'I'm getting used to making people nervous.'

'Yes, well.' The captain clapped his knees and stood up. 'I suppose we can't blame them for that. I would like you to do me a further favour though. Try to think more about those … things. About how you fought them. Something tells me we'll be seeing them again soon enough. I'd like to have a plan of attack next time we run into them.'

With that the captain left, closing the cage door behind him.

Chapter 28

Petron, Nurtle and Jared stood side by side at the foot of the great throne that held Cortis's remains, eyes locked on the shrunken figure, their minds alert, ready for anything.

'Are you sure?' Petron whispered.

Nurtle squeezed Jared's hand in hers. 'It moved, Petron. His hand. It definitely moved.'

'Perhaps it was just the—'

'It wasn't just the wind. Can you not feel it now, the growing pressure? Prepare yourself.'

Nurtle's tone brooked no argument, and Petron sunk to his knees, pulling a large chalk out of his robe and scratching a long line on the ground between them and the throne. As soon as he was done, he stepped back and clapped his hands together.

Immediately the chalk line flashed in response and seemed to burn away, leaving no mark on the stone floor.

'Leave us!' he called to the guards still standing at attention behind them. 'You cannot help here.'

His tone was one of command and the guards responded instantly, hurrying from the room.

'Is it Cortis, or something else?' Nurtle whispered.

'I don't know.' Petron frowned. 'Whatever it is, I mean to have words with it.'

Petron clapped his hands together again and whispered strange syllables as the air warmed and thickened.

Nurtle nodded in recognition of the incantation and stepped back, drawing Jared with her.

'But we can—' Jared protested, only to be cut off with a shake of Nurtle's head.

'We cannot help him. This is Petron's battle. Our presence can only aid the enemy, just as with the guards. Shield yourself, my love.'

With that she finally let go of his hand and wrapped her arms around herself, sinking down to the ground and whispering her own words of power. Jared mimicked her, wrapping himself in a protective cocoon of welds, dropping away from the world and the growing danger spinning into existence before them.

Petron stood alone in front of the throne, eyes twin coals that burned with fury. 'Wrexley,' he whispered. 'They will pay for what they did to you.'

He turned his focus inward, reaching for the power that dwelled there, the knowledge formed from years spent sharing the bond between wielder and ward, and the anger that remained from having that link so brutally severed. Petron was not a true wielder, but he had shared such a deep connection with one for so many years that some of a wielder's power lay within him, and his rage and hurt now helped his mind to fully access it. Inside him a furious whirlwind was turning, growing faster with every moment, urging him onward, waiting to be unleashed. He raised his arm and pointed a single finger at the corpse that sat in front of him.

'Cortis. It's time to answer for your crimes.'

Petron's words seemed to shock the remains on the throne into action. The bowed head lifted to stare directly at Petron, and its cracked lips twisted into an unnatural smile.

A thick black weld shot from Petron's outstretched arm and arrowed into the figure before him, and the surface world dropped completely away.

Petron rushed through the weld, a torrent of power cascading beneath him as his mind tried to make sense of what it was seeing.

The next moment he was through, staring out across a blasted, stricken landscape. A dead world. All that remained of what was once Cortis's mind.

The charge and rush of the weld had disoriented him, and Petron found his mind reeling, trying to grasp onto something to ground itself. What it found was the burning core of anger, the thick wedge of rage lodged in his heart. Rage at Cortis for what he had taken from him, at Wrexley for leaving him here alone, and underneath it all a deep fury at himself for allowing it all to drift out of his grasp.

Just as his mind coalesced back into consciousness, it was blasted away by an all-encompassing voice that seemed to emanate from the welds themselves.

So, finally the time has come. Foolish, petty man. You thought yourself capable of facing me here, in my realm?

The words echoed through Petron's mind, overwhelming it entirely. Suddenly, impossibly, looming above him was what looked to be an enormous serpent, its face twisted into a gruesome approximation of a man. Cortis. It was Cortis's face.

You think your anger at this lackey would somehow serve you? You think your fury can help you here?

Petron knew the truth of the words that blasted through him. How foolish he had been, how arrogant, to think he could face this. To think he could do anything but cower in front of this ancient thing, this lord of the depths, this being from another, deeper realm. This monster that reared up before him, toying with his mind, weighing up the time when it would wrap itself around him and consume him utterly.

Cortis has provided me his final service, bringing you before me to become my next vessel. As a reward I may finally let him die. Petron felt a brush of pure pain, a flash of agony and despair so deep it almost sank him to his knees. It was Cortis, he knew so instantly. What remained of him, suffering in a trapped, eternal sliver of hell.

As soon as the vision passed, Petron felt empty, all anger drained from him, replaced by a hopelessness so deep and all-encompassing he could no longer stand to hold it inside his mind. No one could. No one could stand before such power and survive. No one but—

Petron felt the warmth before he saw it, before his eyes noticed the floating spark of light that seemed to dance in the currents of air just above the great serpent's head. Its sight brought his mind back from the brink, back from the edge of despair it had been about to throw itself from.

As his eyes found it, another voice whispered in his mind. Familiar. One he thought he would never hear again.

Wilt. Remember Wilt, Petron. Remember our pupil. Remember how deeply he delved.

It was Biore's voice, yet changed. Energised, as though whispering to him from a time long before.

Wilt has faced this power before and survived. He has the power to face it again. All is not lost.

The serpent seemed to sense the change in Petron's thoughts, its face twisting in anger as it bent lower, its gaping maw opening to reveal row upon row of sharpened, needle teeth.

Ah. You still resist. You are stronger than Cortis was.

The face of the serpent bubbled and morphed into a new form, and suddenly Petron was staring at an evil facsimile of Wrexley himself.

Cortis loved him too, though he could never admit so. Not until it was too late. Are you stronger than Wrexley was? Can you stand to face death itself? Or will you abandon all just as he did in his final surrender?

Petron almost broke then, at the sight of Wrexley's features, so clear in his heart, now looming over him, spitting words of hate into his face. It was almost too much. Only the single spark of hope saved him. Its random dance in the air above seemed to weave new thoughts into Petron's fevered mind, calming its rush and panic.

Biore's words carried with them a clarity that pulled him back into himself. *Wrexley is dead. He was broken on the rack by a madman, by the human servant of this dark power that stands before you. What remains in his place is your memory of him, of the secrets your minds shared, of the traits he helped instil within you. Nothing else—not anger, not loneliness, not helpless rage at an uncaring universe, none of it can do anything but serve this enemy. You have to let it all go.*

The serpent continued to twist lower, its mouth opening ever wider, closing over him as he stood before it.

Embrace the torrent. Let it free your mind from all constraint. Let it flow through you and beyond. Open yourself to me.

The words no longer filled Petron's mind. They echoed through him, but they no longer blasted all other thoughts clear. He kept his eyes locked on the spark as it sunk toward him, still spinning on its invisible currents of air. The serpent blurred into the background as he reached for it. Petron could feel himself pulling free of the dark mind that threatened to consume him, the connection to the howling depths shrinking into nothingness.

No! I will not allow you to escape. You will remain here! You will become my new vessel!

As his fingers closed around the spark, Petron felt the connection. Biore. Delco. Rawick. Higgs. Daemi. Heather. Frankle. All of them. All who had been touched by Wilt's power, binding them together, interweaving their lives. Linking them within the welds, entwining them in a single rope of consciousness. This was a new form of power, one never wielded before. It was what could finally save them.

You will not escape me. If you cannot serve me, then you will face only the emptiness of death.

The great serpent reared back to strike, and some part of Petron was aware of the heat and stench of the breath that steamed out of its jaws, but his mind was elsewhere now. Within the weld, joined with the others, part of the light that burned the shadows away. He closed his eyes as the jaws closed over him.

Come with me, Petron. Come with us, away from this aberration.

A sharp slap on his cheek shocked him out of the dream, and Petron opened his eyes to see Nurtle's worried gaze staring down at him.

'Petron?'

Another smack sent sparks dancing across his vision, but these faded quickly, they weren't like the—

Like what? What had he been thinking? Where had he—

'Is he—' Jared asked from somewhere behind her.

'He's coming back.'

She raised her hand for another slap and Petron shook his head.

'Enough.' He coughed and raised himself up on one elbow, staring blankly around the empty stone chamber. 'You'll give me a concussion.'

Nurtle's concerned face melted into a smile and she sat back, pulling Petron up into a sitting position. 'You're back.'

Petron nodded slowly, dizzy from more than just Nurtle's over-eager ministrations.

A movement behind them took their attention away, and they turned to see Cortis's remains crumple from the throne, its withered limbs collapsing into a fine dust.

Petron pushed himself to his feet and brushed himself down, watching the dust blow into nothingness as another gust of wind whipped through the chamber. 'Yes. I'm back.'

He watched the last of the dust disappear, then turned his back on it and walked purposefully from the room. 'Come. It is done. There's nothing for us here.'

Chapter 29

The first change Wilt noticed was the sound and vibrations from the wagon's wheels on cobbled stone. After days of soft forest trails and packed dirt roads the hard, bumpy surface sent rattling shocks through the frame of the wagon, and the clip-clopping of horseshoes drowned out all other noise.

You hear that? I was wondering if we'd ever see real civilisation again. Real stone.

Wilt gathered his belongings, strapping the weld blade onto his hip and throwing the forest cloak around his shoulders. He sat patiently in his moving prison, trying to ignore the noise and discomfort, knowing that this particular journey was nearing its end.

Sure enough, only an hour or so later he heard rough voices call out a challenge and answer, and a new noise joined the chorus. Wilt closed his eyes and imagined the scene painted by the sounds, great high wooden gates creaking as they swung slowly open to allow the column access into the capital. Sontair. They had finally made it.

Only minutes later Captain Mont threw back the flap of the wagon, and early afternoon sunlight leaked in as he pulled himself up into the cart.

'So. Our journey is at an end. Thank you for not making it any harder than it had to be.'

Wilt smiled and nodded in reply. 'Thanks for a most comfortable journey. Much easier than walking.'

The captain grunted and swung the gate open. 'Well, the time for relaxation is over. Come.' He waved Wilt out. 'My superiors won't tolerate further delays.'

Wilt stepped out of the wagon, and into chaos.

They were in a large courtyard, a drilling area by the look of the packed dirt and timber training structures scattered about. Most of the column seemed to be here, villagers and guards packed together in the too-small space, pushing and arguing with each other as they tried to organise themselves. Guards bustled back and forth, taking apart wagons, gathering belongings, and loudly farewelling those they had shared the journey with but were no longer part of the same command. Alongside them, young servants and stable boys ducked in and out, scurrying about trying to wrangle horses into some sort of formation, and passing food and drink among the travel-stained troop.

Wilt let the noise and rush wash over him.

Feels like home.

Higgs was right; it was just like Greystone on a busy market day.

'Here. I'm sorry about this.'

Wilt turned to see the captain reaching out to him with heavy iron shackles.

'That's okay.' Wilt offered his wrists. 'You know these are pointless, right?'

'I assumed as much. Must keep up appearances though.'

The shackles locked over Wilt's wrists and the captain wrapped the lead chain around his fist. 'Stay close. Those things can really bite if I have to use this.'

He jerked the chain softly and the heavy iron scraped against Wilt's skin. He nodded and dropped his hands over his cloak.

I don't suppose you want me to help remove those?

Not yet. Just play along. Besides, I thought stone was more your thing.

I'll try my hand at anything.

The heat ring on Wilt's finger blazed in answer, sending fire up his arm.

'Come then, we need not go far.'

Captain Mont marched off across the courtyard, Wilt trotting along behind him. The crowd seemed to part magically for them, every few steps another soldier snapping into a salute. The captain waved each man back at ease wearily as they passed.

'Your men respect you,' Wilt offered.

Captain Mont grunted in reply. 'Most of them need to spend a few more summers training here before they come under my command. Sending these boys out on patrol makes no one's job any easier.'

Wilt paid more attention to the guards they passed. At least half the soldiers were very young, their heavy armour threatening to consume them.

'But this is the price we pay for our current command,' the captain continued. 'You'll no doubt see what I mean soon enough. Perhaps you can help convince them of the reality of the threat we face. Perhaps then they'll give me more than just boys to work with.'

They picked their way across to the far side of the courtyard where a row of low stone buildings squatted in the dirt, huddled together as if for warmth.

No gaudy towers here, Wilt. These buildings were built for one purpose only.

And yet from what the captain tells us those in charge still fail to recognise any threat.

Biore said Sontair hasn't seen any real action in decades, maybe longer. All the trouble has been far to the north.

Are those in power so quick to forget?

Sure they are. You saw that yourself in Redmondis. And what about Greystone? Don't tell me those guards we used to fling rotten fruit at could stand up to what we've seen.

Let's hope they won't have to.

Their thoughts were interrupted by the captain leading them through the first of the low buildings, into another smaller courtyard and toward a large doorway guarded on both sides by formal looking red-cloaked guards. Wilt caught his breath as he saw them, at first glance they looked identical to the Sentinels he'd faced in Redmondis.

They're just men.

Sure enough, it was clear the two guards were just that. Only men, wearing hooded red cloaks and holding long, evil-looking pikes by their sides.

Captain Mont stopped in front of the guards and saluted. 'Presenting the prisoner as the commander ordered.'

The two guards snapped their pikes into a cross formation in front of the door, and the captain stepped back automatically.

After another moment he spoke again, this time his voice a low growl of anger. 'I take it I am to be denied access?'

'Now, now, Captain. No need to get your hackles up.'

A high, giggling voice trickled across to them, followed by a small, hunched old man, his stained and worn red cloak falling loosely about his shoulders and trailing in the dirt behind him.

Guard yourself. This one has power.

Wilt sensed it immediately. An electricity crackling in the air, something he hadn't felt so blatantly since he'd left the safety of Redmondis.

He turned to study the old man shuffling toward them, his hands wringing in supplication, his eyes glowing gold in the fading afternoon light. The sight of those eyes sent a warning thrill of panic up Wilt's spine—they looked so like Cortis's, so like the wolf soldiers he had bent to his command in Redmondis. The scratching presence of a weld skated across the surface of his mind, scanning for a weak point. He held it at bay with ease, watching the strange old man.

Captain Mont seemed displeased with what he saw. 'Vargul,' he grunted. 'To what do we owe the pleasure of the queen's counsel?'

This was rewarded with another high, almost feminine giggle. 'Oh, Captain. You have so much to learn about keeping your feelings hidden. No wonder you're always being sent out to the colonies. You'd never last a day in court.'

'I do not wish to spend five minutes in your court, Vargul. I want to report to the commander as I have been ordered.'

The old man finally reached the doorway and raised his face, giving Wilt his first good look at him. He was mostly swallowed up in the dirty red cloak, the hood pulled tight around a face seemingly entirely composed of wrinkles, as though he were wearing a skin four sizes too large for his body. The dominant feature was his eyes, sneering out at the world and glowing with a power Wilt recognised and no longer feared.

He looks like Cortis, but different. Weaker. Sicker, perhaps.

The scratching of the weld slunk away as those golden eyes burned into him before they turned back to the captain.

'Your orders have changed, Captain. Your queen has received word of the prisoner. Our guest, I should say. She has requested the pleasure of his company immediately.'

'But the commander—'

'The commander of the guard knows his place!' Vargul's high whine was suddenly a bark of command. 'You would do well to follow in his footsteps.'

Vargul's voice dropped back to a thick whisper but his eyes blazed, waiting for any further sign of defiance.

Captain Mont bowed his head briefly and held out the lead chain to Wilt's shackles. 'Very well. I will ensure the commander is informed of this.'

Vargul giggled again as he took the chain. 'Rest assured, Captain, your valiant efforts will be recognised. So many village folk saved. So many more refugees escorted through Sontair's gates to join its already crowded streets. Whatever would we do without soldiers such as yourself?'

Captain Mont seemed about to snap back, but held himself in check and grunted, spinning on his heel and marching away.

Vargul watched him leave, a strangely distant, pondering expression on his face.

Oh, I don't like the look of this one at all.

As soon as the captain had disappeared around the corner, Vargul dropped the chain in the dirt and turned away. 'They tell me you have power.' He threw the words over his shoulder. 'Free yourself from that feeble prison and follow me. We have already dallied too long. Patience is not an affliction my lady suffers from.'

Wilt watched him skitter away into the shadows and held his shackles up in front of his face.

We could just pick the lock.

His hands faded into mist before his eyes, his body taking on its wraith form for a moment before snapping back into solidity as the shackles fell to the ground.

Or we could just do that, I suppose. Little lacking in subtlety, don't you think?

Something tells me this is not the place for subtlety.

Wilt hurried to catch up to Vargul, who was heading toward a small door on the far side of the small courtyard. As he reached the door, Vargul turned to ensure Wilt was following, then pulled it open and ducked inside.

We could just leave. The guards can't stop us.

You saw Vagul's eyes. He has felt the touch of the same power Cortis served, the same power we came here to seek out. Let's see where he can lead us.

Wilt had to bend down to fit through the undersized doorway, and found himself in what looked like a secret passage, cold stone walls closing in on either side of him, and the dim glow of a torch flickering further ahead. A moment later Vargul appeared in the circle of light and waved Wilt on impatiently.

Just don't blame me when you find yourself in trouble again.

Ourselves, Higgs. Ourselves.

Chapter 30

The city walls had been growing taller as Heather, Frankle, and Daemi approached them, tramping through sodden fields, then joining the steady stream of travellers moving along the first wide road they came to; seemingly every villager from the surrounding areas was headed for the shelter of the city.

They had landed further from Sontair than Heather thought; the sheer size of the walls had tricked her sense of distance. It had taken two full days to get this far, and the sun was just touching the western horizon when they made out the shape of the enormous gates standing open, allowing the thickening flow of travellers in and out of the walled city.

Daemi had been trying to hurry the other two along, but they didn't share her history of long marches and physical activity, and though they struggled gamely both Heather and Frankle were close to collapse. She felt for them, but the dimming skies urged her onward. If the whispers she had heard from the various travellers they shared the road with were true, then the city gates would close at sundown, and she didn't fancy trying to find a spot to camp among this crowd of farmers and merchants, each looking more desperate than the last. There wouldn't be much chance for rest if they had to spend the night out here.

'Speed up. We have to make the gates before sunset.'

Frankle recognised the tension in her tone and tried to forget his burning feet and aching shoulders. He took Heather's hand and pulled her onward, trying to lift their pace.

Heather was suffering. Unlike the others her childhood had been one of relative privilege, and she'd never truly had to push her physical limits before. At an early age her parents had recognised her blossoming crafter skills and hired the best tutors money could buy to help her along. Heather's childhood days before Redmondis had been filled with comfort and learning. The result was a young woman who, though not exactly spoiled, had spent too long in a soft life to be expected to suddenly match a hardened soldier in a day's march across muddy fields and hard-packed dirt roads.

Frankle's early life hadn't been so easy, but he too was struggling to keep up with Daemi's demands. His problem was more one of age and size than experience. He had only recently hit puberty, and his muscles had yet to take on the wiry strength required to help him through days like this. He was determined not to show it though, refusing to complain, and most of all rejecting entirely the possibility of failing in the Heather's presence.

'Come on,' he whispered to Heather as he pulled her along. 'We can make it. Can't be much further.'

Frankle's eyes gave his words the lie, the shape of the massive gates only just becoming clear as the three pushed through the crowds, but he ignored that thought and marched on.

Daemi was aware of how much her two younger charges were suffering, but there was nothing for it. They had to make the walls before nightfall. As they pushed their way through the milling crowds, she felt eyes travelling over them, judging them, weighing up risk versus reward. Every second glance was one of greed and cunning, and she knew there would be trouble if they were forced to spend the night outside. Her long cloak marked her as a guard captain of Redmondis, but judging from the mutterings she heard, such trimmings no longer drew the respect and fear they once had.

'One last push.'

Daemi's urgent tone gave her companions a final surge of

energy. She led from the front, shoving travellers out of their path now, ignoring the cries of anger and bluster, carving a wedge of space through the crowd that only thickened as they got closer to the city gates. Heather and Frankle tumbled along in her wake, trying most of all not to trip themselves up with their tired legs.

Finally they were within shouting distance, just as the sky turned from dusty blue to steel grey. The guards that lined the upper barricades shuffled into movement, and Daemi knew what was coming next. The gates were about to close.

'Hold!' She gave the shout every ounce of command and authority she had. It echoed over the general hubbub of the crowd, but the guards on the walls didn't pause in their step.

They were only about fifty feet from the entrance, the last few travellers shuffling in as the gates swung slowly shut. They weren't going to make it.

'Hold!' Daemi yelled again, pulling Heather and Frankle along roughly behind her. 'Hold the gate!'

Daemi's cry drew worried glances from the travellers around them and one or two guards stopped to peer down into the crowd and identify the troublemakers, but the gates didn't halt their slow swing.

She grunted in frustration and shoved a merchant out of her path, sending the unfortunate man flying off the road and tumbling into another group of weary travellers.

'I said hold! In the name of Redmondis!'

Suddenly every eye seemed to turn toward them, some in fear, most in plain curiosity. The gates slowed as the men heaving on the heavy chains that controlled their mechanism paused to see how the guards above them would react.

Daemi took advantage of the confusion to charge through the last of the travellers in their path, sending them sprawling and opening a space at the foot of the gates.

'Who dares speak that name?' A new voice sung out over the crowd, silencing them immediately. Daemi and the others stopped abruptly, responding to the commanding boom. 'Show yourself!'

An enormous guard stepped out from behind the walls and planted himself in the centre of the road. The man had to be at least seven feet tall, his heavy armour spiking up cruelly around his shoulders, the evil-looking helm that covered his face grinning down at the three companions, as if daring them to attack.

Daemi wasn't impressed. She stepped forward, waving Heather and Frankle away, and approached the guard, a captain to judge by the markings on his heavy armour. She stopped six feet in front of him and threw her cloak back over her shoulder, revealing the long knife hanging from her hip.

'I dare. In the name of Redmondis, let us through the gate.' She kept her voice low, but it seemed to echo out in the silence.

The captain made a show of peering down at her. 'A Redmondis guard!' he barked, turning to the guards above him and encouraging the laughter that suddenly broke out. 'Here! At the gates of Sontair!'

The giant of a man finished his pirouette to face Daemi again, not moving from his position in the centre of the road. Frankle stepped in front of Heather, his eyes scanning the jagged ramparts over them.

'What are you doing?' Heather whispered, pushing him out of her way.

'I think we'd better be ready for trouble,' he whispered back. 'That guard looks like he wants a fight.'

Daemi came to the same conclusion, though her response was blunter. She scanned the surrounding guards, making sure every set of eyes was on her, then bent into a formal bow.

The massive guard laughed as she bent low to the ground in front of him, then suddenly choked as Daemi stood up quickly and flung a fistful of trail mud straight into his face.

In the blink of an eye she was on him, following the thrown mud with a high kick that snapped the guard's heavy helm to the side, breaking the clasps that held it in place and blinding him completely. In the same movement her spin continued, her trailing leg sweeping the guard's feet out from under him to send him crashing to the ground with a low boom.

Daemi stepped up to the prone figure, struggling helplessly to right himself in the ridiculous armour that had become his prison, its weight pinning him in place. She placed one boot on his helm and drew her long knife, looking up at the guards above them.

'Anyone else?'

She waited a full ten seconds for someone to rise to the challenge, but the only sounds breaking the silence were the low grunts and sighs of the prone guard captain under her heel.

'Thought not.'

She removed her boot from the man's face and strode quickly through the open gates of Sontair, her head held high, Heather and Frankle hurrying along behind.

Chapter 31

Wilt drifted through the narrow passage, one hand stretched out before him, the other trailing along the cold stone wall to his side. Vargul had disappeared around a bend in the tunnel ahead, and the last torch they had passed was also hidden behind a curve, so that as he walked he was swallowed by an almost complete darkness. He leaned forward, almost tripping over himself, until he realised that the slope of the ground had changed and they were heading deeper underground.

This feels familiar.

I know what you mean.

The passage was very much like the one he and Petron had taken into the Sisters' lair in Redmondis. It wasn't just the confines of the tunnel or the dim light; it was something deeper, a lack of control, of surrendering to a power greater than himself

I was thinking more of the tunnels in Cortis's garrison.

Higgs hadn't been with Wilt when he met the Sisters, and he hadn't been with Higgs when he'd snuck into the garrison. They had been separate people, separate minds then. Now they somehow shared the same consciousness, even the same memories.

His hand moved to the hilt of the weld blade on his hip.

Higgs, do you ever wonder how we ended up here?

Oh, all the time. You don't know the half of it.

In the tunnels of the garrison of Redmondis, Higgs had led a small group of Black Robes into danger, all to save Wilt. As a result,

Higgs had been killed. It was only the strange power of the weld blade and the deep connection between wielder and ward that had allowed some part of Higgs to remain with him. And that sharing of minds, with Higgs and the others, may have been the only thing that allowed Wilt to keep his sanity, keep his very humanity, in those weeks in the Tangle when he'd come so close to giving in completely to the wraith form and the spiralling darkness that called to him.

If Biore was here he'd tell you to focus on what we know and put anything else out of your mind. Now is not the time for dwelling on the past.

But don't you ever feel … robbed? Of what could have been?

Oh, coulda, woulda. We grew up on the streets of Greystone, Wilt. You ever stop to wonder how lucky we were even to live to the age of ten? Ever think about the other kids, the ones we left behind? How long do you think they lasted? All we can do is deal with the world we find ourselves in, the situations that face us. Everything else is for people with too much time on their hands.

Aren't you the philosophical one? I think spending all that time with Biore and Delco has rubbed off on you.

I'm just more interested in what's ahead rather than behind us. You should be too … Wait. Hear that?

Wilt stopped and held his breath, the total silence roaring in his ears. No, not total silence. There was something, just above it, a sing-song tone, almost like a weld but … different.

Guard yourself.

Whatever the sound was, it was getting louder.

Wilt continued walking, focusing his mind, wrapping himself together mentally, ready to face whatever was around the next corner.

Dim light dawned as he walked, an orange glow that grew into flickering firelight. Finally he could see Vargul waiting in the distance, a torch burning on the wall next to him, a closed heavy door blocking the way forward.

Vargul was wringing his hands, obviously impatient to move on. 'Come along, come along.'

As soon as he saw Wilt's shadow appear in the tunnel, he turned to the door and pulled back the heavy bolt. The door swung open slowly, its hinges groaning in protest, and Vargul disappeared through it into the bright light beyond.

Wilt followed, having to duck down again to fit through the small door. For a moment the change in light blinded him, then he blinked the stars in his eyes away and found himself standing in a vast hall, bright sunlight streaming in through enormous, twenty-foot-high windows that lined one wall.

Vargul stood to the side, watching the effect the room had on Wilt. He grinned and waved a hand expansively. 'The queen's private greeting hall.'

Wilt stared open-mouthed. The room seemed to stretch in all directions like a great white desert. The far wall of glass was at least a stone's throw from where he stood, and giant columns shot up from the ground at regular intervals, curving into carved forms of men and beasts, reaching up but not quite touching the high ceiling above. Wilt felt like he'd shrunk in size, or had stumbled into a giant's palace.

Someone's spent a lot of time on this place.

'Most visitors are quite impressed.' Vargul sniffed before hurrying away again.

Wilt hurried into a trot to keep up. *I don't think we gave him the reaction he was hoping for.*

It is impressive. Especially the stonework on those columns. Touch one for me.

Wilt reached out to the first column they passed, brushing his fingers along the cold, shaped stone. As he did so, he felt something else, a spark of recognition.

Life. This stone is alive. Crafters formed this.

Don't go getting any ideas.

Vargul was waiting again, this time by a much larger door at the end of the hall. He was actually tapping his foot, glaring at them, the golden flecks in his eyes glowing in the bright light.

'Once we enter I will introduce you to her majesty the queen. You will remain silent, with your head bowed. Only when she has addressed you directly are you to raise your eyes.' Vargul ended his spiel with another grimace, as though he was sure Wilt would mess up even these simple instructions.

Wilt smiled innocently at him and nodded.

Don't drop your guard. There is power here, real power. I can almost hear it singing in the air.

Wilt turned his senses inward and instantly recognised what Higgs meant. It was as though the air thickened, concentrated on the other side of this door, ready to explode. He wrapped his mind in layers of protection in readiness.

He felt the air change as Vargul pushed the doors open and strode in. Wilt kept his eyes on his feet and followed him.

'My lady, as you requested, I present to you the prisoner that the guard patrols from the north arrived with this morning. The wielder.' He almost spat the last words.

'Ah yes, the one from Redmondis.' The queen's voice was instantly familiar, swooping in and twining itself around Wilt's mind. It brought with it images of serpents and darkness and red-robed figures sitting in judgment upon him.

'Wilt, is it not?'

Wilt raised his eyes and found himself staring into a vision from the past. An impossibly beautiful woman, long, dark red hair cascading over her shoulders, deep green eyes boring into him with an urgency he couldn't resist. The Sister. The Sister from Redmondis. It couldn't be.

A knowing smile curved the queen's lips as she saw the effect her appearance had upon him. 'It is good to finally meet you in the flesh.'

Her eyes remained locked on his, but her voice became one of stern command. 'Leave us, Vargul.'

'But, my lady—'

'Now.' The queen's voice didn't raise in volume, but there was no denying the power behind her words.

Vargul reared back suddenly as if struck, and once again Wilt noticed the strange thickening in the air, as though something more than mere words had passed between the two. Vargul's pale features became even more strained, and a sheen of sweat beaded his forehead. He bowed and backed out of the room.

'Of course, my lady.'

The queen finally broke eye contact with Wilt and watched the councillor hurry toward the doors. There was a dangerous curiosity to her gaze, as though she was considering what specific torments to inflict upon her servant.

The doors swung shut behind Vargul, and the queen turned back to Wilt, her gaze warmer, though still wary. Studying him, weighing his presence.

She looked so much like the Sister in Redmondis, though now that Wilt took the time to stare boldly back at her, he noticed certain small differences. She was just as stunningly beautiful, yet altered. Not as blatant in her knowing stare, not as arrogant. Older, more weathered about the eyes. More worldly, perhaps.

More dangerous.

'Wilt.' Her voice too, now that he heard it again, was not exactly the same. The sense of chorus that had echoed through the Sister in Redmondis was gone, and the tone now was more musical, more human.

'You are familiar to me, of course, though we have never met. You knew my sister in Redmondis. You were with her, in the end.'

It wasn't a question. She smiled at him, though her eyes remained distant and cold.

So they were all sisters then, the nine of them? That goes some way to explaining how they shared such a deep connection.

As soon as Higgs said the words, the queen's gaze changed, warming instantly. 'Your young friend is wiser than his years allow. Perhaps that is one of the benefits of his current position.'

Wilt! She can hear—

'Yes, young crafter, I can hear you. I can sense many things. My powers may no longer be what they were when my sisters and I shared our linked minds, but I still retain some skill.'

Wilt stood stunned in front of her, afraid to think in case any more of his secrets were laid bare. If she could hear Higgs, what else could she know? Was his mind completely at her mercy?

'Fear not, wielder. Your mind remains safe from my touch, though it would perhaps be interesting to test—'

Instantly a spiked probe tried to push into his mind, a shaped, strong weld forcing down upon him, trying to peel back the layers that held his mind separate from the world.

For a panicked moment Wilt felt his control slip, then he dropped into himself, into the silent depths that waited within him, and the probe melted away.

'Ah, you see?' The queen's tone was almost one of regret. 'You remain quite out of my reach.'

'How is this possible?' Wilt finally found his voice, driven on by anger at the sudden attempt on his mind. 'I was there when your sister fell. I was linked with her. I saw the serpents turn … on all of you.'

'You saw much more than we believed any man could see. More than you had a right to. You witnessed the end of our greatest achievement, our true power, our linked minds. Our final folly, perhaps.'

The queen's voice faded as she considered the past. In her drawn features Wilt glimpsed the enormous suffering such a severing must have caused.

'But you did not see my end.' The queen drew herself up, her voice strong again, pushing her memories of pain away. 'Many of my sisters fell that day, perhaps all of them, even I no longer know for sure. Taken by the very powers we thought we could control.'

'You … you cannot sense your sisters at all?'

'No.' The queen's tone brooked no argument. In that one syllable Wilt could hear all the pain and loss the serpents had caused her, the terrifying proximity of death, the endless days and nights that followed spent searching through her own damaged mind, trying to reconnect with those that had become so much a part of herself, their shared links so fundamental that their sudden removal was like losing part of her mind, entire swathes of memory and experience blotted away.

Wilt had been there when it happened, had helped drive the serpents back from the frothing chaos of their feeding frenzy down into the depths where they belonged, but even he had not truly known the suffering they had caused. In that one simple word, the queen had laid all of that bare.

'But come.' The queen smiled suddenly, erasing such dark memories from their presence. 'I did not bring you before me to flounder in self-pity. We each of us have our pain. It does not do to wallow in it.'

That's what I said. Ask her how she can hear me.

'I can hear you, crafter, because you do not shield your thoughts. You do not share our wielder training. You are a trumpet blaring out in the silence. Any wielder worth the name should hear you— it is just our sad predicament that there are no longer many who fit that description.'

The queen brushed imaginary dust from her gown, as though angry at it.

'Redmondis has failed in that regard. We have failed. Time has shown us the folly of our plans for control. Another of the serpents' tricks, perhaps, convincing us to weaken all to shore up our own power. Not realising who we served.'

'And who did you serve? Who did the Sentinels serve? What dwells down there, in the dark, waiting?'

Wilt's bold question brought another smile to the queen's lips, her bright eyes burning once more into his.

'Yes. You know that which dwells below, better than any of us. You have fought its servants and survived. Perhaps you truly are the one the prophecy spoke of.'

'The blood within the stone.' Wilt whispered the words that had been following him since the first time he heard them, a lifetime ago now, choked out by a dying man on the playing field in Greystone.

The queen's eyes only seemed to blaze brighter in response. 'Come, wielder. We have much to discuss.'

Chapter 32

Heather wasn't exactly sure what she had been expecting from Sontair, but it wasn't this.

The streets were filthy, caked mud from the dirt roads outside the city gates seemed to coat every inch of the cobbled street they walked down, and they constantly had to squeeze past travellers who halted in the middle of the road to address one another, oblivious to the obstacle they formed for everyone else trying to get by. Every wagon seemed to be overloaded, axles straining as they inched over the bumps to avoid breaking down completely, the horses and mules that pulled them relieving themselves where they stood adding to the muck underfoot.

And the smell! Heather had never imagined there could be such a stench. Sweat and dirt and other things she didn't want to think too much about mingling together. It was as though they had passed into a new world on walking through the city gates, a new atmosphere, thick and cloying, the stench wriggling into her nose, finding its way into every nook and cranny of her clothes. Heather was sure she'd never be able to get the stink out of her hair. Still, she wrinkled her nose and tried to breathe through her mouth, trotting to keep up with Daemi, who at least seemed to know where she was going.

Frankle was experiencing a different city entirely. He smiled as they walked, a memory he thought he'd lost rushing to the fore as they pushed through the crowds and noise. That was the trigger, he recognised, the sound of the place. A cacophony of action, strange voices calling back and forth across the street, shouting to be heard above the clatter of hooves and general hubbub of the city. It sounded like home. He hadn't come from anywhere as grand as the capital, of course, but the throngs of people, the stench and the chaos they moved through were all instantly familiar.

Daemi wasn't paying any attention to such things. She was on alert. She'd heard stories about Sontair, in particular the lower districts lining the city walls, how they were the haunts of gangsters and thieves, how you should always keep one hand on your purse and the other on the hilt of your sword if you wanted to make it out with your money and your skin intact. Her feet fell into a strange cadence, an unfamiliar rhythm that somehow helped her to move easily past the obstacles in their way, slipping around wagons and merchants, waving away street urchins before they approached, noting every alley entrance they passed. Checking the shadows. It was as though some city dwelling instinct she wasn't aware she had was dredged up to the surface to take control. Heather and Frankle had to hurry just to keep up.

Daemi tried to keep her head high as they walked, aware that she was still supposed to be part of an official delegation. It helped that she seemed taller than most of the crowd, able to see over heads and get a better view of the general area. Her instincts told her that though she was right to stay on alert, there was no immediate danger. Which then led to her next problem—where to now?

If she was honest with herself, Daemi hadn't really thought much past getting to the city gates. From there she'd held the vague hope that they would be met by a court official, who would recognise and respect the Redmondis colours and lead them directly to the king, where they would present themselves and … And what?

Daemi shook her head to dismiss the thought and focused on the now. What they needed first of all was somewhere to stay. A place to rest and recover from their journey—she shuddered as the memory of the flight came rushing back to her—and come up with a plan. Her two companions were soldiering on bravely but they were almost out on their feet. That meant an inn, somewhere cheap and clean and as far from the city gates as they could get. Daemi knew that word of her little display with the guard captain would already be spreading, no doubt becoming more fantastic with each telling. Stories like that attracted certain folk. Gave them ideas.

As the main thoroughfare curved to the left, Daemi saw what she was looking for. Hanging from the side of a building in the middle distance was a battered timber sign, its paint weathered and streaked from years of exposure to the elements. Underneath the dirt and grime she could still make out two crossed keys.

Daemi waved the others on, cutting through the crowd to head toward the shelter of the inn's doorway, just as the skies opened and a heavy, steady rain began to fall.

Once they made it across, she peered through the thick glass windows of the inn. It looked busy, but not too crowded. Patrons were scatted about the various tables in the main room eating and drinking, and a fiddler performed on a low stage.

'This will do.'

She pushed in through the door, Heather and Frankle a step behind, trying not to make their relief too obvious.

Warm, dry air met them as soon as they entered, and the mixed scents of bread and ale and spices filled the room. Daemi spotted an empty table on the far side of the room and strode toward it, ignoring the multiple sets of eyes that followed them.

Frankle noticed the glances too, but kept his gaze down. He knew it often only took a look in the wrong direction to send some folk into a fury, especially when alcohol was involved. He'd learned very early in life that it was often safer never to raise your eyes at all, never to make your presence known. Keep quiet and still and hope to be ignored. It was only recently in Redmondis that he'd broken out of the habit. Now he slipped back into it with ease.

Heather experienced the room differently. She appreciated the warmth and the comforting smells of cooking food, but for her the real wonder was the music. She almost froze when she heard it, the fiddler on stage sending a racing thrill through her heart with his playing. She wanted to stop and watch and lose herself in the feeling, her mind being taken by the hand and led away, swept off its feet by the soaring notes. Everything else was forgotten.

Daemi grabbed Heather by the shoulder and guided her to the empty booth, pushing her into a seat and hunching over to whisper, 'How much money do we have?'

'I've about five silvers in my purse, and some gold hidden in the lining of my boots if it comes to that,' Frankle whispered back.

Daemi rewarded this with a twisted grin. 'Well. A wielder with more than half a brain. Never thought I'd see the day. Heather?'

Heather was in another world, the fiddler's music now a fast trot, the sharp notes buffeting her as they carried her along.

'Heather?' Daemi repeated.

Nothing.

'Heather!' Daemi's fist crashed into the table and half the room jumped.

Heather's eyes snapped back, as though she'd just woken up. 'I—uh, sorry. I was distracted. What were you saying?'

'Money. How much money do you have?' Daemi struggled to keep her voice low.

'Oh, lots. As much as we need, more really.' Heather smiled and pulled her shoulder bag onto the table. 'Bottomless, you know.'

Daemi didn't know what to make of that, and Frankle covered his grin with his hand to avoid angering her further.

Heather's sunny reply had attracted the attention of more than one of the other inn patrons. Daemi sighed and sat back, pulling her cloak free to reveal the long knife hanging from her side.

'Try to keep your voice to a low yell.'

Heather blushed. 'Sorry, it's the music, it's—'

'He's quite good, isn't he?' Frankle agreed, looking to the stage.

The fiddler was an old man, hunched around his instrument,

cradling it in the crook of his shoulder, his eyes closed, as if all that mattered was the music. The bow raced back and forth across the strings, while his other hand danced impossibly quickly up and down the neck of the fiddle, his fingers a blur of movement.

All three watched him for a long moment, taken out of themselves by the music.

Daemi shook her head as though to clear it and sat forward again to address Heather. 'Do you have a way to retrieve enough money to pay for meals and accommodation without making it any clearer how much you're actually carrying?'

'Of course.' Heather pulled her bag off the table and rummaged through it with one hand.

'Frankle.'

Frankle dragged his eyes away from the stage.

'You look like you know these sorts of places.' It wasn't a question, but Frankle nodded just the same. 'Make yourself at home. See if you can siphon up some news. I want to know why the Redmondis name seems to have lost its power.'

He slid out of the booth, heading toward the bar, trying to make himself look older than he felt.

Daemi watched him go, taking note of the eyes that followed him. He'd be okay, she decided. If anything, his small stature would be an asset in this place. He didn't look enough of a threat for anyone to bother with.

'Here.' Heather slid her fist across the table and Daemi covered it with her hand and gave it a gentle squeeze.

'Keep them in hand. Show only what you need to. Dinner for three, and a room. One room.'

This last was a whisper as a large ruddy-faced woman walked up to them, wiping her hands on the front of her apron before placing her fists on her ample hips. 'What can I get you?'

Heather looked up into the unfriendly face, and almost dropped the coins as Daemi released her hand and sat back. 'Uh—a meal please. For three. And a room for the night.'

The woman let out a harrumph as a reply and kept her hands on her hips as though waiting for something.

'Um, how much will that be?' Heather's voice rose in pitch.

'A clean room. Three bunks,' Daemi added, her voice one of command. She tapped three fingers on her shoulder as she spoke, and the serving woman's frown of disapproval instantly melted away.

'Very good, ma'am. That's two silvers in total.'

Heather fumbled out a couple of coins from her fist and handed them over. They disappeared into some hidden pocket in the woman's apron.

Heather stared at the woman's back as she sauntered away toward the kitchen. Two silvers was far cheaper than she'd expected. She'd been willing to pay five at least, perhaps more since they were strangers in town.

'I guess the colours of Redmondis carry some weight here after all.'

'Perhaps,' Daemi replied, rubbing the tips of her fingers together. It wasn't the Redmondis colours that had made the difference; it was the shoulder tap, the sign she'd given without thinking, without knowing what it meant, almost out of some forgotten habit.

She scanned the room again. The eyes that had been locked on them since they entered the inn were all now studiously focused on other things.

In fact, the mood in the tavern seemed to have improved dramatically, and she took a moment to realise that it wasn't her imagination. The music had changed; the jaunty dance from before had been replaced by a lilting ballad, the notes weeping from the fiddler's bow. Daemi and Heather sat in silence, letting the strange music wash over them.

The mood was broken by Frankle plonking three large mugs of ale in the centre of the table. He slid into the booth and leaned forward, his eyes sparkling with excitement. 'We need to be careful.' Daemi sat forward, the music forgotten. 'What do you mean?'

'There are thieves here.' He turned to Heather. 'Keep your hand on your bag.'

'How—?' Daemi pressed.

'You see the two old ones leaning against the bar?'

Daemi scanned the room again, subtly passing over the men Frankle pointed out. 'Yes.'

'Well, they're local. Traders of some sort. Eager for a chat once their tongues had been lubricated. Told me there were members of the thieves' guild here.'

'You mean the two who are openly staring at us right now?' Daemi asked.

Frankle looked up. His drinking companions were looking straight at him, their mouths hanging open. As soon as he met their eyes, they glanced away nervously and gathered their things. 'Uh, yeah. That's weird.'

Daemi sat back. 'I think they were talking about us.'

The music changed again, the sad ballad replaced by a faster song, the mood in the room lightening. Daemi looked up and saw the fiddler bow his head toward the shadows at the side of the stage, then nod directly at their table.

She slid her hand under her cloak and grasped the hilt of her knife.

Frankle tried to explain to Heather what he'd been doing, but his whispers died as a tall, dark-haired man strode toward their table. He studied each of them as he approached, before his eyes returned to Daemi, having obviously decided she was in charge. With a brief wave of his fingers he signalled Frankle to shift over, and Frankle obeyed immediately. He looked like the sort of man used to giving orders.

The man slid into the booth opposite Daemi, his hands resting on the top of the table. 'Now then.' He smiled coldly. 'It seems introductions are in order. I thought I was familiar with all the members of the Grey Guild here in Sontair. My name is Lodan.' He bowed his head in Daemi's direction. 'Who might you be?'

Chapter 33

The two cats danced lightly across the thick ice, skidding and sliding on their padded paws, the larger one moving slowly and carefully, placing each foot with care before shifting his weight, the smaller one moving much less surely, often falling backward before springing back to his feet. Beneath the ice other things moved in the dark. Every few steps, a flash of scales could be seen through the warping lens of the ice, and each time the smaller cat pounced at them, always a moment too late. The larger cat let him play his game. There was no risk of breaking through the packed path.

Above them the strangely lit skies whirled as though a storm were about to break, the clouds twisting and stretching into strange forms, shapes appearing and then blurring away in an instant as they rolled like thick smoke. The larger cat was aware of the faces far above, the eyes that sought them out, the glimpses that broke clear of the roiling storm. These too he ignored.

We ... I apologise for our aspect. It is still troubling to find ourselves here alone.

The cat skidded softly to a stop on the ice and waited.

As you can see, the ages-old defences hold. But they are weakening. Times were that the ice that held back the dark was too thick for any eye to penetrate. Not anymore.

The voice from far above led the cat to peer down through the ice. Another flash of movement slid below his feet, a long serpentine body that sent a shiver of recognition down the cat's spine.

What power formed this defence has long been lost to time, like so much else beneath the surface. All we are left with are hints and snatches of vague prophecies. The blood within the stone. We don't even know the source of that augury, let alone its full text. Was it intended as a warning, or an invitation?

Given this ignorance perhaps we can be forgiven for delving too deep. When our nine linked minds first dove into these depths, we saw a world of possibilities. A challenge. Over time we learned to penetrate the barrier, to release that which dwells below. Now it is clear we were not alone in our folly.

The smaller cat bundled clumsily into the legs of the other as he chased another glimmering shape, and the larger cat turned and swatted him quickly across the snout. In the distance a thick column of steam stretched up from the ice to the heavens above, adding to the chaotic dance of the clouds, thickening the shapes that covered the sky.

This is close enough.

The cat studied the distant steam, watching as a flash of movement shot through it and disappeared into the sky.

This is but one of many such breaks. We do not know who was responsible for this one. Perhaps we all are. Perhaps our meddling has weakened the barriers so fundamentally that it is cracking up. Who is responsible no longer matters. It is just one of the access points that those who dwell below now share.

The cat sat on his haunches. The smaller cat sidled up to him, rubbing his body across the larger one's back.

You say there are others—other weak points?

Many others. And growing every day.

What causes them? How do we plug them? How do we stop those … creatures from entering our world?

This is not the place for such a conversation. Besides, there are other things you need to see.

The next moment both cats were gone, the ice left stark and empty. Wilt floated high above, within the clouds themselves. He didn't try to make sense of the madness; he just unfocused his eyes and let the images roll past.

It was here, beneath the chaos and flux that most who call themselves wielders consider the depths, down in this eternal silence, that we first noticed them.

Them?

Those few still worthy of the wielder name. Those we have forgotten. Those from the true heart of the welds themselves, it is said.

Wait, Wilt—didn't Nurtle mention something like this?

You mean the Eastern Dales. Where the weld blade came from.

Yes, wielder. For I think you too are one of the few who still deserve that title. To the east, across the great mountain range that protects us from their armies, on the far side of the eternal plain, you can still hear mention of it in song if you frequent the right tavern. The Eastern Dales.

But—you saw them here? Wilt took in his surroundings. Above him rolled the impossible storms of the depths, below lay the thick ice barrier protecting the surface world. Here was nothing. *Where?*

Ah! You are close, and yet still do not quite see. The question is not where, wielder, but when.

A flash of movement caught Wilt's eye. A ring of figures sinking out of the roiling chaos above. Nine hooded figures, arms interlocked.

The Sisters.

Yes. Watch.

The circle of women seemed to slow their descent, then stutter to a stop, as if unable to sink any further toward the ice surface below.

We nearly expended ourselves just getting this far. Nine minds stretched to the limits of their endurance, and still did not succeed. It was unthinkable.

But, how is this possible? The Nine Sisters are no more.

Where you are is a place beyond time. What you see is part of a memory, yet here, that no longer matters.

Suddenly another figure appeared, flashing into being right beside the stalled Nine Sisters. It was a figure seemingly composed of shadows, no feature recognisable except a vaguely human shape. It reached out and touched the nearest Sister on the shoulder, and the group sank again.

They knew of our presence, and our struggle, and they gifted us the power needed to proceed. The way to draw up the serpents from below, to bend them to our will.

But … why?

Why indeed? Perhaps they intended for us to fail. To overreach ourselves. I have asked this same question of myself many times.

As the Sisters sank again, one of them reached out as though trying to grab the sleeve of the shadowed figure. It glided away, out of reach, then blinked out of existence.

I have tried again and again to alter this memory. To change what occurred, but such power is beyond me.

What do you mean, alter the memory?

Look to your own experience, wielder. For those who fully control the power of the blood within the stone, what has already occurred can yet be altered. As I said, time is meaningless here.

Like with Red Charley. The dreams we've been having. The way they change with each telling.

Yes. You know the truth of this. Come, wielder, let me show you.

Wilt rose again, the Nine Sisters disappearing as a grey mist filled the air, wiping the scene clear.

He shook the water from his hair and wiped his eyes. He squatted on a rooftop, the rain streaming down upon him, a heavy rain that had set in hours ago and showed no sign of easing. It cut visibility to only a few feet, but that was all he needed. Below him, huddled under a poor excuse for a shelter, lay his father.

He twisted the knife in his hands, the point digging into the callus on his index finger.

It would be so easy to end it here. To never have to feel the brunt of that man's anger ever again.

Do it.

No one would see, not in this weather. There would be no consequences.

Do it.

He leaned over the edge of the rooftop and eased himself down the wall, toward his waiting victim.

No.

The weld snapped free and Wilt stumbled back as he found himself standing in the queen's chamber, at the foot of the dais on which her throne rested. The thick silver weld that had joined their minds faded as he watched, melting into the air.

The queen stared down at him from her throne, her mouth set. 'You do not wish to test your strength in this way? To fully appreciate your potential?'

Wilt shook his head, as much to jolt the troubled memory free as in answer. 'That wasn't … That memory wasn't mine.'

'Oh? Whose was it then? You doubt the truth of what the weld has shown you?'

Red Charley. That was one of Red Charley's memories.

'Future and past entwined. Why would you have access to another's memories, wielder?'

'He is—he was, an enemy of mine. He is no more.'

'Ah! You mean you ended him yourself. This is intriguing. If the welds give you access to other minds, other memories, then the possibilities …' The queen seemed to be struck by this thought, and her voice trailed off. She sat up straighter in her throne. 'Rest for now. I will have to think on this. Your potential may be even greater than we realised. We will have more to show you this evening. I have been assured Vargul has our specimen ready.'

Chapter 34

Petron still felt the echo of the moment when he had held that spark in his hand. The feeling of being more than one mind, in more than one place, in more than one time. It comforted him, though he knew trying to pin down the thought, interrogate it and pick it apart, would only cause it to dance out of reach. It was a breath of wind at the back of his mind, something he was aware of but could not access. Much like the ability to change form, something he could no longer do, a doorway that still existed somewhere in his mind but was now walled off and hidden. He didn't feel this was a loss, however; it was a distant, reassuring memory, vague and unreal yet undeniable.

He shook his head and realised he hadn't been listening to the report the young soldier in front of him had been giving. When the guard finished talking, he nodded and waved his hand vaguely, and that seemed to be response enough. The soldier saluted sharply and marched from the room, pulling the door closed behind him. Petron watched him leave, still amazed at the age of these children acting in the roles of men.

'They seem younger every day, do they not?'

Petron turned to see Nurtle and Jasper standing at the edge of the large opening in his chamber wall. His desk no longer faced that direction.

'You've made adjustments to your quarters, I see,' Nurtle continued.

'Fewer distractions this way.' Petron smiled. 'And there aren't too many with the skills to take me by surprise from the air.'

Nurtle walked toward the fire, one hand still clasped, as ever, in Jared's. Jared looked pale, his face drawn and his eyes distant. He moved stiffly across the room as though no longer comfortable in his own body. Petron held his tongue.

It was Nurtle who spoke first, acknowledging what Petron was polite enough not to voice. 'We are needed elsewhere now. The time has come sooner than we thought.'

'I see. You have been a great help, to all of us here, and elsewhere. I thank you for it.'

Petron's honest, open tone brought a wide smile in return.

'You sound revitalised, Petron. It is good to see our last little adventure has had no lasting effects.'

'No bad ones, at least. I do feel more energised—all of Redmondis does, it seems. We are making progress.'

'Good.' Nurtle nodded. 'You may be needed all too soon.'

'There is time yet. There is hope.'

'Not so much, Petron. Not as much as we need.'

Nurtle turned and pushed Jared down into a chair. He seemed dazed, only half aware of his surroundings. He clung to Nurtle's hand, as though it were the one lifeline remaining that stopped him drifting out to sea.

Petron watched him, that lost, private part of his mind recognising the distance in Jared's gaze, the farseeing sight that was focused on a different way of viewing the world.

'Jared,' he whispered, but the man showed no sign of recognition.

'We have less time than all of us hoped,' Nurtle said, sinking down into the chair beside Jared and patting his hand.

'So soon?'

'I think so.' Nurtle's voice was low. 'Jared and I have spent many years as wildlers, perhaps too many. Too long in foreign minds. I think the only thing keeping us still anchored here all these years was Shade. Now that he's ... no longer with us, our link to this human world is fading. My love can no longer completely find his own way back.'

Petron nodded, recognising the pain in her tone. He was familiar with the risks all wildlers took, the sacrifice they made when spending so long in other forms. He'd felt that pull himself many times when in the eagle form that Wrexley and he had shared, but had always held himself back from the brink. True wildlers such as Nurtle and Jared took things more than one step further and hadn't benefited from the training Redmondis had given him to deal with the dangers of their craft. It was yet one more crime to lay at the feet of the Nine Sisters.

'We have had a good run though, haven't we, old friend? Besides, we have other adventures ahead of us, in other forms.'

Nurtle patted Jared's hand again and stared out over the top of the Tangle stretched far below, the trees swaying as ever in the breeze, waving their subtle invitation.

'You are ready to take that final step?'

'Almost. We fulfilled our last promise to the Guardian to give him some time with our young friends. We have ensured they got to Sontair in good time. Now, well … We shall see. The Tangle itself is much changed. Closed. Wary. Perhaps it is for the best we help bring part of it back.'

'And you are still convinced the Tangle shares our goals?'

'No.' Nurtle chuckled. 'Never that. But I am convinced that we share the same enemy.'

Petron considered her words. 'Very well.' He reached out his hand to her. 'Thank you again for all you have done. For me, and for all of us. I assume we will not meet again.'

Nurtle took his hand and pulled herself to her feet. 'Do not assume so much, Petron. None are wise enough to see so far into the mists of the future. And please, do not waste your time feeling sorry for us. We go where all true wildlers belong.'

She smiled, taking the edge off her words. 'Besides, it's about time our strange young son looked after us. And how many do you know are lucky enough to share themselves completely with their true love?'

Petron stepped aside to let the two wildlers past. He watched them walk to the open window, aware that he was perhaps witnessing their final moments in human form.

'Goodbye, friends. May your winds be favourable.'

'Goodbye, Petron,' Nurtle replied. 'We may yet meet again. One day.'

With that Nurtle and Jared turned to each other, clasped each other's hands and blurred together. A giant eagle let out an exalted cry of freedom before launching into the infinite sky.

Chapter 35

Wilt and Higgs stood on the riverbank under the looming city walls, picking through the rocks and pebbles at their feet, trying to find suitable slinging stones. The wide river bubbled past them, the only movement on its clear surface caused by the breeze from the south, bouncing across the water to ruffle Wilt's hair. On the far bank the thick trees of the Tangle swayed with the same wind, silently watching them.

Higgs was building a small pile of perfectly sized stones—he always seemed to find the right ones so easily—and Wilt took a few steps away to try his luck further down the bank. The toe of his boot kicked a likely candidate and he bent down to grab it, weighing its heft in his hand. Higgs was behind him, out of sight now. He somehow knew he couldn't turn around to see him even if he wanted to.

Wilt pulled his sling out of his pants and dropped the stone into the roughened leather cradle, giving the sling a few practice spins in the air. It felt right. Solid. Much more real than the rest of the scene, which now faded into the strange dim mist of dreams.

Stone and weight. The high walls of Greystone rearing up behind them, containing them. Keeping them safe from the world. And something else, a new presence, a voice.

Wilt spun his sling up to speed and released it with a snap, the stone arcing high over the water toward the trees on the far bank. He watched it disappear into the green and turned to the voice.

He sat up, instantly awake, his breath coming in quick gasps. He stared around the room, taking a moment to remember where he really was. He was in Sontair, in the capital. A guest of the queen. Sleeping in the small comfortable chamber a nameless servant had led him to that afternoon.

Wilt's skin was covered in a thin sheen of sweat, though the air in the room was cool. The small fire in the grate had burned low, almost extinguished, its coals a weak orange glow in the darkness. He swung his feet over the side of the bed and lowered his head into his hands. A dream, just a dream. A nightmare, he supposed.

Greystone. You were dreaming of Greystone. You haven't done that in ages.

You could see it? My dream?

Not while it was happening, but I know what you know. I can see the memory, though it's fading fast. You were dreaming of me and the river and Lodan. The day he approached you about joining the Grey Guild, remember?

Lodan. That had been the voice he heard. The public face of the guild in Greystone, next in line to the Hand himself. Higgs was right, he hadn't thought of him since …

Since before Redmondis.

That's right. When the cantors took us.

An awful lot has happened since then. I wonder what Lodan would think of us now.

Wilt smiled at the thought and felt better. The strange dread the dream had caused him was melting back into his unconsciousness.

What would Lodan think? The last time he'd seen him was on the flagball court, when he was just a scruffy young thief.

A loud knock on the chamber door snapped him out of his musing. He was already pulling his boots on when the door swung slowly open and a servant poked his head in, eyes downcast to save his guest's modesty.

'My apologies, my lord. The queen has requested your presence immediately.'

'I'll be right there.' The servant withdrew to wait in the hall.

She mentioned her specimen. I wonder what she meant.

Wilt stomped his foot to knock his boot into place and started out the door, buckling the weld blade onto his hip as he went.

There's only one way to find out.

As soon as they were on their way, it was clear something was different. It was still the heart of night, for one thing, and the torches hanging at intervals along the stone castle walls threw threatening shadows across the wide hallway, glimpses of tapestries and looming statues appearing suddenly out of the darkness as the firelight flickered. As they passed an open window, Wilt noticed the full moon high in the sky, and the lack of lights from the other buildings stretching out beneath them. It was very late, or very early. A time for secrets.

The servant leading Wilt seemed determined to get his job done as quickly as possible, hurrying along the corridor with his head down, his shuffling trot somehow remaining almost silent. Wilt winced as his own boots echoed in the silence and tried to adjust his gait as he walked to reduce the noise.

Some thief you are. Forgotten everything I showed you?

Wilt grimaced at the thought, settling into the old creeping rhythm of the travellers on the night highway. They hurried along, turning this way and that through gloomy hallways until Wilt knew he was hopelessly lost. This had to be a different path than the one he had taken earlier in the day, so they weren't going back to the queen's audience chamber. Where then?

Wilt was nervous about what he was being led into. The servant stopped in front of a simple wooden door cut into the stone wall. It looked like an entrance to a pantry or storage room. The man opened it outward and gestured Wilt toward the waiting shadows.

Stepping inside, Wilt saw immediately that his expectations for the room were wrong. It was large, larger even than the queen's audience chamber that he'd found so imposing. Flaming torches lined the walls, marking out a wide curve that sunk down into a central pit of shadows, almost like he was standing at the top row of a viewing chamber or theatre. In the centre of the pit the darkness was complete, the flickering light from the torches unable to penetrate it.

Wilt felt his eyes drawn to that point, his wielder instincts alive suddenly, aware that there was more than shadows waiting there.

'Thank you for coming so quickly, young wielder.'

Wilt turned to the voice and found the queen sitting only a few feet from the door, on a row of seats lining the central pit. She looked tense and excited, leaning forward in her seat, eager for the show to begin.

Wilt looked back toward the dark centre of the room, not wanting to take his eyes away from the threat he could feel waiting there. 'What is it?'

The queen smiled and nodded. 'Yes, you feel it too, of course. The pull. The promise of power.'

Wilt was about to disagree that promise was not what he felt at all. What he felt was something closest to dread, but the queen had already turned back to the centre of the room and was waving her hand high in the air as a signal.

At the sign another row of torches in the central pit sprung into life. Wilt blinked the stars from his eyes as this new light blazed into being. These torches weren't lining the walls, they were being held aloft by a circle of robed men. Wilt focused on the closest one, study-ing the hunched figure and the face that danced in and out of sight beneath the shadowed cowl of his hood. It was Vargul, no, another man similar to him. Same drawn features, same glinting, golden eyes.

Wilt turned his attention back to the centre of the pit where impossibly a circle of darkness still resisted the light. He frowned and moved his eyes briefly into their cat form, but even their heightened vision couldn't penetrate the blackness. It was more than just lack of light, it was a viscous, liquid thing, shifting and morphing as the light from the torches bent toward it.

'Wondrous, is it not?' The queen's voice was barely more than a whisper.

Wilt tore his eyes from the shifting mass in the centre of the room to look at the queen. The Sister. At that moment he was most struck by her resemblance to the Sister he had known in Redmondis. Her green eyes shone with a mad hunger.

Watch yourself. She looks like one ready to sacrifice anything for power.

Higgs's voice felt different in Wilt's mind. Quieter, almost muffled, as though it were speaking to him through a thick blanket, all echoes and sharpness buffed away. Instantly he realised what Higgs was doing, trying to hide his shared thoughts from the queen.

You don't need to tell me anything twice, you should know that by now.

It seemed to be working, the queen showed no sign of having heard Higgs's interjection. She was bent forward in her seat, her hands curled into tense claws on the arm rests.

She waved again, impatiently now, and the men holding the torches stepped closer, toward the strange black mass, crowding the darkness in until it would have disappeared entirely were it at all natural.

Wilt watched, aware he was holding his breath.

The next moment the solid bubble of shadow seemed to pop, and something like a massive black spider or crab stood in its place, its evil-looking claws snapping at the air in front of it.

It was another of the shadow creatures that had attacked them in the Tangle, and again from the river. Much larger though, as though the others had only been children and this one was fully grown. Wilt started to draw his blade, but was halted immediately by a stern command from the queen.

'Hold, wielder!' The queen's words were wrapped in power, binding Wilt's arms in place as he strained against them. 'Be still. We have it under control.'

Wilt felt the bonds holding him loosen as he stopped pushing against them, until finally he was free of them entirely, and let go of his blade.

He stared into the pit at the nightmare creature, a shifting mass of limbs and claws snapping at the air, struggling against some invisible barrier that held it back from the men surrounding it.

'A gloomclaw,' the queen whispered, a strange awe tingeing her words. 'Though the legends have given them many names. Dreamflayer, weldreaver. A creature from the nightmare depths. And yet here it is, under my power.'

No. This is wrong. This is—

'These creatures have been attacking townships from the south coast to the very walls of the Tangle for months now, almost entirely unmolested. It seems my success in holding this one captive has only increased the frequency of their attacks. I had hoped my puppet king would remain weak enough to allow time for further study, but news of their threat has found its way into even his befuddled mind. We must act before more concrete efforts are made to repel them.

'You saw the weakening barriers that have allowed their kind through. They attack in moments and leave nothing but death and dust in their wake. They appear from nowhere and disappear just as readily. But we have found a way to leash this one, to hold it on this plane.'

The thing in the pit—the gloomclaw—seemed to react to the queen's words, slowing its angry struggling and turning what Wilt assumed was its face toward them. There were no features to make out, just a shifting jumble of shadows and dark forms. As though a chunk of the chaotic depths had been scooped out and dropped into the surface world.

'The men you see below are more than mere servants. Each is a wielder in his own right, of sorts. Redmondis does not always find everyone who displays power, and rejects some who don't continue to grow into their skills as they age, but I have found a use for these outcasts, these forgotten ones, helping them to link their minds into a chain stronger than the sum of its parts, strong enough to hold even this creature at bay. Strong enough to serve my purposes.'

Wilt was still lost in the shifting darkness of the gloomclaw, unable to take his eyes from it. There was something almost familiar about the pull, much like the call of the dark when he took on the wraith form, the lure of power singing to him in a register he could only barely hear.

Finally he found his voice, though his eyes stayed locked on the centre of the pit. 'Your purposes. What would they be?'

'Don't you see?' The queen's eyes were mad with triumph. 'With this creature I can take the fight back to the depths. Merge with its mind and drive down into that dark centre we Sisters could never penetrate in the past. The past! The past itself is meaningless there. Time has no power in that realm.' Her voice rose into a crazed cackle of triumph as she continued. 'I can bring them back, all of them, all of my fallen sisters. We can be what we were meant to be. The promises of the serpents can at last be fulfilled!'

Wilt felt the words twining around his mind, aware that she was using her powers to influence him. Another flash of memory struck him—the Sister in Redmondis, her green eyes boring into his, her voice holding him down, charming him, winding herself around him like a snake, her tongue flickering into his ear.

He banished the thought and pushed back against the queen's urging voice, feeling the temperature drop as he drew on his power.

'And you will help me, wielder. You have faced them, fought against the gloomclaws and survived. You will join with me and help me form a weld strong enough to break into its mind. Turn it to our uses, our ways. Wield the power of the dark against itself.'

Just like the Sentinels.

Wilt dropped away from them, away from both voices, away from the surface world. The ring on his finger blazed with a sudden heat. Immediately the glowing chain of welds holding the gloomclaw in place became clear, thin silver welds woven together to form a wide mesh that warped and bulged as the creature surged against it. The men forming the weld cage seemed oblivious to all else, sweat coating their foreheads and their eyes shining with a sick golden light.

The queen seemed not to notice or care about the obvious strain the work was having on her men. Her face was in rapture as she stared down at the gloomclaw shifting and morphing in its invisible shackles. Suddenly another weld, a thick black snake, shot out from the queen and struck down on the creature. Wilt watched it twist and flex in the air, its siren song calling to him, compelling him to join with it.

Hold. It's too dangerous.

Wilt could see the strain on the queen's face now as she tried to merge with the thing in the pit. Her face was slack and empty, all thought focused on breaking through to her goal. Her cheek twitched, her features flexing into a horrifying mask of pain. At the same time the gloomclaw seemed to gain a renewed burst of strength, surging against its bonds, throwing its body into the thin silver netting that strained to hold it in place.

Higgs, we have to help her.

You've seen what those creatures from the depths can do. There's no way to help her now. It's inside her mind. It's already too late.

We have to try.

Wilt was already reacting; he reached out to the thick black weld and sunk into it, forgetting all else.

He broke into a raging, frothing sea of panic, dark claws scrabbling for his mind as he struggled to regain his balance. Shadows clawed at him, wrapping around and pulling him down into the depths. He couldn't breathe. He was drowning in chaos.

No. Maintain control. Go with them, use their pull.

Biore? But how are you—

Let the power flow through you. Take them into you, deep down, into where even they fear to tread.

Wilt stopped struggling and let the waters take him, diving with them, pulling the clinging forms into the depths, below the surface world, below the weakened barriers of ice, into the still darkness.

Chapter 36

'Lodan. You're Lodan? From Greystone?' Heather asked.

Lodan turned his cold gaze toward her. 'You've heard my name before.'

Heather nodded quickly, suddenly shy. 'Yes. Higgsy—I mean, Higgs told me about you. About how you helped Wilt.'

Lodan sat forward at the mention of the two familiar names, his eyes gleaming with sudden interest. 'You know Higgs?'

Heather nodded again and dropped her head, unwilling to say any more.

'We knew him,' Daemi explained.

Lodan looked back and forth between the two, digesting the news. 'It seems we have much to talk about. Follow me.'

He walked across the tavern and back into the shadows from where he had appeared.

Daemi found herself on her feet about to follow him before she realised what she was doing. It was his voice, his tone of command. Her soldier's training reacted instantly. Or was it something more? Something familiar, though she was unsure how.

'Should we?' She hesitated, looking at her two companions, who were already hurrying to gather their things.

Daemi led them across the front of the stage, every eye in the place now openly locked on them. As they passed the fiddler, he bowed his head briefly, then struck up another jaunty tune. He jigged across the stage in time with the music, almost physically wrenching the attention away from them, the other customers all drawn to watch him play, their toes tapping in time despite themselves. Before the crowd realised it, the three strangers had disappeared into the shadows and were already on their way to being forgotten.

Daemi and the others passed through a narrow doorway at the side of the stage and down some stairs, the music from the inn fading quickly as the stairs curved downward. Eventually they opened out into a dusty storeroom, sacks of potatoes and grain resting against one wall, boxes of vegetables and herbs lining another. In the centre of the small room, empty crates had been arranged into a desk, two fat candles melted into its top, their flames giving the room a cosy orange glow.

Lodan sat on another crate behind the makeshift desk, waiting for them. As they entered, he waved them toward a pile of rickety boxes in the far corner. 'Find a seat. Make sure they're not too rotten. I don't want to spend another afternoon removing rusty nails and splinters from a clumsy guest's rear end.'

Frankle hurried over and grabbed three crates, eager to be of some use.

Lodan waited patiently for the party to organise themselves before turning once more to Daemi.

'You look familiar to me. These two …' He pointed at Frankle and Heather, his eyes not leaving Daemi's. 'These two are strangers, but you … you I know.'

'How?' Daemi coughed as soon as the word was out of her mouth. Her voice had sounded so small.

'I don't know. That's what I find so interesting.'

Lodan turned away then, and Daemi felt a strange release as his eyes left hers. Eventually they settled on Heather.

'Higgs. Let's start there. I haven't seen Higgs since he saved my new winger's life on the flagball court in Greystone. That winger was Wilt, of course. They both disappeared, taken by the Prefects of Redmondis, so it was whispered. I can only assume by your markings, he nodded at Daemi's cloak, 'that those whispers were true.'

Heather glanced up at Daemi for confirmation, but she was lost in her own thoughts. She didn't know how much she should tell this man. He knew Higgs, from before Redmondis. Could he be trusted with the truth?

Heather stared at Lodan, chewing her lip. Eventually she sighed. 'I knew him in Redmondis. That's where we've come from, all of us.'

Lodan's eyes didn't leave hers.

'It's … kind of a long story.'

Lodan smiled and sat back, gesturing around the empty store-room. 'We have nothing but time.'

'So after all of that, after you recaptured control of Redmondis and started building it back to what you tell me it was supposed to be, why come here? Why Sontair?'

Heather had finally wrapped up her hurried telling of the recent history of Redmondis, of Higgs and Wilt's arrival, of Cortis and his attempted coup, and of the Sisters and what had become of their dreams of power. Frankle and even Daemi had chimed in when they could, and Lodan had interrupted a few times to ask pointed questions that showed he understood more than she had expected about the power struggles of the time. Almost an hour had passed, and the rickety crates weren't getting any more comfortable.

'We're an official delegation, a representative from each of the three main schools sent here to reconnect with the capital, to rebuild the relationship between Redmondis and Sontair,' Heather replied, the words sounding drab and dead in her mouth. 'At least, that was the idea.'

Lodan looked at her silently, then turned to Daemi.

'Because it's where Wilt was going,' Daemi answered, not sure where the words were coming from, but knowing they were true.

'He found something in the Tangle that led him here, some sign he was following. He's the only real chance we have.'

'Chance of what?'

'Of fighting back against the dark.'

Lodan considered her words, his mouth twisting against itself as though he were sucking on something unpleasant. Finally he gave a single quick nod and stood up. 'Follow me.'

He led them out of the storage room, through a side passage none of them had noticed on the way in, and outside into a series of twisting lanes that seemed to be the rear entrance for businesses of all kinds, the clatter and noise of the city breaking over them like a wave as they followed in his wake. The lane was only two men wide, so they proceeded in single file, and every few steps another face appeared in a window or leaned out a doorway to call out a greeting to Lodan as he passed. He acknowledged each one silently, the other three having to hurry to keep up with his long, urgent stride.

Eventually the twisting lanes opened out into a wider courtyard, teeming with people, scattered wagons and tents set up in no particular order or pattern, each trying to claim some small place of their own among the throng. Voices argued back and forth, joining the general hubbub. There were too many people here, too many bodies crowded into a finite space.

Just as they arrived, a large tent to the side of the alley entrance buckled and collapsed under the push of bodies around it, angry shouts rising again as it fell.

Lodan slumped against the stone wall of the alley as he stared at the hopeless commotion. 'Villagers, farmers, merchants from smaller townships. At least, they used to be. They're refugees now.'

Daemi stepped up beside him, her hand drifting to the hilt of her knife automatically as she felt the rising anger and frustration from the crowd. 'From the north?'

'From everywhere. Each with their own wild tale of what happened to their homes. The details differ, but the same central theme remains. Dark things, nightmare shapes that rose from the ground, or came out from the night itself to attack them. Stories too similar to be anything but the truth.'

'Why come here?'

'Where else could they go? The king is supposed to protect them. This is his home, surely it's the safest place. At least, I assume that's their reasoning. There're too many for Sontair to house already, and more come every day.'

They watched the milling crowd in silence, each lost in thought. It seemed so hopeless.

Finally Daemi turned to Lodan. 'And you? You knew Wilt and Higgs in Greystone. What reason was there for you to come here?'

'For the same reason as all these others.'

Lodan returned her stare, and for the first time Daemi recognised the pain behind his eyes. 'Greystone fell months ago. There's nothing left.'

Chapter 37

He watched as Wilt ran down the wing of the flagball pitch, the ball rolling a few feet in front of him. The opposition guard, a heavy-set man who was faster than seemed possible for his size, arrowed straight for him. He wasn't going to stop, that much was clear. He would take both Wilt and the ball out of play in one single, crunching tackle.

The crowd shifted and a tall body moved in front of him, cutting off his view of the pitch. He reached out and pulled roughly at the man's purse, slipping out and around him as the man spun about to catch the would-be thief. He pushed past him, giving himself an uninterrupted view.

Wilt was still running, stepping over the ball now and chopping it from one side of his body to the other with his trailing leg, changing his angle of attack at the same time, cutting back across the charging guard's path. The guard's eyes widened as he realised both Wilt and the ball would be upon him before he was ready, too late to react as Wilt pirouetted, sending the ball curling around the opposite side of the guard, leaving him unable to stop either of them.

The crowd erupted in a cheer at the manoeuvre, and he was jostled almost off his feet as the surrounding bodies surged forward. The guard who Wilt had so easily skipped past lost his footing and skidded into the crowd just metres from where he stood watching.

Wilt was looking up now to spot Lodan waiting in the centre of the pitch, waving for the ball. He lowered his head and curled the ball toward him.

—Wake up.—

Wilt opened his eyes at the command, sucking in a deep breath as he did so, as though breaking the surface after being under water for too long. The present reverberated back into existence, and he was momentarily blinded as a wave of dizziness washed over him.

Higgs. I was dreaming of … I was you. Watching me.

I know. It's confusing. I can't make sense of the memories. That man in the dream I tricked into pushing past. I don't remember that happening. I'm not sure it did.

What is happening to us? Where are we?

A dim orange light flickered at the edge of his vision. He was lying on a cold dirt floor. He sat up, his clothes pulling roughly against his skin. In his hand was the weld blade, the hilt warm and sticky. He looked down and saw he was covered in blood.

The chamber. We're still in the viewing chamber. The queen summoned us here. She was trying to merge minds with the—

Gloomclaw.

Memories surged into Wilt's mind. He had reached out to the weld, joined with it, taken it down into the depths as the queen struggled and lost control.

Biore.

Yes, Wilt. It was him. I heard him too.

But I thought he'd—

He went into the welds, into the depths. Like Nurtle and Jared said, about Rawick. Merging with the welds themselves.

Then how could we hear him?

Perhaps because we followed him down. Which begs the question—

How did we get back out?

Wilt rolled to his feet and held the weld blade up in front of him, pointing out into the darkness. The only sound in the chamber was the faint roar of the flickering torches lining the walls. There was nothing here. Nothing living.

Lying in a wide circle around him were bodies, the robed men he'd seen trying to hold the creature back with their weld net. Wilt bent down to examine the closest man. His faintly golden eyes were blank now, empty of life, a deep gash ripped across his throat. Wilt flexed his hands again, wondering how much of the blood covering him had come from there.

The wound. Could it have been caused by the weld blade?

No, Higgs. The gloomclaw. That's its doing.

Perhaps. But then why are we still alive? And where is it now?

Wilt turned away from the body to study the others. Each looked the same, eyes dead and still, deep cuts across their chests and throats marking their sudden ends. Wilt moved slowly among them, conscious he was searching for some obvious sign it had been the gloomclaw who had done this and not himself.

Wilt. The queen.

At the edge of the circle of firelight lay another body, different from the others. Wilt hesitated before approaching it, unwilling to have his eyes confirm what he knew to be true.

The queen was lying in a large pool of drying blood, her eyes closed, her face at peace. A deep wound bloomed red on her gown over her heart.

She's dead, Wilt. What have we done?

Wilt bent down and pulled her eyelids open. Her eyes were twin pools of black, sending his own blood spatted reflection back to him. He slid them closed again, wiping the image away.

It wasn't us, Higgs. She tried to control it, merge with it, and it broke free. We were there, we were in the weld with them when it happened. Her mind was lost before her body fell.

How can you be sure?

Wilt stood up and looked around the room, at the bodies scattered across the floor.

There's so much blood, Wilt. Why are we covered in so much blood?

Suddenly a bright light burst into the room as a door was thrown open and heavy booted feet stamped in.

'Guards! To arms!'

A stream of soldiers quickly surrounded the scene. More doors were flung open around the outer wall of the chamber, flooding the room with blinding light.

'The queen! The queen has fallen! Seize her killer!'

Vargul. Wilt squinted up at him, standing by the side of an open door, pointing right at him, his golden eyes shining in triumph.

Don't fight them, Wilt. Not now.

Wilt tried to drop his blade, but dried blood held it to his palm. Finally he shook his arm and the blade clattered free.

'Take him alive.'

Let them. We need to work out what we're going to do. What we have done. We can always escape later.

Okay. As long as you're sure.

I'm not. But unless you have any better ideas …

Wilt raised his arms in surrender as the guards moved in. A moment later the world exploded into stars as the nearest guard swung the hilt of his sword into the base of his skull.

Chapter 38

Lodan sat alone in his study, a single private room tucked away on the second floor of the abandoned warehouse the Grey Guild had claimed as its own months before. A week's worth of reports were scattered across his desk, and he flipped idly through them, unable to dredge up the focus required to read them properly. They would all tell him the same thing. Business was bad, the flow of trade into Greystone had slowed to a trickle. Reports of trouble to the south were increasing. Times were hard.

Times have been hard before, lad. They will be again. That's why organisations such as ours exist. That's what the Hand would have told him, were he still alive.

Lodan tossed the report he was holding onto the desk and leaned back in his seat, running the same stream of thoughts through his mind that he did every night. Would the Hand have done anything different? Was he doing enough for the men under his command? Was he missing anything, even the smallest task that would make their lives easier in these dark times?

His eyes wandered along the walls, past the sputtering torch burning by the door, to rest on the shining medallion hanging beside it, flashing glints of silver and gold light. The flagball prize they'd won at the last harvest festival. Almost a year ago now. So much had changed since then. Most for the worst.

The sight of the medallion brought back more painful memories—the guard attacking Wilt, the presentation, and the way the medal glowed bright blue as it was placed over Wilt's head. The two prefects stepping forward to take him away, never to be seen again.

Lodan shook his head to clear the memory and stood up. Wilt was long gone now, taken to Redmondis according to reports they'd had back. Higgs too, his younger friend. Two of the best young thieves he'd come across simply scooped up and carried away.

You have other problems, more pressing worries. Other guild members who need your help.

A scuffled step at the door announced his visitor a moment before it swung open.

'Lodan. Uh, sir.' The boy caught himself and bowed awkwardly. He was panting heavily.

'What is it?' Reave, that was his name.

'There's trouble at the wall. The guard have disappeared, no sign of them anywhere. There's something wrong.'

Lodan watched the boy struggling to arrange his words and realised he was absolutely terrified. 'Calm yourself, Reave. What exactly did you see?'

The boy gulped and tried to catch his breath. He couldn't have been much more than ten years old, the rags falling off him marking him as one of the street rats the guild kept housed and fed in return for information.

'I didn't see nothing—uh, anything, sir. Wendel, my mate, he says he saw a guard fall. I hurried to take a look, but there was nothing. Just …'

'Yes? Spit it out, lad.'

'Just a shadow. Strange like. Like the night was coming alive and moving across the top of the wall. Gave me the shivers.'

'And Wendel and you came straight here to report?'

'Yes sir. They said I should tell you straight away. They said it's an emergency.'

'You've done well, Reave. Sit down. There's bread and water on the sideboard—it's yours. Take some to Wendel as well, then hide yourselves away somewhere safe and secret. Keep out of sight and tell any of the others you know to do the same.'

Reave nodded, wide eyed, unable to shift his gaze from the half loaf of fresh bread Lodan had indicated.

Lodan stepped outside, leaving the boy inching toward the treasure, and closed the door behind him. 'Griggs!'

'Here, Lodan.'

Griggs was standing at the foot of the staircase that led up to Lodan's study. The aged winger from the guild flagball team was doing his best to stand at attention, cracked leather armour draping his thin frame, a battered old short sword hanging from his hip.

Lodan would have smiled at the sight if it weren't so serious. 'You know how to use that?' He pointed at the sword.

'Well enough.'

'Must be important.'

Griggs nodded, his face cold. 'You've heard the stories as well as I. There're too many similarities. Dark shadows, guards disappearing. You know what comes next.'

Lodan strode past him toward the chest that held his weapons and reached for his long sword.

'Well then, let's find out if these wild tales we've been hearing have any truth to them.

Wilt shook his head, fighting against what the dream was showing him, pushing back against the surge of strange memories that flooded his consciousness. Part of his mind was trying to alter what the visions showed him, but he couldn't fight against the force of the past. He rolled over, his cheek resting on the cold stone bench of his cell, and the dream washed him away again.

He stood at the corner, his cheek resting against the rough-cut stone on the wall, watching his townsfolk die.

There was nothing he could do.

The creatures moved impossibly fast, too fast to even get a solid idea of their shape, or what they were. They seemed to be composed of shadows, a blur of black limbs and snapping claws jerking out suddenly to rip into soft flesh before moving on to the next victim, claiming them before the previous body sank to the ground. Even when a lucky strike caught them, it did no harm. Lodan saw two guards strike down together on one of the creatures, their heavy pikes that would bring down a cart horse glancing off the creature's body. The guards both fell almost as soon as their blows had, and the creature moved on.

Some enterprising young thieves had thought to take the high ground, launching flaming bottles of oil down into the fray, but the flames sputtered out as soon as they landed, their heat and light seemingly consumed by the creatures, the acrid smell of burnt hair the only sign they had caused any damage at all. Finally Lodan had got the message to them to flee, that there was no use fighting these things. Not with any weapon they possessed.

That was his focus now, organising what was left of the guild to give the townsfolk as much time as they could to escape, diverting the creatures away from the town gates to allow as many as possible to get away with their lives intact. That meant sacrificing good men by throwing them into the fray, all knowing they had no chance of survival. Still, they followed his orders, making what stands they could and dying in the blink of an eye.

'Griggs!' he called over his shoulder, determined not to look away from the grisly scene.

'Here.'

'Fall back to Tanners alley. Take ten men with you, try to hold them. I'll join you there as soon as I can.'

The last man fell and Lodan finally looked away, turning to meet Griggs's eyes.

Griggs returned his gaze and gave a single nod, then hurried off, calling names as he went.

Another man he'd sent to his death. Another friend.

He pushed the thought down and climbed the wall he'd been leaning against, pulling himself up to the rooftop and hurrying from the fighting, heading toward the south gate. He risked one final glance *back as he ran. Greystone would not survive the night, that much was obvious. The entire northern side of the city was ablaze; silhouetted against the flames, dark shapes poured over the walls like a wave, a tide of darkness that had come to wash Greystone away.*

Lodan slowed his step as he watched it, mesmerised by the sheer hopelessness of what he saw. An explosion erupted as the flames reached a storehouse in the village, and Lodan turned his head to run, blinded by the flash.

'Wakey wakey, Princess.'

Wilt felt the heat and light of a torch push close to his face and reared back from the bars of his cell.

'Leave him be, Deg. They say he's dangerous. Don't bother him. We'll have time enough later.'

The light pulled away from Wilt's closed eyes and stars flashed and burst against his eyelids as he sank back into the dream.

He was standing at the edge of the roof, looking down at another skirmish that was reaching its inevitable conclusion.

A single creature had killed eight men, surging back and forth between them faster than thought. One man was left standing, his sword held hopelessly out in front of him, trying to hold his courage in what he knew were his final moments of life. It was Griggs.

Lodan watched, knowing he could do nothing but determined to bear witness.

The monster slowed, its shape still somehow dancing between forms as it moved toward its final victim.

—No.—

The creature stopped, aware of another voice.

—No more. Not one man more.—

Lodan stepped off the lip of the roof to land on the street below. He drew his sword and pointed it directly at the creature. 'Face me.'

The dark thing didn't turn exactly, but what might have been its face appeared on its back, as though it had morphed its shape.

Twin clawed arms reached out from a central point, an opening that ripped wide to form something like a mouth.

Lodan stared at it, determined not to let the fear that welled up inside him rob him of all fight.

Then it was on him, snapping claws reaching for him, and Lodan felt his blade move in reaction, dancing back and forth impossibly quickly to parry each thrust. His mind felt separated from his body, his sword moving in unfamiliar sweeps and forms, his body seeming to follow rather than direct the blade. Incredibly, the creature seemed to slow, its movements faltering as the blade switched from defence to attack, nipping in to sink into the soft flesh behind its armoured shell. With a final otherworldly screech the creature leaped at him, and Lodan twisted his body backward, one hand holding himself up from the ground, the other thrusting his sword into the centre of the creature's mouth. The screech choked off into a strained yawl and the creature seemed to wrap itself around his sword, shrinking as it spun in place until nothing was left but a small pile of black dirt and an evil, smoky stench in the air.

'You ... you killed it.'

Lodan looked up to see Griggs staring at him, his mouth gaping. He stood up and brushed himself off, a heavy sweat breaking out all over his body as it reacted to its sudden exertions. He felt like he was walking in a dream.

'I guess I did.'

'I've never seen anyone move that fast.'

Lodan stared down at his sword, at the hand that grasped its hilt, struggling to recognise his own flesh. Finally he shook his head. 'Follow me. There are too many of them to fight. We need to get the townsfolk clear.' He trotted out of the alley, Griggs following, leaving the smoking pile of black ash behind

'Something happened then, when the creature attacked me. Something I still don't understand.'

Lodan continued to stare out across the crowded courtyard in Sontair, his eyes unfocused, staring back into the past. 'Have you—' He turned to Daemi, seemingly shaking the memories away. 'Have you ever felt … guided? Controlled, almost. Like there was something else leading your hand? I don't mean in some mystical way like the priests would tell us. I mean really feeling yourself as a vessel for something … other?'

Daemi returned his gaze, not sure how to answer. 'In battle sometimes, my training has taken control. My body acts without my mind getting in the way.'

Lodan shook his head and turned back to the tented village. 'That's not what I mean. Besides, I was never that good with a sword. Never spent much time training as a fighter. This was something else.'

Daemi stepped closer to him, aware suddenly of a silence that seemed to have dropped over them both. 'There was one time. With Wilt, actually.' It was Daemi's turn to gaze into the past. 'We were heading to Redmondis. Wilt was one of the new conscripts the cantors—prefects, you call them—had rounded up. There was something different about him though, even I could see that. We … got into a fight.'

Lodan raised his eyebrows but held his tongue.

'I can't even remember why. But I was angry, angrier than I'd ever been before. Angrier than reason. I wanted to kill him. I would have too, but he used his wielder powers on me. Took over my body. It was like my mind was disconnected, like someone else had stepped in to take the controls and I was just a viewer. My hands were around his throat, and suddenly they just dropped away.'

Daemi shivered at the memory. 'It's part of what wielders can do, the strong ones at least. They can take over your mind.'

Lodan nodded and stared back out at the crowd. It seemed to have grown somehow as they'd been talking, even more bodies cramming into the limited space of the courtyard.

From out of the throng a familiar face appeared, and for a

moment his mind reeled in confusion, split between two conflict-ing memories. Then Griggs raised his hand and waved to him, and the warped feeling faded into his unconscious.

'Ho there, Lodan!'

Lodan waved in return. 'Griggs! Come over here. These are friends. Friends of Wilt's.'

Griggs smiled as he approached. 'Now there's a name I've not heard in a good while. It's good to know he's still alive, at least. How is our star winger?'

Griggs finally reached the edge of the courtyard and Lodan clapped him on the shoulder. 'That's what I was hoping you could help us find out.'

Chapter 39

Wilt felt the world form around him as he floated back up into the present, away from the seething confusion of the past. He kept his eyes closed, the universe an empty slate, waiting to be filled. First came a sound, a drip, a metronomic beat. Then a distant cry for help, the voice far away, muffled by walls of solid rock, the words garbled but the meaning painfully clear. Then a much closer sound, a clink of iron chains and a shuffling, heavy step.

The guards.

Wilt opened his eyes and sat up. In the dim light of the cell he could just make out the far wall, water dripping steadily down from an open shackle hanging from it. The weight on his wrists told him similar shackles bound his hands. He hefted them up in front of his face to study them in the gloom. They seemed heavy, far too heavy for their size. He let his mind sink quickly into the depths to change briefly into his wraith form, to slip from the shackles and free himself, but something resisted, pushing back, holding him up toward the surface and unable to access the depths.

The guards were carrying a torch, and the cell lit up as they approached. Wilt dropped his hands and arranged his features into a blank, open stare.

They know you have power. Be cautious.

As soon as Higgs said the words, Wilt felt the first scratchings at his mind. A fumbling, over-eager clamour that was all too simple to repel. For a moment he considered grasping it, sinking into it to trace it back to its source and attack the foolish wielder who sent it.

Leave it be. Just keep it out.

The shuffling steps had arranged themselves into two distinct gaits as they approached the door of his cell, and Wilt looked up to see two very different characters peering in at him through the thick bars of his cage. Holding the torch that lit the room was a short, immensely fat man, loops of iron hanging across his shoulders and a large keyring swinging from his other hand. The jailer. Next to him was the thin, stooped figure of Vargul.

'Open the door, Deg,' Vargul commanded, and the jailer rummaged through his keys. As he searched, Vargul stared at Wilt, studying him. 'You have found your new accommodation satisfactory, I take it?'

Wilt kept his mouth shut.

'Not tried any of your wielder tricks to escape?' Vargul leaned forward and ran a skeletal hand up and down one of the thick iron bars of the cell.

'The queen—the late queen, I should say—had these cells specially formed many years ago for ones such as you. Iron infused with special stone from Redmondis itself, so they say. Living rock that repels welds. I'm sure you know of it from your time there. Glows green in the darkness. Took the crafters an age to figure out how to get rid of that glow.'

The jailer finally found the correct key and the heavy lock shot back with a thunk.

'Thank you, Deg. You may continue your rounds. Our guest has most likely already discovered these shackles are not so easy to shake free.'

Vargul peered down at the thick iron loops still binding Wilt's hands and flashed a taunting smile.

Wilt stayed silent and blank, refusing to give him the satisfaction of an answer.

'Stand up.'

Wilt was jerked to his feet by his arms, the shackles seeming to respond to Vargul's command. Similar weights clamped around his ankles, joined by another heavy chain to the shackles that bound his wrists.

Vargul's smile grew wider as he saw the growing understanding on Wilt's face. 'Oh yes. We made sure to bind your hands and feet. Can never be too sure, you know, with you Redmondis trained wielders. Had to be quite harsh with some in the past. Count yourself fortunate a collar has not yet been deemed necessary.'

The scrabbling in Wilt's mind intensified, the claws digging in against its protective membrane pushing harder, trying to break through into his thoughts.

He knows you have power, just not how much. Let's keep it that way.

Suddenly the skin holding the foreign weld back broke and Wilt was invaded.

Try not to panic. I'm hiding what's important. Just let him think he's broken you.

Wilt found he didn't need to pretend. He fell to his knees with a cry as a sudden rush of power surged over his mind, a black stain spreading through him, blurring his thoughts and blanking out entire sections of his consciousness.

'You see? Not such a threat after all. Come now. Follow me.'

Vargul turned and strode away down the corridor, confident in the power he held over his prisoner. Sure enough Wilt's feet responded, complying with the command that impelled them to hobble forward.

His mind split, an animal part of him responding to what it was ordered to do while another, deeper part sat in a private space of its own, looking out through his eyes.

Now you know something of how I feel. It's okay, Wilt. Try not to panic. He can't find us here, we're far too deep for his weld to reach.

Wilt tried to respond, but it was desperately hard to form the thoughts required. His mind was a mass of treacle.

What are you doing, Higgs? Why did you let him in?

He needs to be convinced of his power over us. Let him think you no longer a threat. When the time comes, we can shake free of his bonds easily enough.

But the shackles. The strange iron.

Yes, interesting stuff, that. Try to let the iron touch your skin, I want to feel it. Crafter work, surely.

With a supreme effort Wilt raised his arms higher in the air and shrugged his cloak back so the cold iron rested against the skin of his wrists.

Ah. Very interesting. Clever.

Can you free us?

Maybe. Give me some time. Vargul was right, this is from Redmondis. There may be something we can do.

Higgs retreated even further into the hidden depths of Wilt's mind, and Wilt's animal consciousness rose back up to overwhelm him. He became nothing more than a mindless slave, a bound hostage struggling along a dark corridor at the beck and call of his master.

'The assassin, your highness. As requested.'

A part of Wilt rose out of dark, still waters and floated back to consciousness. His vision cleared as he swayed on his feet. He was standing on decorated marble tiles, their swirling pattern adding to the numbing dizziness that threatened to overwhelm him.

'Assassin, Vargul?' The voice was old and weak, the words slurring into one another as though the speaker was drugged.

'Yes, your highness. As reported to you this morning. The queen, she—'

'Oh yes, of course. Silly of me.'

Wilt tried to raise his head to see who was speaking, but his neck refused to obey the feeble command his mind sent.

'From Redmondis, you say? Not dangerous, is he?'

'Not anymore, my king. He is under my command.'

'Good, good. Can't be too careful with those types. Always telling Catherine that, but she never listens.'

'The queen could be stubborn at times, your highness.'

'Ha! Yes, she can be at that. You say she suffered an accident?'

'She was murdered, my king. By this assassin. Sent from Redmondis.'

'Of course. Redmondis. Never did like the sound of that place. Catherine is always trying to—'

'My king? We must present the prisoner to the court. Have the king's justice handed down.'

'What? Oh yes. Yes, of course, as you say. Very good, Vargul.'

There was a pause and Wilt could feel the growing frustration build in the weld that held his animal mind in thrall.

'You must pronounce judgment, my king.'

'Yes. Judgment. Yes.' The voice was fading again, as though the speaker was drifting into a heavy sleep.

'At your command we will call for an assembly of the court in the morning, at which time the prisoner will be sentenced and your judgment made. Have I understood your command correctly, my king?'

'Hmph?' The voice was barely above a whisper now.

'Let it be noted, scribe.'

'Very good, sir.' A new voice, younger, more deferential. Obviously a servant.

'Come now, let us leave the king to his rest. Ensure no one disturbs him until the morning.'

A surge of power pulsed across the weld holding Wilt's mind, and darkness rose around him again.

Careful now, come back down here with me.

Higgs?

I know it's confusing. I'm sorry, you just have to trust me. We had to give Vargul control of some part of your mind. It'll leave you feeling a bit strange.

How ... how are you doing this?

We. We're doing it together. Wielder and ward, remember? We've shared each other's minds before. When the Sisters sought you out in Redmondis and you had to flee, you came into me.

And when Red Charley ... when you—

When he killed me.

Then you came into me.

The blade helped. It merged me into the weld, Wilt, just as I had used it to merge into my form when changing into a cat. I don't really understand how, I just know it worked. Try to think less like a wielder and more like a crafter. As long as it does what is needed, who cares how?

The blade. Vargul must have it.

I think he does. I can feel it, almost hear it. I don't think he knows just what he's got there.

We have to get it back.

That's way down the list of things we have to do, but yes, we'll get it back. I think we've almost reached the limit of what Vargul can teach us.

The weld, I can feel part of his mind through it. He's like Cortis, though not as far gone. I don't think he realises the danger he's in.

He seeks power, and obviously has it now that the queen is out of the way. I wonder how long he waited for one such as you to come along. Someone he could conveniently lay the blame on.

The king, he sounds—

Gone. Too far gone to recover, I suspect. More than simply drugged. The queen mentioned she had him under her power—Vargul and others have probably had their hooks in him for years as well.

But why? To take control? To gain power?

Perhaps. Perhaps Vargul serves his master without fully realising it. Weakening Sontair, surrendering the towns and cities that surround it. Ensuring there is no resistance.

I'm tired, Higgs. My thoughts just seem to race round and round without stopping. I can't get them to focus.

Rest. We'll need all our strength tomorrow. Try to let your thoughts go, a circle of stones falling in order—you remember. I'll wake you when needed. I've got some other things to work on anyway, like these shackles. Sleep.

Wilt was already down, floating in a sea of darkness.

Chapter 40

'There's something … different.'

Heather stared out across the milling crowds in the courtyard, but her gaze was elsewhere, her eyes unfocused and troubled.

Frankle nodded. 'It's the crowd. It's bigger, somehow. Maybe there was a disturbance on the far side of the courtyard we can't see and a mass of people just moved this way all at once.'

'No, it's …' Heather shook her head to clear an unwanted thought. 'It's not just that. There was something familiar.' Her hand fell down to the small pack resting on her hip and her eyes widened. 'Frankle, I need a moment. Can you go see what Daemi's plan is for us?'

Frankle nodded quickly and strode over to where Daemi and Lodan were chatting with another soldier.

As soon as he was gone Heather dropped to her knees and rummaged frantically inside her pack. Finally she found what she was looking for and pulled out a small bowl and a jewelled necklace that glinted sharply in the sunlight. With a furtive glance around to make sure she was alone she placed the necklace inside the sounding bowl and waited.

Sure enough, a moment later a strange music filled the air. Heather snatched the necklace out of the bowl before anyone else could hear it and stuffed the bowl back inside her pack. She held the necklace up in front of her, staring at the strangely cut stone as it spun.

'What's that?' Frankle said as he walked back over.

'Nothing. Just something I made.' Heather pulled the chain over her head and tucked the jewel away under her shirt.

Frankle nodded and waited, expecting more of an explanation.

'Silly of me, I suppose, with all of this.' Heather waved at the crowd, wanting to change the subject. 'What did Daemi have to say?'

'We're staying with Lodan tonight—he's got a few feelers out trying to find out more about Wilt and where he might be. He said if Wilt's still in the city they'll know about it by morning.'

'He is.'

Frankle raised one quizzical eyebrow and Heather hurried to cut off any questions.

'I mean … he must be, right? After all of this.' She smiled suddenly at Frankle, the strange distant look from earlier now completely gone. 'Come on. Let's get moving. I'd like to get away from this crowd.'

Lodan led them to their room for the night, an empty storeroom with three plain bunks lining one wall. It was basic at best, but it was warm and dry and all any of them needed after their travels.

'You know, you remind me of him,' Lodan said to Daemi he ushered them inside. 'The way you hold yourself, perhaps.'

'Who, Wilt?'

'Yes. I thought it was something else at first, but now it's clear.'

Daemi considered Lodan's words for a few moments. 'You thought it was something else?'

Lodan smiled quickly and turned away. 'There's only this one room, I'm afraid. Space is at a bit of a premium right now.'

'It's very kind of you,' Heather interrupted, and Lodan looked at her as though surprised to find someone else in the room with them.

'Yes. Well, rest for now. In the morning I'll find someone to take you up the hill to the castle. The court gathers there each morning. Though I warn you, I don't think finding Wilt will be as easy as just asking around.'

'It never is,' Frankle grunted and dropped his pack on the ground with a sigh.

'Sleep well.' Lodan bowed his head quickly and stepped out of the room, closing the door behind him.

'Something else?' Daemi was still considering his words, a troubled expression on her face.

'Oh, you really are hopeless, aren't you?' Heather laughed, claiming the bed closest to the door. 'He likes you.'

Daemi stared back at her, her face flushing red. 'What?'

'It's obvious. He's been staring at you like a daft cow since we met, can't take his eyes off you. He's quite good looking, don't you think? The dark, mysterious type.' Heather arranged herself on her bed, and Frankle hurried to the far side of the room, eager to stay out of things.

Daemi swallowed and took a deep breath, her face positively glowing now. 'You don't know what you're talking about.'

Heather gave a mischievous grin as she watched Daemi slump down onto her bed. 'Actually, I might have something here that could help. I used to be quite well-known among the other crafters for my love charms.' She rummaged in her pack, pulling out various pieces of jewellery and arranging them across her bed.

Daemi watched with growing horror, then finally sprang to her feet and marched out of the room. 'I'm going for some air. Make sure you rest, you're obviously over-tired.'

She slammed the door behind her as Heather broke into a fit of giggles.

'That really wasn't very nice,' Frankle admonished her.

'Oh, don't be such a stick in the mud. Besides, it will be good for her. You know how she's been.'

Frankle was about to reply, then thought better of it. He'd only really known Daemi since Cortis's invasion, but even after that had all settled down it was obvious Daemi was damaged in some way. Distant. 'Maybe you're right.'

He rolled over and closed his eyes. They'd had a long few days, and he was exhausted, his tiredness welling over him to unravel all thought in the dark tide of sleep.

Daemi stood outside the room, breathing deeply, trying to control the rush of heat that had burned up over her face.

Lodan. Ridiculous.

The passageway was mercifully dark, a single torch burning on the far wall at the top of the staircase. She finally got her breathing under control and crept toward it, suddenly curious to see if she could peer down into the room below. No one else could have heard Heather's ridiculous assertion, could they? The walls didn't look that thin.

She swallowed and inched toward the stairs, half her mind on her task and the other half reeling in circles.

Lodan. He's not thinking like that at all. It's Wilt, something to do with their connection, their link. Something waking up now he's so close.

She stopped and held her breath as a board creaked under her foot.

'Is everything okay?'

Daemi looked up to see Lodan standing at the top of the stairs. 'Oh. Yes. Just wanted to … get some air.' Her voice faded as the excuse dribbled over her lips.

'Some air.' Lodan leaned back and crossed his arms, his face arranging itself to hide the smile that threatened to break out. 'Not much hope of that with these crowds, I'm afraid.'

'Yes.' Daemi drew herself up, trying to regain her composure. 'Yes. Silly of me.'

'That's okay, you've had a long journey. We all have, to find ourselves here.'

Lodan approached her, and Daemi pulled back against the wall, suddenly terrified he was about to—

To what?

Her mind immediately supplied multiple detailed possibilities, and she felt her face burning again.

Lodan stepped around her, continuing on past their room to another door at the far end. 'Time for me to get some rest. You should too, Daemi. I expect tomorrow will be a long day.'

He opened the door and stepped inside, leaving her alone in the dim light. As soon as his door closed she let out her breath in a whoosh.

Lodan. For a second there—

'Enough,' Daemi said aloud to herself, in her best tone of command. She pulled her shoulders back and banished all such thoughts from her mind.

She marched back to their room and threw the door open, ready to snap back at any nonsense Heather might come up with, but she and Frankle were fast asleep.

Daemi closed the door quietly and sat down on her bed to remove her boots.

Lodan.

Ridiculous.

Chapter 41

The circle of stone faces fell one by one, a never-ending wave of movement. Wilt into Higgs. Higgs into Petron. Petron into Daemi. Daemi into Lodan. Lodan into—

—Wake up.—

Wilt opened his eyes and immediately closed them again, squeezing them shut against the bright light that burned through them. He blinked tears away, twisting his face from the source of the light, but even the stone floor was too intense a white to focus on.

'My king, as you have commanded, we present the accused to the court.'

A hand on Wilt's shoulder spun him around and a mailed fist held his chin up to the sun. He screwed his eyes closed as tightly as he could, tears now flowing freely down his cheeks. The sound of a crowd gasping and exclaiming in surprise rose from somewhere below him, and a breeze blew across his face, cooling the hot tears.

His thoughts ground slowly into motion. He was outside. In front of the court. Vargul. Vargul was going to have him killed.

Sorry about this. I was hoping to have things sorted out by now.

Higgs? Where are we? Why do I feel so … numb?

If you would open your eyes we'd both be able to see, but we're outside, in the sunlight. You've been kept in the dark for too long. Your eyes will need time to adjust.

How long have I been—

It's morning. Vargul wanted to hold you longer, but he had no luck penetrating your mind. I think we convinced him he broke you somehow when he took control. Wiped you. All he sees is a blank slate.

But he hasn't—

Relax, Wilt. I've kept you safe.

'Two days ago, our queen was murdered. Her life cut short by a Redmondis assassin. This assassin!'

Wilt's hands were wrenched above his head and he winced as the heavy shackles cut into his wrists.

The shackles.

Still in place, I'm afraid. I've been trying to figure out how to break them, but some very clever crafters were involved in their making.

So I'm stuck here?

I didn't say that. Just trust me.

'The queen's guard caught this spy, this killer, red-handed, standing over her broken body.'

Wilt's hands were shaken roughly back and forth, and the scores of people responded, a massed, angry roar breaking from them. Wilt tried to open his eyes again, but the sunlight was too bright, forcing him to duck away from it, making it look as though he were shying away from the crowd.

The sunlight. Now why didn't I think of that earlier?

'Now we present him to the king for justice to be decided.'

Wilt was spun in place, his face turned away from the baying crowd.

'My king.' Vargul's voice was lower now, gentle, as though talking to a young child.

Wilt, the sunlight. Try to keep the shackles in it.

What?

Just do it. Get as much light on them as possible.

With a grunt of effort, Wilt reached his hands forward, holding them out as if in supplication to the king. His sleeves were pulled back by the movement, and the heavy shackles were fully exposed to the light.

Remember the stone in Redmondis—the stone these were forged from? It glowed green in the darkness. I don't think it was ever meant to be used in the light. I think the sunlight might cause a reaction.

Sure enough, as soon as the sunlight warmed his wrists, Wilt could feel something change, some part of his mind wakened as the shackles loosened ever so slightly.

Vargul called out loudly again, performing for the crowd. 'Look at him, this pathetic creature. Even now he begs for mercy from our king. And he will receive it! The king's mercy!'

The mob responded with another roar and Wilt's hands were slapped down.

There was a muttered noise from the space in front of him and Wilt squinted his eyes open in time to see the aged king slumped across his throne, its high arms holding him upright. Someone's hand waved vaguely back and forth in front of him, but his eyes were blank and staring at something no one else could see. He was trying to say something, but his weak whisper was too soft to be heard.

'The king has made his judgment!' Vargul shouted out again, obviously wanting to get things moving again as quickly as possible. 'Bring the prisoner to the stone!'

Wilt was shoved roughly around and pushed forward, a guard catching him as he fell then marching him away from the throne. Small rocks and rotten fruit peppered them as the crowd lost all semblance of order and threw whatever was closest to hand.

Wilt shied away from the missiles, holding his hands up over his head to protect himself.

That's it. Keep them in the sunlight. Just a few moments more.

Wilt could feel the shackles warming, heating his wrists as they seemed to lighten and stretch, pulling away from his skin.

It's waking up, coming undone. Here. Let me try something.

Wilt felt his lips move and a strange tumble of words spill over them in a hushed whisper. Immediately another block in his mind melted away; his thoughts gathered force now, the vortex of power in his centre spinning back up to speed.

At the same time, his shoulder was wrenched again as he was pulled to a standstill.

'Open your eyes and face your fate, wielder.'

Wilt blinked his eyes clear, the image in front of him blurring back and forth until it locked into place. He was standing at an altar, a solid stone table curved in the centre with black, dried bloodstains telling the tale of its evil history.

'The king's mercy!' Vargul cried out again, and the crowd answered with another shout as a large hooded man stepped into Wilt's view, an enormous axe held at his side. The blade was fully two feet long, curved and glinting cruelly in the sun.

Wilt was pushed forward again, forced to his knees in front of the stone altar, his head angled by rough hands to lie in place in the carved indentation in the centre of the rock.

He saw a shift of movement to his side as the executioner stepped forward.

Any time now would be good, Higgs.

I think it worked. Try to pull your hands free. Once the shackles are clear, you should be able to change.

Wilt forced his hands apart, straining against the stone infused iron that oddly warped and bent around him like thick toffee.

An expectant hush from the crowd told Wilt he only had moments to live. He closed his eyes and pulled the sucking bonds slowly apart, then wrenched his hands free, the weight of the shackles dropping from his wrists.

Now, Wilt. Now!

He dived into the darkness, the world around him shifting into the grey tones of the shadowed world of the wraith. Just in time. The cold axe blade kissed the back of his neck, and the next moment it was through him altogether, the executioner stumbling as the lack of expected resistance sent him sprawling off balance. The heavy axe fell to the ground with a clang.

Wilt stood up, a thousand black welds writhing in his form, a spot of cold silence in the middle of the sudden commotion that broke out as the guards whirled around in confusion. He reached for the nearest body, the nearest flash of life in the darkness, and his hand passed through it, clasping the man's heart in a fist of ice, watching as the light in his eyes faded and was finally snuffed out. Wilt felt the death as a spark of heat that barely registered against the howling hunger for more.

Vargul was standing to one side of the platform, backing away from the horrifying vision that had reared up in front of him. He shook his head frantically, as though trying to deny what his eyes told him.

'No … You were broken … It's not possible, the master—'

Wilt reached into him.

No. Wait. He must know more. Let his memories wash through, let us learn what we can.

Wilt knew Higgs spoke the truth, but his other side, the wraith form that had control, wanted nothing more than to feast on all the life around it, to take as much warmth and light with it to drown in its depths. It wanted no time to be wasted.

Wilt, take control. We have to know more. We have to know—

Wilt's mind wrenched as he willed himself upward and out of the animal hunger that threatened to overwhelm him. His shadowed hand still closed around Vargul's heart, but his grip loosened, allowing a last few seconds of life to flash before the man's eyes.

He stood at the edge of a courtyard, head hooded and bowed but eyes peering out keenly, studying the surrounding group. There were thirteen other applicants, all eager to join the queen's ranks. Queen Catherine, beautiful and terrifying, married to the king these past five years and the true seat of power in the realm. It was said she came from the far north; some even whispered the name Redmondis, though never in her presence. It was said she held the king in thrall, that she possessed strange and terrible powers. Many things were said. He knew better than to believe them all.

He recognised only two or three of the other applicants. They weren't a threat. They had some talent but lacked the hunger to do what was necessary to gain true power. He'd seen others such as these fail, stand in front of waiting victims and waver, too terrified of the consequences to bring their wills to bear, to push down into their victim's minds, smashing their way inside if necessary.

He suffered from no such hesitancy.

Each member of the group snapped to attention, and he hurried to do likewise as a tall, red-robed figure strode into their presence. He started as he saw the figure, almost falling forward in his surprise. Impossible. A Prefect of Redmondis, here, in Sontair?

The prefect strode back and forth, studying each figure as though his eyes had no trouble penetrating the shadows of their hoods. When his time came, Vargul stared straight back, taking in the scarred face, the strange golden eyes, the tight lips that curved into a knowing smile.

'Form a line, gentlemen. Present yourselves.'

From somewhere within his cloak a twisted, clawed staff appeared, and each applicant stood before it, withdrawing their hoods and allowing the staff to touch their foreheads. Vargul watched the first few, saw their shoulders slump in surrender as the staff touched them, saw their blank eyes, their slowly shaking heads as though waking from a dream. He prepared himself.

Centre your mind. Leave the chaos of thought behind. Become cold stone.

When his turn came he was ready, his mind blank and clear. He stepped forward and his eyes fell on the clawed staff. It was a wolf's paw, with long yellow claws. So lifelike.

The prefect held his gaze, the long scar that ran down one side of his face twitching slightly.

The claws flexed and Vargul's control slipped away. It wasn't a staff at all. It was an arm. The prefect's arm. Its claws touched his forehead, and a howl entered his heart.

—Cortis. It had to be. We know the queen was one of the Nine Sisters. He worked for them, before he turned on them. Maybe he was here recruiting, trying to grow their army. But why? Go deeper, Wilt. We have to know more.—

He stared down into the still water of the reflecting bowl, watching his eyes, looking for the flecks of gold that had appeared in them. The light caught one, and he smiled, recognising it. Cortis would be proud.

'The queen, Vargul. She requests our presence.'

He stood and followed his fellow adviser, pulling his hood over his head. Cortis had warned him he would be acting soon, taking advantage of the distracted Sisters and the weakened defences of Redmondis. Perhaps the time had come. Their time.

He walked into the audience chamber and his heart leaped as he saw the tall, red-robed figure standing in front of the king and queen.

The prefect spoke and turned to watch him and the other advisers file into the room, his displeasure clear on his face. Not Cortis, another. Keep your mind shielded.

'As we mentioned to you, Cantor Wrexley, we have our own skilled advisers here in the capital. We have no need of Redmondis' assistance.' The queen's tone dripped with sarcasm, yet remained calm and somehow soothing. She was bending her will, bringing her powers to bear on the strange prefect.

'Yes, your highness, but the surrounding lands—'

'What is he talking about, Catherine?' The king sat up suddenly, as though waking from a doze. 'Has there been trouble in the realm? Why haven't I—'

'Be still, my king.' Vargul could feel the surge of power as the queen spoke, wrapping herself around the king's feeble mind and suffocating all thought. 'Be at peace. All is well.'

Silence fell on the room as the king sank back into his entranced sleep.

'You see, Cantor Wrexley, your visit troubles the king unnecessarily.' The queen's voice was cold now, the threat unmistakable.

Vargul watched the tall prefect, saw the struggle writ clearly on the man's face. The sudden surrender. 'Yes, my queen. I will ... pass on your news to Redmondis.'

The prefect dropped his head and walked quickly from the room in full retreat.

—Wrexley. He was sent to the south before Cortis attacked Red-mondis. The Sisters must have heard reports of trouble.—

—But the queen was one of the Sisters, Wilt. They shared the same mind. Anything she knew was already known by the others. Wrexley was sent on a fool's errand. Moved out of the way—-

—But why weaken Redmondis even further? Why open themselves up for attack?—

—Perhaps they didn't realise how far under the influence of the serpents they had fallen. How twisted their minds had become. More, we need more, Wilt.—

Vargul stood at the door, watching the huddled shape in the far corner scratch and claw at the walls, trying to melt itself into the rock. On the floor, in the middle of the cell, lay a large, dirty sack.

'Will they be missed?' he whispered, not taking his eyes from the shivering form.

'No, sir. Not from here. There are more of the new arrivals, too many of them as it is.'

'Good.' Vargul smiled though his heart remained cold. He could feel himself separating thought from action, washing his hands mentally from what he was about to do. He was no longer in control. He could not be blamed. 'Free the creatures.'

The jailer reached in with a large hook and took hold of one corner of the sack, lifting and shaking it free, leaving behind a writhing pile of black forms. He stepped back hurriedly, putting Vargul between himself and the twisting mound of death now free in the cell. Black asps, the deadliest creatures in all the southern kingdom.

A whimper slipped out from the far corner of the room.

Vargul stared down at the snakes, lost in the dance of their movement. A rush of excitement surged up his spine as he dropped into a weld and sent it into their minds.

Hunger. Pure hunger. Flickering tongue tasting the heat of life. Food is that way. The twist and pull of the others as they too caught its scent.

'Leave me.' His lips formed the words even as his mind forgot its human form and gave itself to the froth and foam of the waters beneath the welds. Where the serpents danced, where the true power lay. Where his master waited for him.

The jailer needed no further encouragement. He'd seen enough of these performances to know what would come next. The sudden strike, the cry of pain choked off in seconds. Then the feast. There would be remains to remove once the work was done, but for now he wanted to spend his time in warmer, friendlier places than this.

Vargul heard the jailer leave and gave himself up completely to the weld, pushing to the front of the writhing pile as it wrapped and rolled itself toward the waiting flesh. In the back of his mind he heard a familiar howl of triumph gathering his thoughts and surging ahead in the charge.

The first set of fangs struck out, spitting their venom deep into tissue, and Vargul tasted the metallic taint of blood and poison that filled his mouth, then all senses shut down as he dropped into the waiting dark.

The world slipped away as he floated in darkness. Ice closed around him, locking time into a single moment. A choking fear wrapped his chest as he waited, aware suddenly that he was not alone, that something other was here with him. Something that knew every thought he had ever had or would ever have, who knew his secrets and dismissed them, who held his mind in its fist and could crush him on a whim.

Something that could foresee the moment of his death and knew who else would be there inside him when it came to pass.

You. I know you.

The voice closed on Wilt like a fist. The world was a frozen instant of time crystallising around him. Then he was pulled below.

The shock of the cold blasted his mind clear, all thoughts shattered. With one final gasp of effort he raised his eyes toward the surface, watching as a blurred form danced and skated on the ice far above, out of reach.

No, Wilt! I'm here. Stay with me.

He felt himself sinking, impossibly heavy in the darkening waters. The shape on the ice above battered at the surface, its four paws clawing uselessly at it.

Wilt, fight it. Stay with me!

He was cold, so cold. So tired. He sank into the darkness, watching the light above fade out.

Chapter 42

Daemi dreamed of water, hidden depths, writhing nests of serpents, and a voice just at the edge of hearing trying to tell her something important, something she had to know.

She opened her eyes and sat up. Something in the changed sounds of the morning had told her body to react. The next moment the door to their chamber swung open and Lodan's face appeared.

'Good, you're awake. Hurry, we need to get to the castle. There's been trouble.'

His head disappeared from view before she could ask anything in reply, so she swung her legs out of bed and kicked the bed next to her where Heather still lay deeply asleep.

'Wake up, princess.'

Heather groaned as she opened her eyes and slowly recognised where she was. 'Oh. I thought I was back in Redmondis. There was—'

'Never mind about that. Time to get going, something's happened.'

Heather's eyes narrowed in recognition of the urgency in Daemi's tone, and she sat up quickly as Daemi turned to wake Frankle.

Minutes later they were out on the streets, munching on hard, thin wafers of trail bread that Lodan had given them to make up for missing breakfast, hurrying along, trying to keep up with his long strides.

Daemi caught up to him just as another soldier saluted Lodan and marched away. 'Trouble?'

Lodan nodded. 'The reports we're getting are strange. Muddled. But the one thing they all have in common is our mutual friend.'

Daemi ducked under a wooden beam that suddenly thrust out of a nearby window, ignoring the angry shouts from behind as other travellers weren't so quick to notice the obstacle. 'Wilt?'

'We'd had word that the latest guard patrol to return had brought along a prisoner, a wielder, according to the whispers. A young man, now a guest of the queen. After we met you we put two and two together.'

'So he's here then, in the castle.'

'He was. Then came reports that the queen had suffered a mischief of some kind. That the guest stood accused, and that court was called to pronounce judgment.'

'So quickly?'

'The king is somewhat … confused these days. Weak. His mind has been fading for some time now, and to be honest it was never that sharp to begin with. The queen has been the true power in Sontair. If the reports are true and she's—'

'Seems awfully convenient that something would happen to the queen so soon after Wilt arrived.'

'Perhaps someone saw this as an opportunity to lay the blame at Redmondis' door. You must be aware of the ill feeling most folk have for Redmondis. It's only grown with the recent troubles.'

'And I thought Redmondis had its intrigues,' Daemi said.

Lodan gave a mirthless chuckle and slapped her on the shoulder. 'Welcome to Sontair.'

A few steps behind them, Frankle and Heather were too busy dodging the various obstacles that kept springing up to spend any time chatting. As they rounded the corner the street opened out, the narrow lane becoming a wide thoroughfare, broad enough for two wagons in each direction, the packed mud hardening into flagstones under their feet.

'This must be the posh quarter.' Heather sniffed. 'Even the air smells nicer here.'

'Where are we going?' Frankle stumbled as he caught the toe of his boot in a rut.

'To the castle, I expect. Do keep up.'

'How do you—'

'I've got two good ears and I use them.' Heather smiled.

'I've been paying just as much attention—'

'You have not. You didn't even notice how Daemi and Lodan have been acting. That's okay though, you're a boy. Boys often miss that sort of thing.'

'Maybe boys just don't want to waste time worrying about other people's business.'

Heather raised a single eyebrow and stared back at Frankle, who immediately stammered out an apology.

'I mean … maybe we just have other things we're—' he stuttered, wilting under Heather's continued glare.

After a long moment of silence, Heather looked away. 'I heard one of Lodan's guards talking about it as we were getting ready to leave. You and Daemi were busy trying to pack up all your things while I,' she patted the small pack hanging from her shoulder, 'came better prepared. There's a trial happening this morning, and I think Wilt's involved. Unless it's some other prisoner from Redmondis they're talking about.'

'Prisoner?'

Heather nodded. 'Come on.'

She broke into a trot just as Daemi and Lodan ahead of them did the same, and Frankle hurried to catch up. This street was quite sparse compared to the cramped lanes they'd been wading through, and it was freeing to move without bumping shoulders with strangers every few steps.

Heather was right about the air too. It was cleaner here, the animal stench of the poorer quarter blown away with the breeze that pushed down the wide street. Ahead of them the street angled upward and curved into a slope, snaking around the central hill of Sontair, leading up to the castle perched on its peak. Frankle stared up at it, its high silver walls gleaming in the sun. How many years and how many men had it taken to build such a wonder?

As they turned the corner, Lodan stopped and drew his sword, reaching out with his other hand to grab Daemi and hold her back. 'Wait.' He crouched in a low fighter's stance, one hand still clasping Daemi's wrist.

Ahead of them the sound of slapping footsteps approached, and a group of three royal guards appeared, running full speed down the hill, their eyes wide and unseeing, obviously in total panic. As soon as he saw the state of the men, Lodan relaxed and sheathed his sword. These men were no threat to anyone but themselves.

The group watched the guards hurry past, their arms pulling at each other in their rush to get as far as possible from whatever they had seen, their sword hands empty.

'Did you see their eyes?' Heather whispered as soon as the men were gone.

Daemi nodded. 'Something terrified those men. I've seen that sort of thing before.'

'In Redmondis?' Lodan asked, realising he still held Daemi's wrist and dropping it guiltily.

Daemi moved on, quickening her step.

In Redmondis. With Wilt.

The courtyard was empty of life.

Two bodies lay on the ground, one a guard and the other a court official, judging by his expensive robes. Their clothes were all that could be used to identify them. Their grey, sunken skin and withered bodies had rendered them otherwise unrecognisable. Both faces were stretched into masks of naked terror, lips drawn back from gums, eyes wide and staring.

Frankle stared down at the ruined body of the guard, lost in thought.

'Don't look at them.' Daemi clapped him on the shoulder,

snapping him out of his daze. 'There's nothing you can do, they're gone.' She moved past him, eyes locked on the ground, searching around the edge of the courtyard for signs of what exactly had happened.

Lodan was doing the same on the other side. 'There wasn't much of a fight here,' he said eventually, bending down to trace a footprint with his finger. 'More of a general panic. I've never seen a sight like this.'

'I have.' Daemi left the edge of the courtyard and moved in to study the bodies. 'It was Wilt. At least, he was involved.'

Lodan joined her in the circle and gestured down at the ruined bodies. 'And these?'

'Drained. I've seen that before too. Wilt did it to one of Cortis's guards, though I don't think he meant to. Something to do with using up the life of his victim to survive an attack from the Sisters. Then later, when he … when he changed. There were others.'

'Changed? What do you mean?'

Daemi shook her head, unwilling to talk any more about it.

'Something happened to Wilt, in Redmondis.' Heather stepped in to explain to Lodan. 'Cantor Cortis—one of the prefects—fell under the influence of a dark power. He took control of Redmondis, took over most of the guards. He started … doing things to the wielders.'

'Wilt stopped him, somehow, by using the welds—that's what wielders call the connections between minds they use to control people,' Frankle added. 'But Higgs—'

'He was killed.' Heather's voice had become distant, as though operating outside her control. 'But Wilt wouldn't let him go. He used the welds—to save him, I suppose—to hold him back from death. But the only way to do that was to give in to the power he needed to use, to let it take him over …'

'He became a wraith,' Frankle finished.

'A … wraith?' Lodan turned toward him.

'A creature formed from the welds themselves, from the other side of life. At least, that's how Petron explained it. It seeks out life and drains it, feeds on it, until all that is left is death. Just like these two.'

'That's not right.' Daemi raised her head, her eyes red and angry. 'Wilt isn't just … He can control it. I know he can.'

Lodan looked back and forth between the three travellers. Each of them carried scars from the past, all centred somehow around Wilt and Higgs and what had become of them.

'So he's dangerous?'

'He might be,' Heather said. 'But we need to find out for sure.'

Lodan watched the others as Heather spoke. Daemi had her eyes locked on the ground again, perhaps furious with their discussion, or with herself and her feelings, or just with the world in general. Frankle was trying to look brave, but Lodan could almost smell the fear on him.

'You're a wielder, aren't you, Frankle?'

Frankle nodded, then tried to explain. 'But I'm not like—'

Lodan waved his protest away. 'Do you think Wilt is dangerous?'

'I think we need to find him, and I think we need to be very careful when we do.'

'Here.' Daemi was now standing at the far side of the courtyard, at the top of a narrow path that led toward the castle. It seemed to curve around and under the building as though hiding beneath it. 'He went this way. I can feel it.'

Heather hurried over to her, her hand clutching something inside her shirt as she stepped next to Daemi. A moment later her face drained of colour, and she nodded. 'Definitely.'

Without looking back, the two women started down the path.

Lodan was left staring uncomprehendingly at their backs until Frankle trotted past, shrugging his apologies.

'Call it women's intuition, if that helps.'

Chapter 43

It was happening again.

The Guardian sat alone on his throne, all senses tuned to the low murmur of the trees gaining in volume, becoming a groan, until the animals themselves sensed it, a sudden scattershot of birds taking flight in the face of the coming storm.

Wilt. It must be. Something has happened.

The next moment even a human could have heard it, the groan becoming a shaking creak as a thousand trees shifted in place, their roots suddenly pulling free, some withering, others reaching ever deeper in a desperate search for sustenance.

A crack echoed across the forest as an elder finally succumbed, its centuries-old trunk shuddering and ripping itself in two, pulling itself up and out of the soil as it fell, laying waste to an entire swathe of forest as it came crashing down.

This is more than before. There's something wrong. Find him, quick.

The Guardian closed his eyes and pulled, down into the depths, down to where the roots reached for life, winding themselves ever deeper into the past.

Stop! Thief!

He ducked under the guard's swinging arm and swerved into the alley, dropping half his haul as he went, not thinking for a moment about stopping to recover any of it. A loud crash behind him told him the guard hadn't been quick enough to change direction and had crashed into the fruit stall that lined one wall.

—*No. Not that way. That's another memory, from another soul. Another life.*—

The Guardian sighed and bent his will even deeper, twisting the roots further down, beyond the past, into the future.

She slung her pack over her shoulder and caught Frankle's hand as he slid down the steep, rocky incline. He was still dazed, his eyes glazed and shadowed, his legs weak. The skies above were already darkening, but they'd only just got out of the twisting cave complex that had eaten up their past few days and nights, so even this ominous sky was a welcome sight.

Ahead of them Daemi waited at the base of the slope, watching them stumble their way toward her with barely disguised impatience. They were only halfway down the mountain, and she didn't want to spend another night close to those caves. Above Daemi's head, perched on a tall boulder, sat a large black cat, its silver claws digging into the stone, its eyes turned to the east, toward their destination.

Another shudder as the roots shrank back from that path, pulling themselves free. The Guardian urged them onward, further into the cold wash of time.

He sat alone in the enormous library, its high vaulted ceilings towering above him, the strange green light that covered everything in this place giving the room a sickly, leprous aspect.

He pushed the parchment flat again as it curled back into a roll and bent toward the words, moving his lips as he read, the air dropping in temperature with each syllable.

Within you and without you
The blood within the stone
Writ for you and about you
Together and yet alone
The roots that sink the deepest
The forked path of the mind
The soul that splits is weakest
Future and past entwined.

He readied his pen to continue the song. The scratching at his mind called to him from the past, their clinging thread pulling at him, wrenching themselves free.

He glanced up at the small looking glass on his desk and froze as he saw the eyes staring back at him.

—Higgs. That was Higgs's face.—

—There. That's the way. But closer, not so far into the—

Daemi ducked and rolled as the creature shot out another claw. The closed scars on her back pulled angrily as she surged to her feet, spinning her blade to deflect the fang that darted toward her, threatening to impale her on its cruelly serrated edge.

Too fast. It was too fast for her. At least she'd die fighting, like a true warrior.

—That's better. Closer. Almost present. Now, another twist.—

The wolf slunk slowly forward, eyes wary, tongue lolling out one side of its jaws and a thick stream of red-tinged drool dripping down to mingle with the dirt and blood at its feet.

She raised her blade, its point impossibly heavy, and tried to form herself into a fighting stance, but her legs didn't want to obey. She was too tired, driven beyond the point of exhaustion.

The wolf stopped its slow, deliberate advance and watched her.

—This is a memory. From the past again, too far back to …—

The wolf sat back on its haunches and leaned its head to one side, openly curious now as it stared at her, all bloodlust and fight drained from its being.

—No. No this is something else. Something familiar. Something more than a memory.—

—I was wondering how long it would take you to find me, Delco.—

—Biore? But how?—

—Not long after you and Rawick helped the Guardian, I too found an outlet for my services.—

—Here? In the wash of memory?—

—More than memory, Delco. You've felt it yourself. I suspect Rawick knew something of it all along. The welds go beyond time, *not just backward but forward as well. And if you can ride them right …—*

—You can move with them. Future and past entwined.—

—That's right. And there's more. Much more. But first we have to bring Wilt back. He's gone deep, deeper than I thought possible. He won't make it back without our help.—

—He was here. We saw a vision of the future, a possible future I suppose. And Daemi. Daemi was fighting one of those creatures.—

—Daemi. Yes, her connection to Wilt is strong. Use that.—

—The dark thing is wrong. It doesn't belong.—

—Well, of course not, Shade. That's what we have been …—

—It came from below. Where nightmares grow.—

—Of course! The boy's right, Delco. That creature, it came from the same place where Wilt is trapped, I'm sure of it. That means there must be a way out. A path. A weakness.—

—Biore, I don't understand what you're saying.—

—Go back. Back into that vision of the dark thing and Daemi. I think I know what we need to do.—

The Guardian gripped the arms of his throne as he focused his mind, sifting through the seemingly endless threads beneath the soil to find the right one, the one that led—

Daemi shuddered with pain. Her right arm was gashed open, her tunic soaking through with blood. She could barely hold her blade, let alone raise it. The creature reached for her, its long, serrated claw flicking out to finish the job.

—Now stop. Back, into the thing itself.—

—But how Biore? Daemi isn't a wielder.—

—But she shares much with one. Use the connection.—

—Just like he did with us.—

—That's right, Shade. It's what the Guardian used Wilt for, to merge your minds with his. Wilt can do it again. He can do more than you can imagine.—

Daemi dropped to her knees as the scars on her back suddenly tore open. Her vision blurred, and for a single moment she thought she could see a figure standing before her, blocking her from the certain death coming her way. Then her mind seemed to warp and bend and with a rush she was elsewhere, hurtling along a thin silver connection into the creature's mind. Into darkness, and silence, and a sudden breath of cold through her core as she dived through a shimmering tunnel, into ice and memory.

'What do you have there, Meat?'

He blinked and time froze, a chill locking everything in place. He could feel tendrils of possibility swimming away from him, urging him to follow, to set them free, but he was stuck inside this one moment, only his eyes able to trace their path.

His shoulder wrenched, a slick, muddy puddle, white bread soaking in the dreck, turning brown and soft.

A shift and a cry as a body hit the ground. A heat spreading up his arm from the warm roll still clutched in his hand.

His shirt pulled tightly around the two rolls he had filched, his other hand pulling out the knife he'd kept secret for so long. It almost pulled him onward, the blade eager to finally be used.

—Wilt, this is not your memory. Leave this to the past.—

—Biore? Where am I? How are you …—

—You are somewhere very deep, out of reach. Only you can bring yourself back. But not this way. Resist it, don't let the nightmare blind you.—

He closed his eyes, forcing the vision away. The ice rumbled and shifted, and he faced another memory, this one more familiar.

'Blade!' someone yelled out in a high voice.

—Higgs. That was Higgs, warning me. This was when we'd won the flagball game.—

—Yes, Wilt. Now watch for the moment, and use it to save yourself.—

The guard that had charged past Wilt into the crowd came stumbling back onto the field of play, a shining dagger in his hand, his eyes wild.

Wilt spun to face the man, the flag still clutched in his hand. Some defence that would be.

—*And Higgs comes out of the crowd and helps save me. I knock the man down and ...*—

A crack in the ice, and the memory shifts.

Wilt stared at the sprawled figure in the dirt. Bolter and Bing had him by the shoulders, and two guards held his legs. Blood covered his face now, but he lifted his head and looked directly at Wilt.

'The blood within the stone!' His voice was deep and rasping, only half human.

—*Stop. Here. This is the place. Now, Wilt. Change the memory.*—

Wilt locked eyes with the man and sent a black weld into his mind.

A wash of panic and fury, chaos pulsing over him, pushing into his nose and throat and choking any life away.

—*No. Control it. Just like the gloomclaw, when the queen tried to use its power.*—

He let the storm pass over him, ignoring the panic and the pull. This man's mind was a hellscape, no human aspect remaining, all blasted away by the power that controlled him. Power that was leaving him behind.

—*Find whatever's controlling him, Wilt. Before it flees.*—

He raced through the collapsing mind, searching out what he knew had to be there. A connection.

—*There.*—

A single golden thread glittered in the distance. A weld, unlike any he had ever seen. He grasped for it, dived into it, and let it pull him free.

Chapter 44

'This way.' Daemi kicked the lock off the heavy wooden door and stepped forward, one hand on the hilt of her blade as the door swung slowly open.

A gust of fetid air rushed out at them from the darkness beyond, and Heather retreated behind Daemi, holding one hand to her nose. 'Ugh.'

Lodan peered over Daemi's shoulder into the shadows. 'Dungeons. And not clean ones, judging by the smell.'

Daemi moved onwards, drawing her long knife as she went.

Lodan fell into place behind her, his hand resting on the hilt of his sword. Behind him came Heather, still holding one hand to her face, and taking up the rear was Frankle, head down, listening to something right on the edge of hearing, something that had grown in volume as the door swung open. Something he knew only he out of the party could hear.

'Check the cells on the left. Make sure none of those bundles move,' Daemi ordered, the captain of the Redmondis guard coming to the fore.

There were cells on both sides of the tight passage, and not all of them were empty. Mounds of rags huddled in their corners, the stench of human waste clinging to them. Lodan reached through the bars to poke his sword gently at one, but nothing moved in response.

The passage split ahead, and Daemi hesitated, both paths leading into further shadows.

'To the right,' Frankle whispered.

Daemi nodded and continued. Only Heather turned to raise an eyebrow at Frankle, who shook his head and kept his eyes down, trying to keep his focus on the strange song that was getting louder and louder with every step.

Weld music. It was something he'd heard before, something from the worst times of his life, from when Cortis attacked Redmondis and he hid in a corner of his room as guards took all his friends away. Not having the courage to stand up and fight. Squirrelled away under a pile of clothes, squeezing his eyes shut and trying to magic himself invisible somehow, barely daring to breathe, only later opening his eyes to find that somehow he'd been missed.

Only this was louder now. Much louder. A siren song from the depths, something all wielders have heard at some stage, and some have yielded to, losing themselves forever in the surge and wash waiting below.

Wilt. It had to be. What had he become, to be heard so clearly?

'Stop,' Daemi whispered, and she held her fist up, signalling those behind.

Up ahead a single door was half open, showing a large lit space behind it. A packed dirt floor. She crept up to it and peered around the door's edge, holding her breath in the silence. Finally she reached out and pushed the door open, stepping into the centre of the frame as it swung clear.

She stood there for a moment, her silhouette framed by the light from the room ahead, both hands clasping her knife now, her feet planted in a fighter's stance, her whole body coiled and ready.

Heather waited, aware that something electric was in the air. She could still feel the vibrations from her bag, the heartstone in its sounding bowl, its song growing in volume with every step. Higgs. Higgs was here, somehow.

Frankle hung back, some part of him watching the others ahead of him, but most of his mind focused on the weld song now filling his ears.

Daemi turned back to them, the weld blade shining in her hand. 'There's noth—'

A giant black shape crashed over her, tearing her out of the doorway and sending her flying across the chamber. A single massive claw tore across her shoulder and down her right arm, leaving a hot wet trail in its wake, and Daemi almost dropped her blade as she crashed onto the packed dirt floor. She rolled clear just as the black creature thumped down on the spot where she'd landed.

Lodan cried out, and the writhing shadows around what could have been the creature's face turned for a brief moment. Daemi rocked up onto her feet and moved away, circling around the beast, her right arm hanging uselessly by her side, her left still holding the weld blade.

Frankle charged into the room, right behind Lodan and Heather as they rushed through. He had no idea what he was planning to do, but the weld song was surging through his mind now, taking it down pathways he'd never been, opening possibilities. He looked at the dark chamber around him, the heat of life calling out in the shadows, brightly lit forms moving through the grey light.

No, Frankle.

The whisper cut through his thoughts, pulling them back from the brink. Higgs. It was Higgs's voice.

That path is not for you, Frankle. Come back.

He had the strangest urge to resist, an anger at being talked down to, a fury at being a child always at the whim of others. *No. It is my time now, my power.*

Heather. She needs your help. Please.

Immediately Frankle felt the pull of the depths fade as he turned toward Heather, the grey light in the room fading out and colours washing back into his vision as the weld song echoed into silence. Heather was backed up against the door frame, eyes wide, her small satchel clasped across her front as though it could shield her from the great black creature in the centre of the chamber.

Frankle hurried over, putting himself in front of her.

'What are you doing?' Heather hissed.

'I'm not sure. Let me know if you have any ideas.'

Lodan charged the creature, both arms swinging his long sword down in a great crashing blow that clanged harmlessly off its armoured shell, his arms ringing from the impact. Like lightning two thin arms shot out from the creature, pointed claws jabbing at Lodan, sending him spinning away, only just making it clear.

Daemi let out a cry and attacked from the other side, but the creature seemed to have eyes in the back of its head and easily deflected her attack, responding even quicker with its own, catching Daemi with a glancing blow at the top of her thigh that dented her armour and sent her staggering backward.

'It's too fast,' Heather whispered, and Frankle could only agree, feeling helpless as he watched.

Both Lodan and Daemi gathered themselves and advanced on the creature from opposite sides, hoping to take advantage of their numbers. It seemed to work; the creature scuttled away as they both stepped forward.

Then the creature split, its twisting shadow now two separate forms, each a whirlwind of movement, driving both Daemi and Lodan away. They now each faced an individual opponent.

Daemi danced backward, just twisting clear of another thrust. Some part of her mind watched herself fight, aware that her training had taken control, knowing it was only a matter of time before another blow landed and she was left exposed, her entire being focused on delaying that moment. Time seemed to slow as she watched herself, feeling her body weaken even as it urged itself ever faster, quicker than she'd ever moved before, quicker than thought itself, but still not quick enough.

Her left arm was a blur of movement, parrying thrust after thrust from the creature, no time anymore for attack. She was losing ground, each blow coming closer than the last before her blade slapped it aside, overwhelming her.

Suddenly, she was alone.

It was as though a screen had dropped in front of her, cutting her off from the world. The light in the room changed, all colour drained out, each shape nothing more than a series of grey shadows against a dark background. The sound changed too; everything became muted and distant, as though she was sinking underwater, away from the surface world, away from the noise and chaos of the life up there.

Is this what it is to die?

Daemi looked down at the weld blade in her hand, its blade glowing blue against the grey world. 'Wilt?'

She fell to her knees, a sudden warmth running down her spine as the scars on her back tore open.

Something moved in front of her, a cold shadow of twisting welds that stepped up to the creature, driving it backward with a glowing sword that seemed to dance around its defences, each cut and thrust sending a spark of light flashing against the grey shadows, driving the darkness away.

Lodan saw Daemi fall and knew he could do nothing for her. He slashed out with a final attack, just hoping to do damage to the creature, to have it pay a price for the life it was about to take. He followed through, aware he was leaving himself hopelessly exposed, that the next moment would bring his death.

But the blow never came. Instead he was pushed backward by an unknown force, away from the dark creature, his breath misting out in front of him as sudden piercing cold seemed to slice into the room, placing itself between him and the shadow monster.

He fell to his knees and rolled away, turning his back on the fighting, trying to find Daemi, to make sure she was still alive. She was on the other side of the room, collapsed on to her knees, her eyes wide and blank. As he watched she pitched forward and collapsed onto her face.

With a grunt of effort he pulled himself back to his feet and stumbled toward her. His entire body seemed locked together, his muscles frozen by the cold and exhausted by the battle. Finally he reached her and dropped beside her, shaking her by the shoulder.

His hand came away from her shoulder stained red with blood. 'Heather! Frankle! Help me!'

Frankle and Heather were mesmerised by the sight of three duelling shadows dancing an impossibly fast dance, but Lodan's desperate cry snapped them out of it. In moments they were beside him, taking position on either side of Daemi and pulling her clear of the danger.

'The door!' Heather called, and they angled toward it, fleeing the chamber. Daemi's feet left twin trails in the packed dirt as they pulled her across the room and out into safety.

As soon as they were clear, Lodan left Daemi in their hands and slammed the door closed. 'Is she alive?'

Heather tried to undo the heavy armour around Daemi's torso. 'She's breathing. I don't think she was hit.'

'Then what—' Lodan caught himself as his voice rose into panic. 'What's all that blood from?'

'It's her scars,' Frankle tried to explain. 'She has wounds from Redmondis that have never healed properly.'

Heather finally worked the clasp of the chest piece open and the armour slid free, revealing two lines of deep scarlet running down the length of Daemi's undershirt.

Heather rummaged in her bag for medicine. 'It's okay. She'll be okay. It looks worse than it is.'

Lodan nodded and turned back to the door, his sword held out in front of him. Whatever had been happening in the chamber was finished now, the sounds of battle had melted back into silence.

'What was that?' he whispered. 'What saved us?'

As if in answer, the door swung open to reveal a large black cat sitting on its haunches and angling its head, studying them.

Daemi sat up suddenly with a gasp, pushing Heather out of the way. For a moment she held her blade out point first, then dropped it as she saw the cat, who hadn't moved.

The black cat trotted toward her, its strange silver claws glinting in the weak firelight.

'Wilt.'

Chapter 45

From the high window Captain Mont had an expansive view of the western side of the city. Stacks of buildings huddled together as if for warmth, then wide open courtyards scattered about, as though some long forgotten giant had stamped its way across the city, flattening everything in its wandering path.

Each open area was teeming with people, and every day the high city gates opened to allow more to stream through. It couldn't go on. Even though each day they miraculously found more space for the new arrivals, every new face meant less food and shelter for those already here. Every new face piled more pressure on to a city already reaching breaking point.

Or perhaps it had already boiled over, and he just hadn't been able to read the signs.

A knock on the door snapped Captain Mont out of his reverie and he turned to see a tall, dark-haired man stride into the room. Immediately he noticed the set of the man's shoulders, the way his eyes scanned the room quickly, the twist of a grin on his face.

Captain Mont set his feet apart and clasped his hands behind his back. He put on his best gruff voice. 'Lodan, I presume?'

Over his many years as an officer, Captain Mont had learned most men found his demeanour off-putting. It put them in a mind of a parent scolding them in childhood, or a superior laying down orders for battle. It had never failed to snap them out of whatever trivial thoughts they had entered the room with and made them instantly receptive to what he had to say. Not so this man.

Lodan strode right up to the captain and offered his hand.

Captain Mont stared at the hand waiting for his, then back up to the man's dark, knowing eyes. Finally he relented and a wide smile broke over his face as he clasped Lodan's hand in a firm grip.

'I see the reports I have been given on you were accurate, at least.'

'Likewise.'

'Oh? You've been holding your own investigations, have you?'

'I've found it best to always learn beforehand something about the man I'm about to meet. Especially one in a position of authority such as yourself.'

Captain Mont relaxed his stance and rocked back on his heels. 'And what is it your spies have told you about me?'

'Spies? Informants, please. They tell me you're one of the few honest leaders left in the city, particularly since the recent troubles.'

'Troubles. Yes, I suppose that is one word for it.'

Captain Mont sat down behind his desk and gestured Lodan toward a seat. 'Another report I've been given has described an assassin, sent here from Redmondis, one who has struck down the queen and left the king at death's door. One who then used some sort of black magic to escape his execution and kill yet another of the queen's advisers before disappearing seemingly into thin air.'

'An "assassin" you yourself brought into the queen's presence, so I've been told, Captain.'

Captain Mont stared at Lodan, all trace of his earlier friendliness gone. When he spoke again, his voice was cold. 'You are well informed. I hope this will not prove to be a problem.'

Lodan held up his hands. 'Believe me when I tell you, Captain, I hold two things of utmost importance in my business. Those who have open ears and those who keep still tongues. You never have to worry about information getting into places it shouldn't. Besides,' he smiled, dissolving the tension, 'I think we both know Wilt was no assassin.'

'So you do know him.'

'Of course.'

'Then you know where I might find him. I'm eager to hear his side of the story.'

'That, Captain, may be more difficult.'

Captain Mont looked down at his desk, at the piles of reports stacked haphazardly across it. None of which contained good news. 'Nothing is ever that easy in Sontair.'

'What I can do for you, Captain, is offer my services. And that of the men and women who serve under me.'

'Oh yes, the "Fingers". And why would I want your help?'

'Because you and I both know this city is on the edge. Even more so now with no guidance from the top. To speak clearly, the king hasn't been able to form a coherent thought in months, and without the queen those less worthy than you are scrabbling for power. It is up to less … ambitious men such as ourselves to do what needs doing.'

'And what is it that needs doing?'

'That is what I came here to talk about.'

Lodan reached into his shirt and pulled out a roll of parchment, standing as he did so. Without a second thought he swept half the papers off the desk and rolled it open, displaying a large and highly detailed map of Sontair.

Captain Mont stood and joined him on the other side of the table, then both men leaned over the map and began to plan.

The cold wind rushed past Petron's open chamber, whistling as it tumbled down the cliff face that formed one wall of Redmondis to create a hollow, mournful piping. Petron stood at the opening, watching the trees far below him move with the wind, feeling it at the tips of his fingers when he reached into the sky.

In the distance he could see birds being buffeted around by the high winds, enjoying themselves in the wash. He smiled, watching them twist in the air, sharing their exhilaration.

'Sir?'

Petron turned toward the voice and stepped away from the edge. The guard was standing just inside the door to his chamber, his body rigid at attention.

'Yes? Oh, relax, won't you?'

The guard shifted himself to an 'at ease' position, his hands clasped tightly behind his back.

Petron sighed to himself. It was probably the most relaxed he could expect.

'Sir, the Battlemaster reports that the final allocation of weld blades has been distributed. All Redmondis guards can now carry the blades with pride.'

'Good, good.' Petron nodded, his eyes moving down to the long silver blade hanging from the guard's hip. 'And how do you find it? The weld blade?'

The guard seemed taken aback by the direct question, but fumbled out an answer. 'I've never seen a weapon to match it, sir.'

Petron nodded again, stepping back over to his desk and the scattered papers that covered its surface. 'Any more reports I should know about? Or has this wind cut off all communications with the outside world?'

As if in response, a stronger gust blew past, raising the constant piping to a higher, more urgent pitch. The guard waited for it to pass before replying.

'We've had no reports from Sontair, though the messenger birds were expected last night. I can speak to the masters in the rookery if you wish.'

Petron frowned and waved the idea away. 'No matter. I'm sure this wind will pass by nightfall.'

The guard saluted again and marched out of the room, and Petron turned back to the opening. He hadn't felt the pull this strongly in weeks, months perhaps. Since before Cortis. The call of the open sky.

One more thing he took away from you. One more thing his master will pay for.

The thought brought him back to the present, to the immediate duties of Redmondis. He bent down to the papers on his desk, sorting idly through them to ensure everything was in order. He knew it was. With the last allocation of weld blades distributed, there was nothing left to do but continue to train, to make sure they were ready, and to wait. Wait for word from Daemi and the others.

In the last few weeks, Petron had spent more time with the students and guards of Redmondis, encouraging them simply by his presence to push themselves, to focus harder on their training. He kept his eyes open and his mouth shut, and it seemed to be working. The wielders and crafters were working hand in hand now, some even moving into each other's quarters to expunge the separation of skills that had built up in the Sisters' time. The guards too were getting more involved, lending their physical attributes to whatever task had been set. The lines between crafter and wielder and guard were blurring, just as Petron had hoped they would.

But would they be ready? Would they be willing to follow him when the time came to lead them out from within these walls?

He tossed the papers back on the desk and scowled at his own thoughts. *You're an old, impatient man, Petron. Give them time. You know you can trust them.*

A heavy wingbeat at the opening behind him announced his visitor moments before the giant eagle landed, its claws scratching into the hard rock floor. Petron turned and smiled, reaching for the container of scrap meat he kept hidden underneath his desk.

'And how do the winds treat you this day, Stax?'

The eagle stared back at him silently, its eyes locked on the bucket.

'No news yet from our other companions?'

Petron tossed a morsel toward the eagle and it snapped the meat easily out of the air, swallowing it in one great gulp.

'I've felt something change down there too. Do you think we can thank Nurtle and Jared for that? Are they even now taking root? Or will they one day come visiting along with you?'

He flipped another hunk of meat into the air and watched the eagle snatch it. 'Tell me, Stax. Do you ever miss these human intrigues?'

As if in answer the giant eagle opened its wings and buffeted a gust of wind Petron's way, pushing his thin hair back from his face. The next moment it had leaped out and was disappearing into the open sky.

Petron dropped the bucket of scraps under his desk with a sigh and stepped toward the opening, forcing his thoughts away from the concerns of Redmondis. He placed the toes of his boots right on the edge of the wall, closed his eyes and leaned out, just touching the cold wind that shot past the window.

For a moment he was flying again, his arms now wings, his mind sharp and focused, his heart free.

A smile played over his lips before he turned and stepped back into the human world.

Daemi lay face down on the bed, her nightshirt pulled up over her shoulders to reveal the angry red scars scratched down her back. As she breathed the scars pulsed slightly, thin trickles of blood leaking out over the raised edges of flesh. Heather reached across and dabbed the blood away, humming.

'I could do without the musical accompaniment,' Daemi grumbled.

'Oh shush,' Heather replied, dabbing directly onto the wounds now, bringing a short gasp of pain out of her patient. 'Sorry.'

'It's okay, just hurry up and get on with whatever you two are planning.'

Frankle took this as his cue and shuffled forward shyly, his eyes on the floor to avoid seeing too much of Daemi's naked flesh.

'And tell your assistant there to man up and get to work,' Daemi admonished.

Frankle looked up and blushed. 'Right. Sorry, Daemi.'

'Here.' Heather held out a dripping cloth, its white fibres stained red with blood. 'Put it with the others. I don't think it's going to get any better until we start.'

Frankle nodded and grabbed the cloth, tossing it onto the growing pile in the corner of the room and wiping his hands down the makeshift apron Heather had given him.

'Are you ready?' Heather asked, looking up at him now.

'I guess.'

Heather smiled at him. 'Just like we worked on the weld blade. Remember?'

Frankle stepped up to the bed, holding his hands out over Daemi's back. Heather moved around to the other side and did the same. Briefly the tips of their fingers touched and Frankle's hands twitched as if shocked.

'Come now, Frankle,' Heather said. 'Try not to be so jumpy.'

'Just get on with it, will you?' Daemi's voice groaned into her pillow.

They closed their eyes and *reached*. Frankle dropped into the world below, the rush of power surging up to him from the whirling chaos of potential welds that rushed below like a raging storm. It was getting easier every time. Too easy.

It's okay, Frankle. You have nothing to fear here.

Frankle almost jerked back to the surface, but maintained control. That wasn't Delco. That was—

Wilt. We haven't met, not formally anyhow. It's about time we changed that. Come, let me show you.

Frankle fell, deeper than he had ever dared go before, falling into the torrent, through it, out into a strangely calm landscape. The weld storm was above him now, twisting and whirling, while below stretched a blank white surface of ice.

Here. Further down. Trust me.

Without meaning to, Frankle drifted closer to the surface. It was pure white, unmarked except for a single black spot. He seemed to be falling straight toward it.

Yes, that's right. Like that.

The black spot arranged itself into form as he neared it. A large black cat, sitting still on the ice, stared up at him. Its tail brushed slowly back and forth.

You see me. I must stay here in this form for now, much like those other wildlers you've already met on your journey. Good. That's close enough.

Frankle stopped in mid-air. A part of him wanted to continue down onto the ice, but he was held back, restrained somehow.

This place is not for you, Frankle. Not yet at least. But you can do something for me. I need you to take something back with you. It will help Daemi. Can you do this for me?

Frankle nodded, though he hadn't intended to.

Good. I'm relying on you to look after them. We both are.

The cat stood up and arched its back in a stretch. As it did so, a single spark of light seemed to pull free of its fur and float up toward Frankle.

Now go, Frankle. We have a long way to travel yet. No time to waste.

The spark danced in the wind in front of Frankle, taking his eyes up and away from the ice, toward the storm rolling above him. He rose with it, unable to do anything else.

In moments he was back above it, Heather's fingers interlaced with his in the surface world, a thin shimmer of silver weaving together in front of his eyes.

'What was that? For a second I thought I'd lost you. Come on, I need your help with this.'

Frankle didn't reply, just bent his mind to the task of weaving the thin silver welds together, knitting Daemi's torn skin back into a whole. It only took moments, as though the welds knew before he did what they needed to do.

He opened his eyes and looked down. Daemi's skin was completely healed.

'Well, that went even better than I expected,' Heather whispered, her eyes scanning Daemi's back for any flaws. She didn't seem to notice their fingers were still locked together.

Frankle stood still, not wanting to move and break the spell.

'We must be getting better at working together.' She pulled her hands from his to stroke Daemi's back.

'Is it … did we do it?' Frankle found his voice was shaking.

'I think so. Keep your voice down. She's sleeping.'

Sure enough a low snore leaked from deep within Daemi's pillow. Heather and Frankle stepped away from the bed.

'I must speak to Petron about this. It seems we make quite the team.'

'Uh, yeah,' Frankle muttered, his face warming again. He stumbled toward the door of the chamber. 'We should let her sleep.'

'Yes. I'll be right there.'

Heather watched Frankle disappear out the door. As soon as he did, she reached inside her shirt and pulled out the glittering heartstone. With her other hand she retrieved the sounding bowl and dropped the heartstone into it. Sure enough, the song echoed out, fading with each moment, until it had died completely.

'Well, well. Now that *is* interesting.'

She looked up at the windowsill where the large black cat sat, studying her with its strange ink-filled eyes.

'I don't suppose you know anything about that?'

The cat angled its head as if listening, then looked over at Daemi, still slumbering away.

'No? Well then. Keep an eye on our patient, won't you?'

As if in reply the cat settled onto its front paws, its eyes locked on the sleeping figure.

'I know you will.'

With that Heather gathered her things and left the room. There was a lot of work yet to do.

Epilogue

The cold wind blew through the clearing, sending sprays of leaves into the air to tumble and spin into miniature tornados as it passed. The trees lining the clearing swayed and danced in the breeze, laughing as the wind tore past. The shadow standing in the centre watched it all, unable to feel the wind itself, but enjoying the reaction it caused in its brothers.

On the southern edge the trees were sparser, and bright sunlight was reaching through the gaps between their trunks from the open sky beyond the edge of the Tangle. The shadow hadn't been this close to the border in weeks, months perhaps, and it enjoyed the strange pull the sunlight had on it, even though it knew it could never survive outside the Tangle's protection. Not anymore.

A child cried out, and the shadow stepped against the nearest tree as a pair of children crashed through the trees.

'You see? I told you there was nothing to fear.'

The larger of the two children stood with her hands on her hips, surveying the area as though claiming new land for her domain.

'But mother said—'

'Never mind what your mummy says. She's spent too much time listening to the village gossips.'

The smaller boy seemed to want to argue back, but dropped his head to whisper as though afraid of being overheard. 'But the Tangle is dangerous. Everyone knows that. Even you've heard the stories of the shade.'

The girl harrumphed and pushed out her chest. 'I say we need to be brave enough to claim what is ours. This forest is part of our land. It's our protection. It's nothing to fear.'

The words sounded rehearsed and foreign on the child's tongue, but she followed them with a glare around the edge of the clearing, as though daring anything to step out and challenge them.

'You're just repeating what Aaron and the others were saying. And I don't see any of them brave enough to step inside these borders.'

'They will. Once they get used to things. It's only been a few days since the trees opened up. Grown-ups always take a bit longer, you know that. '

The boy nodded at her words. They both knew the frustration of waiting for adults to authorise things. 'So you don't believe the stories then? About the shadows that haunt these woods? About the Guardian?'

The girl seemed less sure of herself now that she was being asked a direct question, but nodded stubbornly.

The life is strong in these two. Watch them burn against the grey darkness of the background. The glow and heat of life. So wondrous. So tempting.

'I think the Tangle has its secrets. But I don't believe in ghosts.'

They are not for us to take, Biore. You know this.

Another gust of icy wind blew through the clearing, and both children stepped toward each other automatically, shivering into their cloaks as the wind whipped their hair about their faces.

'It's cold here, Scarlet. Please, can we head back now?'

The girl looked as though she wanted to argue, then nodded and turned her back on the wind, letting it push her along out of the clearing and toward the sunlight.

So close. All it would take is a touch.

The two children walked right past the tree where the shadow stood, clasping the trunk to hold itself back, to maintain some control over the whip and pull of their life force passing by. As they left, the shadow relaxed, able to stand on its own again, master of itself.

You did well, Biore. It is difficult to resist the pull, but we will help you.

Will it always be so hard? Must it always be a battle?

You started yourself down this path long ago. It will take time to gain control.

The shadow nodded to itself and drifted back into the trees, grateful for their constant whispering, their companionship, their guiding hand.

Besides, the Tangle is large. Very large. There will always be trespassers we need not treat with such care. There will be plenty of opportunity to feed.

The shadow faded as the light dimmed around it and the trees closed in. It let itself go, confident it would be called on again.

About the Author

T.R. Thompson is an Australian speculative fiction author. He lives in Belgrave on the outskirts of Melbourne with his wife and two young sons.

When not writing or reading, he spends too much time gaming and taking long meandering walks through the forest that always seem to end up at a tavern.

www.trthompson.com